Also in The Vigilati Series

BLOOD IN THE VALLEY

I0549793

J.K. HOGAN

Praise for Fire on the Island

"Fire on the Island is a paranormal tale that mixes together a good brew of essential elements—love, death, mystery, intrigue, magic and demons, to name a few—that brings the reader into a modern day world with the age old battle of good vs. evil.

The reader will love J.K. Hogan's pairing of romance with the paranormal as she weaves a tale that pulls us into this mysterious and magical world. It is easy for the reader to get lost in the lives of the inhabitants of Arran, an island filled with natural beauty and wonders, simplicity and legends that come to life.

The characters are strong, intelligent and easy to love. Isla is a character who would inspire anyone to become part of her circle of friends. Jeremiah is no less charismatic with his wit, intelligence, strength and New Orleans' charm. In fact, Ms. Hogan spins the varied characters, making up Isla's friends into a story showing they are all an important piece of the whole.

After finishing this first book in the Vigilati Series, the reader will certainly look forward to Book II with great anticipation."

~ Ricki R.

"This is an action-packed paranormal romance book with a very lovable cast."

~Lizzy's Dark Fiction

"I love to read a good paranormal romance. One that will sweep me into it and take me on a magical adventure. Fire on the Island does exactly that and I loved the journey. This book is rich in detail and world building. It has a unique take on witches and demons and I was captured by this story."

~The Book Tart

"Unique, with lots of action, a strong heroine, and a sexy hero, Fire On the Island is a recommended read. I will be picking up book 2 when it comes out in May. Hogan has created a world that I want to revisit frequently and I have high hopes for this series!"

~Romance Reader at Heart, Novel Thoughts and Book Talk

"In a nutshell, I can't wait to read this again. And again. The simple beauty of Hogan's writing transported me from my apartment into the beautiful wilds of the Scottish islands, sitting on the back porch with Isla and Jeremiah. Absolutely stunning. "

~The Canon

FIRE ON THE ISLAND

The Vigilati Series

Book One

J.K. HOGAN

Copyright © 2013 J.K. Hogan

Cover Image by Roser Portella Florit

J.K. Hogan

http://jkhogan.com/
http://twitter.com/JK_Hogan
http://www.facebook.com/OfficialJKHogan
http://www.goodreads.com/jkhogan
http://www.amazon.com/author/jkhogan
http://officialjkhogan.tumblr.com

Dedication

For my husband, James, and my wonderful family for always believing in me.

Thanks to the Dog Haven Crew for your unflagging support and encouragement. A girl couldn't ask for better friends!

A special thank you to Tab Benoit and Jonny Lang, the incredible Blues artists who provided the soundtrack for the story in my head.

J.K. HOGAN

PART I

INCEPTUS

Chapter One
Isle of Arran, Scotland, UK

Isla MacAllan loved her little island with a passion. The tourism industry had branded Arran "Scotland in Miniature" to increase its appeal to travelers, but it was actually quite fitting. The tiny island had the wilds of the Highlands with its rocky mountains and dense forests, the tranquil beauty of the Lowlands, with its farmland and quiet beaches, and everything in between. Isla's own wee cabin was situated in a copse of trees just on the edge of Merckland Wood. The thicket was so dense around the cabin that it kept her comfortably isolated from tourists and travelers on walkabout. Passersby rarely ventured far enough off the path to find it and, if they did, they usually stumbled upon it before they even knew it was there. Isla preferred it that way in part because she valued her privacy, but also because it kept her contact with the local islanders to a minimum.

Ten years ago Isla had moved to Arran from the city of Glasgow where she was born, with nothing but twenty pounds and the clothes on her back. With no money or family to speak of, she had survived by waitressing at the local pub in Brodick and renting the one room flat on the floor above it. Supplementing her meager income by doing odd jobs around the village, like grooming lawns and walking dogs, Isla quickly became well loved by the locals. It was what happened during one of those odd jobs that changed life on the island forever.

Isla was weeding Mrs. Calahan's prized rose garden the first time one of the islanders noticed her mark. It had been a hot day in June, so she had piled her curly, black hair up in a loose knot. It had never occurred to her to hide the mark she'd had on the base of her neck for as long as she could remember. It had never occurred to her that it should matter that Mrs. Calahan's nephew would see it and go on to tell his friend Danny, who would then tell his grandda—such was life on a small island.

The locals in Arran were mostly a friendly, welcoming lot and they had never given her reason to believe otherwise, until she began to get strange looks as she walked by on the street. Until the ladies had begun to whisper behind their hands. Until the men had begun to avoid sitting in her section at the pub.

The older islanders, the ones who had seen and heard so much in their lives, could be quite superstitious and their opinions had weight with the others. No one seemed to know what to make of Isla's brand, but that didn't stop anyone from speculating about what it meant.

Suddenly talk of how Isla just appeared on the island one day, and no one knew who her people were, ran rampant in town, as did ideas about the meaning of the peculiar symbol. From one day to the next, Isla never knew if she was in a satanic cult, a witches' coven, or if she was the child of the devil himself—those seemed to be the most popular theories.

Isla tried not to speculate on how she got the curious marking. Her father had left Isla and her mother when she was still too young to understand, and her mother had been a raging alcoholic who couldn't be believed about anything. Having never known her grandparents, Isla was alone in the world, which left her no explanation for the eye surrounded by three circles that was imprinted on her neck.

Eventually Isla had squirreled away enough savings to purchase her *Taigh na Beinne,* or mountain house, and it had been her refuge ever since. Her cabin and the business she had managed to start over three years before, an outdoor excursion company called Expeditions, were her safe havens in an uncertain and solitary world.

෨෩

"Put yer hands on either side of the pot, little one," Mhairi Mackay *said to her four-year-old granddaughter. They sat at the shabby kitchen table of their small home in the "Low-End" area of the Ruchazie district. Mhairi smiled as the tiny, dark-haired child cupped the pot in her hands, concentration knotting her brow. The child wouldn't really be able to do magick until she came of age and received her signa, but it was never too early to teach.*

"Imagine takin' off a twig from yer spirit tree and givin' it t' the seedling. We'll need tae give her some of our energy tae help her grow." Mhairi *placed her hands atop the child's, and the signa on her wrist began to glow and rotate.*

"Say the words with me now, child."

The little girl's voice joined her grandmother's, strong and true, to recite the growing spell. "Sume spiritum meum, sume incendium meum, accipe terram meam, aer meae spiro. Da te vitae."

Mhairi watched as the child's eyes widened in wonder as the little bean sprout pushed through the soil and expanded its leaves. Isla tossed a toothy grin at Mhairi, but it quickly faded as she focused on a point just over Mhairi's shoulder.

Mhairi turned to see her daughter Eileen glaring at them from the entryway, cradling the bottle of bourbon that had become a constant companion since her husband had left. Eyes dull and glassy from the drink, Eileen slowly approached the table, swaying only a little.

"Go to yer room, Isla," she said, and Mhairi winced at the cold tone directed at Eileen's own child. The woman who had rocked the child to sleep after nightmares and bandaged her cuts was gone and had been for some time now. All that remained was an empty shell, clutching a bottle like it was a lifeline.

"B-but Mum — " Isla was silenced by the now empty bottle hurling past her head to shatter across the faded wallpaper behind them. Knocking over her chair in her haste, she fled from the room as if the devil were on her tail.

"I'll not have that magick absurdity in this house!" Eileen shouted. Mhairi held her hands out, palms up, as if approaching an agitated cougar.

"You can't deny our heritage, my daughter. The child needs to learn about what she's tae become."

"Your ridiculous drivel of witches has taken enough from me. You drove my Charlie away, and I won't let you corrupt my daughter too!"

Mhairi sighed and scrubbed a wrinkled hand over her face, and she spoke calmly to the stranger who was once her daughter, knowing it would do no good. "Eileen, the only thing that drove yer Charlie away was yer love affair with th' bottle! I'm no' tryin' to take yer daughter from ye'. I'm only tryin' to prepare her for the life she is tae lead."

For what seemed like several minutes, Eileen stared at the floor, and Mhairi began to wonder if she would speak again at all. Slowly she raised flashing jade green eyes to Mhairi, and her once pretty mouth twisted into a snarl.

"Lies!" she shouted and slapped Mhairi across the face. "I'll not have it in my house any longer!" While Mhairi was momentarily stunned into silence, Eileen took a deep breath and seemed to collect herself. In a voice that was flat and devoid of emotion, she continued. "You are not welcome in this house. You will not see my daughter, and your lies will die with you. Get. Out."

Knowing that Eileen was lost to her now, Mhairi gathered her meager possessions from the small alcove she slept in. She feared what would happen to Isla with only her drunken mother for guidance, but she could only hope the child would contact her when she was able. Casting a sorrowful glance down the hallway where no doubt Isla was eavesdropping, she slung her rucksack over her shoulder and walked out the door.

Chapter Two

Dr. Jeremiah Rousseau had hit a wall in his research. He stared at the scans of an ancient text he had been struggling, to no avail, to translate for long hours into the night. He had found the tome on a dusty shelf of a private bookseller in Rome and had the inexplicable urge to take it with him. What had attracted Jere to the book, which he had found in the mythology section, was the symbol on the cover. There had been a niggling spark of recognition as if he had seen the symbol before, and it galled him that he couldn't quite remember where.

The book appeared to be written in some form of Latin, in which Jeremiah was fluent, but he could only distinguish a few words that he understood. He suspected it was some form of Old Latin and had gotten excited when he saw the word *Latium* come up several times. So even though he couldn't read it, he had paid the bookseller an exorbitant amount of money and left Rome with book in hand.

Jeremiah had scanned several passages from the book so that he wouldn't damage the ancient text while he worked on his translations.

Jeremiah removed his wire-rimmed reading glasses and rubbed his tired eyes. "This is hopeless," he said as he closed his laptop none too gently. Ever since he had acquired it, he'd had a feeling this book was going to be paramount in his research for his current project. Desperate to get the pages translated, he'd sent an email to his old friend Drew, a.k.a. Dr. Andrew Deveraux, an anthropologist who was also an expert on antiquated languages.

While he had earned his Doctorate in Psychology from the University of Edinburgh, the focus of Jeremiah's studies and now his work was parapsychology—the study of paranormal phenomena. Currently he was a world renowned paranormal researcher and author. He was well known for debunking, or proving the existence of, famous ghost stories and sightings.

Often when he wrote a book on his investigation of a paranormal phenomenon that turned out to be genuine, he simultaneously released a suspense novel about the events investigated and sometimes the investigation itself. Because of this, he'd gained notoriety in not only the parapsychology field, but also in the world of fiction writing.

His most recent investigations included the fabled *Le Petit Ange* of New Orleans, the ghost of a little girl who had fallen to her death off the second story balcony of a French Quarter mansion, and the ghost of Zebulon Jackson, who had been rumored to haunt the Blue Rock Motel in Boone, North Carolina. He had come away from the former with several pieces of evidence proving her existence. The latter had been debunked as a long-running prank by the staff to try and draw a bigger tourist crowd.

His current project was something that had been with him since his time at University, when he had come upon a mention of a particular sect of witches called the *Bruixi* in one of his research materials. When most people thought of witches, it brought to mind Medieval castle towers and Salem witch trials, but anthropologically they were a much more dynamic and diverse group of people than they were ever given credit for. As he researched the *Bruixi* further, he became fascinated by what little information he could find. What he did know for sure was that this society of witches predated the Roman Empire and possibly even existed in the ancient region of Latium which later became modern-day Rome. As far as he could tell, this was the oldest sect of witches known in history today.

Ever since this first discovery, Jeremiah had been searching for more information about the *Bruixi*, determined to prove their existence in the modern world. Strangely it had never occurred to him to try and disprove their existence because he had a bone-deep feeling that they were out there. He had located several people that he believed may have had information about modern *Bruixi,* but each time he tried to set up an interview, something got in the way. Out of four women he had located based on family names that had come up during the research, two had refused to speak with him, one had gone off the grid, and one had passed away before he could speak with her.

Frustrated but compelled to continue his quest, he focused his attention on the last name on his list. Mhairi Mackay, a seventy-year-old Scottish woman living in a retirement home in Glasgow, had no known living relatives, so

Jeremiah decided to contact the facility where she lived. Dialing the number for Sacred Hearts Assisted Living, Jere mentally crossed his fingers and waited for an answer on the line.

"Sacred Hearts, how can I help you?"

"Yes, ma'am, my name is Dr. Jeremiah Rousseau. I am trying to contact Mhairi Mackay, one of your residents. Is there any way I can speak with her?"

Jeremiah heard the soft tapping of computer keys as he waited for an answer. "Sir, Ms. Mackay is receiving inpatient treatment for dementia. If you aren't a family member, you'll have to leave a message for her doctor before you can speak with her. Would you like to do that now?"

Jeremiah sighed and tried to remind himself that this was farther than he had gotten with any of his other leads. "Sure, that would be great. Thanks." He was transferred to the voicemail of a Dr. MacLaren, and he left a brief message explaining who he was and why he wanted to see Mhairi. He didn't want to go into too much detail over voicemail, and besides, anyone could run a web search on him and find out what he did for a living.

A beep sounded from Jere's phone, letting him know he had new email, so he unlocked the screen and opened his email program. Excitedly, he clicked on a new email from Drew. As usual, it was short and sweet:

Email scans. Will have a look. U know I can't turn down a challenge! D.

Relieved that his friend was willing to help, Jeremiah reopened his laptop to continue his online research. Earlier that morning he had come across a travel blog post about an island off the Southwest coast of Scotland called Arran. The majority of the post consisted of descriptions of the blogger's hikes and excursions during her stay on the island, but at the end there was a section on the island's myths and folklore.

Jere read about the *Pookas*, the *Bocans*, and other faeries and ghosts with mild interest. He perked up a bit when he began to read the more modern story of a supposed witch that inhabited the island. According to the islanders, the woman lived alone in the woods like a hermit and rarely came down the hill to the town below. Some believed her to be a harmless eccentric, while many of the older villagers believed her to be the devil's own daughter because of a rumor of a peculiar runic-like tattoo on the back of her neck.

At the mention of the tattoo, the hair on the back of Jere's neck rose, and he began thinking this could be another possible lead. He typed in a search for the Isle of Arran to find that it was a popular vacation spot that still maintained an old world feel because of its protected woodlands and beaches. Next he typed *The Arran Witch* into the search bar and was surprised by how many hits the search got.

Jeremiah was jarred out of his thoughts by a bluesy Tab Benoit guitar riff that he used as his ringtone. Checking the caller ID and seeing his friend and editor, Ian Scott, was calling, Jere rolled his eyes and answered. "Rousseau."

"Jere, where have you been, man? You know I hate when you go AWOL like that!"

"I'm still here in Chicago, at The Drake. Just finishing up the research on the Archer Avenue investigation." Jere had finished up his investigation of Chicago's Archer Avenue ghost days ago but had taken advantage of some quiet time in his richly appointed room at the Drake Hotel to go over some of his other projects. He knew Ian wasn't crazy about the witch angle he had been working, so what the guy didn't know wouldn't hurt him.

"Bullshit! You're still working on that hocus pocus nonsense, aren't you?"

"Look, Ian—"

"No, you look. This witch thing is nothing but a fairy tale, and you're wasting your time. The ghost hunts are the money makers. This thing is consuming all of your attention. I have no idea why you are so caught up in this, but you need to take a break and get back to reality. I want you to take a vacation," Ian said in a tone that brooked no argument. However, Jere had always been told he was a stubborn little fucker, and he wasn't about to let Ian pull rank on him.

"Ian, I'm fine," he snapped. "I'm wrapping it up here today and I'll be on a plane back to New Orleans tomorrow morning."

"No, Jeremiah. This is non-negotiable. Let me rephrase—the publisher wants you to take a vacation, and if you want to keep pulling in a paycheck, you'll do it."

While Jeremiah's first instinct was to tell Ian and his publisher where to stuff their orders, he thought about the little island in Scotland that was rich with folklore and rumors of a reclusive witch and smiled. Half listening to Ian's diatribe about the perils of pissing off your publisher, he flicked his tongue over one of his long canine teeth that, much to his mother's dismay, hadn't been fixed by braces. He had caught hell about it from his peers in school, being called everything from *Dracula* to *Teen Wolf*, and he had picked up the habit out of self-consciousness. His wolfish grin had gotten him a fair share of dates growing up, but it lost some of its charm with the ladies once they realized he wasn't batting for Team Edward or Team Jacob.

Interrupting Ian's tirade, Jere cut him off. "You're right, I've been a workaholic lately. A vacation will probably do me a world of good. In fact, I know just the place."

Jeremiah placed a couple of calls, one to his travel agent to book a flight to Scotland, and the other to a neighbor to look after his place for a couple of weeks.

Lying down on the fluffy hotel mattress, Jeremiah finally succumbed to hours of exhaustion and fell into a fitful sleep.

CRED

Orleans Parish
October 31, 1991

Twelve-year-old Jeremiah Rousseau was shivering with so much youthful excitement, he was practically jumping out of his skin. He was about to embark on his first *solo voyage*, as he saw it, into the unknown. He was going on an outing with his older friends, without his mom. Words failed. As a single mother, Esme Rousseau could be embarrassingly overprotective—at least, if you asked Jeremiah. He had spent weeks begging, promising, wheeling and dealing, until she'd finally given in.

Tonight was the night. Jere was to go on a ghost tour of St. Louis Cemetery #1, New Orleans' most infamous hotspot of the paranormal, with his friends Drew, Josh, and Josh's older brother, Beau. They weren't wearing costumes—dressing up for Halloween was so elementary school. So Jere pulled on his rattiest, and therefore most comfortable, pair of jeans with a Pearl Jam tour t-shirt and ran a comb haphazardly through his mop of sandy brown hair. His mom had been at him to cut it for weeks because it had begun to flop down over his forehead and curl at his collar, but Jere had a natural talent of being selectively deaf.

Giving himself one last cursory glance in his bathroom mirror, Jere flashed a snaggletoothed grin at his reflection, rolling hazel eyes at his abnormally long canines that Esme seemed sure braces would fix. Satisfied with his appearance, Jeremiah briefly contemplated bringing a jacket, then decided against it. He got to the front door just as Beau honked his horn from the street. Jere was halfway out the door when his mother's voice stopped him in his tracks.

"Jeremiah David Rousseau, I know you are not walkin' out that door without kissin' your mama goodbye!"

Jere pulled a quick about-face and plastered an angelic smile on his face, determined not to jeopardize his epic Halloween plans. "Of course not, Mama. I just wanted to wave to Beau to let him know I was comin'."

With a look that said she didn't buy that excuse for a second, Esme bent down to kiss his cheek. Grasping his shoulders and squeezing a bit for emphasis, she looked him dead in the eye. "You be careful now, hear? Stay with the group, mind Beau, and call me if you have any trouble."

"Yes, Mama."

Esme sighed and for a second, Jeremiah almost wanted to say he would stay just to take the worry out of her eyes. But the appeal of a night of independence was too much for an adventurous young boy to ignore.

"Go on now. Be safe."

"I will, Mama."

Jeremiah ran down the front walk and climbed into the backseat of Beau's beat up Honda, high-fiving Drew who sat on the passenger side. "Seatbelts!" Beau shouted over Nirvana blasting from the one working speaker. Once the boys were buckled in, they were off, racing down Gentilly Boulevard toward the cemetery and their ghost adventure.

"...Marie Laveau died in 1881 and she was reportedly buried here in the Glapion family tomb. Many believe that her spirit still walks the grounds here and that she haunts any who try to disturb her," the guide droned. Jeremiah tried to concentrate on the older man who was fully regaled in top hat and tails—and fake vampire teeth for the Halloween crowd—but the tour was turning out to be not at all what he expected.

Jere wasn't sure what he had expected, exactly, but he'd assumed a ghost tour would be, well, scary. It turned out that it was more of a history lesson than anything, and how lame was that? Though he did think it was kind of neat that in New Orleans the dead had to be buried in above-ground tombs because the city was below sea level. Still, while Beau and the boys paid rapt attention, Jere was bored. He had always been more interested in science than history anyway.

Catching a flash of movement out of the corner of his eye, Jeremiah turned to scan the dark perimeter of the cemetery. His view was blocked by the monstrous marble tombs that St. Louis #1 was famous for. As it often did, curiosity got the better of him and he stepped away from the tour group, ignoring the little voice of caution in his head that sounded remarkably like his mother.

Already committed to exploring, Jeremiah cast a brief glance back at the small group gathered around the tomb of Marie Laveau. Satisfied that no one would notice his absence, he began his exploration of the macabre matrix of New Orleans' *City of the Dead*. Jeremiah froze when he heard the scrape of a boot heel on the gravelly concrete. He couldn't explain why, but dread curled in his gut like a fist, yet he was helpless but to follow.

Turning a corner almost at a run, Jeremiah skidded to a stop when he noticed the shadowy figure of a man leaning casually against an ancient looking pediment tomb. An eerie fog wafted up from the ground and around him to mingle with his cigarette smoke, and an orange dot appeared in the shadows as he took a drag. The figure stepped through the fog slowly—like a predator—into a patch of moonlight, causing Jere to cringe in fear. The stranger was dressed unremarkably enough, sporting a black leather biker jacket, ripped jeans, and black cowboy boots—although it was rather odd that he was wearing sunglasses at night. Jere stared at the strange tattoo on the man's forehead. It looked like a peace sign without the circle. Curious but still wary, Jere took a cautious step forward.

A wave of pure, unfiltered evil blasted into him, and immediately a single thought stabbed through his brain. *RUN!* He had no idea how he knew, but this was not a man. As if in response to Jere's thought, the...*thing*...removed its sunglasses and turned grey eyes, so pale they were almost opaque, to Jere's face. Unable to help himself, Jeremiah stared into those bizarre eyes and thought he saw shadows swirling inside them. The creature opened its mouth in a gruesome parody of a smile, revealing a row of menacing serrated fangs.

Jeremiah's heart leapt into his throat and his survival instinct galvanized into action. As he was preparing to flee, he felt a stabbing sensation in his temples. Jere tried to back away from the creature, who was now slowly approaching him like a cougar stalking its prey, and he quickly realized that his feet wouldn't move. Panicked now, Jere futilely tried harder to force his body into motion.

As the creature approached Jeremiah and placed skeletal hands on either side of his head, Jere's eyes rolled back in his head. Another shot of pain glanced through his skull, jarring him back into consciousness.

So this is how it's going to be. He's going to kill me and he wants me to feel every last bit of it. Jere thought of his mama having to deal with losing one of her sons so soon after the death of his father, and a single tear slipped down his cheek. He had to swallow back the bile that rose when the creature tugged him closer and licked the tear off his cheek with a snake-like tongue.

Jere's head was swimming in the battle to lose consciousness, causing all of his thoughts to slow as if they were wading through muddy water. As soon as it occurred to him to test his voice and try to scream, a circle of fire erupted out of the ground to surround the two of them. Jeremiah didn't know if he was hallucinating—perhaps he was already dead—or if the fire was real. All he knew was that it was close enough for him to feel the heat of it on the back of his neck, and it burned him when stray embers landed on his bare arms.

The pain in Jeremiah's head intensified and his whole body began to go numb. Against his will, he again turned his terrified gaze to the creature's greedy one, where the shadows almost appeared to be leaping out at him. Jere's vision narrowed until all he could see were those peculiar opaque eyes, and he felt a tingling sensation inside his head. Compelled against his will, his muscles relaxed and he felt his mind opening to this being.

Just when Jeremiah thought for sure he was about to be consumed—in body or soul, he wasn't sure—the creature was abruptly jerked out of the fiery sphere and the flames dissipated. Trembling violently, Jere tested his legs, and sure enough, they were working again. Knowing he should take off running like a bat out of hell, but unable to tamp down his morbid curiosity, he cautiously looked around to see if the creature was still nearby. Turning slowly in a circle, Jeremiah's eyes locked onto an astonishing scene.

A tiny, dark-haired woman had petite hands locked around the creature's throat, and a radiant glow emanated from the contact. She swiveled her head around to look at Jere, and surprisingly he recognized her as the gypsy tarot card reader he often saw in Jackson Square. He usually avoided walking too close to her table because she looked at him like she knew too much—he never knew why that scared him so much, but it did.

There was something different about her tonight, Jere realized. She was dressed in a gold and white silk robe and had a trio of nesting circles that covered most of her left cheek that he had never seen before. Baffled by the appearance of the mark and the way it seemed to writhe and glow on her cheek, Jeremiah started to back away.

"*Ne t'effraie pas,*" she said to him. *Don't be afraid.*

"*Je suis ici pour vous protéger.*" *I am here to protect you.*

Before Jeremiah could puzzle out how he could understand her perfectly when he didn't speak a lick of French, she turned her gaze back to the creature, and ghostly blue flames leapt out from her eyes to lick at the creature's face. The creature let out a mournful howl and disappeared in a burst of smoke that smelled of flint and death, leaving nothing but a small white serpent slithering on the ground.

The gypsy woman picked up the snake and tucked it into her knapsack, then turned milky white eyes back to a terrified Jeremiah and winked. Having tested the limits of his consciousness to take in the impossible, Jere's brain finally checked out and he dropped like a stone.

A groggy, fuzzy headed Jere awoke minutes later, finding himself curled up at the foot of one of the massive tombs. Unsure of how long he had been out and anxious to return to his friends, he dusted himself off and shot off like a bullet to rejoin the tour group. He was ready to get the hell out of that cemetery and never look back.

Jeremiah's red Chuck Taylors slid to a stop when the tour group came into view, crowded around another tomb. Not wanting to alert anyone to his absence, he crept up silently to stand behind Drew and Josh, trying to hold in his panting breaths. Beau turned to study him and chuckled.

"Dude, tell me this is not actually scarin' you."

Jere looked down at his toes and mumbled, "Nah. Just not feelin' so good." It was all he could do not to run screaming to the car and lock himself inside.

Concern replaced the amusement in Beau's face, and he nodded. He tapped Josh on the shoulder and motioned for the boys to follow. "Let's get outta here. This is totally lame. Besides, it's almost over anyway." Not wanting to be considered lame for wanting to stay, Josh and Drew trailed behind Beau when he placed a hand on the back of Jere's neck and urged him forward. Normally Jeremiah would protest cutting the tour short on his account, but he couldn't bring himself to stay in the cemetery one second longer.

Once they were loaded up in the car and on their way back home, Jeremiah was finally able to relax slightly. He leaned his head on the cool glass of the window, closed his eyes, and went over the events of the night, trying to sort through the details. He remembered the strange entity and the gypsy woman, but details that should have been crystal clear were now hazy, as if seen through a dream. He tried harder to remember until a piercing throb in his skull caused him to back off. The analytical, science-nerd part of his brain took over, and he tried to figure out a reasonable explanation for what little he remembered. *What was that thing? What was it trying to do to me?* There were too many questions and frustratingly few answers. Jere knew without a doubt, however fuzzy the details, that the gypsy woman had saved him from some kind of horrible fate. He wondered how she had come to be in the cemetery and how she had known what to do to help him.

Unable to come up with any theories to explain his frightening encounter, Jere sighed and stared out the car window. His heart rate had finally returned to normal and the trembling had stopped, but he knew the events of Halloween '91 had changed him in ways he couldn't yet imagine.

Chapter Three

Isla drove her battered, old pickup truck down the dirt road that led from her cabin to the office of her company, Expeditions, located in the small village of Lamlash. The business was housed in an A-frame cedar building that nestled into the landscape at the foot of one of the great hills on the island. To the left of the building were canoe and kayak racks, and on the right were three sheds that stored equipment and apparel for various outdoor excursions.

Isla was dressed for work in cargo trousers and a black tank top, and she had braided her curly, black hair into a thick rope to keep it out of her way, but also to cover the mark on her neck. To her way of thinking, the fewer people who saw it, the fewer questions there would be. Swiping at the thick fringe that framed her jade green eyes, she entered the lobby, waving at two of her guides who were looking at maps and going over the schedule for the day's events.

"G'morning girls. How's the day looking for us?" After ten years of living on the island, Isla had picked up the lilting country brogue.

Brynna, a young Irish girl with flaming red hair and green eyes, was the first to speak. "Mornin' boss lady!" Brynna knew Isla hated to be called that—especially since she didn't make it known to the public that she was the owner of the company—which was exactly why the impish girl said it. Isla never failed to be touched, and slightly surprised, by the good-natured ribbing when she got it.

Their American import, Amy, spoke up next. "I've got two sea kayaking tours, Bryn has a half-day cycling trip, and Kieran will be taking a group up to the summit of Goat Fell."

"Who's got office duty today?" Since they both preferred to be outdoors, Isla and her manager, Callum, alternated running the office and leading excursions because someone had to stay back and check in customers.

"Looks like Callum pulled the short straw today. You have two waterfall tours on the books today, one at ten and the other at three this afternoon, both to Glenashedale," Amy answered. Glenashedale was Arran's tallest waterfall, towering at over 100 ft, and it was one of Isla's favorite hikes to lead.

"Lovely! Is Callum in the break room?"

"Yeah, he said come on back when you got here. He's got some news."

Interested to find out what gossip Callum had to share, Isla turned the corner and headed back to the small kitchen the staff used as a break room. He was worse than the little old ladies in the church knitting circle.

Callum, her best friend and business partner, sat at the kitchen table staring into his coffee. Isla didn't miss the slight twitch of his mouth and the sparkle in his eye that always gave him away when he had something interesting to share.

Pulling out a chair and turning it backwards to straddle it, Isla tapped Callum's tanned arm. "Spill it. What've you got?"

His dark-skinned face split in a huge grin, revealing even, white teeth, and his blue eyes twinkled. "We've rented out our summer cabin for two months! Some fancy American author needing to find himself, or some such thing. Who really cares why?"

"That's wonderful, especially this late in the season. That will be a nice chunk of change for you and Jack. Maybe you can finally run away together!" Jack was Callum's partner of twelve years. Callum always talked about how they were going to make it big and ride off into the sunset. Their vacation home in Lochranza, on the northern coast of the island, was just one of their many ways of doing so.

"When will your tenant arrive, then?"

"If all goes to plan, he'll be arriving on the ferry tomorrow afternoon. I've also got him booked on a hiking tour on Saturday. I threw that in as part of the rental agreement, hoping it would sweeten the pot."

"Who's on hiking on Saturday?"

Callum cleared his throat and fixed his eyes to a point on the wall to the right of Isla's face. She had a sinking feeling that this would turn out to be one of Callum's many plots to *socialize* her. Bless his damn fool heart, he meant well, but he didn't entirely understand why Isla kept to herself. "Callum...," she said in a warning tone.

"You're on hikes for Saturday, love. Please don't be mad, you just always seem to me more comfortable around tourists than you do around locals —"

"With good reason."

"Yes, of course. No arguments there. So what would it hurt to get to know a tourist who will be around longer than a week? You might like him. Hell, he might even be good looking. Even you have to scratch that itch occasionally."

"Callum!" she exclaimed, swatting him in the shoulder. He twirled a lock of sun-streaked blond hair and widened his eyes innocently. The bell on the front door jangled, signaling the arrival of the first tour group of the day, and Callum made his graceful escape. "Duty calls!" he shouted as he disappeared down the hall.

Shaking her head and chuckling to herself, Isla put Callum's forgotten coffee cup in the sink to wash it. She knew Callum loved her and didn't want her to be alone, but all she wanted from this American was his business and for him to stay out of trouble on her tour.

∞∞

Isla sat bolt upright in her bed, sweating and trembling, still in the grips of the nightmare. She could still feel the hand in her hair, the knife at her throat. Flailing her arms madly to get away from the imaginary threat, she scrambled back across the bedspread to flatten her back against the headboard.

Taking great gulps of air, reality finally started sinking in. She was alone in her cabin in Arran, in her own bed, with her two cats, Atticus and Smitty sitting side by side, regarding her curiously. They were both Savannahs, a large breed closely related to bobcats and often highly expressive.

"What?" she replied to their questioning looks. "Never heard of a nightmare before?"

Flicking his tail like a rattlesnake, Smit gave her his back and jumped off the bed. Atticus rose to follow, glancing back at her before leaping gracefully to the floor. Her alarm clock chose that moment to start screeching to signify that, yes, it was indeed time to get up.

Pushing sweaty bangs out of her eyes, Isla swung her legs over the side of the bed and padded to the bathroom.

"Talkin' to me cats now," she said to the empty house. "I'm the crazy cat lady. Pure dead brilliant."

After brushing her teeth and tying her hair back, she headed out of the bedroom, when she paused to look at the full-length wall mirror beside the door. A long, jagged crack ran from the top of the glass to the bottom and smaller cracks branched off to create a web of broken glass.

"Now how in the hell did that happen? Great, need a new mirror now, too."

Trudging through the open great room and into the adjoining kitchen, Isla filled the tea kettle and set it on the stove. She thought she would need something stronger than tea after the night she'd had, so she got out her french press and coffee grinder as well. As she reached for the sack of coffee beans, her hand skimmed across the steam piping out of the spout of the teapot.

Yelping, Isla jerked her hand away and then whirled around when a framed photograph came crashing down from the wall. Isla blinked, looking at the picture, then at the tea kettle, then back at her hand. Shaking her head, she returned to the mundane task of grinding beans and making coffee.

Atticus prowled around her legs while Smitty leapt onto the kitchen island and settled in for a nap in a sun spot. "Maybe I'm losing it. People have been calling me crazy for years, maybe I'm just finally living up to it." After slowly sipping her allotted one cup of coffee, Isla gathered her gear for the day's tours and stuffed it all in her rucksack, grabbed her keys, and headed out the door.

Out on the stone porch, Isla turned her face to the sun and breathed deep of the fresh island air. She started down the porch steps but froze at the bottom when she saw a shape at the edge of the woods. Shading her eyes with her hand, she strained to see what sort of animal would come out of hiding in broad daylight with a human about.

She sucked in a sharp breath when she realized it appeared to be a grey...wolf. "Impossible," Isla whispered. Everyone knew that wolves had been hunted into extinction in Scotland back in the 1700's. And even if there were still wolves on the mainland, how would they get to the island? Swim?

Taking a few seconds to admire the creature, she took in the light grey, almost white fur, soft sky-blue eyes rimmed in black, like eyeliner, and three black strips of fur around the wolf's neck. Isla thought this wolf had to be the most unusual animal she had ever seen, but it could pose an extreme danger to the islanders if it was a predator gone rogue.

Making no sudden movements, Isla side-stepped to her pickup as the wolf calmly watched. Locking herself inside the vehicle, she shifted into reverse and backed out of her gravel drive by muscle memory, her eyes never leaving the mysterious wolf.

₧₧₧

Isla was still rattled when she rushed into Expeditions headquarters like the devil was on her heels.

"Oi, where's the fire, lass?" Callum called from behind the check-in desk. "You're over an hour early, don't worry!"

Still panting, Isla walked up to the opposite side of the desk and slapped her palms on the glass surface. "Oh. My. God. You won't believe what I saw up at the cabin this morning," she exclaimed, her brogue more pronounced in her excitement.

"What's that?"

"A wolf. A fucking wolf, Callum!"

"Bollocks!" Callum rolled his baby blues at her, and turned his attention back to the appointment book.

Annoyed, Isla snatched the ledger from his hand and waved it in his face. "Hand to God, Callum. Cross me 'eart and all that. It was there just staring at me from the edge of the woods when I left for work!"

"Sweetie, you know there aren't any wolves in Scotland. Haven't been for centuries, much to the disappointment of the conservationists."

"Yes, I know. I thought the same thing when I saw it, but it was there just the same!"

Callum flicked a skeptical look at her, and she could tell he didn't believe her. "Well, wolf or no wolf, the show must go on. You have a hike in an hour and ten. Remember that my tenant, the good doctor himself, will be on this one, so make it good. We want him to come back."

"Aye, we do," Isla agreed, waving at Amy who had just entered the room. "And bring his money with him."

She patted Callum's shoulder, and then turned to the other woman. "I'm going to take a quick climb in the cave before the troops arrive. Belay for me?" Amy nodded and followed her through a door off to the right of the lobby that led to *the cave*, Expeditions' indoor climbing room.

The unique structure looked exactly like its name implied—a cave. All four walls and ceiling were covered in simulated rock and also indoor rock climbing handholds. Isla was an expert climber, and she loved using the indoor structure for exercise, but when outdoors, she preferred rock scrambling, a type of climbing rocky faces using nothing but the body.

Jeremiah was half an hour early for his hiking tour. This was more due to a need to explore his surroundings without the bustle of tourists about rather than any kind of punctuality. He pulled his rental car into the parking lot and unfolded his long legs from the compact vehicle. He turned in a slow circle to survey the landscape. The Expeditions office was a lovely log and stone structure nestled into the valley created by the three small mountains that surrounded it.

Whistling, Jere stuffed his hands in the pockets of his cargo shorts and ambled about the grounds, checking out kayaks and poking his head in equipment sheds. Finally he pulled open the heavy glass door to enter the lobby. The room was charming, all wood paneling and natural log benches. Since no one was around, he walked around to study the framed maps of Arran on the wall.

Jeremiah turned as the man he recognized as Callum, his new landlord, strolled into the lobby from somewhere in the back. "Oi, Dr. Rousseau! Welcome to Expeditions. I trust you settled in alright yesterday?"

Jere had arrived on the Caledonian MacBrayne ferry at three in the afternoon yesterday and Callum had been waiting for him. Jere had followed him up to Lochranza to find the cottage he had rented, and they had sat on the porch and talked a bit over a pint. Callum liked the younger man, and one never knew when you could use a friend.

"Jeremiah, please. I settled in just fine, thanks. The place is gorgeous."

"Ye're a bit early, the rest of the group won't show up for a little while. Make yourself at home."

"Mind if I look around?"

"Not at all. I'll just be over here paper pushing if you need anything. I lost the coin toss today." Callum grinned and winked, as if there were some inside joke that Jere was supposed to get. Shaking it off, he turned his attention to exploring.

Finding a gift shop, Jere browsed for a bit before getting bored and moving on. He popped his head into the locker room, eyes lingering on the door to the sauna with longing. "Maybe later, buddy. Gotta do the outdoorsy stuff first," he told himself. While he didn't consider himself a city slicker by any means, he was no outdoorsman, and he hadn't had the heart to turn Callum down when the man had generously offered to throw in a hike at his outdoor company.

Turning left, Jere found himself in a room that resembled a giant mountain cave. He saw a tall blonde straining to hold a climbing rope. She turned to smile at him briefly, her eyes making an appreciative trip from his face to his toes and back again before turning her attention to what was going on above.

Allowing his eyes to travel the direction of the rope, he looked up...up...up, until he finally caught site of a tiny woman suspended from the ceiling. She was in a precarious position with one foot still on the vertical wall, one hand and the other foot clinging fast to holds on the ceiling of the cave, and the other hand clipping her rope into an anchor.

Even knowing the other woman was spotting her, Jere's heart leapt to his throat as he imagined her plummeting 30 feet to land flat on her back. The woman, however, didn't seem to be phased by the danger at all. Hell, she wasn't even breathing hard—as if defying gravity was somewhere between reading on the couch and having a cup of tea.

From his vantage point, Jere couldn't see her face or much detail at all, but what he could see was magnificent. Long, black curls were doing their best to escape a waist-length braid that now hung down away from her body as she executed a horizontal spider crawl across the ceiling. Her skin looked as though it would have been pale, but was a toasted, golden brown dusted with freckles from the sun, and it was glistening with a fine sheen of sweat. Well-defined muscles in her arms and legs bunched and strained from maintaining her handholds, but he had a feeling she would be soft to the touch.

Get a grip, man, Jere told himself, shaking his head. He breathed a silent sigh of relief when the woman reached the opposite wall and began to repel down to the floor.

"Thanks, Amy. I needed that," she said, dusting chalk off her hands and wiping her face with a hand towel.

"No problem, Bo — er, Isla."

Jeremiah watched as the blonde sashayed her way over to him with a seductive bounce in her step. Feeling like meat on a hook, which made him a bit uncomfortable, he looked down at his feet and shuffled them a little.

The woman came to a halt about two feet in front of him and stuck out her hand. "Hello there! My name's Amy Wyatt. And you are?"

Jere felt the familiar twin spots of red appear over his cheekbones, disconcerted by the woman's predatory gaze.

"Dr. Jeremiah Rousseau, ma'am. I'm here for the hiking tour. I'm a little early, so Callum said I could look around." There were times when Jeremiah cursed his smooth Cajun drawl, as it often attracted unwanted attention.

Amy's eyes lit up and she sidled so close, Jere had to take a step back. "Ooh, a doctor!" she said excitedly, placing her hand on his arm.

Shifting uneasily, Jere tried to dispel her misconception. "PhD, ma'am. Not a medical doctor."

Seemingly unaffected by that revelation, Amy looked up at him and Jere actually thought she batted her eyelashes. "Where's that accent from? Too cute. And polite too!"

The smaller woman had finished cleaning up and walked up behind Amy. Clapping a hand on Amy's shoulder, she gently tugged the blonde away from him. "Down girl, give the man some breathing room. You're sucking all of the oxygen out of the room."

Amy just grinned unapologetically and bounced off to collect the equipment. Unaccountably grateful for the save, Jeremiah raised his eyes to her face to thank her.

"Thanks, I—" His words stuttered to a halt when huge jade green eyes looked up at him from under a thick fringe of bangs, and he felt as if he'd been punched in the gut. He thought she'd been magnificent while climbing, but up close, she was breathtaking. Her face was dainty and heart-shaped, with high cheekbones and full lips, the lower one slightly larger. It was her eyes that struck him, though—a clear, sparkling green rimmed in thick, black lashes, slightly turned up at the corners. It was the shadows under them, however, that reached out to him.

Shaking himself out of his reverie, Jere cleared his throat and held out his hand. "Jeremiah." *Eloquent, dumbass.* He hadn't been this flustered by a woman since, well, ever.

That gorgeous mouth quirking up on one side, she took his hand in a firm grip and shook it.

"Isla MacAllan. You must be the tenant."

"Huh? Oh, right. Yes, I'm renting Callum's cottage."

Jeremiah had a chance to look at her some more while she bent to remove her harness and other gear. She was short— the top of her head barely came up to his chest—and what little height she had was mostly legs. While on some women such muscle definition would make them look masculine, on her it was just unbelievably sexy.

Isla straightened and gave him a slightly impatient look. "You're a wee bit early. I've got to hit the showers and change for the hike. Callum will be back in the lobby if you want some company."

"Isn't Callum leading the hike?"

"Nope. He wanted you to have the best. That'd be me."

"Modesty. Always a good quality," he said with a wink, inwardly groaning at his lame comment.

She just raised an eyebrow, did that half-smile thing, and turned to leave. Jere followed her out, hoping his tongue wasn't lolling out of his mouth like a happy puppy dog. He began to wonder how he was going to get through a half-day's hike staring at the back of her.

Chapter Four

Isla drove the Expeditions tour van and its five passengers to the town of Whiting Bay to find the trailhead for the Glenashdale Falls. She had originally planned on taking the group to Machrie Moor, which is a much easier walk, but all of the people in her group were experienced hikers — with the exception of Dr. Rousseau.

Part of her wanted to take him there because the falls were magnificent, and she wanted to show him the best their little island had to offer. Another part of her wanted to push him because of the way he had affected her. He had gotten under her skin from the minute she saw him. His embarrassment over Amy's flirting had been endearing, but when she'd gotten close enough to see him, she couldn't stop looking.

When Callum had told her about his new tenant, she had expected a white-haired, professor type — not tall, tan, and gorgeous back there. The man had sharp chiseled features that were softened by the mop of sun-streaked, brown hair that was just a bit too long. His hazel eyes were sparkling and friendly, with laugh lines crinkling at the corners. But it was his smile that had stunned her. She had no idea how he managed to look boyish and predatory at the same time, but somehow he pulled it off. He had sensuous lips that covered a decidedly wolf-like set of pearly whites, which naturally had Isla thinking back to her wolfish encounter that morning and brought her back to reality.

No one rattled her. No one. So if she wanted to push the good doctor a little bit on a not-exactly-easy hike, who could blame her. *He's a big boy, he can handle it.* As the devil on her shoulder laughed its head off at that thought, Isla found a parking spot and began to unload passengers and gear.

The rest of the group consisted of Ethan and Katie, a pair of honeymooners from North Carolina, and a father and son duo. Robert and Fletcher were mainlanders on holiday from Edinburgh.

"Right then," Isla began when they were all unloaded, "we need to go over some safety precautions." She motioned for everyone to gather around so they could hear.

"The most important rule is to stay with the group. Don't go wandering off alone. It can be very dangerous if you don't know the terrain. If there's something you want to stop and look at, just yell up ahead for me and we'll all stop. Got it?"

She waited until the five of them nodded before she continued. "This isn't a climb by any means, but it is a steep trail. Keep well hydrated and signal me if you need to take a rest."

"Lastly, remember the hiker's code: 'Take nothing but pictures, leave nothing but footprints.' And don't touch anything that looks poisonous!"

Isla checked everyone's pack to make sure they had everything they needed and then started down the side road that led to the trailhead.

When they first set out, Jeremiah was having trouble concentrating on the scenery — and the ground he walked on — because he was too busy watching Isla up ahead. She moved with the same cat-like grace that she had on the climbing wall as she negotiated the steepening trail. His eyes traveled from her slender ankles to her shapely calves and thighs then promptly came to rest at her denim cut-off clad backside.

Jere stumbled for about the fifth time, so Isla stopped the group and turned to look at him. Lifting her chin a notch and raising her eyebrow, she said, "Need a break, Doc? Can't have you tumbling back down. Expeditions frowns upon losing hikers."

He mumbled that he was fine to continue and did his best to pay attention to where he was going. Soon he became so absorbed in the rugged landscape of the forest that he almost forgot there was anyone with him.

Jeremiah thought he heard rustling in the brush off to his left. Thinking it could be some wildlife, he took one step toward it and then another.

"Dr. Rousseau, stay on the trail please," Isla said firmly without turning her head.

Did the woman have eyes in the back of her head or just supersensitive hearing?

"Yes, ma'am," he drawled when she peeked over her shoulder at him to make sure he'd heard. It was insane that he had known this woman for less than a day and already one look from her set his heart racing.

The forest became thicker with moss-covered birch trees and tufts of fern and the trail sharply sloped upwards. Jeremiah began to hear the mighty rush of the waterfall. He also began to notice something strange.

He had glimpsed a couple of red squirrels that he learned were indigenous to the island. The squirrels that would normally be darting about and skittering up trees seemed to be...following the group. Or, more specifically, following Isla. The animals slinked through the ferns that lined the trails, always keeping about three feet behind her.

Jeremiah was interested in the curious squirrel behavior, but he was also starting to breathe harder from the extra strain of the incline, so he focused back on the trail.

Finally Isla drew them to a stop in front of a wooden overlook. "We can stop here for a bit of a rest and some pictures," she said, making a sweeping gesture toward the valley beyond. There, across the valley, was an enormous waterfall that came plunging down over a rocky outcrop to the river below. A smoky cloud of mist rose up from the rushing water, giving the scene an ethereal quality.

The other hikers gasped and chattered excitedly as they all crowded onto the structure to get a better look. Jeremiah hung back and stepped up beside Isla, who watched the group with a small smile tugging at her lips.

"I never get tired of seeing that," she said so softly Jeremiah wasn't sure she knew it was aloud.

"Tired of what?"

"Their sense of wonder."

"Is that why you work for Expeditions?"

She turned to look at him, her mouth twitching. "Something like that."

Jeremiah walked over to the overlook to look over the railing, giving Isla a chance to study him. The man was two parts bookish professor with his clumsiness and childlike interest in everything around him and one part bad boy with his bulky, muscular physique. He had impossibly wide, well-muscled shoulders that formed a V down to a trim waist. He was wearing cargo shorts and a sleeveless t-shirt that showed off his darkly tanned arms.

On his left arm he had a tattoo of a snake wrapping around his forearm that went halfway up his bicep, where it coiled around a large bird with flaming wings. Isla had never been a fan of tattoos, especially with the mystery surrounding hers, but on him she found it incredibly sexy. Isla found herself quelling the urge to reach out and trace it with her fingers.

As if sensing her scrutiny, Jeremiah looked back at her and smiled like a kid in a candy store, obviously enjoying the waterfall as much as the others. Ignoring the little flutter in her stomach, Isla cleared her throat. "All right everyone, time to head back. It's getting late and we don't want to get caught up here when the storm comes."

Fletcher, a baby-faced boy who looked about twelve but was probably close to sixteen, looked at her like she had grown a second head. "What storm? The sky is crystal clear. What makes you think it's going to storm?"

"I can smell it," Isla said, only half teasing. "I can always tell when the weather is going to change. But also, there was a cloud over the summit of Goat Fell. That almost always means a storm."

As the group started the descent back down the steep trail, Jeremiah sped up to fall into step beside Isla. "So what do you do for fun on the island?"

"We have kayaking, abseiling, rock scrambling, and horseback riding to name a few. Obviously the most popular activity is hiking. There are dozens of beautiful walks."

"That's helpful, but I actually meant what do *you* do for fun?"

"I do all of those things, for work and pleasure. I'm almost always either at Expeditions or at home. Expeditions only has four full-time guides, so I keep pretty busy working."

There was a note of sadness in her voice, but Jeremiah didn't push. He had a tendency to come on pretty strong when it came to mysteries. He could tell from the guarded way Isla spoke that she wouldn't be an easy egg to crack, which only made him more interested.

When the group made it back to the trailhead, they were all pretty winded, with the exception of Isla. The six of them piled back into the van and headed back to Expeditions. As Isla drove, Jeremiah tried to ignore the honeymooners necking in the back, and he chuckled when he saw Fletcher trying not to fall asleep against his dad's shoulder.

They pulled into the parking lot of Expeditions where all the passengers were unloaded and all the gear was put away. Jeremiah hung back while the other hikers said their goodbyes and drove off in their rental cars. Once they were gone, Isla turned back to go inside and Jeremiah followed. He found her at the front desk, presumably going over the next day's schedule. She was chewing on the eraser of her pencil, a line of concentration forming between her brows. He thought she looked hauntingly beautiful and unbearably lonely.

"Come have a drink with me," he blurted before he thought better of it.

Her head flew up, her gaze colliding with his, and she looked genuinely surprised. "Pardon?"

"I'm on sort of a forced vacation here. My publisher thinks I need to 'clear my head.' The only other person I know on the island is Callum and" — Jere made a show of looking around the empty lobby — "he's not here. I could use the company."

She gave him a sympathetic smile, and he thought her eyes lingered just slightly on his lips, but he probably imagined it. "I appreciate it, but I don't think that's a good idea," she said, shaking her head.

Not willing to give up so easily, Jere leaned on the counter and cocked his head at her. "Why not?"

"I've still got some things to finish up here."

"So tonight then," Jere said, flashing her that toothy grin. "Meet me at the pub around six?"

She simply stared at him for a few moments and it looked like she might refuse. But then she sighed, and gave him a tentative smile that made his heart flip-flop dangerously.

"Alright, six it is then," she said.

Chapter Five

Isla walked into Brodick's Pub at 5:59 and scanned the dim room for Jeremiah. She spotted him in a booth toward the back, reading a newspaper, and her stomach did that fluttering thing again. Catching a few dark glances from locals at the bar, she muttered to herself, "What the hell am I doing here?"

She started to turn around and make her escape when he raised sparkling hazel eyes to her face. As heat coiled inside her, Isla swallowed and began to make her way through the gathering crowd. *Oh, you're in big trouble,* she told herself.

Isla reached the booth and slid onto the cracked vinyl bench across the table from him. He smiled at her and the rest of the world receded just a little.

"Hi," he said. "Glad you came."

She gave him a wry smile. "Didn't get any better offers."

Jeremiah barked out a laugh and she relaxed ever so slightly. As was her habit, Isla pulled her legs up and sat cross legged on the bench and propped her chin on her hand.

"Want a drink?" he asked, signaling for a waitress.

"Scotch, neat," came her reply. He regarded her with curiosity, but ordered one for each of them.

Although she had visibly relaxed since first sitting down, Jeremiah noticed Isla kept sneaking nervous glances around the room as if she were waiting for something to jump out at her. Following her gaze, he noticed a pair at the bar looking at them with disdain and whispering to each other.

Shrugging it off, he turned his attention back to his reluctant date. While clad simply in an Arran Outfitters t-shirt and skinny jeans, she was stunning. Her face was absent of makeup, except for a touch of lip gloss, her skin naturally smooth as marble. She had her hair down tonight, a heavy mass of midnight curls tumbling down over her shoulders that Jere longed to sink his fingers into.

Jere cleared his throat and leaned back as the waitress set their drinks in front of them. He took a deep whiff of the scotch and then tasted it, rolling the amber liquid around his mouth before swallowing. "That's incredible."

"The Arran twelve-year malt, distilled here on the island. You should try the fourteen year, it'll knock your socks right off," she said, laughing. "So what really brings you to our island, doctor?"

Jere rolled his eyes. "Oh, hell...Jeremiah, please. It's like I said. I'm a writer and I just came off a big project. My editor and publisher ganged up on me and forced me to take some time off."

"You poor thing," she said sarcastically, taking a sip of her scotch and briefly closing her eyes.

"How about you?" Jere asked. "Were you born here on the island?"

"Glasgow. I moved here ten years ago." Her smile disappeared and her face closed up, so Jeremiah decided not to press her on her past. This time.

"Oi, if it isn't Beauty and the Yank! I wouldn't have believed it if I hadn't seen it with me own eyes!" Callum hollered at them, causing several heads to turn. He dragged Jack across the room to the booth. Callum took Isla's hand and pulled her up, spinning her gracefully over to Jeremiah's side, and sat her down. The two men sat down together on the now empty bench. Callum and Jack were both in their early forties, but while Callum was slender and wiry, Jack was brawny and compact. He had dark brown hair buzzed military style, golden brown eyes, and an affable smile.

"I'm from New Orleans, brother, no Yanks there!" Jere shot back good-naturedly.

"So that's where the accent comes from," Isla teased.

"What are you talking about? Y'all are the ones with accents," he retorted, making them all laugh.

Callum introduced Jack to Jeremiah and the men shook hands. He glanced over at Isla and winked. "Doc, I can't believe you actually got our lass to come out. She's not a very social animal."

Jere smiled at that, but the smile faded when a man and woman walked by glaring at them and shaking their heads. Callum and Jack exchanged worried glances while Isla suddenly became very interested in her left thumbnail.

Turning concerned eyes back to the couple across from him, Jere questioned them gently. "Do y'all get a lot of trouble here, being gay and all?"

Jack shook his head. "Not too much. It's not that...they —
"

Isla shot out of the booth like she was on fire. "Look, I have to go guys. Cal, see you Monday. Jack, Jeremiah, good to see you. Have a good night." As she rushed for the door, Jere thought it odd how the crowd parted for her.

"Jack!" Callum snapped. Jack slapped his forehead with his palm. "I'm such an idiot."

"What the hell just happened?" Jere demanded, looking back and forth between the two.

Callum sighed and scrubbed a hand over his face. "Those people aren't looking over here because of us, Jeremiah."

"Okay," Jere prompted, drawing out the last syllable.

"Isla has kind of a reputation here in town," Callum said, obviously choosing his words carefully.

"What kind of a reputation?"

"A lot of the people living on the island grew up here, as did their families. Isla just showed up one day out of the blue, with no known family, while a lot of the residents here will tell you how they can trace their ancestry back to the Bruce himself. People fear what they don't understand. Somewhere along the way, rumors began to surround Isla. The talk is what caused her to retreat to where she spends most of her time either working or at her cabin. Unfortunately, doing so just fueled the rumor mill, so she tries to avoid the popular local spots. That's why I was so surprised she came out tonight."

"Shit." Jere didn't know what else to say. He could tell Callum was leaving out a lot of details, but what he'd revealed was bad enough.

"Look," Callum said, pegging him with a fierce stare, "the girl is tough. Tougher than most men I know. But she's also lonely. I think it would do her some good to get out some, maybe have some nice guy show her a good time." He waggled scruffy eyebrows. "That's why I set you up on her tour."

"Manipulative bastard," Jere teased.

"Damn right. I'm hoping you'll be a friend to her and bring her out of her shell a bit. But make no mistake, mate. You hurt her, I hurt you. Got it?"

"Understood." Jere thought about all he had learned that night and became even more determined to find out more about the mysterious Isla MacAllan.

⌘

When Isla settled into bed that night, her mind was racing. All she saw when she closed her eyes was Jeremiah's devilishly handsome face. Frustrated, she yanked the quilt tighter around herself, dislodging Atticus and earning a hiss. She slapped at the covers with both hands, trying unsuccessfully to get comfortable.

"I do *not* need to get involved with a tourist!" She said aloud, causing Smitty and Atticus to look at her curiously. It was a complication she just didn't need. Eventually she would have to tell him why she never wanted to go into town, if Callum hadn't already, and that would only lead to more questions. Maybe he would even shun her like the rest of the people on the island.

Something told her that the intelligent Dr. Rousseau would not jump to conclusions so easily. And just like that, he was back on her mind again—his sexy mouth in particular. She drifted off to sleep imagining what it would be like to press her own lips against it, just once.

Isla was jerked awake by a loud thud coming from the front of the house. She sat straight up in her bed and listened for a few seconds, but all remained quiet. While she needed to check things out, she prided herself in not being an idiot, so she grabbed her twelve-gauge shotgun from her closet and loaded four cartridges.

She methodically explored every corner of the tiny cabin and checked the locks on all the doors and windows. When she found nothing, she unlocked the front door and cautiously poked her head out, looking first left toward the rocking chairs, then right toward the wood pile.

At first, she didn't notice anything out of the ordinary, until her gaze rested on the porch in front of the wood pile. Two logs appeared to have rolled off the top of the pile—which was now taller than Isla herself—and toppled to the ground.

What the hell? The logs were probably ten pounds each and the night air was still as a grave. There was no reason for the logs to have fallen, unless something had knocked them down. Isla scanned the tree line around the clearing that housed her cabin for any signs of life.

Seeing nothing but foggy darkness, Isla gave up and turned to go inside. She had just leaned the shotgun against the wall just inside the door when she heard an unusual sound. The distant music of children's laughter echoed faintly through the trees. Startled, Isla turned sharply back around, just in time to catch a glimpse of a bright red shirt of a little boy disappearing behind a hazy shrub of rhododendron.

Alarmed for the child, Isla quickly shut the front door and took off into the trees after him, no longer concerned with her own safety.

She chased the boy through the murky forest for what seemed like hours. Occasionally he would stop and wait for her, a gap-toothed grin splitting his pale face, only to dart away again when she got close. She almost caught him once, her fingers barely grasping the collar of his thin shirt, but it slipped away just as quickly around the bend of the path.

When Isla didn't see him again for a few minutes, she almost gave up, hoping the boy had sense enough to go home to his parents. She had just decided to turn back when she stepped into a clearing and saw, not the boy, but a man casually leaning against a tall pine.

Mildly confused to find another person out in the middle of the night, Isla approached cautiously, hoping the man was somehow related to the little boy. Her surroundings began to go out of focus as the grey fog closed in around them, and Isla tried to hang onto the memory of what she had been doing. Her mind suddenly felt as foggy as the clearing.

She stared at the man as he stood there, watching her watch him. He was so handsome, with black hair and pale blue eyes set deep in dark sockets, skin smooth and white as the driven snow. His face was sharp and chiseled, cheeks hollow. His full, red lips quirked up in an easy half-smile. Trying to pull her gaze away from his mesmerizing, shadowy eyes, she shook her head and forced her brain to think.

"Did you see the boy?" she asked, her voice sounding strange to her own ears.

The man merely smiled. And watched.

Inexplicably, Isla found herself compelled to approach him. A hint of alarm caused her stomach to clench because she didn't want to fight the urge—she wasn't normally so cavalier about her own safety.

Pushing off from the tree, the stranger walked forward to meet her. He stopped a couple of feet in front of her and waited. Isla was dimly aware of her state of dress, pajama bottoms, tank top, and bare feet, but she couldn't bring herself to care.

Her eyes met his and she saw shadows twisting and turning in his opalescent gaze. She felt as if she were being pulled in, her mind being separated from her physical body. Frightened, Isla tried to back away and found that she was no longer able to move. Panic blossomed and Isla tried to break eye contact with the stranger, but she wasn't able to do that either.

As she stared, unable to break away, the man's face began changing. Before her eyes, a sign manifested on his forehead, a primitive glyph that resembled a human eye. It looked eerily similar to what the Celts called an "evil eye." His eyes flashed and his lips pulled back into a deadly snarl.

Isla trembled uncontrollably, knowing that she was in danger, but unable to move a muscle to do anything but shiver. The malevolence reached for her face with bony fingers and began to caress her cheek, making her skin crawl. She could practically feel the evil rolling off of him in waves.

Just when he extended razor sharp claws from the tips of those corpse-like fingers, a horrific howl pierced the night, and she was jolted out of the trance the creature held her in, feeling those claws slicing her skin just as the vision dissipated.

Suddenly fully aware, Isla looked up to find that she wasn't in a clearing in the woods, but on one of the moors where she stood in front of a primitive stone circle. She had believed herself familiar with all of the ancient ruins on the island, but she didn't recognize this one.

She turned in a slow circle, taking stock of her new surroundings, wincing at the pain in her bare feet. She froze when she locked her jade green gaze with the wolf's pale blue one. Remembering the howl that had broken the creature's hold on her, she had the feeling that the wolf meant her no harm. As she watched it, the wolf cocked his head at her, and then slid down until his belly rested on the cold ground and bowed his head.

Isla recognized this as a submissive position, so she relaxed slightly. Quickly she reminded herself of her vulnerable position alone out on the moor, and remaining here would risk the depraved creature returning. As if coming to the same conclusion, the wolf let out three short barks and a growl in her direction.

Not needing to be told twice, Isla took off running in the direction she hoped was home.

Chapter Six

Jeremiah sat stretched out on the couch in the living room of his rented cottage, staring out the window that looked out to the sea. He had his most prized possession, a '72 Fender Telecaster Thinline guitar — gorgeous lady that she was — sitting on his lap, and he was teasing out a run from Jonny Lang's *I Am*. Listening to and playing the blues always reminded him of home and helped him clear his mind when he was trying to puzzle something out.

And Isla MacAllan was most definitely a puzzle. The woman was beautiful, ripped, and clearly very good at her job. From what he could tell, she was also highly intelligent and fiercely independent. The few friends that she had loved her dearly and were highly protective of her.

So why would she shy away from interacting with the locals? Why were they so unwelcoming to her after she had been on the island for so long? Jeremiah couldn't help but feel as though there was a piece he was missing.

Further thought was cut off when his wailing ringtone clashed with the notes he was playing. He carefully set aside his guitar, reached for his iPhone, and hit answer. "Hey Drew, where y'at?"

"Hey brother," Drew said. "I wanted to give you an update on these scans you sent me."

Jere immediately scrambled off the couch and searched for a notepad. "Hold on, man, let me get something to write on." Finding what he was looking for, he took a seat at the kitchen bar and put Drew on speaker. "Okay, go."

"First of all, it's definitely written in some form of Old Latin, but one I've never come across before. I gotta tell ya, it's slow going."

"What do you have so far?"

"Well, I think you were right. I think this could indeed be a collection of oral myths from ancient Latium. That in itself is incredible, but the subject matter is...unusual."

Drew paused, causing Jeremiah's pulse to speed up in anticipation. "What do you mean, unusual?"

Jeremiah heard him take a deep breath, as if preparing himself to deliver bad news. "There are a lot of references to," Drew paused, "witches."

"Go on," Jeremiah urged.

"What do you mean, go on? I just told you we have an ancient text about witches, and all you can say is 'Go on'? You — shit. You were expecting this, weren't you?"

Jere chuckled. "I had hopes, but I didn't want to make assumptions," he said with a smile in his voice. "I have seen that mark on the cover used in conjunction with accounts of witches before."

"I should have known. You are the ghost doctor, after all. Not too much of a stretch."

"Get to the point, Drew."

"Alright, take it easy. Like I said, I am unfamiliar with this dialect, but I have been able to translate a few passages. They all center around this particular group of witches called *Bruixi*. It is referred to as more of a race than a coven, as if it's something they are born into rather than join."

When Jeremiah didn't comment, Drew said, "Aaaand you know this already, too."

"Just bits and pieces. I was hoping this book could give me some new information."

"There *is* something else," Drew continued. "Within the *Bruixi* race, there is a particular family lineage — they are described almost like royalty in the passages — called the *Vigilati*. Roughly translated, it means "Guardians." While all of the *Bruixi* are supposedly born with the power to use magic and manipulate the elements, the *Vigilati* are much more powerful."

"This is new," Jere interrupted. "I haven't come across this in any of my research."

"The *Vigilati* are spoken of like they are some sort of *spirit warriors* — for lack of a better translation. Supposedly throughout the world there were believed to be gateways — called *Locuses* in the text — between the spirit world and the human world. Sort of like the vortices we hear about with ghosts. They believed in certain types of demons that would try and cross over through these gateways when they gathered enough energy to become corporeal."

Jere began to feel uneasy, though he couldn't explain it. "Where would they get this energy?"

"The *Bruixi* believed that these demons, referred to as *auchrim*, would lure humans to cross over to their side of the gateway, where they would drain their energy and channel it to the strongest among them, the *Lochrim*."

"What does that have to do with these *Vigilati*?" Jere asked, writing furiously on his notepad.

"This is where it starts to get interesting," Drew said, chuckling. "The *Vigilati* were bred with these special powers to keep the demons contained. Mainly they just had to guard the *locus* to keep humans away. However, if a *Lochrim* manages to escape, it was the *vigile* guarding that particular gateway who was charged with trapping the demon and sending it back."

"Couldn't they kill it?"

"From what I've read so far, it doesn't seem like any of them have that ability. Like I said, I haven't gotten very far."

"No worries, what you've given me already is great. I'll have much more to go on in my research now. Can you email me your translations?"

"F'sure. Hey, one more thing."

"Yeah?"

"You mentioned the symbol on the cover. I think I know what it is."

Jere sat up straight, instantly at full attention. "What?"

"This *Vigilati* line apparently passes from grandmother to granddaughter. It was written that each *vigile* has that brand—called a *signa* in the text—somewhere on her body. Thing is, they're not born with it. It supposedly appears sometime during early adolescence, around the same time they gain use of their powers."

"That's amazing, Drew. I can't wait to read the rest," Jere said. "Well, I don't want to take up any more of your time. You've been such a big help—"

"Hey Jere?"

"Yeah, Drew?"

"Look, I'm not sure I believe in all this *witches* and *demons* shit..."

"But?"

"Well, if my grandmother is to be believed, demons are much worse than spirits. They can actually harm you." Drew came from a big family of hardcore Catholics. "Just be careful, man, hear?"

"Always," Jere said cheerfully, knowing Drew wouldn't believe it for a second. "Thanks again."

⁓֍֍

It had been two days since Isla had seen Jeremiah, not that she was counting. It was probably for the best, anyway. She had been especially jumpy since her dream—or whatever it was—the other night, and it was embarrassing. She got startled by the silliest things, like Smitty jumping up on the back of the couch by her head or Callum clapping her on the shoulder when she was busy working on the schedule.

She had come back from her only tour of the day, a beginner's hike, had a quick climb in the cave, and decided to try relaxing in the sauna. She hoped that the steamy heat would unknot her tense muscles.

After ten minutes, Isla caught herself nodding off, so she left the humid room to hit the shower. She had slept precious little since the incident the other night, almost afraid to let herself surrender consciousness. She had the most disturbing feeling that her mind was no longer entirely her own. Because of the lack of sleep, Isla had been jittery and snappish, even with her employees, and dark circles bruised the area underneath her eyes.

Isla heaved a shuddering sigh and stepped out of the shower to towel off. As she stared at her drawn face in the mirror, she barely recognized herself. For the first time in years, she truly wished she had someone to talk to. Someone who understood.

Jeremiah had spent the last two days since their outing to the pub buried in research. He had received the translations from Drew, and he had been so absorbed in them that he sometimes even forgot to eat.

Finally dragging his eyes away from his computer screen, Jere decided it was definitely time for a break. He gathered his keys, phone, and a light jacket and jogged out the front door. Hopping in the rental car, he debated with himself over where to go, but when he pulled out onto the coastal road, he automatically headed south to Lamlash.

When Jere arrived at Expeditions, Callum was on his way out. The smaller man waved at Jeremiah and walked over to meet him.

"How goes the vacation, Doc?" he said, grinning.

Rolling his eyes, Jere ignored the *doc* part. "Still working too damn much."

"Can't get away from it, eh?"

"Something like that."

"Wish I could stay, mate, but I got a hot date," Callum said, waggling his eyebrows comically.

Jere chuckled. "Oh, boy, does Jack know?"

"He'd better, it's his treat! Hey, Isla's inside. Would you mind keeping her company until she closes up? I hate it when she's here late by herself."

Since he had been planning to do just that, Jere nodded and clapped Callum on the back. "No problem. I can probably annoy her into leaving anyway," he said with a wink, then turned to go inside.

"Jeremiah?"

"Yeah?"

"Do me a favor and keep an eye on her, okay? She's been in a strange mood all day, but she won't talk to me about it. I'm worried about her."

Frowning, Jere nodded again. "Will do. Have a good night."

When they parted ways, Jeremiah headed into the lobby of Expeditions and began to search for Isla. He checked the cave first, and not finding her, he poked his head in the breakroom. Still nothing. Finally he decided to check the locker room, where he found her sitting on a bench with her back to him, brushing her hair into long silky waves.

"Hey, Isla, Callum told me to come on back. Hope you don't mind."

"Son of a *bitch!*" she screamed, popping off the bench like a jack-in-the-box. She whirled around to face him, assuming a defensive stance and breathing heavily. "Damn it, Jeremiah, you scared the holy hell out of me. I thought I was alone."

"Clearly," he said, quirking an eyebrow at her, pretending to clear out his ear. "I think I'm partially deaf now."

"Well, what did you expect, sneaking up on a body like that?"

"I didn't sneak! Why so jumpy?"

Her eyes darted to the right and she bit her lip, sending a shot of heat straight to his groin. Not wanting to embarrass himself, Jere studied the lockers just to the left of her.

"I'm not jumpy, I just wasn't expecting you." She didn't sound all that convincing.

Against his better judgment, Jeremiah stepped closer. Bad idea, now he could smell her. Hers was an intoxicating mixture of her mint shampoo, soap, and clean skin, and Jere briefly closed his eyes before he spoke.

"I was hoping you'd have dinner with me."

Her brow furrowed and, to her credit, she at least pretended to think it over before she turned him down.

"I'm sorry, I don't think that's a very good idea."

"Why not?"

"I try and make it a habit not to date customers," she said, pushing past him to head for the door.

"I'm not a customer anymore. I want to hike, I'll hike by myself," he said, grinning widely.

She gave a weary sigh, and Jeremiah noticed how tired she looked, how her beautiful face seemed more full of shadows than usual. "Look, I'm just not interested, alright?"

Turning away from him, she grabbed the door handle and pulled it open. In a lightning-quick move, he grabbed her free hand and spun her around until she came chest to chest with him. He snaked one arm around until his hand rested on the small of her back, and he buried the other deep in her ebony curls. Ever so gently, using his hand in her hair, he urged her to look up at him.

"Bullshit." His mouth came down on hers surprisingly gently, considering the way he'd grabbed her. He placed little kisses first on her upper lip, then her lower, his tongue teasing at the corners.

Her hand came to his chest and tensed to push him away, and she opened her mouth to protest. Taking the opportunity presented to him, Jere slid his tongue inside her mouth, urging her deeper into the kiss.

Finally, just when he thought she might really push him away, she began kissing him back. The hand on his chest relaxed, and her other hand slid around his waist. Groaning, he pulled her closer, slanting his head to deepen the angle of the kiss.

Then, as quickly as it started, he ended it with one last peck on her nose. Isla's eyes opened slowly and she blinked, looking a little dazed.

Jeremiah smiled down at her and raised an eyebrow.

"You may have your reasons for not wanting to go out, but you're definitely interested," he said. "But I won't push. Not yet, anyway." He winked at her and pushed past her out of the locker room.

"Bastard," she muttered, but smiled a little to herself. While she knew seeing Jeremiah could complicate her life immensely, she was grateful to him for taking her mind off her scary encounter for a few minutes. *And, let's face it,* she told herself, *he's incredibly hot.*

Isla joined him a few seconds later in the lobby, and she felt her cheeks heat when he gave her a knowing smile. He was leaning on the front desk, scribbling something on a notepad. Tearing the sheet off, he folded it and handed it to her.

"My cell number. In case you change your mind. I'm gonna go for a hike."

She looked at the paper skeptically, then shrugged delicate shoulders and took it. "You shouldn't hike by yourself," she said automatically.

"I'll be fine."

Typical man, she thought, rolling her eyes. "Well don't stay out too late, it's going to rain."

"Hiker's intuition again?" he asked.

She shrugged again. "Take it or leave it."

Before she could protest, Jere kissed her on the cheek and stepped forward to open the door for her. Isla exited the lobby ahead of him, headed to her car, and then she turned back to him. "Jeremiah."

"Ma'am?" he drawled, giving her goosebumps.

"Stay on the trail."

Chapter Seven

When Jeremiah began his hike on the southeast side of the island, it was a beautiful, clear day. The trails were devoid of travelers due to a sailboat race in Brodick Bay. He had wandered up a rough trail that sliced through the heart of the Merckland Wood.

He'd been walking for nearly two hours when the first clap of thunder rang in the sky. He told himself he would just go a little bit further, knowing the canopy of the forest would give him some protection from the rain.

The trail curved sharply to the right, then disappeared. Just up ahead, Jere noticed several primitive-looking stacks of sticks cut from saplings. They loomed in the darkening forest like ghostly monuments. He remembered reading somewhere that the locals would build these structures as offerings to the faeries. They believed the faeries would take up residence in the makeshift houses.

Jere had lost track of time wandering through the *faerie village* when the deluge broke. Rain poured down from the sky in buckets, and he laughed at himself for thinking the trees would protect him. The sun had gone down fast, aided by dark thunderclouds, and Jeremiah suddenly found himself in a very dangerous situation.

Calmly, he began to retrace his steps in what he thought was the direction he'd come from. The rain was pounding so hard that he couldn't see a foot in front of his face, except when a bolt of lightning lit up the sky.

Making his way slowly, carefully through the woods, Jeremiah began to question his direction. He should have made it back to the trail by now if he was going the right way. No sooner than the thought crossed his mind, Jeremiah stepped out into thin air.

He had stepped off of some kind of bluff and found himself half rolling, half sliding down a shear embankment. He flailed desperately, trying to grab a branch or a root — anything to anchor himself — but there was nothing but mud and rocks.

He managed to stop the alligator roll and maneuvered his body so that he was sliding on his back. Just when he thought he would never stop sliding, the ground beneath his back dropped off and he was falling. He hit the ground feet first. Hard. Pain shot up his right leg as his ankle gave way beneath him.

"Damn it!" he yelled out into the storm, agony causing his vision to narrow. He didn't know how long he lay there on the ground, panting, until finally the pain receded enough that he was pretty sure he would stay conscious. Gingerly, he pulled his battered body into a sitting position as the rain slowed to a light drizzle.

"Figures," he muttered. "Now what am I gonna do?"

He quickly took stock of his injuries — sprained, possibly broken ankle, bruised ribs, bleeding cut over his right eye. Next, he surveyed his surroundings, trying unsuccessfully to find any identifying landmarks. He did, however, see a faint glow off in the distance.

Thinking the light could be from a house, but barely daring to hope, Jeremiah scooted over to a tree to try and pull himself up. He was able to stand briefly on his good leg, but when he tried to take a step, he dropped like a stone.

Jeremiah pulled his good knee up and rested his forehead on it, closing his eyes briefly to stave off the nausea. His head snapped up when he heard a low-pitched rumble that sounded a little too much like a growl. He gaped as a silvery shape appeared out of the darkness.

"Un-fucking-believable," Jere breathed, staring at the large wolf that stalked closer to him, jowls pulled back in a snarl. Its ice-blue eyes were locked onto Jeremiah as it took one step, then another.

Jeremiah held his breath and tried not to move a muscle, waiting to see what the wolf would do. The huge animal turned its head and glanced behind it, and Jeremiah cringed when he saw four more wolves step out of the shadows. Now, he didn't know all the statistics on it, but he was pretty damn sure the odds of finding one wolf, much less five, on an island in Scotland were about one in a billion.

The leader of the pack tipped his head back and howled to the wind, and then he lowered his big body into a crouch, as if he were preparing to attack. Jeremiah flattened himself against the tree line and felt around for anything to use for a weapon. His fingertips brushed across a sharp rock and he picked it up. It wasn't much, but it was all he had.

Jeremiah braced for impact as the wolf's muscles coiled and bunched, preparing to strike. He jumped when a shotgun blast echoed through the trees. Four of the wolves melted into the surrounding darkness, leaving only the alpha. In fact, they left so fast Jeremiah couldn't even track the movements. It was as if they just disappeared.

Hearing footsteps approach, Jeremiah looked beyond the remaining wolf to see Isla emerge from the trees, twelve gauge aimed right at the wolf. She looked like an Amazon, thick ropes of wet hair tossed by the wind, clothes soaked to the skin, hard eyes fixated on the wolf. And she was well-armed, from the shotgun to the wicked-looking bowie knife sheathed at her belt.

"What the—"

"Shh!" she commanded without looking at him. "Don't give it any more reason to bite you."

"Isla, it could kill you."

The wolf growled and inched toward Jeremiah.

"Jeremiah. Shut. Up." Isla pumped the shotgun again. The sound drew the wolf's attention, and it turned around to regard Isla with curiosity. Isla merely stared back, right into the creature's eyes, which Jeremiah was pretty sure was the last thing you're supposed to do with a wild animal.

Ever so slowly, the wolf lowered his haunches to a sitting position and bowed his head.

"*Facile esse*," Isla whispered, "*bene est*." Be of ease, all is well.

Jeremiah looked back and forth between Isla and the wolf. To his disbelief, the wolf rose to his feet, and after one last piercing look at Jeremiah, he loped off into the trees.

At a loss for words—as there was so much *what the fuck* in what just happened, he didn't know where to start—Jeremiah finally said the first thing that came to mind. "You speak Latin?"

"Huh?"

"Never mind. Look, we've gotta get out of here before that thing comes back!"

Isla shouldered her shotgun and walked over to where Jeremiah sat slumped against a tree. "Can you walk?"

"With your help, I think I'll be able to manage," he answered, trying not to wince when he shifted positions.

Isla crouched down beside him so he could sling one arm across her shoulder. With Jere levering his body up on his good leg, they were able to pull him upright. "My cabin is just around the bend. Think you can make it?"

"Gonna have to," Jere said in a tight voice, clenching his jaw against the pain. He had to lean heavily on her when he took a step on his bad leg.

"Damn, you're heavy!" Isla teased.

"Not really, you're just tiny," he retorted, which wasn't entirely true—at six foot four and nearly two hundred pounds of muscle, Jere was pretty sure he felt damn heavy as dead weight.

"You know, I think someone warned you not to go off by yourself *and* not to stay out too late."

"Don't remind me," Jere said, groaning.

Isla patted his hand sympathetically. "We're almost there. It's just up ahead."

Jeremiah breathed a sigh of relief, because his good leg was shaking so badly from holding his weight that he was sure he would collapse if he had to walk much farther.

§)(§

When they made it to the cabin, Isla helped Jeremiah hobble over to the couch where he flopped down with a grunt.

Isla took one of the throw pillows and placed it on the coffee table. "Prop your foot up here and I'll get you some ice."

She moved off to the kitchen where Jere could hear her digging around in the ice bucket. She returned with a towel wrapped around a handful of ice.

First, she ran her hands gently over the injured area, thoroughly soothing the muscles, and Jere felt a curious warmth begin to tingle up from his toes to his throbbing ankle. Bringing out her first-aid kit, she wrapped a bandage around the towel to hold it firmly to his ankle.

She sat next to him and used an alcohol swab to disinfect the cut over his eye. He sucked in a sharp breath at the sting.

"Sorry," she said sympathetically. "This could probably use some stitches, but we'll have to make do with a bandage." She opened an adhesive bandage and applied it to the cut. "That should at least stop the bleeding."

"Thanks. I don't want to impose, though. If you could just drive me back to town, I'll get out of your way," he said with a self-deprecating smile.

Isla snorted out a less than ladylike laugh. "In a storm like this, the road will be flooded for a couple of days. We're stuck with each other for the time being. Can I get you anything?"

"Beer. Aspirin. Sleep. In that order," he said, eyes closed.

Isla returned from the kitchen with two bottles of Tennent's. Handing him one, she set hers on the coffee table and pulled the aspirin bottle out of the first-aid kit and tapped out three pills into his hand. He tossed them in his mouth, chased them with a swallow of beer, and leaned his head back on the couch.

"Thanks," he said on an exhale. "And thanks for...well, saving me."

"You're welcome. I'm glad I found you in time." She sat down next to him on the couch again and pulled one leg up under her. A huge spotted cat jumped into her lap and stared unblinking at Jeremiah. Another one slinked its lithe body back and forth behind Jere's head, and he tried to convince himself that he wasn't looking at a miniature leopard.

"Isla, have you ever seen a wolf on the island before?"

She looked him in the eye and tugged on a curl. "No. They're supposed to be extinct in Scotland."

"But you didn't seem surprised."

"I've seen that wolf a couple of times since your hike at Expeditions. He's never threatened me—it almost seems as if he's protecting me in some way. I know it sounds crazy, but I think that may have been why he tried to attack you. You got too close to my cabin."

"You're right, it does sound crazy," he said, smiling, "but I've heard crazier.

"Well, it's been a long night. We should probably get some sleep." Isla walked to the hall closet and pulled out an extra blanket and pillow and handed them to Jeremiah. "I hope you'll be alright on the couch. The guest room is sort of being used for storage. I've been meaning to clear it, but I keep finding better things to do," she said, smiling guiltily.

"I'll be fine. I'm just grateful to be dry and in one piece," he said, and he meant it.

Isla yawned and stretched like a cat. "Just yell if you need anything," she said while tying her mass of hair up into a topknot. "Goodnight."

When she turned around, Jeremiah got a good look at the back of her neck and nearly spit out a mouthful of beer. She had a tattoo on the back of her neck that exactly matched the symbol on the cover of the *Bruixi* text, except hers had a glyph shaped like an eye inside the smallest circle.

He had just found the Arran Witch, and he had no idea what to do about it.

Chapter Eight
Glasgow, Scotland, UK
Milton District
October 31, 1991

Isla sat in her favorite chair by the window of the one-bedroom shack she shared with her mother, and stared out at the rain pelting the dirty window. The old chair had three and a half legs — the half-leg was propped up with a stack of books — and was upholstered with dodgy plaid fabric, but it was the most comfortable thing in the building.

A mother and her son hurried past on the street below, huddled under a big umbrella, and Isla half-heartedly wished she could go with them. Feeling much older than her eight years, Isla knew she would never have a mother like the one on the street. One who cared about her child and wanted to see him safe and warm inside. Her mother did the best she could, the drink having stolen half her mind and all her beauty, but Isla longed for a normal family. One with a mum and a da and a nice house without the stink of alcohol, cigarette smoke, and bitterness in the air.

Eileen MacAllen had led a hard life. Her husband had left her when Isla was just two years old. Eileen blamed it on the psychotic ravings of her now-dead mother, when Isla felt sure it was probably the booze and the anger that had driven him away. She would probably never understand why her mother was so angry at the world, so the best she could do was stay out of her way.

Isla wished she could be out guising like the rest of the kids her age would be on Halloween, but she'd never been allowed to go. And the children certainly didn't come to their neighborhood to beg for candy. Absently, she reached under her black, curly hair and rubbed at a sore spot on the back of her neck. Her neck had been aching lately, probably because of the lumpy bed and flat pillow she slept on, and today it had kicked up a notch.

"Something wrong with your neck, girl?" Eileen barked from the old couch.

Isla knew better than to complain in her mother's presence. "No, ma'am. Sure I just slept on it wrong."

Eileen rose and walked over to Isla, batting the girl's hands away, ignoring her protests. "Let's 'ave a look, then." Surprisingly gently, Eileen lifted Isla's hair off her neck. With a gasp, she dropped it again and backed away.

Hearing Eileen's sharp intake of breath, Isla turned to face her. "What is it, Mum?"

Her mother's eyes grew shuttered, her face strangely expressionless. "Nothing to worry over, it's just a bit red. We'll put a salve on it before you go to bed." Eileen said and hurried out of the room. Isla caught the image of Eileen crossing herself in the wall mirror but thought she must be mistaken. Eileen had lost her faith years ago.

Curious about her mother's reaction to her sore neck, she went to retrieve a hand mirror off the dingy bathroom sink. Turning away from the mirror above the sink, she angled the smaller mirror so she could see the back of her head in the reflection. Lifting her hair up with her other hand, Isla inspected the back of her neck, expecting to find a rash or a cut. She froze in disbelief, stunned and confused by what she saw. A mark had appeared on the skin of her neck, about two inches in diameter, so clearly defined that it could have been a tattoo — only it wasn't. The edges of it were raised as if it had been scored into her skin.

The image that appeared was three concentric circles, nested inside one another, with three slashes across them, one at twelve o'clock, one at four, and one at eight, like they formed the points of an invisible triangle. Inside the smallest circle was a primitive-looking glyph that resembled an eye. Isla was at a loss to explain the appearance of the strange brand or why her mother hadn't told her about it. She knew she was out of time to figure it out when Eileen called her to the kitchen area for the evening meal.

Eileen placed a bowl of lukewarm oatmeal on the kitchen table in front of Isla — her idea of supper. "Eat this and run along to bed."

"Yes, Mum," she said, and forced down a spoonful of the thick slop. The sooner she ate it, the sooner Eileen would leave her alone to puzzle over the bizarre turn of events. Isla finished the oatmeal as quickly as she could stomach it and took her dirty bowl to the sink.

"G'night, Mum," she said, and placed a quick kiss on her mother's sallow cheek. She merely nodded, and Isla noticed that Eileen wouldn't meet her gaze. As Isla walked down the small hallway to the single bedroom, her eyelids began to droop and her mouth felt fuzzy. Feeling unaccountably sleepy after a lazy Saturday at home, Isla hastened into the tiny room. When she reached the foot of her trundle bed, the room spun madly, and she collapsed face down on the lumpy mattress.

Isla was driven awake from a groggy stupor as a white hot flash of pain lanced across her neck. She tried to sit up, but there was a dead weight atop her, pinning her to the bed. Her face was turned to the side and pressed against the pillow, but she recognized her mother's leg at her side, and she thought she heard sobbing through the heartbeat pounding in her ears.

Pain radiated from the center of her neck, and Isla instantly became fully aware of what was happening. Eileen was straddling her back, holding her down, and carving at her neck with what Isla could only assume was a kitchen knife.

"Mama, NO!" The plea came out as a keening wail as Isla tried to wrestle away.

"Shh, be still," Eileen whispered through her sobs. "Ye've got the devil in you, child. He left his mark on you, plain as day. I've just got to get it out. Then you'll be alright. We'll be alright," she said as she continued to dig the knife into Isla's tender skin.

Screeching incoherently, Isla drew on adrenaline and a well of strength she didn't know she had, and surged her little body upwards, dislodging Eileen from her back. As Eileen tumbled to the opposite side of the bed, Isla slapped a hand over the bleeding wound on her neck and tore out of the room.

Isla skidded into the kitchen on her stockinged feet, hearing a thump and a muffled curse from the bedroom, and she knew Eileen would be coming after her again. Looking around frantically for any kind of weapon to stave off another attack, she picked up a chipped coffee mug from the counter.

When Eileen appeared in the doorway, Isla hurled the mug at her, but in her drunken state, Eileen had listed to the right so the mug merely glanced off her shoulder and shattered on the floor.

Eileen's eyes widened madly and her face contorted into a mask of dark rage. "You little bitch!" she screamed. "You're the devil's own daughter! I tried to save you. I tried to be a good mother to you, but he's *in* you! Don't you see?"

Isla began to slowly back away from the crazed woman, inch by agonizing inch, while Eileen laughed ferociously. It had finally happened—Eileen had lost what few marbles she had left, and now Isla's main concern was getting out of that house.

As Isla continued her torturous exit, Eileen began pacing and mumbling to herself. "He seduced me. I should have known he wasn't my Charlie. He was too beautiful. Too....perfect. By the time I did, it was too late. Can never tell Charlie, never tell. He wouldn't understand."

Still backing away, Isla gasped as her back connected with a door frame hard enough to rattle the few pictures on the wall. Eileen stopped dead in her tracks, her gaze snapping back to Isla's face. As if they were stuck in a suspended moment in time, neither of them moved. Breaking out of her trance, Isla whirled into the living room and lunged for the front door. The moment she reached it, Eileen was behind her, yanking her back by the hair, knife still in hand.

Eileen forced Isla down onto her knees with a hard push to her shoulder. With her hand still in Isla's hair, Eileen jerked her head back to a punishing angle and held up the knife with the other.

"I'm sorry, my girl. But I see now that the evil has already taken you over. I can't allow his child to survive."

Isla's eyes rolled and strained, trying to follow the direction of the knife. Before she could even scream a protest, the knife swiped across her throat and Eileen dropped her only child like a bag of dirty wash.

When Isla came to, she was sprawled in front of the door where Eileen had left her. Isla's hand went immediately to her throat and came away wet and sticky. Taking a testing breath and swallow, she realized that not only was she alive, but her throat still worked relatively normally. It seemed that during Eileen's manic rage, she had pulled Isla's neck back so far that the knife had made a very shallow wound, leaving a vicious cut but no mortal damage.

Hearing Eileen smashing plates in the kitchen and screaming, Isla realized that she had to get out before her mother noticed that she was still alive. She quietly reached up, opened the door, and crawled out onto the sagging porch on her hands and knees. She had made her way to the front walk when police cars came flying down the block and skidded to a halt in front of their house.

Disoriented and dizzy from the steadily bleeding wound, Isla idly wondered if one of the neighbors had heard the commotion and called the police. She heard more sirens as an ambulance pulled to a stop behind the police cars. Strong hands lifted her up and carried her to the back of the ambulance, where she was laid out on a gurney. A medical technician bandaged her neck, checked her vitals, and started an IV.

Isla couldn't see them removing her mother from the house, but she could hear Eileen's enraged screams and deranged mutterings as she was led to one of the squad cars. She was dimly aware of a pair of officers talking outside the ambulance. She couldn't hear much, but words like "committed" and "orphanage" drifted into the vehicle. Knowing her life had just taken a turn for the worse, Isla gave in to exhaustion and blood loss and drifted off into a fitful sleep.

℮)ℂℛ

Jeremiah was awakened by the entire cabin faintly shuddering. It happened so quickly that he thought it must have been a low-flying plane going by. He sat up and began unwrapping his ankle, removing the wet towel so he could check it out. It was bruised and a bit sore, but it wasn't nearly as bad as it had appeared last night, and at least it wasn't broken.

Wiggling it experimentally, he was relieved when he got sharp discomfort rather than nauseating pain. He levered himself up off the couch and tried putting some weight on it. It didn't feel good by any means, but he thought he would be able to walk with a limp.

Looking around the cabin, Jere observed the small kitchen with vintage appliances, the quaint living room with the hodgepodge furniture, the cast iron wood burning stove in the space between the two. The little house was charming, and it suited Isla perfectly.

Feeling the rumbling again, this time longer and powerful enough to rattle the windows, Jeremiah grew concerned. He hobbled down the small hallway and poked his head into the first door he saw. Bathroom. He turned and opened the door on the opposite side.

There he saw Isla, a tiny lump under the quilt on the king-sized bed, tossing and turning as if locked in the grip of a nightmare. The bed frame beneath her shivered and creaked, causing the rumbling noise. Not sure what to make of it, Jeremiah approached the bedside and sat down on the edge.

When she didn't wake up, he put his hand on her shoulder and shook her gently. He had to duck when she came up swinging, a gut-wrenching shriek tore from her throat. Jeremiah had to use both hands to pin her arms to her side, keeping her from taking off his head.

"Isla," he said, giving her another quick shake. He watched as she turned unfocused eyes to him and touched her throat. He'd never noticed it before, but she had a thin, jagged scar there. She shook her head, and her gaze slowly became sharper and the tension in her body eased slightly.

Jeremiah pulled her into his arms rubbing his hands up and down her back. "It's okay." She relaxed into his embrace just a little more.

Isla drew in a shuddering breath and pulled back to look up at him. "Sorry to wake you."

"Don't worry about it. At least I was able to walk in here." She smiled at that. "Do you want to talk about it?"

"Probably not," she answered. "Definitely not before coffee. She hopped off the bed and shuffled into the kitchen, presumably to brew said coffee. Jere remained where he was, staring at the bed, and wondered what kind of power it took to shake a whole house in your sleep. It appeared to Jeremiah that if Isla was indeed *Bruixi*, she had no idea, and that could be very dangerous for her.

When he joined her in the kitchen a few minutes later, she had pulled out two cast iron skillets, a package of bacon, and a carton of eggs. "Care for some breakfast?"

"Sure, I'll help."

She handed him a mixing bowl and he began cracking eggs into it. "You know, for being a Scot, you sure do have a lot of American habits. Coffee, hearty American breakfast" — he looked pointedly at the bag of shredded cheddar she pulled from the fridge — "cheese in your eggs."

"A lot of the nurses at the orphanage were American," she said, then swallowed visibly and wouldn't meet his eyes when he turned to look at her. He could tell she hadn't meant to reveal that little tidbit.

He put a hand on her delicate shoulder and gave it a gentle squeeze. "I can't imagine what it must have been like, growing up without knowing who your family was."

She dropped the last piece of bacon into the pan and braced palms on the counter. Taking a deep breath, she turned luminous, haunted eyes to him. "I didn't say I didn't know who they were," she said, her voice devoid of emotion.

He thought she would continue, but she turned back to the stove and busied her hands with the task of cooking. They worked in silence until the cooking was done, and Jeremiah carried their plates to the rough-hewn kitchen table. When Isla just stared down at her plate, pushing the food around, Jeremiah knew that something was still troubling her.

"Do you want to talk about it? Your parents, I mean."

"No, not really. But I guess I probably should. It's supposed to be therapeutic or something, right? I'm just so used to being on my own when the memories crop up. You'd probably be running for the hills after hearing about my childhood, anyway."

"Isla, I have a psychology degree. It would take a hell of a lot to shock me. No pressure, but I'm here if you want someone to listen."

She gave him a small smile that made him want to pull her into his lap and kiss her until she forgot everything, but he knew she wouldn't accept his sympathy. Not about this. Taking a deep breath, visibly steeling herself against whatever memories still haunted her, she began to speak.

"My da left us when I was too young to even remember him. After that we lived with my grandmum, until Eileen, my mum, finally kicked her out. She blamed her for driving Da away, although I'm sure it had more to do with the fact that Eileen was a drunk. I was told Grandmum died shortly after she left our house."

Jere reached out his hand to cover hers on the table, squeezed a little. "What happened? How did you end up in an orphanage?"

Isla's chest rose and fell with a deep breath and she continued. "My world fell apart on Halloween night, when I was eight." She twisted her torso in her chair, gave him her back, and swept her curls off her neck.

Jeremiah cleared his throat, not sure how to react. "That's a nice tattoo," he said.

"You'd think that's what it was, wouldn't you? Only I never got a tattoo—this is where you start to fit me for a straight jacket."

"Like I said, takes a lot to shock me."

"That mark just appeared on my neck that morning. It stung and I was rubbing it, and Eileen saw me. She wanted to see what the problem was so I showed her. At the time, she showed no reaction, just told me we'd put a salve on it.

"Of course, I didn't believe her, so I went to the bathroom to check it out, and this is what I found. We ate dinner shortly after, if you could call it that, and then I headed for bed. As far as I can tell, Eileen drugged my oatmeal with something because I barely remember hitting the bed. Intense pain in my neck woke me up, and I found her straddling my waist, trying to cut out the mark."

"God," he breathed, free hand curling to a fist so tight, three knuckles cracked.

Nodding, Isla went on mechanically, her eyes fixed on his face, but he could tell she wasn't seeing him. "I've no idea how, but I managed to throw her off and run into the kitchen. I tried to stave off another attack by throwing things at her, but that only made her angrier. She had some kind of crazy notion that she had been seduced by the devil and that I was the result of the unholy union. She said he put his mark on me."

She took a sip of coffee, trembling hands cupped around the mug like a lifeline, and then turned her head and dashed a hand across her cheek.

"I almost got out. I left her in the kitchen and had made it to the front door when she grabbed me by the hair and slit my throat." It came out in a rush, as if she were afraid of lingering on the words too long lest she have to relive it.

Jeremiah's big body jerked violently in his chair in response to her revelation, but he remained silent, clenching his jaw so hard he was sure she could hear his teeth grinding.

Silent tears streamed down her cheeks and her mournful eyes finally focused on him. She gave him a shaky half-smile. "She wasn't very good at it though. She cut me but not fatally," Isla said, fingering the scar on her throat.

"Thinking she'd killed me, Eileen went back to trashing things in the house and I was able to slip out the front door. A neighbor had called the police, and they were there by the time I made it to the front yard. Eileen was taken to an institution for the criminally insane, and I ended up in the orphanage."

Expelling a long, slow breath to give himself time to formulate a response, Jere rose from his chair and pulled her up with him, wrapping her in his arms.

Isla stiffened at first, as if not wanting to have to lean on anyone, but then she relaxed into him and began to sob. As he stroked her hair and cradled her, Jeremiah wondered if she had ever really allowed herself to grieve.

Sniffling a little, Isla finally pulled back, wiping her face with a sleeve. "Thanks," she said sheepishly. "I guess I needed to let it out a little."

"My pleasure," he said, and meant it.

They settled into an easy rhythm throughout the day, with Isla working on the accounts for Expeditions at her antique cherry wood desk and Jeremiah doing internet research on his iPhone. Isla was unsettled at how quickly she had become comfortable having him in what had always been her space.

He sat slouched on her overstuffed black leather couch with his feet propped on the coffee table, tap-tap-tapping on the screen of his phone, and he looked as if he belonged there. Isla's heart did a little flip-flop in her chest when he caught her staring and gave her a lopsided grin. Running his fingers through his thick mop of hair that was beginning to curl, he turned back to his web-surfing.

Isla shook her head and tried to concentrate on the ledgers. The soulful wailing of his ringtone cut through the silence, and when he checked the caller ID, he excused himself out to the porch.

Jeremiah took the phone call outside so he wouldn't disturb her.

"Rousseau."

"Dr. Rousseau? This is Dr. Stephen MacLaren from Sacred Hearts Assisted Living."

Instantly on full alert, Jeremiah answered the older man, "Yes, Dr. MacLaren, what can I do for you?"

"I'm calling to inform you that I've decided to allow you a short visit with Ms. Mackay. I can't guarantee her lucidity or how long it will last. But if you can make it here tomorrow at three, you may speak with her."

"I'll be there. I really appreciate it. See you at three."

When Jeremiah ended the call, the sun was starting to set below the trees and the sky was soaked in vibrant reds and yellows. He entered the house to find Isla curled up on the couch in her pajamas with a book on her lap. She looked so young and frail that it was hard to believe she had survived so much.

Isla turned to look at him, smiled, and patted the cushion beside her, inviting him to sit down. He took the seat and slid his arm casually onto the back of the sofa, behind her but not touching. "Tell me about your childhood," she said with a smile in her voice. "Maybe it will make me feel better to hear a little normal."

"Not much to tell really. I grew up in New Orleans with my mom and my younger brother, Matthieu. My dad died when I was nine years old, and Mom never remarried. She threw all of her energy into raising us up to be good boys," he said with a smile tugging at the corners of his mouth.

"You were close, though." It wasn't a question so much as a statement.

"Yeah, we were. Are, really. I travel a lot for work, so we don't get to see each other all that often, but the love was always there."

He gave her an apologetic smile, but she just shook her head. "Don't. You having a happy childhood has nothing to do with me having a bad one. Please, go on."

"I graduated from high school a year early and did my undergrad at Tulane. After that, I went to the University of Edinburgh to get my PhD in psychology."

She looked surprised at that, so he laughed and tugged on one of her curls. "This isn't my first trip across the pond! I had actually planned to stay in Edinburgh to start working on my research."

"Why didn't you?"

Jeremiah closed his eyes against the flood of images that always remained just below the surface—broken houses, broken lives, a city buckling under a shroud of muddy water. "When Katrina wiped out the family home in '05, I moved back home to take care of my mom for awhile. Matt was still in college, and Mom was hellbent on him staying put. Eventually, I got her settled in a nice house outside the city and I started traveling more for my research."

"So where do you live now?" Isla asked, leaning toward him. She seemed appreciative of the distraction.

"I still have an apartment in New Orleans, but I mostly live out of hotels. Between my research and book tours, I'm always traveling somewhere."

It sounded so much emptier when he said it out loud, and he knew he'd find it hard to go back to such a singular existence after even such a short time of basking in her light.

Changing the subject, Isla said, "The road should be passable by tomorrow, so if you can stand me one more night, I can drive you back to town. I'll hike down at first light to make sure we won't get stuck."

Jeremiah slid his hand to the back of her neck, feeling the ridge of the scar her mother had left above her mark, gripped the base of her neck, and pulled her closer. "I think I can stand it," he said right before he closed his mouth over hers.

80CR

It was an unseasonably cold night, so Isla had started a fire in the old cast-iron stove. She and Jeremiah sat at the kitchen table with glasses of wine, sharing a companionable silence. Jeremiah was contemplating how to bring up the subject of how the locals treated Isla and the real reason behind it. He wanted to be able to bring up the subject of witches, without revealing too much about his profession.

People often reacted with skepticism and even derision when they found out what he did for a living. "I have an appointment tomorrow in Glasgow," he blurted, mentally kicking himself for opening himself up to questions about why he was going there.

Her mouth quirked in an uneven smile, her dimple peeking out, causing him to lose his train of thought. "Vacation, eh?"

"What? Oh. Yeah," he said dumbly. *Charming, dumbass.* "I was hoping you'd have dinner with me when I get back."

Her smile faded instantly as she studied the stem of her wine glass. "I can't."

Realizing that she wasn't going to elaborate, he tried a different tack. "How about a hike?"

On more comfortable ground how, the smile returned, again causing his heart to stutter. He willed himself to stay on track. "Sure, that would be nice."

"So it's only public places you have a problem with."

Startled, her eyes flew to his face and her brows knotted. "What do you mean?"

"Are you embarrassed to be seen with me?" He knew she wasn't, but he needed her to admit what was really going on.

"No. God, no. Jeremiah, why would you think that?"

"Do you really have to ask?" To her credit, she had the grace to blush.

Isla set her glass down and took a deep breath. "Look, I don't like going to town. The locals aren't exactly friendly to me."

Jere nodded noncommittally. "I did notice that the other night. At first I thought it was directed at Callum and Jack, but they set me straight. Why is that, exactly?"

"Part of it is the fact that I have no family, I'm sure. Family lineage is important to a lot of people. The larger part of it is because of the mark."

"You mean, the one that just appeared," he said genuinely.

"That'd be the one," Isla replied with a bitter laugh. "People around here are very superstitious. They can't all seem to agree on what exactly they think it means, but most think it's something between a motorcycle gang member and devil worshipper."

This made Jeremiah smile, because those two things were about the last things he could imagine her being.

"The most popular theory is that I'm a witch," she said, watching him closely as if she were waiting for him to run screaming from the room.

"Are you?"

Isla snorted indelicately, nearly choking on a sip of wine. "Hell, no! Well, not that I know of any way." The last part was said sarcastically, but it set Jeremiah's wheels turning. Now we're getting somewhere, he thought.

"So what if you were?" he asked casually, watching her from beneath his lashes. She looked at him as if he had suddenly grown a second head.

"Are you havin' me on? There's no such thing as witches!"

"Isla, I'm from New Orleans, arguably the supernatural capital of the US. I've seen a lot of crazy shit that most people don't believe in. All I'm saying is that everything happens for a reason. A tattoo doesn't just appear on your skin one day without having some sort of explanation. Magick doesn't seem too farfetched when it comes to something like that, now does it?

"Jeremiah."

"Isla," he said, emphasizing by drawing out the word.

"You are a highly educated, rational, sane human being. You can't possibly believe in witches!"

"I'm not saying I do," he hedged, "but I'm not saying I don't. What I am saying is that it doesn't hurt to examine some of the inexplicable things that have happened to you, not the least of which is the locals' suspicion. When you were having your nightmare this morning, the whole house was shaking."

She seemed startled at that, wouldn't quite meet his eyes, but didn't comment. It led him to believe strange things like that had happened to her before.

"There are always animals around you, from your freakishly human-like cats" — she gave him a genuine grin at that — "to wild animals that follow you on your hikes. And then there's that wolf. I'm no wildlife expert, but that was definitely not normal alpha dog behavior — let alone the fact that there aren't supposed to be wolves in Scotland at all."

Isla pursed her lips and set down her wine glass with a thud. She scraped back her chair and rose to stare, unseeing, out the window. She rubbed her arms with her hands as if she had caught a chill, and suddenly Jeremiah was afraid he had pushed her too hard.

Taking her hand, he led her to the couch and gestured for her to sit down, and then returned to add another log to the stove.

He heard her draw in a long, shuddering breath and let out an exaggerated exhale. "You know," she said, "while whether you are in possession of all your marbles remains to be seen, it is nice to have someone to talk to who doesn't think I'm a freak."

Barking out a laugh, Jere came back into the living room and flopped down beside her and, just like that, the tension dissipated.

Jeremiah found that he really enjoyed her company. They talked easily about movies and music to outdoor adventures. He even thought at one point he had agreed to a kayak race at which he was quite sure she would kick his ass.

Sometime during the course of the conversation, things began to change. Jeremiah found himself watching her mouth, that beautiful bee-stung bow, while she talked — it was driving him to distraction, to the point where he'd had to ask her to repeat herself several times.

As she talked, she began unconsciously fiddling with the zipper to one of his cargo pockets, zipping it back and forth. His thigh muscle tensed and bunched under her pseudo touch, while his brain was wishing like hell that he could feel her hand on his skin.

"Jeremiah." Tearing his eyes away from her hand and how close it was to touching him, he forced his hazel eyes to meet her feline gaze. Slowly, so slow he had to wonder if it was deliberate, her tongue snaked out to moisten her lips, and she caught her bottom lip in her teeth, causing her dimple to wink at him.

Taking what he hoped he hadn't misinterpreted as an unspoken invitation, Jeremiah reached for the back of her neck and dragged her to him with a growl. They met with an explosion of passion, tongues pushing and wrestling, teeth scraping.

The scent and the feel of her were so intoxicating that Jeremiah's head swam. Her hands had crept up his neck to bury in his shaggy hair, causing him to shudder. Leaning back to lay longways on the couch, he pulled her down on top of him and began pressing open-mouthed kisses to her neck.

He hoped he wasn't moving too fast for her, but the small mewling sounds she made deep in her throat were an encouragement. He slipped his hands under her shirt to caress the small of her back and captured her mouth again, feeling her respond deliciously.

Unhurriedly, his hands massaged and kneaded her back, and then slid down inside her yoga pants to grasp her curvy backside and pressed her against his nearly painful erection. They both groaned in unison.

Jeremiah lifted his hips, pushing himself more firmly against her, and she squirmed, sending shockwaves straight to his groin. They stayed that way for a few minutes, just moving against each other, engulfed in a heated kiss, until Jeremiah noticed the lamp beside him flickering.

In his daze, he thought it must be a bad bulb. Realizing there was more important business at hand, he focused his attention back to the beautiful woman in his arms. He broke away from her lips to lick a trail up the side of her neck, from the hollow of her shoulder to her ear, and then he latched on to her earlobe and sucked.

All around the room, lights began flickering violently, and the light bulb in the lamp beside them shattered with a loud pop. Isla jumped away from him like she had been caught stealing and stood there in the middle of the living room, chest heaving, eyes searching the room wildly.

"What just happened?" she asked, her voice high and tinged with hysteria.

While Jeremiah was shaken up as well as still painfully hard, he didn't want to alarm her, so he forced himself to remain calm.

"Isla, come sit down," he said in a gentle voice.

She sat, doubled over, with her face in her hands. "What the hell is wrong with me?" she murmured, voice muffled through her fingers. Leaning back, she took a coin from her pocket and began swiftly weaving it through her fingers.

"Listen to me." He waited until she turned to look at him. "Nothing is wrong with you. But there is something strange going on, and we're going to figure it out."

"I can't...you know. Not now."

Jeremiah nodded, understanding that she was too shaken up to pick up where they left off. He looked at the silver coin glinting between her fingers.

She handed it to him so that he could have a closer look. "It's the only thing I have of my grandmother's. I don't know what it says, but it always makes me feel better just to have it close."

Inspecting the coin, Jeremiah saw a crude engraving that was written in Latin. "I can translate it, if you want."

The brilliant smile she gave him was worth more than translating a few lines of a dead language, but Jeremiah was glad to have it. He looked back at the etching on the coin.

Quae signo gerit opposita inter virum et monstrum.
Filia deorum, mater hominis, protector omnis vitae.

Jeremiah sighed, knowing the translation would raise more questions than answers, but he told her anyway. "It says: She who wields the mark is the barrier between man and monster.

She is the daughter of gods, the mother of man, protector of all life."

Isla just shook her head and rubbed her eyes, looking worn out and scared. Jeremiah looked back down to the coin, and flipped it over to check out the opposite side, and what he saw there shocked him to his core and made his blood run cold.

Vigilati Usque Ad Mortem
Mhairi Siobhan Mackay
Glasgow, 1961

PART II

CONCITATUS

Chapter Nine

Isla slid between the covers of her bed, hoping for the quick, blessed oblivion of sleep. But it was not to be. All of the bizarre happenings of the past few days played across her mind like a movie reel. She found herself wondering if Jeremiah might be right. Not about witches, necessarily, but about the events being caused by some metaphysical or preternatural phenomenon.

Or she could just be going crazy like her mother. God knew it probably ran in the family. Sighing, Isla rolled over to face Atticus curled up on the pillow next to her. She smirked at him. "Do *you* think I'm a witch?" Atticus almost appeared to roll those huge slanted eyes at her, and then he went back to grooming himself.

Clearly not finding any wisdom of the feline variety, Isla turned her thoughts instead to Jeremiah. She knew it was stupid and risky to get involved with a tourist, especially an American who had no ties to Scotland other than University, but he was slowly but surely charming her until she couldn't seem to remember why it was such a bad idea.

Bringing a picture of him into her mind, she imagined his ragged mop of sandy hair that begged for a cut, his subtly arched brows over twinkling hazel eyes. She thought of his straight patrician nose and his supple, full lips over a dimpled chin. And that smile, that wolfish shit-eating grin that she was coming to love, caused delicious shivers to ripple under her skin.

Sighing contentedly and in a much better mood, Isla floated in the twilight state between wakefulness and dreaming with the image of Jere's smiling face fresh on her mind. Just as she was starting to surrender to sleep, the face slowly began to morph into something else entirely. Features sharpened, eyes and skin paled, hair turned jet black, and a small eye appeared in the center of the forehead. As she felt a familiar paralysis sink into her bones, her mouth locked into a silent scream and she realized with horror that she was no longer looking at Jeremiah at all.

Jeremiah had made his pallet on the couch just as he had the night before, but he had fallen asleep sitting up with his feet propped on the coffee table. He was dreaming about Isla, her skin, her hair, her killer curves.

He began to feel hot kisses on his neck, a warm tongue dragging from his collarbone to his ear. Still unable to open his eyes, he felt the delicious weight of Isla straddling his lap, grinding on his erection. In the haze of half-sleep, the thought crossed his mind that while she was an independent woman, this was definitely forward even for her, but then it flew out just as quickly as her hands found the hem of his shirt.

She tugged at his shirt, and he sleepily raised his arms to allow her to pull it over his head. Her nails kneaded the muscles of his chest like cat's claws, causing his hips to buck involuntarily under her. Laughing seductively she captured his mouth in a savage kiss, her tongue delving deep into his mouth, her hips rocking against him.

Shockwaves rippled through Jeremiah's body, and he dimly thought that he hadn't been this close to coming in his pants like a damned teenager since he was, well, a teenager. Her fingers reached between them to unbutton his trousers, to draw the zipper down tantalizingly slowly. When Jeremiah finally pried open his heavy lids, he took in the sight of her. She was wearing nothing but an oversized t-shirt and panties, straddling him like a cowgirl, hair tossed and wild, bangs hanging down over her eyes, face flushed.

He'd never seen a more erotic sight. Gripped with the sudden urge to see her face clearly, to look into her eyes, he slid his hand across her full breast and up the column of her throat to her cheek. Pushing aside the curtain of her long hair with one hand, he swept her bangs back with the other and looked up into her eyes. In place of her jade green gaze were soulless opalescent orbs that swirled with darkness, and a glyph of an eye had emerged on her forehead.

"What the *fuck!*" he shouted, jumping up like he had been electrocuted and dropping her unceremoniously on the floor with a thud.

He stood in the middle of the living room shirtless and panting, pants opened and hanging down to reveal the tops of his boxers, and hands buried in his hair. Isla dragged herself off the floor and onto the couch, hugging herself and rocking back and forth.

Although his body was still vibrating and his mind was still scrambled with a huge helping of WTF, his heart lurched for her. He walked back to the couch and pulled her into his arms, squeezing her tight and tucking her head into the crook of his shoulder. She was shaking like a leaf and sobbing so hard that all that was coming out were little hiccups.

She looked as if she was trying to speak but couldn't. She took a shuddering breath and tried again. "I-I don't know what's happening to me. I'm really afraid, Jeremiah."

Not wanting to reveal that he was too, he just stroked her hair and murmured encouraging words against her ear. "I know, baby, I know. We'll figure it out. You're going to be okay."

She pulled back slightly to look up at him, her eyes — they were hers again — were huge and haunted, shimmering with tears.

Without a word, Jeremiah lifted her into his arms and carried her back into the bedroom. Laying her on the bed, he drew the covers up to her chin and kissed her forehead. "You need to try and get some sleep. We'll figure this out tomorrow."

She nodded, but when he started to leave, she reached out and snagged his wrist in a surprisingly strong grip. "Stay. Please? Just...I don't think I can be alone."

Not wanting to her to feel pressured, but also not willing to sleep in his two-day-old clothes, he stripped down to his boxers and got on top of the covers, pulling the throw up to cover his legs. He turned on his side and stroked her hair until he felt her finally relax into sleep.

Jeremiah snuggled farther into the warmth of the bed, smelling sweet lavender and spices. He was again dreaming of Isla. She was wrapped in his arms and he had her pinned with one of his big thighs across her legs. He nuzzled into the crook of her neck and breathed deep of her unique scent. He felt delicate fingers winding into his thick hair, felt them tug slightly on the strands. Giving a grunt of approval, he squeezed her closer and scraped his teeth across the side of her neck, savoring the enticing little shudders that racked her in response.

A chuckle rumbled through her throat against his ear, and those fingers in his hair gave another tug, this time hard enough to hurt, causing him to blink into awareness. It wasn't a dream. He was draped across her, their bodies entwined, with his face buried against her neck.

He slowly disengaged his arms and legs from her but didn't move away. Instead, he lay facing her, looking into those bright eyes. "Hi."

"Hi," she whispered with a small smile.

"How'd you sleep?"

"Good actually. Better," she said, looking at him shyly from beneath her lashes. "I'd love to stay here all morning, but I've got to go to work."

Jeremiah captured her lips in a brief but electrifying kiss. "Work? What kind of slave driver do you work for?" he asked with a laugh. "I'm sure Callum wouldn't mind if you take the morning off. He seems like a pretty laid back boss, and you work all the time."

Isla toyed with a curl and her eyes darted away before returning to his face. "Actually, I'm his boss," she said after a long pause.

"What? I thought Callum owned Expeditions."

"He manages the day-to-day operations, and we let everyone assume he's the owner. It keeps the locals' mistrust of me from affecting the business negatively."

"Wow," Jere said, astonished. "That's amazing. And convenient. See, I happen to know your boss, and I think she has a soft spot for big, clumsy Cajuns. Now I'm sure you can get the morning off."

"Nice try. But I've got two tours booked this morning, and you have that appointment in Glasgow today, remember?"

"Worth a shot," he shrugged and tackled her, causing her to break out with uncharacteristic giggles. "Guess it's back to reality."

හ෬

As usual, Isla arrived at Expeditions an hour before her first tour. She'd decided to go in early that morning to do a little internet research on the odd things that have been happening to and around her.

She had her own laptop, although she kept it at the office since she didn't have an internet connection out at her cabin. Taking the sleek, compact machine with her, she settled at the breakroom table, flipped it open, and connected to the internet.

First, she pulled up the Arran Daily News website to skim it for happenings on the island. It was always good for Expeditions to keep up on current events so the guides could inform tourists of interesting facts and events around the island.

Frowning, Isla read the first headline that had caught her eye. It said in bold lettering: *Honeymoon Couple Disappears While Hiking.* Isla was astonished when she went on to read that the missing couple was Ethan and Katherine Redding, the same honeymooners who had been on her hiking tour.

Skimming the article, Isla learned that they had left word with their landlord — smart kids — two days ago, that they were going walking on Machrie Moor. When the older woman didn't hear from them the next day, she went to check on them at the one-room cottage she rented to them. They were gone, and she found no sign that they had been there recently. The investigation was ongoing.

Isla made a note to herself to call the chief of police after her tours that day to offer her services in the search. As an expert tracker, Isla often assisted the local police in locating missing hikers.

Opening a new browser window, Isla started to do a search on paranormal activity, but instead she typed Jeremiah's name in the search bar—she came to find out the two were more closely related than she ever would have thought.

The first link was a *Wikipedia* article on Dr. Jeremiah Rousseau. Smiling to herself, Isla clicked on it and dug into the article. She perused the basic background information that he had already told her— grew up in New Orleans, son of Paul and Esme Rousseau, younger brother Matthieu, attended Tulane and then the University of Edinburgh.

That's when it started to get weird. According to the article, Dr. Jeremiah Rousseau had earned his PhD in psychology with a concentration in *parapsychology*. Curious at the unfamiliar term, Isla opened a new search page and typed *define parapsychology*.

Parapsychology: a field of study concerned with the investigation of evidence for paranormal psychological phenomena .

She went on to read about Dr. Rousseau's numerous successful investigations, proving and disproving popular paranormal myths and ghost sightings across the world. He had written several research studies on his investigations and several fiction novels as companions. His last known project was an investigation of the Archer Avenue ghost in Chicago, IL.

Well, fuck. Isla stared at the screen in disbelief, unsure of what to think or what to do. Was this why he came? Did he make up the whole vacation story? Is that why he brought up the subject of witches and the locals opinion of her? Isla began to wonder if somehow he had heard of a supposed *witch* living on the island and had come to investigate.

The idea that he had lied to her and she had bought it caused a knot of fury to boil in her gut. This is what she got for letting her guard down. You just couldn't trust anyone. No one.

Chapter Ten

Jeremiah entered Sacred Hearts Assisted Living through tall oak doors that were probably as thick as his forearm. The hallways were lined with worn, peeling wallpaper circa 1965. Dr. MacLaren, who met Jere in the lobby, was a short, affable looking man in his seventies with thick, white hair and a full mustache that brought Col. Sanders to mind.

The two men introduced themselves, shook hands, and Dr. MacLaren gestured for Jeremiah to follow him down one of the dimly lit hallways.

"You're in luck. Ms. Mackay has actually been quite lucid today. More so than usual. Even so, I must warn you that it takes very little for her to become agitated. She also tends to slip back and forth from present to past, or even to unreality, so you'll want to fact check anything you get from her."

"Of course," Jeremiah answered, not bothering to mention how little *facts* there actually were on the subject.

The older man gestured to the left down an intersecting hallway. "Of course, we do try to limit visitor contact to fifteen minutes or less so as not to overwhelm our patients." He stopped in front of a dingy door labeled 517. "And please, do try not to upset her," the doctor said sternly, eyeing Jeremiah skeptically from under bushy eyebrows.

"I'll do my best," Jere said, giving the man what he thought of as his good ol' boy smile.

Dr. MacLaren opened the door and motioned Jeremiah inside. The room was small, spartan, and sparsely furnished. There was a twin bed with a wrought iron frame, a crucifix mounted on the wall above, a writing desk, and a small dresser. There was one window with a mesh cover across it that obscured most of the sunlight.

A tiny, frail-looking woman sat almost curled in a rocking chair, halfway facing the window, her profile visible to him.

Dr. MacLaren cleared his throat. "Good afternoon, Mhairi. You have a visitor."

She didn't move a muscle. If she heard him, she gave no indication.

"This is Dr. Rousseau. He is here to ask you some questions regarding his research that he thinks may involve your family lineage."

When again she made no response, Dr. MacLaren nodded to Jeremiah and left them. When they were alone, Jere waited a few seconds to speak. Then a few seconds more.

He had finally gathered his nerve, when she slowly turned her face to him and pegged him with a sharp, extremely lucid, and knowing stare. "What took ye so long?" she asked in a thick Scots brogue.

Unsure of how to respond to that, Jeremiah crossed the room and took a seat on the bed opposite her. "Ms. Mackay —"

"Mhairi, lad."

"Uh, Mhairi. I had planned on coming here to ask you about the *Bruixi*. I have been researching them for quite some time, and I traced one of the family lines here to you. I think you know what I'm talking about. But now I need your help. The situation has…escalated."

"Escalated?"

"Yes, ma'am. I've met a young lady I believe to be *Bruixi*, but I don't think she has any idea. I'm afraid she may be in danger."

Mhairi nodded, tapping a finger to her chin once, then again. "Aye, if she is *Bruixi* by birth but has no' been taught how t'use and control her power, she could very well be in grave danger."

Jeremiah was glad that she didn't waste time pretending she didn't know what he was talking about, but he was even more afraid for Isla. "Tell me about the *Vigilati*."

The brief widening of her eyes told him he'd surprised her, but she recovered quickly. She regarded him silently, head cocked to one side, as if deciding how much she should tell him.

"She has a brand," he said, hoping to encourage her to tell him the truth. "Just here." He palmed the back of his neck.

Mhairi rolled up her sleeve and presented him the inside of her rail-thin wrist that bore a brand remarkably similar to Isla's. "It is called a *signa*. Is hers like this?"

Jeremiah nodded. "Exactly like that. Except hers has a symbol inside the circles. He rose to approach the writing desk, finding a pen and paper there. He scratched out a quick sketch of the symbol and handed it to her.

Glancing at the paper, Mhairi hissed in a breath and dropped it like a snake. "*Alastore.* The baleful eye."

"Who? The what?" he asked, returning to his seat on the bed.

Leaning forward, Mhairi lowered her voice and spoke excitedly. "Listen, we hav'nae much time. All o'er the world there are *locuses*, or gateways between the spirit world and the world of man. There are harmless spirits, those we know as ghosts, and then there are malevolent spirits, those we know as poltergeists. Then there are the *auchrim*. They are sort of a cross between an evil spirit and a demon. They are'nae in possession of a corporeal form, but they can channel energy t' materialize and interact with the human world."

"But they have to pass through a *locus* to do so," Jeremiah interjected.

Nodding gravely, Mhairi continued. "These *locuses* are located at spiritually charged points in our world called ley lines, or the intersection of several landmarks or monuments. These spots genuinely possess an overabundance of energy on which the *auchrim* feed."

"So what does the symbol mean?" Jeremiah asked, gesturing to the piece of paper on the floor.

"I'm gettin' there, boy! So there isn't enough energy tae support all these beings in a corporeal form, so they are led by more powerful demons called *Lochrim*. The others channel energy into the *Lochrim* so it may enter our world through the gateway, often by luring humans in an' draining them.

"The *Vigilati* are a family line of the *Bruixi* that are charged with monitoring the *locuses* and keeping the *Lochrim* from getting through. While a *vigile* does no' have the ability to kill the *Lochrim*, she can keep them from stealin' energy — and if one gets through, she has the ability to trap him.

"Every *Lochrim* has a symbol that is unique to it, called a *seal*. I've heard tell of a phenomenon where a *vigile* is born with the symbol of a *Lochrim* inside her *signa*. This woman, called a *praeda*, will be more powerful than any of us, possibly even havin' the ability t'kill the *Lochrim*. But the price is steep. This ability comes from being of the blood of the Lochrim, therefore leavin' her more susceptible to him. An *embulibruixi*—a repressed witch, one who is not aware of her heritage—could easily be possessed and even killed by the *Lochrim*."

"Damn," Jeremiah breathed, raking a hand through his hair. Mhairi reached down to pick up the scrap of paper with his drawing on it.

"This symbol belongs to *Alastore*, one of the most evil *Lochrim* that exists. If yer lady friend bears this *seal*, she is in mortal danger."

"How can I help her?" Jeremiah's voice was tinged with desperation, and he still sounded calmer than he felt.

"You must bring her t'me. I must speak wi' her immediately. Also, you will need t'find her *feradux*. He will be able to assist her."

On information overload, he gave an exasperated sigh. "What the hell is a *feradux*?"

Mhairi looked at him as if he were a schoolboy who was always two steps behind. "An animal spirit guide. A protector. Each *vigile* will have one. They are a race within the *bruixi* who have great power and the ability t' take the form of an animal. They serve as protectors for the *Vigilati*.

"However, those who've committed misdeeds or betrayals are given the chance to redeem themselves. If they're able t'protect their charge and assist in defeating the *auchrim*, the *vigile* will regain the ability t' stay in their human form, t' give them another chance at life."

"So I'm looking for an animal."

She quirked a wry smile at him. "Try t'keep up, Dr. Rousseau."

"Well, she has cats."

"A witch who has cats?" she exclaimed in mock surprise. "And ye call yourself a scientist? Think of something that would'nae normally belong."

"The wolf!" he exclaimed, pleased with himself. He glanced up at Mhairi, only to see her staring out the window with vacant eyes as if they had never spoken.

Assuming he had gotten everything he would out of her, and grateful for it, he rose to his feet and turned to leave.

Her hand snaked out to grab his wrist in a punishing grip, and he turned back to her. Her eyes which had once been coal grey were now a milky white. With her other hand, she grasped his shirt to pull him down close to her face. "*Ne t'effraie pas*," she whispered, drawing back a little to wink at him.

His mind was immediately seized with the memory of that Halloween when he was twelve, every harrowing detail became crystal clear from the face of the creature that had stalked him to the gypsy woman and the mark on her face.

"Motherfucker!" he shouted tearing from her grip, stumbling back away from her, heart pounding and hands shaking. She simply turned back to the window and sighed.

❧❦

Isla was still seeing red when she got the text from Jeremiah that evening.

Meet me at the pub. Need 2 talk!!

"I'll meet him at the pub, all right," she growled through gritted teeth. Grabbing her purse and keys, she ran out the door and headed for her truck.

Jeremiah sat in the same booth as he had a few nights ago, anxiously waiting for Isla to arrive so he could tell her all he learned. He hoped she would trust him and let him help her.

He felt her presence before he saw her. It came in the form of an overwhelming pressure wave of fury and hurt. It spread through the room like wildfire, and he could tell the other patrons felt it when they began to fidget nervously, some even physically jerking in their seats.

And then she was there, stomping into the room like a tempest, and once again, the crowd parted for her. He stood up when she approached him with hands fisted at her sides, eyes flashing.

He never saw it coming. She smacked him with a vicious right hook in the mouth, so hard that his head snapped back to send him stumbling backwards into the booth, seeing stars. The large ring she wore on her middle finger had cut into his lip and he tasted blood.

He sat there on the old leather bench, panting and staring up at her with astonishment and not a little awe. She'd sure rung his bell but good.

"You...first...rate...bastard!" she ground out through clenched teeth, anger reaching a fever pitch. "Did you think I wouldn't find out?"

He scrubbed a hand over his face, still unable to string two thoughts together, but he had a sinking feeling he knew what she was talking about. "Listen, Isla, it's not what you think."

"Shut up! You've no idea what in the hell I'm thinking! Did you think that because I'm some small-town Scottish island girl that I didn't know how to use a computer? I can spell Google!"

"Of course that's not what I think," he said, willing his voice calm so as not to aggravate her even more.

"So what, did you hear a rumor about some crazy witch living on the island and come to check it out?" she spat. He winced, her words hitting too close to home. "Well I'm not going to be anyone's science project," she hissed and turned on her heel to storm out, slamming the door in her wake.

Heedless of the blood streaming down his chin, Jeremiah jumped up from the booth and ran after her, catching her just as she was getting into her car. He grabbed her and spun her around to face him.

His voice remained calm but his bright hazel eyes were fierce with determination. "Alright, you got your shot at me," he said, licking at the blood on his lip. "You had your say. Now it's my turn to talk." He could tell she wanted to argue—she was still fuming—but she wisely held her tongue.

"I'm sorry I didn't tell you about my profession up front. At first, I honestly didn't think we would get this close. I never know how much to tell people about what I do because, as Callum said to me, people fear things they don't understand. I take a lot of heat from nonbelievers, and some react very strongly."

"Do you deny that you came to the island to investigate the rumor of a witch living here?" she accused, poking a finger into his chest.

"No, I can't deny that. I was honest with you about my publisher demanding I take a vacation. I did choose this place because of the rumors. But I swear, I had no idea the rumors were about you until you told me last night."

She looked skeptical but crossed her arms and remained silent.

"Now that I know you, this is personal for me. I want to figure out what's going on for you, not for my work. That said, I found out some things today that we really need to talk about, sooner rather than later."

She hugged herself, huge, haunted eyes looking everywhere but at him, and his heart hurt for her. "I need some time."

"Sure," he said, cupping her cheek. He kissed her on her forehead and stepped back. "Don't take too long. I don't want anything happening to you."

Chapter Eleven

Isla drove around the island for hours, not wanting to go home but also not trusting herself to see Jeremiah. She was tied up in knots, a mass of jumbled thoughts and emotions. She wanted to allow herself to believe in Jeremiah, and that had never happened to her before, but she was so afraid to open her heart only to get cast aside again.

Traveling the coastal road, she had circled the island nearly twice. When she passed through the little southeast town of Sliddery for the second time, she decided to take the risk. Continuing on in her original direction, she set a course for Lochranza, and Jeremiah.

By the time she reached Callum's wee cottage by the sea, her stomach was flip-flopping with nerves. It may not mean a thing to Jeremiah that she was crossing all kinds of personal boundaries to trust him, to give him another chance, but to her it was everything.

She approached the house hesitantly, not sure of what to say or do, but wanting to make Jeremiah realize the importance of this step for her. Instead of going for the door, she went to the front porch first, with its picture window that faced out to the beach.

A sultry, melancholy melody floated out to her, aided by the gentle sea breeze, piercing straight through her and making her shiver. Peering into the window, she saw Jeremiah reclining on the couch facing away from her, a sleek, but well-worn, black guitar cradled in his lap. He stroked the neck like a lover with long fingers, and Isla found herself wishing her body was the thing his hands caressed.

Needing a little distance and not wanting to disturb his playing, Isla chose to go for a walk on the shore for a little while. Though the late evening chill had a bite, she took off her shoes to dab her toes in the water.

Jeremiah felt a tickle at the back of his neck, and his hackles rose as if he was being watched. Setting his guitar aside, he propped himself up on his elbows and craned his neck around to look at the window. Seeing nothing, he heaved himself off the couch to peer through the glass.

He didn't see her at first in the fading light, until he caught a glimpse of movement at the water's edge. She wore snug jeans and a white peasant top that fluttered in the wind. Her long mahogany curls waved behind her like a curtain tossed in a spring wind.

Sliding open the back door, Jeremiah strolled out onto the porch and leaned a shoulder against one of the columns holding up the pediment. As if sensing his presence, Isla turned her face into the wind to lock eyes with him. Raising a hand high in greeting, she started back toward the house, and he walked down the porch steps to meet her.

When she approached him, she looked so lost and uncertain, gaze pinned to the ground in front of her that he just wanted to hug her. So he did. "Hi," he murmured.

"Hi." Her voice was muffled by her face pressing against his chest and that made him smile. They stood like that for a while, with the sea softly tossing behind them, and the wind whistling her *banshee* song through the trees.

Inhaling a deep shuddering breath, Isla finally relaxed into his hold and her hands came up, ever so cautiously, to clasp around his waist. Leaning back just enough so that she could meet his warm hazel gaze with her own, she gave him a small smile.

"I'm not very good at this," she said. He wasn't sure whether she meant trusting someone to help her or letting her guard down enough to be intimate. Maybe it was both.

"I know," he said, tucking an errant black curl behind her ear, and gave her a lopsided grin. "S'ok. I totally am."

She laughed a little, a merry tinkling sound, and he was glad he could give her that, although the sound had sent a jolt of pure lust southward, and he knew she would be able to feel the evidence of it.

Clearing his throat, Jeremiah took a step back to put a little space between them. The last thing he wanted was for her to feel pressured by him and his traitorous body. "You'll always be safe with me. You know that, right?"

"Yes, I do," she answered without hesitation. Her eyes widened and her mouth fell open—clearly she had surprised herself with her conviction as much as she had Jeremiah. As he watched her, Jeremiah saw the truth of her statement slowly dawn on her.

As if a switch had been flipped, her gaze dropped to his mouth, she unconsciously bit her lip and her eyes grew heavy lidded. With her left hand, she hooked two fingers through the belt loop at his hip and jerked him toward her so that their lower bodies were flush. Her right hand slid up from his belly to his chest, where she grabbed a fistful of his shirt to drag him down for a kiss.

She crushed her mouth to his, biting his bottom lip just hard enough to sting. Her surprising aggression sent shockwaves of electricity up and down his spine. Lust coiled in his belly, causing him to groan. Isla broke the kiss reluctantly with one last nip.

Reaching up, she gingerly touched the cut on the side of his lower lip caused by her earlier blow. She pursed her lips, but her eyes were twinkling with an utter lack of remorse and more than a little amusement.

"Small, but mighty," he chuckled.

Fire sparked in her eyes, and she used both hands to jerk him harder against her. "You know it," she said, lifting her chin almost as if to challenge him to prove just that.

Control slipping away from him, Jeremiah's vision dimmed around the edges as he filled his mouth again with the taste of Isla. Sliding his hands down from where they had rested on her back, he cupped her curvaceous ass and lifted her off the ground.

He let out a grunt of approval when she immediately hooked her legs around his waist because he was too busy feasting on her sinful mouth to speak. Turning to carry her back into the house, he grudgingly tore his mouth away from her so that he could see where he was going.

As he carried her up the steps to the porch, she turned her attentions to his neck, kissing and nipping a path from collarbone to ear and back again. When she bit down on a particularly sensitive spot over his leaping pulse, the pain/pleasure sensation went straight to his groin—and he was pretty sure his eyes actually crossed.

Crossing the threshold, he kicked the door shut, and Isla immediately slithered down the front of him until her feet rested on the plush carpet. Jeremiah tugged at the hem of her gauzy top, and she obediently raised her arms to allow him to draw it up her torso, his palms sliding across her taut abdomen along the way.

Tossing the shirt aside, Jeremiah quirked an eyebrow at the lacy, white scrap of fabric that covered small but full breasts. The woman was just full of surprises.

Isla's head was spinning with the release of all her pent up frustration and lust. She had tried to hold back and keep herself closed off from him, telling herself that it was a bad idea to get involved with any man, much less one who was just passing through. She had told herself to be sensible and responsible, that it hadn't been that long. But it had.

Never one to do anything halfway, she made the decision to give in to temptation and share with Jeremiah both her body and her trust. And besides, she thought, the man was hot.

Muscles bunched in his arms and chest as he whipped off his t-shirt, and before he had even finished, she had begun to unbutton his jeans.

Batting her hands aside, Jere kicked off his shoes and pulled off his jeans while Isla did the same. Pushing her up against the door, his mouth came down on hers again, this time hotter and more insistent.

Her hands massaged the taut muscles of his back, and slid down to grip his muscular ass. He groaned against her mouth, a sound that she mirrored when his questing hands found her breasts, his fingers dipping inside the silk to tease and stroke.

Chest heaving, he broke away long enough to gasp, "Bed?" Equally as winded, she gulped in a breath and gave him a quick shake of her head. "Too far."

Sealing their mouths again, Jeremiah half pulled, half dragged her to the lush rug in front of the stone hearth. Laughing, they tumbled to the floor in a tangle of limbs.

All laughter stopped when Jeremiah rolled on top of Isla, bracing his forearms on either side of her head to take some of his weight.

Her face was flushed, her lips were reddened from his kisses, and her eyes looked decidedly dazed. Perfect, he thought. Pushing him off of her with the flat of her hand, Isla sat up and reached around behind her back to unhook and discard her bra.

Gently, Jeremiah pushed her back down on the rug and slid down her body, licking a path from her neck all the way to her breasts. Taking one sensitive peak into his mouth, he sucked hard, and his hand slid down her side to dip into her plain cotton panties and cup her firmly.

Jeremiah struggled for control as he continued working her body that way for what felt like hours but could have only been minutes. His hands and mouth were everywhere at once, stroking, nibbling, worshipping, while her body burned beneath him. Just when he thought he couldn't take much more, he watched in awe as she shattered in an extraordinary release, her body growing taut and bowing up off the rug.

Jeremiah leaned back to make quick work of his boxers, and then he drew the thin cotton down her long legs until she was completely exposed to him. He froze for just a moment, taking in the sight of her.

Her skin was fair, but sun kissed and freckled in areas of frequent exposure. Her dark curls fanned out from her face, looking deliciously tumbled. That lithe, muscular body still quivered with the aftershocks of her release, and her heavy-lidded, feline eyes watched him from beneath their thick, black fringe.

The last of his control gone, he covered her body with his own. Settling his hips between her strong thighs, he surged inside her with a sound akin to a growl.

Jeremiah felt her shudder as he sheathed himself inside her wet heat. He held still at first, reveling in the sensation of being joined with her. After a few seconds, she squirmed beneath him and he was dying to move.

Finally, he did. He wasn't gentle with her—he didn't think that was what she wanted. He pounded into her again and again, placing mindless kisses and nips against her neck and ear as he lost himself to sensation.

Never one to be passive, Isla ran her hands over his powerful back, felt the muscles there bulge and ripple. Wrapping her legs around the back of his thighs, she surged up to meet him thrust for thrust. When he bit down on the fleshy area at the crook of her shoulder, and began to pound into her even harder, she felt her muscles contract and her belly quiver with the beginning of another crest.

As she gripped him through her release, Jeremiah felt her hand slide down to his abdomen, where the muscles flexed with exertion and lust, and she dragged her nails up from where they were joined, along his belly to his chest to scrape across his nipples.

The movement sent a bolt of pleasure rippling up and down his spine, and he exploded. His hips rocked into her as his own release overtook him.

Collapsing on top of her, Jere panted and waited for his pounding heart to slow down. He felt rather than heard the rumble of laughter that bubbled up from her as she stroked his back gently.

Tugging on his hair lightly as had become her habit, she urged him to roll off of her.

"You're heavy," she said, with laughter in her voice.

"That's because you killed me. I'm just dead weight now," he said, grinning at her. "But what a way to go!"

"A man after me own heart."

They lay there together, side by side, until breathing calmed and heartbeats normalized. Jeremiah propped himself up on an elbow to look down at her face and kiss her sweetly on the lips. "Thank you," he said.

"For what?"

"For trusting me—giving me another chance."

She gave him a long look, and he got the feeling she saw much more than the surface. Smiling, she tapped a finger on his dimpled chin. "You know, I think you might just be worth it."

After they had dressed and settled themselves at the kitchen table with cups of coffee, Jeremiah explained to Isla everything he had learned about the *Bruixi* through his research. He told her of the old book he'd found in Rome and of his frustration at the slow progression of the translations. She sat in pensive silence as he recounted most of the details about his visit with Mhairi.

"So she believes that your life could be in danger if we don't figure out how you can use and control your powers."

"Assuming that I believe that I am one of these...*vigile* things—because I'm not saying I do—how am I supposed to figure out how to fight these demons when all we have to go on is your research and the word of a woman who suffers from dementia?"

"That's another thing she said. Apparently the *Vigilati* have spirit guides or protectors that are supposed to help guide them in their...quest—for lack of a less clichéd phrase. We just have to find this person."

"That shouldn't be too hard, it's a small island. I know just about everyone here." Jeremiah cleared his throat and looked away. "What?"

"Well, the spirit guide will be in the form of an animal. She called it a *feradux*."

"Oh, for—"

"I think it's the wolf," he interrupted. "She said it would be something that seemed out of place. Not like your cats or something."

Pinching the bridge of her nose, Isla took a deep, calming breath. "So I'm supposed to approach this wolf, and what? Talk to it? Damn it, Jeremiah!"

"I don't have all the answers, yet. She wants to see you. I'm hoping she can tell you what to do." He held up a hand to stop her when she opened to her mouth to protest. He reached out to take the coin out of her hand that she always flipped between her fingers when she was troubled.

"There's something else." He flipped it over and slid it back to her, facedown. He pointed to the name inscription on the worn silver. "That's her name."

Isla stared down at the coin, unsure of what to say or think. Her grandmother, alive? Was it possible? She hadn't seen Mhairi since she was six years old. She only had Eileen's word to go on that the woman had passed away. That, in itself, was her answer.

Jeremiah covered her hand with his and squeezed. "I didn't tell her. She wasn't...lucid...toward the end of our conversation. But she asked if I would bring you to her as soon as possible. Tomorrow, if you can."

Shaking her head to clear it, Isla pulled herself back down into reality. "I can't tomorrow. I'm the best tracker on the island. I'm assisting with the search for the missing hikers."

Jeremiah's brows drew together, and he frowned. "Missing hikers?"

"The honeymooners that were on the hike with us. They went for a hike a couple of days ago and no one's heard from them since."

"Stay with me tonight. I'll go with you. We can stop by your place at first light to get your gear."

"You don't have to—"

"I want to. I'm sure the search party could always use another pair of eyes. And besides," he said, brushing a stray curl away from her face, "I'm not ready to let you out of my sight yet."

Standing up, he held out a hand for her. "Stay," he repeated. She nodded, taking his hand, and allowed him to lead her into the bedroom.

Chapter Twelve

They woke before dawn and dressed silently in the dark. Jeremiah had followed Isla down the coastal road, up the winding gravel street that led to her cabin. There they collected Isla's search and survival gear — first-aid kit, water, energy bars, flashlights, flares.

Dressed simply in cargo pants and a white tank top, Isla tied back her mass of curls into a messy bun on the top of her head. Though her eyes kept drifting back to Jeremiah, her mind kept remembering, she willed herself to focus on the task at hand. They had a pair of honeymooners to find.

As she hooked the leather sheath for her machete to her belt, she caught a glimpse of Jeremiah sporting a comical look on his face. "What?"

He said nothing, just raised an eyebrow and looked pointedly at the machete now hanging at her hip. Isla shrugged and went back to stuffing her rucksack full of gear. "Never know," she mumbled.

After two packs were filled with all of the survival gear they could comfortably carry, Isla handed her bowie knife, sheathed and ready, hilt first to Jeremiah. "That wolf could be some kind of spooky spirit guide. But more than likely, it's just a wolf. We need to be safe. You never know," she said again, more forcefully this time.

Nodding, Jeremiah took the knife from her and clipped it to his own belt. They carried their packs to Isla's old truck and took off for the rendezvous point in the heart of Machrie Moor.

Chief James Sinclair of the Arran Police Department didn't believe in voodoo, hocus pocus, evil spirits, or any of that other spooky shite that the islanders went on about whenever anything out of the ordinary happened.

More than likely, a couple of hikers went missing, they'd gone and gotten themselves lost, or gotten themselves dead, or both. But it never had anything to do with any of that other nonsense.

So he didn't have any problem calling in the girl the locals called "The Arran Witch" to help in the search. Lass was the best tracker he'd ever come across in all his days in law enforcement.

She never said how she came about her special skills, and he never asked, but she'd delivered on every search he had put her on. So when he saw the volunteer searchers turn to each other and whisper behind their hands as Isla approached with the visiting Dr. Rousseau, he did the exact opposite and walked over to greet them.

Offering his hand first to Isla and then to Dr. Rousseau, Chief Sinclair gave them a warm smile. "Marnin,' Isla, Dr. Rousseau."

"Jeremiah, please."

"Awright then, my name's James but most people just call me Chief. I really appreciate the help. Isla, you said you had the couple on one of your hikes. What would you say about their experience level?"

"From what I could gather, they were both athletic, kept in shape. They'd done a bit of hiking back in the States but nothing too difficult. What they lacked in experience, they made up for in enthusiasm, so it wouldn't be too much of a stretch to imagine them going off the trail."

Chief frowned at that, rubbing a hand over the back of his neck. "Gonna have a quick briefing over there by the stones in five. I'll give everyone their routes after that and we'll be off."

Isla turned in a slow circle, scanning the flat, shrub-covered pastures of the moor, edged in all directions by mountains that mirrored the highlands of the mainland. This was her home, she thought. Two people were missing and she was going to find them.

The spot Chief Sinclair had chosen for the rendezvous point and base camp was the site of a trio of standing stones. The ruins on the moor, and the stones, were a popular stop for tourists on walkabout. Since it was not a difficult hike from the public parking in Blackwaterfoot to the stones, the Chief had felt sure that the hikers would have made it here before getting lost.

Isla motioned for Jeremiah to follow as she went to join the small group of volunteer searchers. Seeing Callum and Jack among the group, they smiled and waved their hands in greeting.

Callum sidled up beside Isla and bumped her with his hip. "Mornin,' Little Bear," he said, tugging on her hair.

"Little Bear?" Jeremiah asked, cocking an eyebrow at the two of them.

Jack approached from behind, and he cuffed Callum lovingly on the back of his head and kissed Isla on the cheek. "Don't mind Cal, he has to have a nickname for everyone. He calls her Little Bear because she reminds him of Bear Grylls, only tinier and prettier of course."

Laughing at that, Jeremiah pulled Isla toward him and wrapped an arm around her, placing a kiss atop her head.

He raised his hazel eyes to meet Callum's shrewd stare and raised his chin a bit, as if challenging Callum to say something about his familiarity with her. After studying Jere's face for a moment, Cal nodded once and gave him a crooked grin. "So that's the way of it then?"

"Looks that way," Jeremiah answered.

"Good. Don't make me regret it."

Isla looked back and forth at the two men and wondered at the exchange that passed between them. She was about to ask what the hell was going on when Chief Sinclair stepped up to the group and cleared his throat.

"Awright everyone, we'll have a quick briefing and then we'll get this search started. We're searching for Ethan and Kate Redding, newlyweds from Asheville, North Carolina. He's a computer programmer, twenty-nine years old. Six foot, athletic build on the thin side, blond hair in a military buzz, blue eyes."

Chief Sinclair took out a picture of the couple that had been found in their suitcase and passed it around the group. "She's a graphic designer, originally from Colorado. Twenty-six, long blond hair, also blue eyes, five six, medium build."

When all the searchers had gotten a good look, Sinclair took the photo back and handed it to Isla. When she gave him a puzzled look, he just smiled. "You're most likely to get to them first so you keep that with you."

"The couple was last seen two days ago when they left word with their landlord that they were going out to hike the moor. Isla, Cal, and Jack, since you are our more experienced hikers, you head east toward *Gleann Dubh*. Take the good doctor with you if he can handle it."

"What is it with you people and the doctor thing?" Jere asked to nobody in particular. Isla just laughed and pulled him over to where an officer was handing out two-way radios. They each took a radio, checked the battery, and clipped them on their belts.

Once he had divided the rest of the searchers into teams and chosen their routes, the chief spoke again. "Keep your radios on, but keep the chatter to a minimum unless you have something important to say. We're on channel two. Everyone ready?"

Nodding at the chorus of affirmative answers, Sinclair delivered a few last minute instructions. "Radio in to base if you find anything that may be a lead — clothing, hair, blood — give us your coordinates, and we'll bring out the dogs. Let's go!"

Each group set off in their assigned directions, moving slowly, scouring the land for any signs of the missing hikers.

Isla, Jeremiah, Jack, and Cal checked their supplies one last time and then set off eastward at a brisk pace. Allowing Callum and Jack to lead the way across the moor, Isla hung back with Jere. Keeping her eyes on the path in front of her, always looking for signs of the wayward hikers, Isla addressed Jeremiah in a hushed tone.

"This will be a difficult hike, even for us. I want you to tell me if you feel out of your depth. It will be safer for everyone. Last thing we need is to lose a searcher too," she said, in her blunt trail guide voice. She was all business now, Jere thought.

At first he bristled, somewhat offended that she didn't think he could handle himself. But he knew that—in her special Isla way—she was looking out for him. So he pushed his bruised manly pride out of the way and nodded at her. "Got it."

Making their way slowly across the flat, grassy moorland, the group searched for any signs of the missing hikers. It was understood that it wasn't likely they'd find anything on the moor, as it was open and flat with few hazards, but they needed to be thorough.

The moor was bordered on the east by vast pastureland. Many of the trails on the island cut through the sheep pastures—it was allowed by the farmers as long as the hikers were respectful of the livestock and closed gates behind them.

Following the most commonly traveled route, Isla took the lead, driving the group at a fast clip, anxious to get to the meat of the search. Just when it seemed like the endless flats would go on forever, they came upon the String Road.

After crossing it, they walked through several more acres of moorland, awash in blooming heather and rowan trees, until they came upon the edge of a thick wood.

Hitching her pack up higher on her shoulders, Isla stopped and looked back at the three men. "This is where it gets dodgy. The Machrie Moor trail would have ended back at the road for a less experienced hiker."

Isla closed her eyes and raised her face to the wind. When Jeremiah took a step toward her and looked as if he would speak, Callum stopped him with a hand on his shoulder. Giving his head a quick shake, he whispered, "Just wait."

She stood with complete stillness, clearing her mind of all distraction. The forest would speak to her as clearly as any person could, drawing her in, giving her direction. She could hear the creaking of the tall pine trees as they swayed in the wind, smelled the crispness of the island air. And when she opened her eyes, she saw the tracks distinctly as if they were painted on the ground in bright red paint.

"They came this way," she said, entering the woods at a fast pace and leaving the men to follow.

Although this was not like any kind of tracking he had ever heard of, Jeremiah wisely kept silent and followed.

She did use some traditional tracking methods, finding broken branches and scraped trunks on trees. She pointed out the two sets of tracks to him, one looked like a man's hiking boot about his size, a twelve, and the other was probably a sneaker, about a woman's size seven.

He could barely make out the tracks when they were pointed out, so he couldn't imagine how she found them. Still studying the prints, Jeremiah and Isla whipped their heads around when they heard Callum call out.

"Oi, got something over here."

Hurrying to his side, they saw a small pink backpack at the foot of an Arran Whitebeam tree. It wasn't a hiking pack, to be sure. The pink Jansport looked more like what a student would carry to school. But it had *Kate* written in black marker on the front pocket.

"Damn it!" Isla hissed. "What would have made her drop her pack?" None of the men spoke, but they all knew the answer. Nothing good.

Isla unclipped her radio and pressed the talk button. "Team one to base. Over."

"Base, come back," came the crackling reply.

"Got a pack here, got *Kate* written on it. Over."

"What's your twenty, team one?"

Isla read off their coordinates from her handheld GPS.

"Roger that. We'll send out a canine team. Over and out."

"Team one, out."

The foursome continued on due east, Isla again taking the lead. They traveled through the dense forest for hours, getting whipped by branches and clawed at by briars. Finally, Isla stopped them for a rest.

Finding moss-covered stones to sit on, they each took their canteens out of their packs to rehydrate. Isla radioed to base that they were taking a short break, again reading off their coordinates.

They could hear the distant baying of the hounds as they made their way to the location of the pack. The dogs would take the scent and do their work, but they couldn't track the scent through water or across the craggy mountains like the search team could. They all had their strengths and their weaknesses, and hopefully they would work together to find the missing.

After recharging with energy bars and water, they set a course east by northeast as Isla followed her clues unseen by the others. The forest cleared and the ground in front of them dropped away into a deep glen.

"*Gleann Dubh*," Callum supplied for Jeremiah's benefit. "The Black Glen."

"Keep your eyes on the ground ahead and mind your feet," Isla said. "She's more treacherous than she looks."

Battling their way carefully across moss-covered rock, they struggled down the western decline into the glen. Reaching the lowest point, Isla paused, lifting her face to the craggy cliffs up the eastern face.

Closing her eyes again, she stretched her senses, searching for signs of life, listening for changes in the air. When they opened, the trail the hikers had taken glowed for her, a bright blood red that filled her with an overwhelming sense of dread. Swallowing down her fear, she squared her shoulders and continued on.

Now unable to separate her unusual tracking skills from Jeremiah's paranormal theory, she gave into it, summoning her power as best she could, calling on her extra senses that she had never questioned before.

Shading her eyes with her hand, Isla pointed to a particularly treacherous looking cliff before them among the rocky ridge that separated *Gleann Dubh* from the *Sheeans*, or the Faerie Hills as the locals called them. "They headed toward the Raven's Rock."

Callum cursed colorfully under his breath. "Hell of a climb, that. That would be hard for an experienced hiker without climbing gear, much less a couple of tourists. No offense, Jeremiah."

"None taken."

"We'll follow the route they took until we can't go anymore. Or until we find something," Isla said. No one questioned how she knew what route they took.

As they walked, the land began a steep incline until they were practically crawling up the steep eastern face. Isla was impressed by the way Jeremiah kept up, although they were all bruised and bloody from scrapes and falls.

Whenever she stumbled or had trouble finding her footing, he was always there to lend a hand. Her heart tripped over itself a little when they finally made it to the rocky ridge where they could stand upright, and he shot her his shit-eating grin, flashing pearly whites from a tanned and grubby face.

Following the ridge northward, a jaggedly pointed peak rose above them, blocking the sun and casting itself in a raven-black silhouette. Maybe that's where the name came from, Isla thought, but she wasn't sure.

When they reached the foot of the craggy monolith, they examined the trail that led to its peak. It wasn't so much a trail, as it was a thin chimney corridor between two flat rocks. They would have to crawl up, bracing their arms and legs on either wall, a technique called *stemming*. This was a dangerous climb without gear.

"I'll go first," Isla declared. "Anyone feels unstable, turn back, no questions asked. We don't need an accident out here." She looked pointedly at Jeremiah until he gave her a quick nod.

Taking the lead, Isla found handholds to pull herself up into the corridor, squeezing her body into the tight space. Levering herself up with her legs braced on either wall, she inched her way up.

Sweat dripped down her neck and pooled between her shoulder blades. Her muscles shook from the exertion, but she gritted her teeth and kept ascending. Jack began climbing underneath her, to be followed by Jeremiah, and Callum to bring up the rear.

It was an agonizing climb. Their muscles burned and screamed, but they kept on going. Isla's hackles rose as her sense of dread increased, but they had no choice but to press on.

Finally, Isla took her final handhold and pulled herself up onto the flat peak of Raven's Rock. What she saw there caused her heart to trip.

A woman stood about a foot from the edge of the rocky cliff. Her face was bruised and bloody, her blond hair, dark and matted. Her head hung, as if she didn't have the energy to hold it up, so Isla couldn't see her face clearly. But instinctively Isla knew that this was Kate, one of the missing hikers.

Holding her hands out, palms up, Isla approached her slowly, afraid she would startle the girl into taking a step back.

"Kate," she said softly. "Kate, we're here to help. We've got you." Isla stepped closer, inch by agonizing inch. Hearing a sharp intake of breath behind her, she knew that Jack had reached the summit and taken in the precarious situation, and Jeremiah would be close behind.

Mere feet away, Isla reached out to the girl. "Kate, take my hand. We need to get you to safety."

The girl finally stirred, raised her face to the sun that caused her pale — too pale — eyes to glint and sparkle. Her mouth twisted into a gruesome smirk as she looked straight at Isla.

"He'll come for you too," she sang in an eerie, lilting voice. She took a small step back, then another. Spreading her arms, she launched herself backwards into empty space.

"No!" Frantically Isla lunged after her, staggering on the edge, only to have Jeremiah yank her back towards him. He held her there, bracketed in his steely embrace as she punched, kicked, and clawed, trying to break away so that she could try and save the girl.

"She's gone." He gave her a little shake. "Isla, she's gone." The fighting gave way to sobbing.

Jack crept carefully over to the edge, looking down. "Damn," he breathed.

Callum paced angrily back and forth behind him, raking hands through his hair. "God*damn* it! What the fuck was she thinking?"

That was a question no one but Kate would ever know the answer to. Jack was the quickest to recover, unclipping his radio to deliver the news.

"Team one to base."

"Base, go ahead."

"Found the girl up on Raven's Rock, west of the *Sheeans*."

"Do we need to send a medic?" A discreet way of asking if she was still alive.

"Not anymore. She jumped." He heard nothing but static from the radio, and then, "Come again?"

"She jumped. We found her on the summit of the Raven, and she fucking jumped."

More static. "We'll send a team to recover the...remains. Your team good to keep searching?"

Jack looked over at Isla who stepped away from Jeremiah and furiously scrubbed at her ruddy cheeks with the palms of her hands. Her eyes sparked, as if daring Jack to say she wasn't fit to continue.

"Team one? Come back."

"Yeah, base, we're going to continue on, look for the husband. Over and out."

Carefully making their way down the western face of the craggy ridge, they came to a wild area overgrown with shrubs and brush that led into another dense forest. The wilds of the *Sheeans*, as Callum had called them, were thought to be a playground for the faeries.

They pressed on, through brush so thick that Isla was forced to unsheathe her machete and cut their way through.

Callum called out from behind them, "Isla, are you sure this is the way he came? There are no signs that he cut a path through this." He made a broad sweeping gesture toward the thick undergrowth.

She turned fierce eyes back to him. "I know it."

No one questioned her again. Jeremiah watched her cutting her way through the brush, muscles flexing, sweat rolling. She moved with the grace of a mountain cat, no obstacle slowing her down for long. More impressed than he wanted to be, he continued to follow.

As the sun began to sink below the trees behind them, Isla stopped in a small clearing amidst the thick brush. "We should make camp. Don't want to lose the light while cutting our way through this."

It was a warm night, so they opted to spread out their bedrolls under the forest canopy and forgo the tents. Seeing no need for pretense anymore, Isla and Jeremiah zipped their bedrolls together. Jack and Callum did the same, and they all settled in.

An evening fog rolled in, blanketing the clearing, as they all tried to block out the memories of the day long enough to sleep. Finally, with her head resting on Jeremiah's shoulder, Isla drifted off.

She dreamed of an eagle, soaring through the sky over the island on a cloudless day. The sky darkened to an angry grey and the eagle's feathers blackened, until she realized it had become a raven. It dove toward her, hurtling through the steely clouds, and just before it would have impacted her, she sat straight up in her sleeping bag, panting.

Needing to walk it off, Isla took a flashlight and her machete and left the campsite, cutting her way through a thin curtain of brush to another clearing she hadn't seen in the daylight. She turned in a slow circle, shining her light to check out her surroundings.

A hand snaked around from behind her, and the flashlight clattered to the ground, illuminating the clearing with a sickly glow. Another hand reached across her body to pull her machete from its sheath and hold it to her throat.

The hand left her mouth and buried deep in her hair, pulling hard, sparking long dead memories of another horrible night, nearly twenty years ago. Isla drew in a deep breath in preparation to scream, when she was stopped by a sharp nick from the blade over her jugular.

"Now, now. We wouldn't want me to slip, would we?" he hissed into her ear.

His accent. American. *Please don't let it be him!* But she knew it was. "Ethan, you need to let me go. We're here to help you."

The answer she got was a crazed cackle that she felt rumble up in his chest that was pressed against her back.

"The devil's own daughter!" he wailed in a high-pitched voice. "Gonna cut the devil out, bitch!"

Nausea rolled in Isla's belly as her mother's long ago words were thrown back at her. Fighting it down, she calmed her breathing, willed her body into action. With a sudden flick of her neck, she smashed her head back, connecting with the man's nose.

Surprise and pain caused him to loosen his hold slightly, and it was just enough. Isla lifted her feet off the ground so that he carried all of her weight and twisted her body to wriggle out of his arms, which had loosened even more with the additional strain.

Hitting the ground hard enough to knock the wind out of her, Isla rolled onto her back and crab-crawled away from the man who was clutching his broken nose as it gushed blood. He recovered quicker than she expected, stalking toward her with the machete raised high above his head.

Standing over her prepared to strike, he turned his pale, demented eyes to her face and smiled. Raising her hands defensively, she braced for the blow. It never came.

With a feral growl, a silver shape streaked out of the mist and pounced on Ethan, knocking him sideways. While man and wolf grappled, Isla backed away and got to her feet.

An almost supernatural speed and strength lent itself to the fight, and Ethan was able to swipe at the wolf with the machete, across its ribcage, as it lunged for his throat. The blow propelled it off of him, and with an agonized whimper, the wolf crumpled to the ground.

Isla let out a strangled cry and started toward the wolf, only to draw up short when the men exploded into the clearing, each armed with a hunting knife.

Realizing he was cornered and outnumbered, Ethan held out both hands in a submissive gesture, though the right one still held the machete. He threw his head back and laughed to the trees, the sound sending chills down Isla's spine.

Pointing the machete at Isla, he curled his lip at her and spoke in that high-pitched whine. "He's *in* you. Don't you see?" Isla's hand flew to her throat, and she backed up until her back hit the solid wall of Jeremiah's chest.

Before any of them had time to speak, Ethan cast one last wild, shadowed look at the four of them and drew the machete across his own throat. Blood ran like a river, and his lifeless body collapsed onto the forest floor.

With a choked scream, Isla turned her face into Jeremiah's chest, and he held her tight. Jack went back to the camp and returned with a bedroll to cover the body. Isla could hear Callum's hushed voice as he radioed their position to base camp.

In her daze of shock and horror, Isla suddenly remembered what had saved her. "The wolf!" she shouted, breaking out of Jeremiah's hold and running for the spot where the wolf had fallen. There was nothing there but a pool of blood. No trail, no tracks—nothing.

Hearing footsteps behind her, Isla turned toward Jeremiah and swiped at tears she didn't realize were falling. Placing both hands on her shoulders, Jeremiah spoke in a calm, soothing tone. "Sun's rising. They're going to send out a retrieval team. We need to go home."

Chapter Thirteen

It was full afternoon by the time Isla and Jeremiah finally stumbled through the front door of the cabin. There had been hours of hiking back to base camp, and then hours more of being interviewed and questions from the police about the night's events.

Their clothes were dirty and torn, their bodies bruised, their minds traumatized. Without a word, they both headed for the bedroom to the roomy tiled shower. Jeremiah started the water running, allowing it to heat up and fill the room with soothing steam.

Quickly, silently, they discarded their ruined clothing and stepped into the spray. Isla moaned as the scalding water washed over her aching muscles.

She wanted to close her eyes and give herself up to the comfort of a warm shower and a strong man, but every time she tried, the gruesome images from the search would flicker through her mind like a bad drive-in film. She could feel the dull edges of shock scraping against her consciousness. She needed something to ground her into reality, and safety.

She opened her eyes and blinked as water droplets clung to her lashes. Looking at the man in front of her, it suddenly dawned on her. This was her lifeline, her reality. She had no doubt that he would do anything to keep her safe, and the realization was nothing short of life altering. Sliding her arms around Jeremiah's neck, she captured his mouth with hers and tried to pour every ounce of her depth of love for him into one searing kiss. Feeling his need as strong as her own, she explored his body with hands and lips until his breathing sped up to match hers.

He let out a sound halfway between a groan and a growl, and she felt his big body shudder. Taking a deep breath, he pushed her away gently. "Isla, I don't think this is a good time to be—"

"Shut up." Again, soapy hands lathered and caressed him, teasing and arousing along their wicked path. When he tried to back away, she stayed with him, continuing her exquisite torture. His head fell back against the tile wall, and his muscles twitched and rippled.

"Isla, you've had a tough night," he breathed. "You shouldn't be—"

"Shut. Up. Let me." She ran her tongue up and down the length of his neck, reveling in his delicious shudders. "Isla," he said her name on a sigh, and he was losing the fight. He'd let her have her distraction.

Turning her deep, green eyes up to his face, his skin flushed with desire, lids at half mast, she quirked a small smile at him. "Jeremiah."

"Hmm?"

"Shut up." She reveled in having such a strong, powerful creature willing to give up complete control to her whim. She rained kisses all over his neck and torso, smiling at the gasp he let out when she grazed him with her teeth. Teasing him with mouth and hands, she drove him almost to the point of no return, until his fingers were clenching—but never pulling—in her hair.

The essence of him swirled around her in a cloud of vanilla-scented steam, and her mind spun with want as he turned her to face the ceramic tiled wall. Biting down on the back of her neck, right over her *signa*, he filled her—more than just physically—he filled a part deep inside that she hadn't known was empty.

Resting her forehead against the cool tile, she allowed the feel of him to swamp her.

The beautiful agony of calloused hands sliding over slick skin, lips caressing, brought her to the ultimate surrender—body and heart.

He followed her shortly after, shuddering over her as his own body was overcome with sensation. They stayed where they were, joined and panting, for quite a while before Jeremiah eased back to let her up. Turning around, Isla took his mouth again in a deep, lazy kiss.

"What was that for?"

"For being exactly what I needed."

Smiling, he kissed the tip of her nose. They leisurely lathered up and washed each other, lingering longer on certain parts than was exactly necessary. As the water began to cool, they stepped out of the shower to towel off.

Isla went to the bedroom to change into clean clothes and dug out some of Callum's old sweats he had left over one day for Jeremiah to wear.

By the time they were fully dressed and had made a pot of coffee, the sun was setting. They were just settling down on the couch with their mugs, when they heard a shrill whine and a loud thump from the front porch.

Still overwrought from the events of the night before, Isla flew off her couch and had her shotgun trained at the door before Jeremiah even stood up.

"Easy," Jere coaxed. "Probably nothing. I'll go check."

She was embarrassed by her reaction, and by the way the barrel of the gun was shaking, but not enough to put it down.

She watched as Jeremiah crept up to the door, unlocked the deadbolt, turned the handle, and peeked out.

"What the—? You've got to be kidding me." He flung the door wide, so that Isla was able to see the motionless mound of blood tinged grey fur that lay on the doormat.

"Oh, my God," Isla gasped, running to the prone form and kneeling beside it. "Help me get him inside!"

"What? Isla, are you serious? That's a wild animal!"

She rounded on him, ready to go to bat for the wounded creature. "He saved my life."

With a sigh, Jeremiah knelt down and carefully scooped up the wolf and brought him inside. Up close, the animal was smaller than she'd imagined, leaner.

Dragging the coffee table out of the way, Isla laid a blanket over the scratched hardwood floor and motioned for Jere to set the wolf down. Disappearing for a moment into the bedroom, Isla returned with her first-aid kit, just as she had when Jeremiah had been injured.

Checking the wolf's gum color, she saw that he was pale from blood loss and his breathing was shallow. She gingerly probed the deep gash across the wolf's ribs. "This needs to be sutured. It's not very deep, but we've got to stop the bleeding."

"So, what?" Jeremiah asked, at a loss. "We take him to a vet?"

"No need. Jack's the island's only vet, so I help him out with assisting whenever I need extra quid. I can stitch it."

Taking an electric clipper out of a drawer in the kitchen, she painstakingly shaved the fur around the wound. She pulled out a pair of surgical scissors from her kit and trimmed the jagged edges of the gash.

After cleaning the area with an alcohol swab, she meticulously stitched the edges together until it was completely closed. She then placed a dressing over the site to keep it clean and dry for as long as possible.

"He's lost so much blood, he'll be out for hours, if he makes it through the night at all. We should get some sleep while we can."

Turning out the lights, they retired to the bedroom to rest. Long after Isla had fallen asleep, Jeremiah lay awake listening to the sounds of the night. He had almost lost her today, he thought, as he watched the gentle rise and fall of her chest. It surprised him just how much that scared him.

The sound of shattering glass woke them both from a sound sleep. Jeremiah stumbled out of bed, grappling for the shotgun he'd placed underneath it. "Now what! How the hell long have we been asleep?"

Pressing a button to illuminate the display, Isla checked the bedside clock. "Only three hours. I can't imagine he would be recovered enough to move around yet."

"Well, something's moving in there. Damn it, I told you this was a bad idea. There's a wolf in your living room."

Isla clapped a hand over her mouth to stop the hysterical laughter he heard bubbling up to the surface. "Okay,

okay, let's figure this out. Maybe one of us can distract him while the other slips by to open the door. Then we can, sort of, shoo him out."

Tossing an annoyed look over his shoulder at her, Jeremiah padded to the bedroom door. "Stay here."

"Be careful," she whispered.

Cracking open the door, Jeremiah squeezed through the opening to slip into the pitch-black room. While waiting for his eyes to adjust, he listened for unusual sounds in the darkness, keeping still so as not to attract the animal's attention.

Hearing first a muffled thud, then what sounded like a whispered curse, Jeremiah's finger tightened on the trigger of the twelve gauge, and he reached out his other hand to flick on the lights.

The shadowy darkness quickly dissolved to reveal an impossible scene. A young man, nineteen, maybe twenty at the most, stood naked in the middle of the living room. Frozen like a deer caught in headlights, his glittering, blue eyes were wide and fixed on the muzzle of the gun.

"What. The. Fuck." Jeremiah started toward the kid, and he backed away in fear.

At the same time, Isla burst through the door, machete drawn—the new one Chief Sinclair had given her, as hers was still evidence.

Not expecting to see a stranger stark naked in the middle of her house, she stumbled to a stop, squealed and covered her face—but peeked through the cracks between her fingers. "Oh, dear God."

Seeing Isla, the boy's expression calmed. Smiling, he made as if to approach her when he was stopped by the shotgun barrel nudging his chest. "Easy there, partner," Jere said in a deceptively flat voice.

After casting another wary glance in Jeremiah's direction, the boy lowered his eyes and began to tremble. An inexplicable protective instinct sparked inside Isla, so she placed a hand gently on the shotgun barrel, forcing Jeremiah to lower it.

Walking to a wooden rack next to the fireplace, Isla pulled out a quilt and returned to wrap it around the boy's naked body. "Sit," she ordered gently, gesturing to the couch. "You too," she told Jeremiah, indicating the worn recliner in the corner of the room.

Ignoring her suggestion, Jere sat on the coffee table directly in front of the young man, while she sat next to him on the couch.

Jeremiah pinned the boy with a hostile glare. "How the hell did you get in here?" he growled.

Patting his hand where it clenched the couch cushion, Isla encouraged him to speak. "It's okay, just tell us. We won't hurt you."

"Yet," Jere interjected, earning a quelling look from Isla.

Looking back and forth between the two of them, the boy contemplated his answer with an odd expression on his face, as if they had asked him a ridiculous question. When he finally spoke, his trembling voice was lightly accented. Mediterranean, maybe Italian. "You...you let me in."

Isla turned to look at Jeremiah and saw her own confusion mirrored in his face. Had they left the door unlocked? Had the boy somehow considered that an invitation? Leaning in to study him closer, Isla noticed how his Siberian blue eyes contrasted sharply with his olive skin and dark brown curls.

He had a peculiar tattoo of three bands around his neck, just above his collarbone. Looking lower, over a lean—

bordering on emaciated—but well-muscled chest, she gasped when she saw a jagged, angry gash across his ribcage that looked like it had been clumsily stitched. Several of the stitches had pulled out, and the wound was slowly leaking blood.

"You're right. We did," she answered, and Jeremiah's eyes snapped up to meet her gaze.

"Isla, what—"

She held up a hand to stave off his reply. "Look at him, Jeremiah. Look at these markings on him. This wound. I think he's right where we left him."

"That's ridiculous. This kid obviously must have broken in!"

"You were the one that brought up the idea of the wolf being the *feradux*. Isn't that right, *Doctor* Rousseau?" At least he had the grace to look sheepish.

Hearing an obviously familiar term, the boy brightened instantly, turning luminous, blue eyes toward Isla. "*Domina mea, veni ut auxilium*," he said, earnestly sliding closer to her.

"All right, pal, that's close enough," Jeremiah growled, causing the boy again to shrink back.

Isla turned snapping jade eyes back to Jeremiah. "Don't pull that alpha male shit with me. You're scaring him."

Jeremiah cleared his throat and looked away. "I'm sorry. After last night, I just..."

Giving him a sympathetic smile, she saved him from finishing the thought. "We're all safe and alive. Now we just need some answers. I assume you understood what he said?"

"He said he's here to help you."

Nodding, she turned her body to face their guest and smiled at him. "What's your name?"

Pausing for a moment, his brows drew together as if he were thinking, and Isla realized he was probably translating her words in his head. When he smiled at her, her stomach leapt into her throat when she realized he still had fangs like the wolf that he was.

"Marduk."

"Last name?"

Another pause. Another smile. "Just Marduk."

Speaking in a calm, even voice, Jeremiah addressed Marduk. "So you are a *feradux*, then?"

"Yes," he answered. "I have been watching the lady ever since she came to the island."

"Well, that's not creepy at all," Jeremiah muttered under his breath.

"Ten years?" Isla exclaimed. "How old *are* you?"

Frowning, Marduk looked down at his hands and seemed to be ticking off fingers. "Twenty...five."

"Are you serious? You don't look over twenty."

He gave her a small smile. "From what I can tell, I do not age physically while in beast form. Since I can only retain a human shape for short periods of time, I guess I have not aged much."

Seeming to forget his original trepidations, Jeremiah leaned forward, fascinated. "Mhairi said that the *feradux* were *Bruixi* who had committed some kind of crime and were given the opportunity to redeem themselves. What did you do?"

Withdrawing into himself, Marduk turned to look out the window. His eyes took on an ancient, haunted look. Turning back, he met Jeremiah's questioning stare with one of his own and cocked his head to the side.

"I killed my father." His brows drew low over the arctic stare, and a muscle jumped in his clenched jaw.

"How come you never approached me before? Or... changed?" Isla asked.

"You did not know what you were then. I am not allowed to force you to believe."

"I only noticed the wolf a few days ago."

"Things have...escalated."

"Damn right they have," Jeremiah bit out. "Can you tell us about the threat to her?"

Marduk yawned so wide his jaw cracked, and then he flashed his fangs at Jere. "Yes. I can."

"Can you help her learn to use her powers to fight this thing?"

Another yawn. "Yes."

"Jeremiah, he's tired. I'll bandage his wound and we can all get some sleep." Encouraging Marduk to lay down longways on the couch, Isla made quick work of covering the bloody gash with a thick bandage. The boy's eyelids drooped shut, and soon his breathing had evened out.

Putting away her supplies, Isla stood on her tiptoes and kissed Jeremiah on the lips. "Let's go to bed."

Leaning into the kiss before breaking away, Jeremiah nodded. "Be right there." Isla disappeared into the bedroom, while Jeremiah walked back to the couch and pulled the blanket up to cover Marduk's shoulders.

"If you can help me keep her safe, then kid, you're my new best friend." As he turned to leave, a hand snaked out from under the blanket and grabbed him with an iron grip. He looked down to see clear, blue eyes boring into him from down below.

"*Protegam eam cum vita.*" I will protect her with my life.

"Why?" Jeremiah asked, not really expecting an answer.

"Because our survival depends on it."

"Whose?"

"Everyone's."

Awaking early as usual, Isla shuffled groggily out of the bedroom and into the kitchen to start a pot of coffee. The dim early morning light was diluted to a diffused, green glow as it filtered through the kitchen curtains.

It was when she was leaning down over an open fridge, trying to find the makings of a decent breakfast, when the macabre events of the past twenty-four hours came rushing through her head like an old movie reel.

Shit. Man-wolf-person. In her living room. Swallowing, she skirted around the cast-iron stove and tiptoed up to peer over the back of the couch. Sure enough, there was a silky, grey-furred lump curled up on the cushion where the man had been hours earlier.

She shifted her weight from one foot to the other, wondering what she would do. Finally, she decided on the direct approach. "Hey there, buddy," she whispered. *Idiot.*

Tentatively, she reached down to stroke the thick pelt across the animal's back. It was warm and soft as a newborn kitten. The wolf stirred, causing her to jerk her hand back, but did not awaken, making her feel silly for jumping.

Feeling a little bolder, she cleared her throat and spoke louder. "Marduk. Wake up." She had to cover her face when a blinding white light filled the room. When she felt it was safe to open her eyes, she looked down to the wolf and saw the young man in its place.

"Uh...good morning," Isla said tentatively.

Marduk uncoiled his long, lean body from the couch and stretched like a cat. "Morning!"

"Gonna have to see about getting you some clothes today. Jeremiah will have an aneurysm if you keep walking around like that.

The boy just smiled at her, unaffected by his own nakedness. Isla handed him the blanket and he wrapped himself up just before Jeremiah shuffled in.

Isla drank in the sight of him. He looked bleary-eyed and deliciously rumpled. The three of them returned to the kitchen, and Jeremiah grunted when she handed him a mug of coffee. Sitting at the kitchen table, the two men regarded each other silently while Isla busied herself making breakfast.

When she placed plates in front of them, they both dug in like starving men. After they had finished eating, Jeremiah collected the dishes, washed them in the sink, and put them away.

Still silent, he walked back to take his seat, carefully folding his napkin and placing it on the table. He pegged Marduk with an inscrutable stare. "You ready to talk?"

Unfazed, the boy flashed them what Isla was beginning to learn was his signature smile—it kind of reminded her of a puppy that didn't know when to be cautious. "Of course. Ask me anything and I will try to answer as best I can."

Seeming satisfied, Jeremiah leaned his chair back and steepled his fingers together. All scientist now, Isla thought with a smile.

"What are we up against?"

"An entity of great evil," Marduk answering, his face impassive.

A muscle in Jeremiah's jaw ticked, but he showed no other reaction. "Can you be more specific?"

"I shall try." He scrunched his brows and looked off to the side, as if thinking of how to begin. "His name is Alastore. It is said that he may have once been a god, although it is disputed as to which pantheon. Corrupted by evil, he was banished to the *caligo*—the space between Heaven and Earth, dreaming and waking—to live as a *Lochrim*. He remains trapped there, and his only goal is to hoard enough energy to support his corporeal form. If he is able to do so during one of the few days of our calendar year in which the veil between our world and the spirit world is lifted—Samhain and Beltane—he could escape for good, to wreak havoc among man."

"And supposedly it is Isla's job to, what? Kill him? Contain him?"

"Kill him, no. In my time, I've never seen it done. But to contain him, trap him, yes."

"Says who?"

"Jeremiah," Isla warned.

Marduk merely gave them a secret smile. "She was born to it."

Isla spoke in a determined, if quiet voice. "How will I know how to do this?"

"The power to do so is in you, has always been in you. None other than an act of the gods could take it from you. Now that you know this, I can try to show you what to do."

Jeremiah leaned forward to rest his elbows on the table. "This Alastore," he said, punching each syllable through a clenched jaw. "Can he kill us?"

Raising his head, Marduk turned cool arctic eyes to Jere's face. "Yes. He can. Alastore feeds off of energy—primarily negative—and he must consume this energy to be able to create and maintain a corporeal body. Once he has, everyone is fair game, physically."

"Where does he get the energy?" Isla asked.

"There is always latent energy from times past lingering in the atmosphere, plus what is produced by the local flora and fauna, but that is not enough to sustain him. His goal will be to draw humans to him, to his *locus*, to trap them there and feed.

"He'll prey on the worst parts of them, their fears, anger, frustrations — trying to extract the evil from them. He magnifies and enhances those thoughts and feelings until they just have to come out, to explode, and then he consumes the malevolent energy. There is usually nothing left to save after that.

"The more energy he consumes, the more power he has to attract more. He can possess people, even animals sometimes, and force them to do his bidding, until he is able to materialize completely and do it himself."

Isla turned troubled eyes to Jeremiah. "That's what happened to the hikers, isn't it? They were being controlled, in the grips of some evil creature." She lowered her eyes, wrung her hands. "And it was after me."

"No," Marduk said firmly. "Alastore is after them, all of us, really. He'll come after you because you are an obstacle to that, but he wants to destroy everything. This isn't your fault."

In that moment, Marduk's brows drew together into a frown. "You said hikers, plural. I only saw the one who attacked you."

Taking Isla's hand, it was Jeremiah who spoke up. "We found his wife first, out on Raven's Rock. She jumped."

Shaking his head sadly, Marduk looked to Isla. "That's how he'll come after you. He knows you have defenses against him, especially in a one-on-one battle. He'll try to catch you unaware, during sleep — through dreams — or in moments of intense emotion, and take hold of your mind."

Isla and Jeremiah shared a nervous glance.

"What?" Marduk asked, looking back and forth between the two of them. "Has that happened?"

"Twice," Isla said. "Once in a dream, before I really knew Jeremiah. Then after I started spending time with him, it escalated. I think he possessed me...briefly," she said, flicking her eyes back to Jere's face.

"*Cazzo!*" Marduk said, and they certainly didn't need a translation for the outrage. "It's worse than I thought. For an *embulibruixi*—one who was not raised in the order and who's powers are repressed—it takes a significant disruption or emotional change in one's life to fully unlock them. If Alastore sensed that happening, it follows that he would try to make a move. It seems like meeting Jeremiah might have been your *concitatus*."

"My what?" Isla pinched the bridge of her nose and closed her eyes.

"Your catalyst," murmured Jeremiah, who seemed deep in thought. "If this...entity has already made a move on Isla, we need to get her up to speed, like yesterday."

"Agreed," Marduk said. "And one more thing. Make no mistake, Alastore is *not* human. While still a target, Isla has natural defenses against him. Jeremiah, you do not, so take care."

ഇൟ

After breakfast, the three of them congregated on the cabin's faded front porch. Marduk said being out in the open air would allow Isla to center herself quicker, but Jeremiah thought they were all probably just a bit claustrophobic.

Reclining in an old, plastic patio chair, Jeremiah watched Isla and Marduk through slitted lids in the soft midmorning light. They ambled about the front lawn as Isla explained the strange things that have happened around her.

Beautiful, he thought. Pure. And in that moment, as he watched her earnest face and animated gestures, he would do anything to protect her. As the pair wandered back over to seat themselves on the porch steps, he wondered just what that said about his feelings for her.

With his body angled to face Isla, Marduk sat on the porch with his back against a column. Holding his left hand out, palm up, he smiled brightly at Isla. "Watch closely, Grasshopper."

When Isla flicked a confused look up at Jeremiah, he just flashed her a crooked grin. The kid was growing on him. The grin faded to a slack-jawed look of wonder as Marduk settled his right hand above his left, and a small ball of blue flame licked up from his upturned palm.

"As an order of natural witches, the *Bruixi* need not rely on spells for our magick. Spells can sometimes enhance the effects, but they aren't necessary. I don't know all the physics of it, but it feels like an extra reserve of energy. When you open your mind to it, you can control its movement."

He held out his hand to Isla, and she waved hers through the flame. "It's not hot."

"It's just an illusion. Not the David Copperfield kind, but a sort of projection. Not that I can't make real fire, but I figured we should start slow," he said, making her laugh.

"Let's try something easy." Taking the spoon out of the empty coffee mug that sat beside him, he set it on the weather-roughened wood. Cool blue eyes stared at the spoon for a few seconds, and slowly it started spinning. "Your turn!"

Her eyes grew huge, but they gleamed with excitement as she scooted closer. "What do I do?"

"Imagine the atmosphere around you as...a giant Jell-O mold. If you push on it, there is a ripple effect that runs through it causing it to move in other places. Because it's nearly solid though, it still returns to its original form. With me?"

"I guess," Isla answered, frowning.

"You have to empty your mind, create a stillness around you, to search for the right spot to push to have the desired effect. Give it a try."

"Do I need to look at the spoon to do it?"

"There is no spoon."

From his patio chair, Jeremiah snorted loudly, causing Marduk to flash him a wicked grin. He had to bite his lip to keep from laughing when Isla sent him a sharp look. They really needed to school her a little on pop culture, he thought. He waved his hand in the air at them. "Sorry. As you were."

"Close your eyes." Isla listened closely as Marduk continued. "You need to create a shield in your mind from other energies that would influence your thoughts. Imagine a deserted island in the middle of the ocean, or a fortified castle. Anything that represents keeping unwanted presences out."

Slowing her breathing, Isla closed her eyes and thought of where she would feel the most isolated and still comfortable. In her mind's eye, she imagined herself on top of Goat Fell, the highest peak on Arran, a sleeping warrior watching over the island.

Alone on the summit, a grey mist swirled around her to where she could barely see down to The Saddle, the valley between Goat Fell and Cir Mhòr. Not wanting to break her concentration, she gave Marduk a small nod.

"The next part can't really be taught. You have to find your power. Concentrate on finding the core of your energy, where your essence comes from. When you find it, there will be something extra, a little burst of color, a little flash of light. If you see that, grab hold of it. Wrap yourself up in it like a blanket."

He paused as if to allow her to follow his directions. Taking a deep breath, she imagined a mirror image of herself standing on that mountain ridge. In her mind, her own body was transparent, radiating a yellow glow from her heart. Reaching into the opaque form, she closed her hand around the glimmering orb.

Power bloomed like a cresting wave, up her arm and into her body. Her skin vibrated with it, her gut clenched around it. "Open your eyes," Marduk whispered.

Blinking against the hazy sunlight, she looked around. Everything was brighter, more saturated with color, and radiated with tiny pinpoints of light.

"Try pushing at the energy around the spoon, see what happens."

She tried concentrating on the spoon, but nothing happened. "There is no spoon," she muttered to herself, inciting another muffled bark of laughter from Jeremiah. Reaching out with her mind, she bore down on the space around the spoon.

It started with a quiver. Then it shot across the porch, narrowly missing Jeremiah and nearly causing him to topple out of his chair. "Holy shit!" he exclaimed, leaping off the chair and staring wide-eyed at Isla.

"It worked...sort of."

80CR

The Caledonian MacBrayne was a massive vessel that ferried travelers back and forth from Arran to the coastal town of Ardrossan, on the mainland. It was the first leg of their trip to Glasgow to meet with Mhairi.

Jeremiah thought back to his conversation with the stuffy Dr. MacLaren. The man had been none too pleased when he'd requested another visit, but telling him he had possibly found the woman's next of kin quieted him right down.

He looked over at Isla as she leaned on the railing to look out over the bow, taking in her wind-whipped curls, her delicate pixie face, the strong set of her chin, and his heart tripped a little. They had been through so much together already — insane adventures, amazing sex, terrible tragedy, and there was so much more they had yet to face — and in that moment, he knew he would support and protect her through anything.

It had only been a few weeks, but the woman had him completely wrapped around her little finger, and he was sure she didn't even know it. He loved her. He had never loved anyone, save his family and the few friends he let close enough to see the real him, but somehow he knew.

When she turned and smiled at him, white teeth flashing against sun kissed skin, he knew she loved him too. He just had to convince her that it was safe to feel what she felt.

Drawing her into the circle of his arms, he rested his chin on the top of her head and stared out at the choppy waters of the Firth of Clyde. A hazy fog enveloped the coast of Ardrossan, giving the grassy, rolling hills a bluish tint. White windmills dotted the fields, reminding him of looming giants through the curtain of mist.

"You don't have to do this, you know. I can meet with her myself, tell her all we've learned, see if she has anymore advice for us."

Looking up at him with brilliant jade eyes, she gave him a grateful smile and shook her head. "Yes, I do. I wouldn't be able to live with myself if I didn't find out for sure."

She stepped back from him and squared her shoulders. "She could be family. My blood. That matters. It's all I have left."

Taking her hand, he pressed a kiss to her knuckles. "No. You've got me too."

"That I do." Raising up on her tiptoes, she brushed a kiss to his lips, lingered there for a moment, and then turned back to the rolling sea.

When the ferry docked, they piled into Jeremiah's rented sedan and drove down the ramp. They spoke little during the hour long drive into Glasgow, each lost in their own thoughts. When Jeremiah finally pulled into the long, tree-lined drive that led up to the main building of Sacred Hearts, Isla let out a long breath she was unaware she'd been holding.

Studying the building, she thought it looked quite cold and stark. It caused her heart to clench to think of the grandmother she had loved so much as a child wasting away in an institution.

Jeremiah rounded the front of the car to open her door, ushering her toward the looming building with a supportive hand on the small of her back.

This time, Dr. MacLaren was nowhere to be found. The receptionist behind the peeling Formica counter and dingy glass window gave them directions to Mhairi's room, and then swiveled around in her chair to turn her attention back to a soap playing on the ten inch black and white.

Hand in hand, they walked the dimly lit hallways that reminded Isla of a twisted imitation of a rat race. When they reached the room indicated by the disinterested receptionist, Jeremiah knocked softly. Receiving no answer, he turned the knob and eased the door open slowly. It gave a tired creak, then flung wide to reveal a drab grey room with sparse furniture.

This time Mhairi lay on the bed, arms crossed over her chest like a corpse at a viewing, face turned away from them toward the wall.

Jeremiah spoke gently. "Ms. Mackay? Mhairi. It's Dr. Rousseau. Remember, we spoke a few days ago? I've brought someone with me."

She turned her head sluggishly, as if they may have drugged her. Her grey-streaked, red hair was a wild halo around her head, eyes sunken and face deeply lined.

"Dr. Rousseau," she said, with a voice that was much stronger than she looked.

"Afternoon, Mhairi. Nice to see you again. I've brought you another visitor," he repeated. He stepped aside to allow Isla to come approach.

Edging toward the bed, Isla looked at Jeremiah briefly, eyes wide with apprehension as she could feel herself start to panic. He gave her an encouraging smile, so she gathered herself and turned to face the woman he believed was her grandmother.

"Hi," she said lamely.

The woman's eyes rolled up to look at Isla's face, and her wrinkled mouth formed a small O of surprise. "Eileen?" she asked incredulously, looking at Isla with nothing short of blatant contempt. Isla knew in that moment that this was indeed her Mhairi.

Pulling up a chair, Isla sat by Mhairi's bedside and moved her face into the light from the small window. "Not Eileen. Isla."

Tears pooled in Mhairi's tired eyes, and she reached out a gnarled hand for Isla's. "My girl," she whispered. "My beautiful girl."

A broken sob escaped, and Isla felt Jeremiah's reassuring hand on her shoulder. "Eileen told me you were dead."

Nodding, Mhairi patted Isla's hand, clasped in her own. "She would have. She caught me teaching you a spell, threw me out o' the house. I tried tae keep in touch, found out how ye were doing, but she wouldnae tell me anythin'. Heard she'd been carted off to the loony bin, so I called around to find out what happened to ye. She'd already told everyone ye had no kin left."

"Yes, she did get taken to a mental institution — after she tried to kill me when I was eight."

Sucking in a breath sharply, Mhairi's aging features grew fierce and Isla saw a glimpse of the woman she had once been. "Crazy bitch. What'd she go an' do a thing like that for?"

Rubbing the back of her neck, Isla looked her in the eye when she answered. "It was the night my *signa* appeared. She didn't take kindly to it. Claimed I was the child of the devil."

Sitting up in the bed, Mhairi shifted back so that her back rested against the headboard. "Let me see it."

Obediently, Isla twisted at the waist and lifted her thick hair off her neck. Mhairi tossed him a scathing look over Isla's head at Jeremiah. "She is the one you were telling me about. My Isla? When were ye going to mention that?"

Raising his hands in submission, Jeremiah sat down at the foot of the bed to face Isla and Mhairi. "I didn't put it together until Isla showed me the coin she carries that her grandmother had given her. It has your name on the back. I'm sorry, I wish I had found out sooner."

Seeming to accept that reasoning, Mhairi looked back at Isla and pursed her lips. "I hate to say it, my wee bairn, but there is a kernel of truth to Eileen's words."

Isla shot a wary glance over to Jeremiah, who just shrugged and shook his head. "What do you mean?"

Removing her hand from Isla's grasp, Mhairi twisted it around to show Isla the mark on the inside of her wrist. "This is what the *Vigilati signa* looks like."

Studying it, Isla's brows drew together and she frowned. It was almost identical to hers. Almost. It had the three nested circles, the three slashes forming points of a triangle. But the center circle was empty.

Looking toward the door nervously, Mhairi lowered her voice. "The outer and inner circles represent the spirit world and the earthly world. The one in between represents the barrier between the two, that which we are charged to protect."

When she paused, Isla nodded to indicate she was following. "The three perpendicular slashes represent the *locus*, the gateway. It is said that the glyph is a representation of a set of standing stones, which were almost always pathways for spirits and demons to pass through—although *locuses* can manifest in many different structures."

"Why is mine different?" Isla asked cautiously.

Taking a deep breath, Mhairi rubbed her temples before continuing. "I believe your *signa* is different because you are a *praeda. Praedos* are *Vigilati* who have the blood of a demon running through their veins. So they say, anyway. I've never actually met one."

"I'm sorry, what?" Isla said through clenched teeth, clearly losing patience.

Much to her relief, Jeremiah took charge of the conversation. "How would that happen?"

Mhairi shook her head. "I'm no' sure. Like I said, this is all legend. My guess is that the *lochrim* was able to hoard enough energy to not only take on corporeal form, but to disguise himself with glamour. He may have come to your mother with your father's face, seduced her, impregnated her. I hate to say it, but if that's what happened to her, it's probably a blessing that her mind is gone."

"But why do that? What does he gain?" Jeremiah asked.

"I don't know," Mhairi said, her tone rising in frustration. "Why does evil do anything? Maybe he believed he could destroy the *Vigilati* from the inside out. This is an age-old war, one that has no lasting victory for either side, only destruction."

Isla steeled herself for what was coming. "What do I need to do?"

"You must engage him. Alastore. That is his seal—the evil eye—inside your *signa*. I wish like hell I could fight this fight for ye, m'love, but as a *praeda*, you have the best chance of anyone to face him.

"He will torment you, try and trick you into coming to him. He can't physically hurt you until Samhain, when the veil is lifted—he must wait until then t' try and break free. But he can gain power, possess people, animals, and they *can* hurt you. And he can come after those ye love," she added, cutting her gaze to Jeremiah and back.

"Can Isla fight him, trap him, whatever, before Samhain?"

Mhairi shook her head sadly. "No. She can only defend."

Jeremiah clenched his fist where it lay on his knee, but said nothing.

"Ye've found your *feradux*." It wasn't a question.

"Yes, Marduk. He revealed himself to us yesterday." Her mouth quirked up into a smile. "Went to bed with an injured wolf in the house, woke up to a naked boy in the living room. Very disconcerting. Especially for Jeremiah."

Mhairi chuckled, then grew serious once again. "Let him help you." She looked at Jeremiah pointedly. "Both of you. He can teach you how to defend yourself, how to harness your power. Somethin' I wish I could have been there t' do."

Dashing away an errant tear, Isla kissed her grandmother's cheek. "I have you now, and I'm grateful for that."

They all flinched when the door creaked open loudly to reveal Dr. MacLaren's wrinkled face. "Time's up. The patient needs rest."

Jeremiah rose, took Isla's hand, and they turned to leave.

"I'd like a word with my granddaughter. Alone, please." Three pairs of eyes turned to Dr. MacLaren. He scowled, but nodded shortly.

"Two minutes. Dr. Rousseau and I will wait in the hall.

Effectively dismissed, Jeremiah followed the old man outside to wait. When they were alone, Mhairi motioned to Isla to come closer, and Isla could see that her eyes had become glassy and unfocused. She gave Isla a dreamy smile "He's a nice young man."

"Yes," Isla said, smiling. "Yes, he is."

"*Bruixi* mate for life, Isla. If he's the one, your fates are intertwined. Always have been. Something led him here. If he's the one, you'll know."

Thinking they may have passed the point of lucidity, Isla just nodded and gave Mhairi a quick hug. "I'll come see you again soon." Mhairi smiled sadly, and Isla got the feeling she didn't believe her.

As she turned to leave, Mhairi touched Isla's hand lightly, and Isla looked back. Mhairi's eyes were wide and unseeing, pupils dilated. "The blood is the key."

"What?"

"*Vincere* Alastore. The blood is key." Rolling away from Isla, Mhairi lay on her side, facing the wall. Heaving a sad sigh, Isla quietly left the room.

The afternoon sun radiated from a crisp, clear blue sky. Isla turned her face up to the warm September breeze and sighed deeply.

"You okay?" Jeremiah asked as they walked hand in hand.

She nodded, smiling toward him. "I will be."

"What'd she say, after I left? You don't have to tell me, if you don't want to," he added when a thin line creased the skin between her brows.

"No, I want to. I'm just not sure what she meant. What does *vincere* mean?"

"To defeat," he supplied.

"Well, then she said 'to defeat Alastore, the blood is key.'"

Raking a hand through his hair, Jere looked pensive for a moment, and then just shook his head. "Not sure what to make of it. I guess she was just elaborating on the idea that you may be able to do more damage to him because you're...well...related to him." He gave her a sympathetic smile.

She was unsure of whether or not to tell Jeremiah what else Mhairi had said, but her thoughts were interrupted by the jangling of her cell phone from her purse.

"What? Some people's phones just ring," she said when he cocked an eyebrow at her. Checking the caller ID, she flicked a worried glance toward him. "It's Chief Sinclair. I wonder what he needs."

Hitting the send button, Isla answered warily. "Hi, Chief. What's goin' on?"

"Evenin' Isla. I wish I had a happier reason t'be callin' you, but I need your help. Someone else has gone missin'."

"God," Isla breathed, closing her eyes briefly and causing Jeremiah to look at her sharply. Clicking a button on the side of her phone, she put him on speaker. "Chief, I've got you on speaker. Jeremiah's here too. Tell me what happened."

Heaving a ragged sigh, the older man cleared his throat. "Myra Frasier's boy, Rory. He took off yesterday with some neighborhood kids to go fishin' in Lamlash and he didn't come home last night. The other boys made it back, but when Myra called around, they said they had parted ways at the Glenashdale trailhead when they came back down. No one seems to know what happened."

"That's horrible! Myra must be beside herself," Isla said sympathetically. "Of course I'll help track. Where's the rendezvous point?"

When the chief hesitated, Isla looked at Jeremiah, frowning. "Chief?"

"Yeah, I'm here. Listen, I need you to work on this one by yerself. Rory's been missing barely twenty-four hours, so there won't be an official search on until tomorrow."

Sure that there was something he wasn't saying, her stomach knotted in apprehension. Another brief glance at Jeremiah's tense face told her he was having a similar thought.

Nervously clearing his throat again, the chief continued. "That's not all. There's been some...talk...around town."

Of course there was, Isla thought. "What kind of talk?"

"Everyone's nervous, after the first disappearance ended the way it did. I'm not sayin' they have any right to be, mind you. I was there when you came back down from *Gleann Dubh*. I saw how traumatized you were."

"Get to the point, Sinclair," Jeremiah growled. Isla could tell that Jeremiah was losing patience by the muscle twitching in his jaw.

"Uh, yes. Well, you see, some of the townspeople are talking about how both those kids killed themselves when you were there, Isla. You seemed to be the common factor in those scenarios, and that's got everyone rattled. Some of the more…outspoken people have hinted that you might even be involved somehow."

"You have *got* to be kidding me!" Jeremiah exclaimed, seething.

Hurt flashed through her at the implication, but she kept calm for Jeremiah's sake. He was mad enough for the both of them.

"Oi, now listen, I didn't say I agreed with them! I'm just telling you because the other folks are refusing to search with you. But I know you're the best, and I just want to find the boy. So I'm asking if you'll still help me out with this, go solo this time."

"I'll do it—for Rory—and damn the talk. I just hate that they can't see past their own superstitions to realize that the only ones they are hurting are the Frasiers."

"Thank you," he said sincerely. "You're good as gold. Can you meet me at the station in an hour?"

"We're in Glasgow so it will be just over that. I'm going to want Callum and Jack on this too. They know the terrain better than anyone."

"You got it. See you soon."

After hanging up, Isla turned to him with her chin lifted. "Let's go, we have a kid to find."

Jeremiah's heart stuttered a bit, a feeling he was becoming all too familiar with, and he was staggered by how overwhelming his feelings were for her after such a short time. The woman had more bravery in her little finger than any of those crazy bastards on the island.

He smoldered with fury when he thought of the things they were saying about her, but if she could push past it, he sure as hell would too. Opening the passenger side door of the rental car, he gestured for her to get in.

They remained quiet on the drive back to the dock, each lost in their own thoughts, but both wondering if this would just be a case of a mischievous boy getting lost, or if he was just another pawn in Alastore's twisted game.

Chapter Fourteen

They met Chief Sinclair at the Strathclyde Police Station in Lamlash just over an hour later, along with Callum and Jack, who Isla had called on the drive back to Ardrossan.

The nearly hundred-year-old structure looked more like a cottage than a municipal building, with its whitewashed brick face and neatly kept lawn, but such were most places on the island.

Gathering in a small conference room adjacent to the chief's office, the five of them took seats at a scratched wooden table that was probably as old as the building. Though most of them knew Rory Frasier, Sinclair passed around a picture for Jeremiah's benefit.

Smiling gratefully, he studied the image of the boy's smiling face. He was a cute kid, from his strawberry-blond hair that stood out at all angles from his head, to his sparkling, kelly green eyes and charming smattering of freckles across his cheeks.

"Rory Frasier, age eleven," Sinclair began. "Last seen by his friends at roughly two in the afternoon at the Glenashedale trailhead, where they parted ways. I figure you should follow the trail to the falls, see if you pick up anything from there."

Looking thoughtful, Isla shook her head. "No, if they went fishing, they probably followed the river up to the base. Maybe he saw something, went back to check it out."

"That's a good point," Jack chimed in.

"Why don't Jack and I take the trail to the top and, Isla, you and Jeremiah can travel upriver. We'll have two ways in case either pair finds something," Callum suggested.

"Sounds like a plan." Sinclair handed them each a fully charged radio, and they all clicked over to channel two. They decided to dash off to their respective houses to collect their gear and meet at the trailhead in a half hour.

As September rolled in, the weather had begun to cool, so when the group converged at the mouth of the trail in Whiting Bay, they were all dressed similarly in cargo pants and long sleeved thermal shirts.

Lifting worried eyes to the sky, Isla seemed to measure the angry grey clouds rolling in. "I think we should meet back here by six. The weather may turn soon."

Callum nodded, and he and Jack set out on the steep, upward incline of the trail to the top of Glenashedale, while Isla motioned Jeremiah to follow her to the right, into the dense woods. Finding the river, they followed almost due west.

Jeremiah studied the flow of the river, as it snaked in a slow curve over smooth rocks and fallen tree trunks. While it was fast moving with excess water from the recent storms, it wasn't rapids by any stretch of the imagination. A boy Rory's age who had grown up fishing on the island would have known how to handle himself on the bank. Unless he had run into something—or someone—he couldn't handle.

When Isla quickened her steps, he could tell she was no longer merely following the path of the river but had picked up a trail somehow. She moved at a brisk clip, and Jeremiah found himself struggling to keep up.

Slowing, she lifted her face, sniffed the air, and looked back at him. "I was right. He came this way. After he left his friends," she turned sorrowful eyes to Jere's face, "but he wasn't alone."

Gut clenching, Jeremiah fell into step behind her again, nearly at a run this time. He almost fell face first into a shallow rock pool after tripping over a hidden tree root, and he forced himself to be more careful. As the land to either side of the dark artery of water began to ascend, they could hear the sound of the roaring of the falls filling the silence. Dread filled him when, rising above the din of pounding water, was the unmistakable sound of crying. Sobbing, in fact.

No longer needing a tracker when he had his own ears to rely on, Jere surged ahead of Isla, feet pounding on the densely packed forest floor, leaping over obstacles. Knowing Isla was right on his heels, matching him stride for stride, filled him with urgency.

Suddenly, the thick tree line cleared and the river widened, and just feet ahead of him was the cloud of mist that surrounded the pool of water at the base of the falls, generated by the hammering fall of water from the cliff a hundred feet above their heads.

Stopping so abruptly that Isla nearly collided with the back of him, he searched the dim clearing for the source of the sobs. Frustrated, he saw nothing at first, and then he saw a flash of red in his periphery.

To his horror, Jeremiah glimpsed Rory standing at the edge of a jutting outcrop about twenty feet above the churning water, his back to them. A squeak of surprise from behind told him that Isla had seen it too.

His heart leapt into his throat when he saw the boy take a step back, then another, causing pebbles to come tumbling down from the shelf of rock. Slowly, the shape of a woman emerged from the shady curtain of trees just beyond Rory.

Hair ragged, clothes torn, the woman stalked toward the boy with the single-minded focus of a predator. Even from their vantage point from below, they could see the wild look in her opaque eyes.

"Shit," Jeremiah whispered. "He's got the woman, not the boy."

Isla nodded, knowing exactly who *he* was. "That's Penny. She works the checkout at the Co-Op," she said, referring to the local grocery store in Brodick.

Turning a stricken face to Jeremiah, Isla shook her head furiously. "This can't happen again. We have to do something!"

"If we try to climb up there, she'll push him off before we make it."

"I know it," she said sadly. They turned in unison when movement behind them drew their attention. Marduk approached them cautiously from the tree line, his eyes flicking back and forth between them and the bluff.

Moving to stand just behind them, he spoke in a whisper. "Isla, I know you've just started discovering your powers, but you are going to have to try to stop her. It's the only hope that boy has."

"What do I do?!"

"Reach out with your mind, try and isolate Alastore's energy. Push at it, like the spoon."

Seeing the crazed woman move closer to Rory, Isla gave a jerky nod. Flanked by the two men, she closed her eyes and tried to clear her mind. As Marduk had taught her, she put up her mental barriers by imagining herself at the top of the mountain, alone.

When she felt the prickle of power start to roll under her skin, she allowed her thoughts to focus on Penny. Drifting outside of herself, in her mind's eye she stood in front of the woman on the bluff. The entity that had a strangle hold on Penny's mind danced above her like an eerie spectre, glaring at Isla with its pale, shadowy eyes.

Suddenly unbearably angry, Isla felt a flush of energy rush down her arms, into her hands, and down to her fingertips. Not quite sure exactly what she thought would happen, she raised her hands, palms out, and imagined herself pushing at the air around the spirit.

She had been prepared for movement—some sort of action like what had happened with the spoon. The bluish-white flames that leapt from her fingers out to the creature like cloud-to-cloud lightning were definitely unexpected.

When the flames licked over the shadowy figure, it let out an inhuman screech and dissipated into thin air. After giving one final lunge at the boy, Penny's eyes rolled back in her head, and she collapsed onto the moss-covered rock.

The next few seconds seem to unfold in slow motion. As Penny went down, Isla's consciousness slammed back into her body so hard, she fell to her knees—exactly the same time that Rory lost his footing on the ledge and tumbled backwards into the churning water below.

Seeing the streak of red from Rory's jacket as he plummeted, Jeremiah strained to find where he hit the water. Looking back at Isla who was kneeling on the ground, gulping in huge gasping breaths, he was torn between the woman who owned his heart, and the little boy struggling to keep his head above water.

Still shaking and seemingly unable to speak, Isla turned blazing eyes to his face and mouthed the word "go." Nodding once, he kicked off his shoes and shrugged out of his windbreaker. Leaving her in the capable care of Marduk, Jere dove headlong into the deep pool at the foot of the falls.

While the river wasn't overly wild, the weight of the hundred foot column of water hitting the pool below caused a surprising downward current that threatened to pull him under. It took all of his strength to keep himself above water and the little bobbing blond head in his view.

Just as he got within feet of Rory, the head disappeared. "Damn it!" he shouted over the cacophony of water beating down on him. Taking a deep breath, he submerged himself in the cold, murky water.

The water was so dark, it was nearly black, so he had to grope blindly with his hands, scraping his knuckles on rocks as he searched for any sign of the boy. Struggling to hold his breath, Jeremiah began to see spots in his field of vision from lack of oxygen. Just when he thought he would have to resurface for air, his fingers brushed against what felt like an arm.

Grabbing a tight hold, he fought his way to the surface, pulling the boy with him. Lungs burning, he struggled to swim back to the bank one handed, his other arm wrapped around Rory's torso. He breathed a shuddering sigh of relief when he finally clawed his way to the water's edge and collapsed on his back, chest heaving.

Jeremiah noted Marduk fading back into the trees as Isla knelt beside Rory, who was now furiously coughing up water from his lungs. Wrapping him in Jeremiah's windbreaker, she rubbed the boy's arms and wrapped herself around him.

Rory was shivering and letting out little gasping sobs. Isla met Jeremiah's eyes over the top of the boy's head, her relief and gratitude shining clearly in her own.

Once he caught his breath, Jere reached for his discarded radio to call for help through chattering teeth.

"Sinclair, c-come in."

"Sinclair. Go ahead."

"We've g-got him. We got Rory. He's alive. Over."

"Thank God. Where are you? Over."

"Down at the base of the falls. Get someone here fast with blankets and dry clothes. He's been in the water. He'll be hypothermic before too long. Over."

"Be there as soon as we can. Hold tight. Over and out."

ഉ)രു

The next few hours after the rescue passed in a blur of policemen, medics, difficult questions and answers. Rory had been rushed to the hospital, but Jeremiah had refused. Just needed to warm up, he'd said.

Isla drove them back to her cabin, as Jeremiah appeared to be exhausted. Thinking he looked just a little too pale and drawn, she motioned for him to sit on the couch while she busied herself making a pot of tea.

Return to the living room with a steaming mug in each hand, she nearly dropped them both when she caught sight of Jeremiah. He was deathly pale with dark circles under his eyes. Clutching at the quilt he had wrapped around himself, he shivered violently, and Isla could hear his teeth chattering from where she stood.

"Jeremiah! I think you're hypothermic. We need to get you warm!" Tugging him up from the couch, she hooked an arm around his waist to help support his big, shuddering body. She cast him a worried glance and saw that his eyes had a glazed, vacant look to them, and his lips were faintly tinged with blue.

Isla scrolled through all of her survival training she had been through before starting up Expeditions. Somehow, now that it was someone she cared about, everything she knew seemed to have flown out of her mind.

"We need to get you in the shower," she said decisively. Guiding him into the bathroom, she pushed him gently down to sit on the covered toilet. Placing the mug of tea in his hands, she frowned when the liquid sloshed around from his trembling as he tried to take a drink.

When he looked up at her, his eyes were wide and unfocused. "I'm...I—"

"Don't try and talk, love. Let's just get you in the shower." Setting the mug on the marble countertop, she quickly helped him to undress and step under the steaming flow of water. He let out a shuddering sigh when the heated spray hit his chilled skin but just stood with his head hanging, droplets of water dripping off of shaggy strands of hair to roll down his face.

Quickly shedding her own clothes, Isla stepped in behind him and wrapped her arms around him. "What can I do?" she asked.

Saying nothing, he turned around and buried his face in the crook of her neck, strong arms snaking around to clamp around her back as tense muscles shifted and bunched with each shiver. "Feels like I'll never be warm again," he said, voice slurring from the shivers.

"I knew I should have made you go to the hospital."

He just held on tight as his body quaked. Finally the water began to run cold, so Isla helped him step out of the shower and wrapped him in a towel. She took his hand to lead him into the bedroom, and he followed along numbly.

Peeling back the covers for him, she waited while he climbed into the bed. She then changed into her pajama pants and t-shirt to slide in beside him. Turning on her side, she watched him intently. "Jeremiah."

He gave her no response at first, so she repeated herself, and he finally turned his head to look at her. She thought he looked sick, and she was seriously beginning to worry. "Tell me what you need."

"Warm. I—I've just gotta get warm." The slurring was worse now. Isla sat up and quickly shed her clothing. Scooting closer to him under the covers, she wrapped her whole body around him, rubbing his arms with her hands, his legs with her legs.

After what seemed like hours, but was probably only minutes, the shuddering slowly began to ease, and his breathing slowed. As he slept, she kept herself wrapped around him, afraid of letting him get cold again. She studied his profile in the dark for long moments, felt his chest rising and falling steadily under her hand. He looked younger under the veil of sleep, worry lines eased and thick, dark lashes dusted over chiseled cheekbones. He had become so dear to her so quickly, she didn't want to let go for fear that he would slip away from her. Once she was satisfied that he had slipped into a deep, healing sleep, she closed her eyes and allowed herself to drift.

Jeremiah awoke with Isla still twined around him, naked and warm. Taking a moment to bask in the blissful warmth that he thought would never again permeate the bone-deep chill, he buried his face in her hair and breathed deeply.

When she burrowed closer in response, he raised his face to take her mouth in a slow, leisurely kiss. She sighed into his mouth when he pulled her leg higher to hook over his hipbone and slipped into her where they lay.

Unlike the white-hot flash of passion that they had experienced before, this was a slow burn smoldering between them, but no less potent. It was a slow dance of lazy strokes and easy kisses set to a symphony of skin sliding against sweat-dampened skin.

When she began to clutch at his lower back and graze his shoulder with her teeth, he knew she was close, and that caused his own release to build at a fever pitch. Just as he felt her body bow, taut muscles shuddering, his climax gripped him as he matched her thrust for thrust.

He kissed her deep, enjoying her unique flavor. "Mornin'," he said with a smile.

Her brow furrowed, and that full lower lip stuck out just a bit in a sort of pout, making him want to nip at it. So he did, enjoying the little whimper that she tried to hold in. Placing a hand on his chest, she angled her upper body back so that she could look in his eyes.

"You really scared me."

A line of worry formed between her brows, and he reached up to smooth his fingers over it. "I know, I'm sorry. Scared myself a little there, actually."

"Why didn't you tell anyone how bad off you were?"

"I didn't really know right away. I was all caught up in helping get Rory to the hospital, and worryin' about you—you looked so pale and tired after—well, you know. It didn't hit me that I might be in trouble until the ride back over here. At that point, there was really nothing left to do but ride it out."

She seemed to mull that over for a moment, and then launched herself at him, embracing him with a surprising strength. "God, don't scare me like that again," she whispered. "Don't know what I would do if anything happened to you."

While it wasn't exactly a declaration of undying love, her words sent his spirit soaring. He returned her hug and kissed her hair. "I'll try to oblige."

Disentangling herself from him, she rose and walked to the bureau to gather her clothes for the day. When she was heading out the door toward the bathroom, Jeremiah's voice stopped her.

"Where're you going?" he asked, stretching like a cat and tucking his arms behind his head.

Chuckling, she tossed a pair of his pants at him, which happened to hit him in the face. "I'm going to brush my teeth and get dressed. Some of us have to work, *Doctor* Rousseau."

Giving her an exaggerated eye roll, he dragged himself out of bed and dressed. When they met again in the kitchen, he captured her mouth in a tender kiss that caused her toes to curl in her sneakers.

"Got a tour today or are you riding the pine?"

"I have a kayak tour this morning, then I'm off for the afternoon. Amy's on desk duty, Brynna's got the afternoon tours so she can break in our new guide, Braeden, and Cal's off today."

Jeremiah pulled a chair out from the kitchen table and gestured for her to sit down. Taking his own seat across from her, he fixed her with a serious gaze. "Good. That's good.

There's something I've been wanting to run by you, but...well, we've been busy."

"Okay," she said, eyeing him a bit warily.

"I think we should tell Callum what's going on. Jack too, I guess, since Cal will probably tell him anyway."

She narrowed her eyes at him. "Jeremiah, they're my best friends. I can't afford having them thinking I've gone 'round the bend."

"Darlin', those boys love you. Even if they did think you were crazy, they'd love you anyway," he said, giving her his signature crooked grin. "Besides, I think they'll surprise you. I'm sure they can tell something strange is going on."

Isla chewed on her fingernail absently as she thought it over. Reluctantly, she heaved a sigh and nodded. "Alright, we can fill them in. I just hope we won't regret it."

"I don't think we will. We need all the backup we can get. You get to work, I'll call Cal and set it up."

Gathering up her things, Isla pressed a chaste kiss on his lips and turned to leave. Snaking out a hand, he grabbed her wrist to spin her around. He closed his mouth over hers in a hot branding of lips on lips and slid his tongue inside, caressing her velvety softness.

Sighing, she slipped her hands under the hem of his shirt and raked her nails up his back, giving him chills. He pulled his mouth from hers with one last nip at her lower lip. "Have a nice day."

Chapter Fifteen

As Isla headed off to work, Jeremiah put in a call first to the Expeditions office.

"Expeditions, this is Amy," came the bright reply.

"Mornin' Amy, this is Jeremiah Rousseau."

"Hey, Jeremiah! I heard there was trouble yesterday. How's our girl?"

"Still truckin', as usual. She's on her way in right now. Said she had a kayak tour this morning?"

"Uh huh. She's taking a family of five around the fisheries in Lamlash Bay, out by the Holy Isle. Why?"

"Got room for one more?"

"Sure! Can't get enough, huh?"

"Something like that," Jeremiah agreed. Of course he wanted to see Isla, but he also worried about her. Who knew when and where Alastore would strike again.

"Alright, I got you booked. Better get a move on, van leaves in an hour. Oh, and no discounts for sleeping with the guide."

"Oh, come on, Amy!" he said, laughing.

"Just sayin'. See you soon."

"Bye, Amy." Shaking his head, he ended the call and opened the keypad to dial Callum. It was time to fill the boys in on everything that had happened.

Callum's loud voice boomed over the end of the line. "Oi, mate! What's shakin'?"

"Hey, Cal. Got a couple of questions for you."

"Sure thing, Doc. Shoot."

Barely suppressing the eye roll at the *doc* moniker, Jere chuckled. "First, I need to keep my hands busy at home so I don't bury myself in my work and make my editor have a conniption."

He continued when Cal grunted out a laugh. "You mind if I do a little work on the porch? I found a couple of loose boards, so I thought I could fix them, maybe refinish and paint it. What do you say?"

"Sure thing, brother. I'd be stupid to pass up some free home improvement."

"Great! The other reason I was calling was to see if you and Jack wanted to get together with me and Isla tonight. We have some things we'd like to run by you."

"Must be a mind reader, my friend. We were actually going to invite you two to dinner tonight. Our place at six. How's that sound?"

"Perfect. Thanks, Cal. We'll see you tonight."

Isla was in the equipment room pulling out wetsuits and life preservers for her kayak tour when Amy came in, smiling like the Cheshire Cat.

"Added one to your tour," she said, clearly trying to act innocent.

Not taking the bait, Isla continued checking over the equipment. "That's good. We're heading into the slow season so we can use the business."

Pouting, Amy studied her fingernails for a moment then turned around and flounced out of the room. Isla rolled her eyes and turned her attention back to preparing for the tour. Whatever hot guy Amy booked on the tour or juicy tidbit of gossip she had, Isla wasn't interested. She was too busy worrying about the upcoming powwow with the boys.

Jeremiah had texted to tell her that Callum had invited them to dinner. No turning back now, she thought, stomach turning a little somersault.

Hearing the bells on the front door jangle, she rose from the cedar bench in the equipment room and walked out into the lobby to greet their guests. Amy was checking in the Roarke family, a middle-aged couple from Wisconsin and their three boys, when the door opened again.

Squinting her eyes, Isla watched as a large form filled the doorway, backlit by the early morning sun. Tall, she noted passively, head barely clearing the top of the door frame. Massive shoulders nearly filled the width of the door. This must be Amy's "plus one," she thought.

The man stepped into the lobby, out of the glare of the sun, and her breath caught when she glimpsed the mop of shaggy brown hair and devilish grin. Jeremiah. When he winked at her, she returned his smile despite herself.

Amy bit back a smile as she made her way over to Isla to introduce their patrons. "Cheryl, Tom, this is Isla. She'll be your guide today."

Isla shook hands first with an average-looking man with an amiable smile, and then with his plump, pretty wife. "Good to meet you. I'm glad you could join us, looks like we're going to have perfect weather."

"Oh, yes, it's lovely," Cheryl said, then gestured toward the three clean-cut boys behind her. "These are our boys, Isaac, Jacob, and Caleb."

Flashing each boy a smile, Isla shook hands with them as well. "Is this your first time kayaking?" she asked. Isaac, the oldest at fourteen, looked at her shyly. "Yes, ma'am."

"None of that," she said, dimple flashing. "You can call me Isla."

Isaac cut his eyes over to his mother, who nodded discreetly. "Thanks, Isla."

"Guys, this is Jeremiah. He's a friend of mine and he'll be joining us."

After they all got acquainted, Amy led them into the equipment room to gear up, leaving Isla briefly alone with Jeremiah. Without a word he pulled her into a tight hug and smiled down on her. "Missed you."

"You saw me less than an hour ago," she teased, laughing.

"What can I say? I got it bad." The sudden heat in his gaze gave her goosebumps as she raised her face for his kiss.

When they finally drew apart, she narrowed her eyes suspiciously at him. "Are you here because you want to see me, because you are dying to kayak, or because you want to keep an eye on me?"

"Can't it be all three?" he asked.

"I guess so. You'll have to keep up with me."

"Duly noted," he said, looking decidedly unworried.

"Come on, let's get you suited up."

Taking his hand, she pulled him into the equipment room where Amy was fitting everyone with life preservers. The

Roarkes were all grinning like kids and checking each other out in their wet suits.

Amy tossed Jeremiah a suit and jerked a thumb at the door behind her. "Changing room's back there. Hurry up!"

When everyone had suits, windbreakers, life jackets, and appropriately sized paddles, Isla headed for the door. "Follow me outside and we'll pick out your boats. You can choose a single or a double."

They made their way to the boat rack where multi-colored kayaks were carefully stacked one on top of the other. Cheryl and Tom chose a double boat, while the rest of them picked out singles. Isla, together with Jeremiah, Tom, and Amy, loaded the boats onto a trailer that was hitched to the company van.

With everyone piled in, Isla maneuvered the van on the short trip to the small, sandy beach at Lamlash Bay. Once the boats were unloaded onto the beach, she gave a quick overview on steering and paddling and assisted the Roarkes with casting off.

Wading into the water, Jeremiah climbed into his own kayak and paddled in a slow circle while Isla launched hers. He had kayaked a few times, and while he was by no means an expert, he could hold his own.

They circled the shallows of the bay while the family got the hang of paddling. Finally, when Isla felt that they were comfortable enough, they forged on, following the curve of the coast.

Relaxing, Jeremiah took in the scenery. Two thirds of the bay was cradled by Arran's coast, while the passageway out to open water was interrupted by the looming bulk of the Holy Isle, a small mountain island that housed a monastery and a colony of monks.

Off in the distance, he could see large circular structures made of pipe and netting, which Isla had told him were the fisheries — breeding areas for farmed salmon. He breathed deep of the salt sea air and paddled on, enjoying watching Isla helping the kids to straighten out their boats.

Eventually, they were all skimming the water at a fast clip, heading toward the southern tip of the Holy Isle. He had skirted the group and was paddling side by side with Isla. He smiled when he heard the boys giggling behind him.

Turning his face to Isla, he saw the pure joy written across hers. When the small group neared the fisheries, the salmon started breaching in earnest. Hundreds of the fish flopped into the air and landed with great splashes, causing the Roarke boys to hoot with laughter. That explains the nets, Jeremiah thought.

They remained there for a while, paddling back and forth between the three structures, watching the antics of the fish and taking pictures. After a half hour, Isla motioned for the group to follow her again, and they rounded the fisheries to head back toward the beach from the other end of the bay.

Jeremiah and Isaac started an impromptu race, taking deep strokes into the cold water to push themselves onward, their boats skimming over the water. Afterwards, they floated, bobbing with the subtle current generated by the gently blowing breeze, and waited for the others to catch up.

Because he was ahead of her, Jeremiah saw it first. Flames sparked on the surface of the water some twenty feet from where his boat drifted and traveled in an arching line like a lit fuse.

"What in the hell?" he mumbled, looking helplessly over his shoulder as Isla and the others approached.

"Hmm?" Isaac asked, looking over at him with a lazy smile. Confused, Jere glanced back at Isla and she gave an almost imperceptible shake of her head. Jeremiah examined the faces of the other kayakers as they laughed and joked with one another. They didn't see it, he thought as the wall of fire rolled into a wide circle around the six boats.

The sound was deafening, the ring of fire creating a leaping, roaring cauldron around them. Jeremiah reached out with his paddle so that Isla could grasp it and pull herself closer. They floated there in the water, boats bumping against one another, and watched in horror as the flames closed in.

The Roarkes had lashed their boats together with some bungee cords Isla had brought and were busying themselves with snacks from their drybags. They were seemingly oblivious to the ominous circle of roaring fire. "It's not real," Isla whispered, but her death grip on Jeremiah's hand belied her confidence.

Breathing hard, Jeremiah nodded. "Just a trick."

"Oh God, what if he possesses one of them out here? It could get us all killed." Her breath hitched in a silent sob.

Jeremiah squeezed her hand tightly. "You saved Rory, you can save them too."

He watched as Isla stared hard at the wall of fire around them, and she seemed to reach deep inside herself to hidden reserves of energy. Marduk had taught her to visualize energy as solid objects so, best he could figure, she would imagine a wall between them and the unholy fire, and use her own energy to create it.

A hissing sound filled the air, and a slender form slipped through the crackling fire to hover before them, feet never quite touching the water. Alastore, or his projection of himself, was dressed all in black so that his pale white skin seemed to glow in contrast.

Hard, translucent eyes glared out at them, with their shadows jumping and swirling from a handsome but sharp face, black hair swept back away from a high forehead marked with a glyph of an eye. As they watched him warily, thin lips peeled back to form a ghastly smile, revealing razor sharp teeth.

As Jeremiah looked on in horror, he was instantly transported to that Halloween night twenty years ago when he faced a very similar creature. He had begun to remember it in more detail since visiting Mhairi, but seeing Alastore brought it all back in vivid detail.

Jeremiah wasn't a witch, but even he could feel Alastore's power, his hatred, straining against the barrier Isla had formed between him and his ring of fire and their small group of kayakers.

When he spoke, they could hear his human voice, but also the demon inside him. "You will never defeat me."

Just as quickly as they had come, the fire—and Alastore—were gone. Isla pinched the bridge of her nose as if she had a headache. They were both shaking and panting from fear and shock, but the Roarkes were blessedly unaware.

"Alright guys, let's pack it in," she said, pointing her boat toward the shore and beginning to paddle briskly. The other kayakers fell in behind her, talking back and forth to each other over the sound of the surf hitting the hulls of their boats.

After they pulled their boats ashore and stowed them in the boat rack at the beach, ready for the next tour, they all piled into the van for the ride back.

ജരു

When Isla arrived at Callum and Jack's cottage, she was tired and more than a little irritated. The house was a charming brick two story, with a patio off the back—half of which was walled in with floor-to-ceiling windows.

Hearing laughter and music drifting through the air from the backyard, she decided to forgo the knocking and meet them out back. As she rounded the back of the house, the scene she encountered was enough to melt away the worst part of her sour mood.

Callum and Jack sat at a small table in patio chairs, feet propped up on a cooler. With an ice cold bottle of Newcastle in each of their hands, their attention was directed toward Jeremiah, who sat sprawled out in a reclining deck chair. He had brought along his guitar and a small portable amp and was teasing out a wailing stream of blue notes—something Isla had come to realize he did to help him work through his thoughts.

Isla pulled out a chair and placed it across from the men, turning it around to straddle it. Folding her arms over the back of the chair, she rested her chin on her forearms and silently regarded Jeremiah.

It was as if man and instrument were one and the same. His left hand slid deftly up and down the neck of the guitar, bending the strings as he picked the notes with his right— creating the classic bluesy sound that he loved so much.

As the muscles flexed in his wrists and forearms, Isla found her gaze drawn to where his hands stroked the guitar, his fingers long, thick, and muscular from years of playing. She had no idea why she found them so unbelievably sexy, but she did.

Her gaze drifted up to his face, and she found that his eyes were closed. He followed the rise and fall of the tune with subtle movements of his head, slight changes of the expression on his face. Whenever he would get really deep into the song and he would pick a particularly complex riff, his eyes would squeeze shut tight, he would bite his lip, and his face would twist in an almost pained expression.

Suddenly his eyes opened, and she was caught in his deep hazel gaze. She could feel herself blush at being caught staring, and he confirmed it by smiling knowingly at her and finishing the song with a long slide down the entire neck of the guitar.

"Hey there, pretty lady," he drawled.

"You make a lot of faces when you play," she pointed out, still flustered.

"It's not blues if it don't look like it hurt a little bit," he said, flashing those wolfish teeth at her again.

Callum removed his feet from the cooler to dig out another beer, flicked the cap off with his bottle opener, and passed it to Isla. She smiled gratefully at him. "I need this after the day I've had."

"Did something happen at work?"

Not ready to explain the nightmarish kayaking trip yet, Isla simply explained that they'd had a difficult tour. Jack shrugged and excused himself to go check on dinner.

When he returned to tell them the food was ready, they all rose to help him carry the dishes to the patio table. They ate in easy companionship, entertaining each other with stories and jokes. Once the food was finished and the dishes were done, they reconvened on the patio and sat in pensive silence, each lost in their own thoughts.

It was Jack who finally broke the silence. "So, what did you want to talk to us about, Jeremiah?"

He took a long, slow sip of his beer and glanced over at Isla. She drummed up a smile for him, even though her heart wasn't in it. "Well...I don't know if you noticed that some...uh...strange things have been going on around the island."

Jack nodded solemnly while Callum—being Callum—chose the sarcastic approach. "Hmm, like disappearances, suicides"—he narrowed his eyes at Isla—"wolves. No, nothing's strange there."

Jere chuckled, then sobered quickly. "Isla and I think we may have discovered the cause of it all. But it's not my story to tell," he said, wrapping a supportive arm around Isla's shoulders.

Breathing in a shuddering breath, Isla opened her mouth to speak and then clamped it shut so hard that her teeth clicked.

Sarcasm forgotten, Callum leaned forward in his chair, his face a mixture of interest and profound concern that was mirrored on Jack's. "Love, you know you can tell me an' Jack anything, right? Nothing could make us love you any less."

Her eyes welled but the tears never fell. Instead, she squared her shoulders and began to speak. "It really is a long story," she said apologetically.

"We have all night," Jack assured her.

Nodding, she took another deep breath. "It all started in 1991, when my mother tried to kill me."

Callum drained his bottle in one chug and slammed it down on the table. "I'm gonna need another beer."

Jack and Callum sat in intense silence as Isla related first the appearance of her *signa* and her attempted murder, and the strange events that had begun to happen around her. She and

Jeremiah took turns explaining the hypotheses from Jere's research and the information they had learned from Mhairi.

There was a long, tense silence as they tried to absorb all that they had just heard. Finally, Jack covered Callum's hand with his own, where it lay on the patio table, and gave Callum a short nod.

Leaning back in his chair, Callum steepled his fingers together and pegged Isla with an inscrutable gaze. "So," he started slowly, "you're telling us that, first of all, you're a witch. You have supernatural powers imbued upon you from some unknown source to assist you in the fight against soul-sucking demons. Do I have this about right?"

Isla gave him a curt nod, but said nothing.

"And the good doctor here," he continued, "makes his living researching and writing about paranormal activity." Callum flicked his eyes over Jeremiah's ashen face. "Rumors of a witch on the island brought you here, unsure of what you'd find. What you did find was a woman who has powers that even she didn't know about. And, the rest is history, yes?"

Wincing, Jeremiah rubbed his tired eyes with the hand that was not occupied holding Isla's. "That about covers it."

"Right then. I'll allow it."

Isla, who had just taken a nervous sip of her beer, had to slap a hand over her mouth to keep from performing a classic spit take. Looking over at Jeremiah, she saw her own surprise mirrored on his face. She narrowed her eyes at Callum. "You'll allow it? Just like that?"

Jack finally broke his own silence. "Isla, love, we've known you for ten years. In all of that time, do you think we wouldn't realize there's something different about you?"

Isla ducked her head and studied her fingernails. "I didn't know," she said in a small voice.

"Oh, honey, of course you didn't. You had no one to teach you any different. You were just you, and you'd always been that way. You had no reason to think anything was unusual about yourself."

Nodding, Callum spoke up. "And we live in Scotland, m'dear. Jack and I have seen enough strange things in our lifetime to know that there are plenty of unexplained phenomena in the world. Hell, this isn't even the strangest thing we've heard this year!"

Stunned into silence, Isla glanced at Jeremiah, who merely shrugged.

"I said it before, and I'll say it again," Callum said fiercely, "nothing you could do would make us love you any less."

Giving them a watery smile, Isla rose to hug first Callum, then Jack. She returned to her seat, sighed and leaned into Jeremiah. "You boys are the best."

"There is a missing piece to the story, though," Jack said thoughtfully.

"What's that?" Isla asked.

"Jeremiah, you said that you had been researching the *bruixi* off and on for several years before you came here, which was why the rumor of a witch on the island intrigued you so."

When he paused, Jeremiah nodded. "I had come across veiled references while researching other projects, and my curiosity was definitely piqued. So I kept an ear to the ground for more information, which eventually led me here."

"Mmm," Jack grunted, tapping his chin with the tip of the finger. "The question is why, though. What was it about the story that intrigued you so? You'd have to have run across quite a few legends and myths in your line of work. Why this one?"

"That's a fair question. And up until about a month ago, I wouldn't have been able to answer it. I think I have an idea now."

Isla glanced over at him sharply, narrowing her eyes. He smoothed a hand down her arm, reassuring her. "I haven't hidden anything from you, darlin'. This is just an idea I've been chewing on. Now seems as good a time as any to talk it out."

He seemed to wait for her to relax before he began. "When I was twelve years old, I had my first paranormal experience. I guess trying to explain it was the main reason I became interested in the field of parapsychology."

"What did you see?" Isla asked in a sharp tone, bordering on accusatory.

"I was never completely sure what exactly I *saw*. After it happened, the memory almost immediately became very hazy, as if something was blocking it out. I've only recently been able to remember more detail."

"Do you think that the sudden clarity is associated with coming to the island?" Jack asked.

Jeremiah nodded slowly. "I do, but I'll get to that. Let me tell you what I remember first. I was on a tour of the St. Louis Cemetery #1 in New Orleans. You know, one of those where they walk around and tell you about all the ghost stories associated with the graves and such."

When the others nodded their understanding, he continued. "I was actually getting pretty bored. I had been expecting it to be, you know, scary. Anyway, I saw a suspicious looking guy skulking around, so naturally I had to follow him and see what he was up to."

Callum snorted out a laugh at that. "An investigator is born."

Jere gave him a lopsided grin. "Pretty much, although that night I definitely came to regret it. When I finally caught up to him, he was just kind of standing there—almost like he was waiting for me to catch up. In hindsight, I should have probably taken that as a bad sign. I immediately had the feeling that something was off, like I was in the presence of something not quite human. Then it proved me right by showing me its fangs and creepy swirling eyes."

He turned to Isla. "Actually he looked an awful lot like the guy from the lake, but he had a different symbol. He approached me, and I realized that I couldn't move. No matter how hard I tried to send a signal to my arms and legs to work, nothing happened.

"So he stepped up to me and put his hands on my head. What happened then is still really fuzzy, even as the rest of the memory has come back. He did some sort of demon mind meld thing on me. I tried to fight it, but I could just feel my brain checking out. He raised a ring of fire around us, just like at the lake. It was so real, I could feel it burning me."

He gave Isla a grateful smile when she squeezed his hand. "So how did you get away?"

"I didn't see much of it. All of a sudden, he was snatched backwards out of the fire and I was alone. When the fire disappeared, I saw him a few feet away, basically being strangled by a woman. She had a mark just like Mhairi's, except it was on her face." He placed his own hand on his left cheek. "Just here. But it was moving, writhing almost, and kind of...glowed."

"This is where it gets really weird," Jere said, this time earning a laugh from Jack.

"Relatively, of course," Jack pointed out.

"Naturally," Jere acknowledged. "So this woman had her hands around his throat, and she was probably a buck ten soaking wet, yet she seemed to have complete control over this creature. She stared him down until I saw flames literally shoot out of her eyes and basically — for lack of a better term — zapped him. He went up in smoke, and all that was left was a small white snake on the ground, with opaque eyes just like he had.

"The lady turned to look at me, and I actually recognized her as a gypsy fortune teller from the park. I used to be kind of scared of her as a kid. So then, she picks up the snake and stuffs it in her bag. Then she winks at me and smiles, and that was kind of the last straw for my poor twelve-year-old self. I bit the dirt, hard. When I woke up, I was alone and scared shitless."

"You said this happened when you were twelve. You're positive about that?" Isla asked.

"Completely. Why?"

"If you were twelve, then this would have happened — "

"Halloween night, 1991," he finished for her, understanding dawning. Jere rose to pace angrily around the patio, raking a shaking hand through his hair.

Callum looked at Jack then turned his attention back to Isla. "What are we missing here?"

Visibly steeling herself, Isla reached out to grab Jeremiah's hand and pull him back down into his chair, linking her fingers with his. "Halloween night '91 was the same night my mother tried to kill me."

"Bloody hell," exclaimed Jack. "What are the odds of that?"

Jeremiah turned fierce eyes toward the pair. "Probably a billion to one. This was no coincidence. We're like pawns in some twisted game!" Isla saw the rage that bubbled up, white hot and angry, but he seemed to hold it together.

Troubled, Isla thought back to their visit with Mhairi and what had been said after Jeremiah left the room. "Bruixi *mate for life, Isla. If he's the one, your fates are intertwined. Always have been. Something led him here. If he's the one, you'll know.*" She knew she should tell Jeremiah, but she was afraid of what he might say.

The haunting words echoed in her head, causing her throat to clench and her heart to thump. Was she really ready to be tied to someone for the rest of her life? Someone whom fate had chosen for her? She didn't know, but the idea of it seemed to suck all of the air out of her space.

She wanted to be with someone because she loved them and they loved her. Not because of some ancient writing on the wall. Did she love him? Maybe. She thought she was beginning to, but they'd only known each other for a little over a month.

That didn't stop him, she thought. He loved her. She could see it shining in his eyes every time he looked at her, and that sight never failed to make her heart flutter. But the idea that this was all out of their control was enough to blur the lines of her vision with the dull edge of panic.

Gulping for air, she shot out of her seat and backed away from the group slowly. Jeremiah rose and reached for her, but she twisted out of his reach, chest heaving.

Hurt flashed in his eyes but disappeared just as quickly as it came. "Isla—"

"Please." She silently pleaded for him to give her the space she needed. If they talked now, she was afraid she would say something she couldn't take back. "I just need some time to process. I'll find you later." Without waiting for a response, she turned and dashed away.

Jeremiah stood transfixed, staring at the spot where she had been until he heard her ancient pickup cough and sputter its way down the drive.

Grabbing his keys where he had tossed them on the table, he started after her, only to be blocked by a hand on the center of his chest. Callum stood in front of him with Jack flanking his right side.

His hand was firm, but his eyes were filled with sympathy. "Just give her a little space, mate. It's a lot to take in, findin' out that your life may not be entirely your own. She just needs a minute to wrap her head around it."

Jere sighed and his broad shoulders slumped just a bit. "Yeah, I know. It's just hard not to try and fix it for her."

"That's how it is when you love someone, man. Get used to it," Jack said, clapping one big hand on Jere's shoulder and the other on Callum's. "Why don't we all just sit down an' have another beer."

Giving him a small smile, Jeremiah shook his head. "I appreciate it, but I think I'm just going to head back to the house, maybe do some work on the deck. It will give me time to wrap my own brain around all this new information. Do me a favor? You hear from her, just call me so I know she's all right."

"Will do. Take care, mate."

Chapter Sixteen

After three days, he still hadn't heard from her. Jeremiah had kept himself mindlessly busy during that time to keep himself from calling her or going to see her. He had managed to repair all of the loose boards on the deck and refinish it to remove all of the splinters that kept stabbing him.

After that, he moved on to painting it a nice, crisp white to match the trim and shutters of the little cottage. Having just finished the job, he stomped into the house barefoot and shirtless—covered in paint—wearing nothing but ragged, paint-splattered jeans.

Padding into the kitchen, he snagged a half empty bottle of single malt off the counter. He had polished off the first half somewhere between refinishing and painting.

Exhausted and more than a little buzzed, he flopped down on the couch, only pausing for a second to hope that all of the paint on him was dry. He took a swill of the cheap scotch and looked around the room. Realizing that he had just run out of projects to keep his mind off of Isla, he searched desperately for something — anything — to do. He spotted his guitar in its scratched black case across the room.

Old friend, he thought. Heaving his big body up, he walked over to it and flicked open the case. He stroked a loving finger down the neck of his worn, shabby Fender, and lifted the instrument gently out of the case. She may not be pretty, he thought, but she still sings like an angel.

Returning to the couch, he propped his feet up on the coffee table and closed his eyes and began plucking a tune. Without opening his eyes, he reached out to snag the cord connected to his portable amp and plugged it in to the bottom of the guitar.

Squeezing his eyes shut even tighter, his fingers began to fly on the strings and the guitar began to wail. He often lost himself in the music when he had a lot on his mind. He would put himself into a kind of trance, where nothing existed but the music.

As he played a riff from one of his favorite country blues songs, Jeremiah realized that for the first time in his life, he wasn't transported by the music. Try as he might, he couldn't keep his thoughts from drifting back to Isla. Where was she now? Why hadn't she contacted him?

He tried to tell himself it didn't matter, he would be going back to the states in a month anyway, so he had no use for personal attachments. He almost believed it. Shifting on the couch, he picked up the bottle and took another drink, played another riff.

Losing track of time, he continued on that way for what could have been hours — or only minutes — until he began to drift off, fingers still poised on the guitar.

Isla had worn a track in front of her fireplace, pacing back and forth, worrying over her situation, over Jeremiah. The idea that unseen forces were pushing her toward someone as a foregone conclusion terrified her, and yet she knew she'd had feelings for Jeremiah before she found out about their intertwined fates. How much of what she felt were her own emotions and free will and how much was destined? How could she know—how could anyone know?

She kept thinking in circles, a self-perpetuating cycle of worry. The one conclusion she could manage to come to was that, regardless of the why or how of it, she had come to love Jeremiah and when it came down to it, that was all that mattered.

Stopping in her tracks suddenly enough to startle the cats out of their slumber, Isla realized that she had just admitted to herself that she was in love for the first time in her life, and she hadn't spoken to the man in question in three days. She would be lucky if he'd even see her. Stuffing her feet into scuffed brown hiking boots—a stark contrast with her wispy mid-thigh-length tunic dress—she grabbed her keys and ran out the door.

Parking the old truck on the street, Isla climbed the slope of the neatly manicured lawn and went around to the back of the cottage. It never occurred to her to go to the front door, as she had been coming this way for nearly ten years.

She stopped when she came to the back porch, taken aback by the gleaming whitewash and the mended boards. He'd been busy, she thought, wondering if worry for her had caused this burst of productivity.

The next thing she took note of was the silence. The cottage was curiously absent of any ambient noise, no footsteps or music, no movement coming from inside. Still shaken from their encounter at the lake, Isla was instantly worried for Jeremiah. Her heart leapt into her throat and her pulse pounded in her ears.

Not wanting to give an enemy the advantage, she crept up the steps to the back porch, her well-worn boots tapping softly on the refinished boards. Easing the glass door open, Isla tiptoed inside. The only sound came from her dress ruffling around her legs as she turned to shut the door behind her.

The back door opened to the dining room and kitchen area, which she found empty and silent. Afraid to call out, Isla crept around the corner into the large, open living room. Her whole body sagged against the wall as she breathed a huge sigh of relief. Jeremiah was seated on the couch with his long legs stretched out and the guitar still in playing position resting against his stomach, sound asleep.

Taking a moment to just look at him, Isla raked her eyes over the thick, muscular chest that narrowed to a trim V underneath the guitar, which his slumping posture had hitched up higher on his belly. She swallowed as she glimpsed the trail of fine, dark hair that disappeared into the waistband of his jeans, where the top two buttons were left undone.

She trailed her gaze along the length of his long, paint splattered legs to his bare feet, which she found strangely endearing. He truly was a specimen, she thought, as her pulse leapt and heat pooled in her belly.

Frowning, she took in the two empty bottles of cheap scotch and several beer bottles on the coffee table. Studying his face more closely, she saw the dark shadows under his eyes that brushed against his sharp cheekbones and the worry lines around his mouth.

She did this. In the short time that she had known him, she had brought the man nothing but trouble, from her enemies attacking him to sending him mixed messages and shutting him out. It cut her deep that she had caused him so much pain and worry that he had resorted to drinking too much to drown it out.

Jeremiah deserved better than this, she thought. He deserved a woman that stood by him and let him help her, who shared everything with him. Flawed though she was, Isla just didn't have it in her to give him up to someone else. He was too wonderful to let go. So from that moment on, she resolved herself to be everything he deserved and more, and she knew without even thinking about it that he would do the same.

Isla knelt before him, situating herself on the floor between his knees, and placed her hands gently on his thighs. His left hand, still resting on the body of the guitar, twitched reflexively on the strings.

Peering up at him, Isla saw that he was watching her through slitted lids. He seemed groggy, but she could tell that the haze of alcohol had receded a bit with the rest.

He watched her through barely open eyes, his expression guarded and wary. Isla felt another stab of guilt for wounding him, however unintentional. Searching his angular face, she dared hope to see forgiveness and acceptance.

Seconds passed and finally his body relaxed again. He began to pick a tune on the guitar still across his stomach. The melody, soft and twangy, floated through her like a wandering spirit. She remembered him playing the song before—he had called it Shining Moon—said it reminded him of her.

Taking it as a good sign that he was playing for her, she sat there for a moment, suspended in time, and let the music fill her with warmth. While the song was an olive branch of sorts, Isla wanted more of him.

Leaning forward slightly, she placed both palms on his rigid abdomen. She traced the lines and grooves of muscle there, silk over steel, and still he watched her, his expression veiled. Isla let her fingertips follow the dusting of hair to the open buttons of his jeans, and she slowly released the remaining buttons.

Parting the V of worn denim, Isla reached inside and freed him, causing his breath to hitch slightly, but his fingers never faltered on the guitar. He said nothing, just watched her and continued to play. Isla's mouth quirked up in a half-smile, considering his feigned indifference a challenge that she would gladly meet.

Lowering the waistband of his jeans slightly, Isla allowed her hands to roam, gauging his reactions. His eyes closed briefly, and then turned their fierce hazel glow back to her face. She'd hurt him. She could see it in his eyes. But he'd forgive her. She saw that there as well, and she closed her eyes as she was swamped with love for him. Wanting him to relax in a way that he hadn't been able to in days, she smoothed her hands over him.

His hands shook slightly and his chest hitched up and down as his breathing sped up—all the while, the guitar's wistful siren song continued. She leaned over him, brushing her silky curls over his belly, causing the muscles there to ripple and bunch. Oh yes, she thought. Her man needed her, wanted her badly.

His head sagged back as his eyes reflexively closed, and he allowed her to do as she pleased. She felt her own body respond, relishing the skin-on-skin contact, and she dug the nails of her free hand into his jean-clad thigh which tore a strangled groan from his lips.

Finally, as if just remembering it was there, Jeremiah slid the guitar off of him to rest safely on the couch beside him. He brushed her curtain of mahogany curls aside with one big hand and stroked her cheek with a calloused thumb.

She literally purred. She sounded feline and satisfied, and if she wasn't so mesmerized by him, she'd have laughed at herself. The sound seemed to have lit a fire under him, and he had to gently push her away. Unable to help it, Isla could feel her lips form a pout, and he chuckled at her.

"Unless you want this to end right here, right now, you're going to have to stop," he said, chest heaving.

Isla got to her feet and her lips parted with a sly smile. Jeremiah swallowed visibly as she prowled toward him, sliding her hands up the sides of her slender thighs to her hips, and raising the hem of her dress along the way.

His eyes were riveted to her hands as she hooked her fingers into the elastic of the scrap of silk that covered her and slinked it down her legs. Stepping out of the garment with first one foot, then the other, she came toward him—stalked him with fluid grace.

In one easy movement, she climbed up on the couch and straddled his lap, slowly lowering herself onto him. Jeremiah's eyes drifted closed as he gripped her hips and thrust up to meet her downward movement. His hands were everywhere, cupping her breasts, molding her curves.

Isla set the pace, pushing him faster as she took her pleasure from him. Looking down to where their bodies joined, Isla found it incredibly erotic to see that they were still mostly dressed. She'd never wanted anyone—or been wanted—that desperately. It was a heady feeling.

Heat spread through her body and she knew she was close. He kept one hand on her hip while splaying the other between her breasts, riding it down her torso, which was stretched tight as a bowstring.

He began to stroke her in time with the movement of his hips. She threw her head back in a rain of curls, as her release exploded within her. In the glow of her own passion, she felt the exact moment he lost himself to her, and rode the wave of his own release.

Isla collapsed against his chest with her arms around his neck, both of them taking great heaving breaths. They stayed that way for an interminable amount of time before she drew back to peg him with her jade stare.

"Hi."

"Hi," he answered, releasing a satisfied, lopsided grin. "I missed you."

She smoothed soft fingers over the worry line between his brows and frowned. "I know. I'm sorry I freaked out."

"S'ok. I'm not that easy to get rid of." He winked at her and flashed those wolfy teeth. She knew he was making light of the situation, forgiving her and comforting her all at once. Her heart tripped, and fell.

"I don't deserve you," she said, placing staying fingers over his lips when he tried to protest, "but I love you anyway."

He blinked and started to speak, then stopped and blinked again, making her laugh. The movement of her body made her acutely aware of their intimate position, and the fact that he was still inside of her.

"What did you say?"

"You heard me," she said with a smile. He ran his hand up her neck to fist in the hair at her nape, and dragged her forward, crushing her mouth in a possessive assault. As their tongues danced, Isla was astonished to feel him harden again inside her.

He pulled away, breathing heavily. Cupping her cheek, he looked at her with those deep hazel eyes. "I love you, too." Her breath caught, released, and caught again. Slowly, her gaze dropped to his mouth, and she rolled her hips against him.

Isla loved the way his eyes crinkled at the corners as he chuckled at her. "Down girl! A man can only take so much." She felt a blush creep over her cheeks before she realized he was teasing her.

Rolling her eyes at him, she swatted him on the shoulder. "Jackass," she muttered.

Sobering, she turned to face him and stroked her hand over his face. "I really love you, you know. I probably shouldn't, but I do."

Taking her hand, he kissed each of the knuckles in turn. Then he yawned so big that his jaw cracked. "Me too," he said sleepily as he drifted off to a contented sleep.

Isla lay awake for a while longer, thinking about the man asleep next to her. About how she had come to love him so much so quickly, and how their future was more uncertain than ever.

⃝⃝

Hours later, Isla awoke alone on the couch feeling deliciously sore and yet unbelievably relaxed. She could hear the shower running from the master bathroom, and she smiled at the thought of her man in the next room. Her man. Imagine that.

Snagging her underwear and Jere's oversized Tulane t-shirt that was draped over the arm of the loveseat, she dressed and headed into the kitchen to see about breakfast. There wasn't enough in the cupboards to make a true hearty Scottish breakfast, so she popped some toast in the toaster and set a few strips of bacon to frying.

As she was turning on the burner, she heard the house phone ring. Having no caller ID—people on the island just didn't have need of such things—she picked up the cordless handset to answer, assuming it was Callum or Jack. "Hello?" she said.

The line was silent for a moment and she was about to end the call when the person on the other end cleared her throat. "I...I'm sorry, I must have the wrong number."

The woman on the call had a southern drawl that was much thicker, but extremely similar to Jeremiah's, so Isla knew it had to be a friend or relative from back in Louisiana.

"It's alright, ma'am. Who are you looking for?"

"I am looking for Jeremiah Rousseau. I thought this was the number he gave me, but I must have misdialed."

"Not at all, ma'am. This is Jeremiah's vacation house. I'm a friend of his."

"A friend?" the woman asked with an obvious smile in her voice, and Isla knew instantly that this had to be Jeremiah's mother.

"Aye. My name's Isla."

"You can call me Esme. Oh and what a darlin' accent you have there, sweetie. Listen, I'd love to talk to you more, but I really need to speak with Jere. It's very important."

Momentarily stunned at the woman's change from timid to bouncy southern lady, Isla shook herself to recover and remembered what the woman had asked.

"Jeremiah just got into the shower, actually. I'm not sure if he takes long ones or not but it will be at least a few minutes. Shall I have him call you back?"

Again the tone of the conversation changed, and Esme went from bouncy to worried in the blink of an eye. Her voice shook as she said, "No, baby, I need you to go get him...please."

It was the *please* that did it, spoken in that trembling tone one gets when she is struggling to hold back tears. "I'll get him for you. Just hold a few moments, I'm going to put the phone down."

"Thank you," she answered, sniffling. And damn if that didn't cause Isla to tear up herself. She had never had a normal, or even sane family life, and here is Jeremiah's family already treating her like one of the flock just because she said she was a "friend."

Putting the phone down, Isla crossed the living room and went down the hall to the master bedroom and into the bath...with the large, triple-headed shower that could fit an entire football team inside. She swallowed convulsively at the idea of that, at the uses they could think of for it.

Snapping herself back into reality, she wrapped on the glass to get Jeremiah's attention. When he turned, though, her mind momentarily blitzed out. Her man was magnificent, from his huge shoulders that could fill a doorway, to his washboard abs, thick thighs, and ropy calves. He looked like a golden god with water sluicing over that beautifully tanned skin.

His unruly hair was plastered down over his eyes, but she could see their hazel depths and their expression hit her like a ton of bricks. He wanted her badly. Again. They had made love three times that night, and here the man is staring at her like he was starving and she is the last piece of bread. Her body responded instantly, as did her mind as she remembered why she had come in the first place.

"Jeremiah, you have to get out and dry off. Your mother's on the phone and she says it's urgent."

"You could have said I'd call her back."

"Oh, I did. That was when she started fighting back the tears and I caved. She was so sweet to me and I didn't have the heart to tell her no."

They walked into the kitchen together, Jere rubbing himself furiously with a giant bath towel which he then wrapped around his hips.

"Mama? Mama, what is going on that you had to have me drug out of the shower."

"Jeremiah, this is important. Matty's gone missin' again."

In a bid for patience, Jeremiah pinched the bridge of his nose. His brother Matthieu had a habit of running off when shit got critical. But he always came back—when he was good and ready and not a moment sooner.

"What happened this time?"

"That girl that he was 'engaged' to"—Jere could practically hear the mental air quotes—"took off with another man. Matty was devastated. Said he had to get out of here. I'm not sure if he meant our house, Baton Rouge, Louisiana, or the country. I have no idea where he's gone!"

Her voice started to take on an edge of hysteria, which never failed to split his head with a migraine. Matty was always pulling shit like this. And Esme always bought into it.

"Mama, you need to calm down. Matt is a grown man and he can take care of himself. He'll come home when he's ready. Or he won't. Maybe he'll settle somewhere else and be happy. If he does, you're gonna have to get right with that, yes?"

A deep sigh and static followed before she answered. "Honey, I know you're right. But I worry about y'all, Matty especially because he's still drifting..."

"Okay, how about this. I'll make a few calls, use my limited hacking skills, such as they are, and see if I can draw a bead on him. I'm not going to tell him to come home. Hell, I may not even tell you where he went, but I'll make sure he's safe. Deal?"

Esme pouted for a moment, but she really had no choice to make. "Deal. Now who's your Scottish lady friend there? Answering your phone already?"

"Mamaaaa," he warned, a growl in his voice.

"Oh relax, Jeremiah. I just spoke with her briefly and she seems right friendly. So I hope whatever it is works out for you."

"I hope so too, Mama, because I'm in love with her."

"Oh...my. Well bless her little heart, she was so sweet. I can't wait to meet her!"

"One thing at a time. We have some work to do over here for a while, and I've got to find Matthieu, so I'm going to be busy. We'll figure out when and if we can all get together once we've got all our loose ends tied up.

"I gotta go now, my little woman's in the kitchen cookin' breakfast."

"Oh go on, you little joker. Bet you don't say that to the 'little woman's' face!"

"True enough. Hey, Mama?"

"Hmm?"

"Don't get your hopes up, okay? You know as well as I that if Matty doesn't want to be found —"

"I know, son," Esme said in a tired voice. "I know."

Jeremiah heaved a weary sigh as he ended the call and pinched the bridge of his nose with two fingers to stave off the threatening headache. Damn his brother for doing this to them again. He guessed it wasn't really Matthieu's fault, but it still pissed him off that the boy caused their mother so much worry.

Making his way to the kitchen, he leaned against the doorjamb and just looked at Isla frying bacon in nothing but his old college t-shirt. Damn, if she wasn't spectacular. And didn't it just give him a surge of possessive pride to see her wearing his clothes.

He walked up behind her and wrapped his arms around her trim waist, resting his chin on her shoulder and inhaling her scent. Momentarily, she let herself lean into him before she cut off the burner.

"Have a seat, breakfast is ready."

Slumping into one of the kitchen chairs, Jere stared unseeing out the glass patio door. He had so lost himself in his thoughts that he jolted when she placed a plate in front of him.

Sliding into the seat across from him with her own plate, she nibbled on a piece of crisp bacon and regarded him, silently waiting.

It dawned on him that this was what a relationship was about—being able to share your joys and your pain with that other person, and knowing she would support you unconditionally and without judgment, but knowing she'll love you anyway.

"It's my brother," he started, actually feeling himself gearing up to tell her the whole story. "He's MIA...and it's not the first time."

Matthieu Rousseau was a wayward soul. That was really the best way Jere knew of to describe him. His brother had a brilliant mind, but he was always too restless to put much time into realizing its potential.

After high school, Matt actually got a partial scholarship to LSU where he was pursuing a double major in criminalistics and forensics. He just had a knack for working out puzzles—he could see patterns and clues where others could not.

Ever restless, he dropped out after two years to join the Marines. Shortly after finishing boot camp, he was shipped out to Afghanistan, then Iraq, where he was a member of a special ops team. Jeremiah still didn't know exactly what he did for them, but he knew it had ruined his brother. What was left of him to ruin, anyway.

A year after he was deployed, the G9X Ops team was blown sky high by an IED underneath their tank. Matt lost a kidney, gained a Purple Heart and a medical discharge.

After the war, his brother had come back broken, even more mentally than physically. He drifted around from one contract job to another, utilizing his military training and forensics education, first as a hired mercenary, and then as a private investigator. He was probably still doing both, which was why Jeremiah knew that Matthieu was perfectly capable of ghosting, and staying that way, if he wanted.

Constantly seeking belonging but unable to settle into any kind of routine, Matt sought to fill the void left by their father's passing, and the one created by the atrocities of war, not only with dangerous living, but with unhealthy relationships as well.

Matt was more handsome than any one man should be, and lord, some women loved a broken man. He attracted the clingers, the whiners, the controllers, even the gold diggers—the mercenary business had been quite lucrative.

It was a normal pattern for him to fall in love too quickly with the wrong woman, seeking to fix what was broken in him, and ended up getting his heart stomped on every time. The result was always the same, the cracks deepened and Matt went off the grid.

Jeremiah had long since given up trying to fix things for Matt. His help was neither effective nor welcome. All he could do was be there when and if his brother needed him.

Blinking down at his empty plate, Jeremiah realized that he had just spewed his family problems out loud to Isla over breakfast and didn't give it a second thought. She had become his solid ground, the place he could lay his burdens when he couldn't, or shouldn't, bear them alone.

Isla had just finished dressing in her own clothes and was getting ready to head to work, when her cell phone rang. She brushed a swift kiss over Jeremiah's lips, went in for a nibble when she wanted more, and then hit the send button on her phone to answer the call.

"Hello?"

"Isla? It's Chief Sinclair."

"Hey Chief, how are things going?" Isla said, then clicked the phone on speaker mode so that Jeremiah could listen in.

"Not too good, I'm afraid. I don't really know how to say this...but we've had five more people go missing in the last forty-eight hours."

"Dear God! What can I do to help? Where do you need me?"

"Listen, Isla," he started, the tension in his voice striking a chord of anticipation in her. "I need you to come in to the station."

"Of course, Chief. Anything we can do to help," she said, and hearing her say "we" just caused Jere to stand up a little straighter. "Is that going to be HQ for the search?"

"No, I'm afraid not....I'm going to need you to account for your whereabouts during the last forty-eight."

The implications hit her like a ton of bricks, just as she heard Jeremiah clamp his jaw shut so tight his teeth were grinding. "What?"

"Not sayin' I agree with it, but there's been talk around the island, about how all these things going on seem to be connected to you...and when we find folks, dead or alive, you're always right there."

"That's because she's on the motherfucking search party, Chief! She's your only tracker," Jere exploded, obviously unable to hold in his outrage any longer.

"Believe me, I know. Like I said, doesn't mean I buy into all the talk, but I have to follow all the leads. Otherwise folks will say I'm giving you special treatment."

Her lips thinned and her face hardened. "I understand. Give me a few minutes to make some arrangements to cover me at Expeditions, and we'll be right over.

"I'd appreciate it. I'm sorry, Isla."

"Me too," she said flatly, ending the call without a goodbye. She had some calls to make.

&)Q&

Drumming her fingers on the worn wooden table of the interrogation room, chin in hand, Isla rolled her eyes toward the ticking wall clock. She had been sitting in this cinderblock icebox for half an hour, and no one had come to question her.

She knew this had to be some kind of tactic they used to unnerve a suspect, get them to spill their guts just to get the hell out of that room. Which meant, naturally, that they considered her a suspect. Maybe even a criminal.

Leaning back in the cold metal chair, she narrowed her eyes at a black, ballpoint pen that had been tossed on the table. The pen began to spin furiously, and then flung itself across the room. Tossing a glance up to the closed circuit security camera, she had the fleeting thought that she should be careful about displaying her power, and then shrugged it off. Everyone already thought she was a witch any damn way, so there was no use in hiding it.

And the witch was pissed. A sneer tugged at the corners of her mouth as she continued to stare at the camera. She wondered if they realized that she was indeed what they thought she was, and because of that, no four walls could hold her if she didn't want them to.

The video feed zoomed in and Isla's smiling face filled the screen — just before the picture fuzzed out and the camera went dead.

Jeremiah poured himself a cup of coffee from the carafe in the main room of the police station. Looking down into his cup, he blinked in horror at the black, oily swill. So the cliché of bad PD coffee was true, he thought. Damned if he didn't doctor it up and drink it anyway.

He had been pacing the dirty brown, low-pile carpet for nearly half an hour, all the while glaring daggers at the various officers seated at their desks. "Chief got held up," they had said. Bullshit. Jeremiah knew that they had left Isla twisting in the wind to try and scare her into giving something up. Problem was, there was nothing *to* give up.

All it was really going to do was piss her off and make her less cooperative. He could practically feel her energy simmering across his skin. He wondered if the officers couldn't feel it too.

He turned his head at the perfect moment to catch sight of Isla's falsely angelic smile fill the closed circuit monitor. As quickly as that happened, the feed snowed out and switched off. And the wires running to the monitor sparked, just for good measure.

Cursing under his breath, Jere looked around to see if anyone saw what happened. A tubby officer got up from his desk to slap the monitor a couple of times, shrugged, and sat back down. Thank fuck he didn't make any connection with the woman in the room. *Keep it together, Isla,* he thought.

Finally, Chief Sinclair emerged from his office looking grim. He nodded to Jeremiah but said nothing as he made his way down the hall to the interrogation room. As the Chief disappeared behind the beat-up metal door, Jeremiah clenched his fists and resumed pacing. This was not going well.

Isla was careful to keep her expression impassive as Chief Sinclair wordlessly entered the room. She wasn't sure what questions the older man was going to ask, but she knew that she probably wouldn't have a good answer for him.

Since she had taken off and secluded herself for the past few days, only leaving the house to go to work during the day, the only one who could verify her whereabouts couldn't speak for her. She had spent her time at home working with Marduk to help her learn to harness her powers. There hadn't even been time to let Jeremiah in on that.

Sinclair cleared his throat, and Isla heard the scraping of the chair legs on the floor as he sat down, but she didn't look at him.

"Isla," he said softly, waiting for her to meet his eyes. "I'm no' happy about this either, so let's just get on with it, okay?"

When he got no response but a curt nod, he sighed and his shoulders sagged a little. "I need you to account for your activities since Wednesday night."

Clenching her fingers and releasing them, Isla turned her eyes skyward as she called up her memories of the last forty-eight hours. Those that she could share, anyway. "Wednesday night I had dinner at Callum and Jack's, stayed there until about seven. Went straight home after that."

"Alone?" Sinclair interjected. Isla flashed him a glare and nodded again.

"Thursday, I worked the desk at Expeditions from nine to four. Again, I went straight home. Alone. Yesterday was exactly the same schedule. Work. Home. Except, instead of staying at home last night, I went to Jeremiah's. I was still at his place when you called me this morning."

Shaking his head, the chief looked at her pointedly. "Is there anyone that can verify that you were at home during the times you say you were?"

Struggling with what exactly she should say about Marduk, Isla hedged. "You know I live alone, Chief. And the cats aren't talking."

Clearly not amused, Sinclair closed his eyes briefly and then looked back at her. "That's not what I asked and you know it. You need to be honest with me, Isla. I can't help you otherwise."

Mind on rapid fire, trying to figure out how to spin the Marduk thing, she wished like hell that Jeremiah was with her. He'd know what to do. "I had a friend staying with me from...out of town," she said after a long pause. "But he's gone now, and I'm not sure I can get in touch with him."

"You're goin' to have to. This is serious, Isla. I'm not blind here, lass. All of these disappearances and incidents seem to revolve around you in some way. If you can't provide me with an alibi, I may be forced to hold you on suspicion. Just give me your friend's contact info, and I'll run 'im in."

"I need to speak with Jeremiah. He may know where my friend is, and he can probably get to him faster."

Jere pushed the door open slowly, not sure what kind of state he was going to find her in. "Hey darlin'," he said, seating himself in the chair that Sinclair had just vacated, and taking her hands. "How'd it go?"

"Not well, Jeremiah. He said they have enough to hold me for a little while. Sinclair might actually think I have something to do with this."

"Why do you say that?"

"The time I spent away from you was either at work or at home. The only person who can verify that I was actually home can't exactly come in for an interview."

Closing his eyes briefly, he raked a hand through his brown mop of hair. "Marduk." He'd had to suppress a growl at the thought of Isla alone with another man...wolf...manwolf—whatthefuckever—he had working parts. Then he reminded himself that Marduk was just a kid and saw Isla as more of a master than a conquest.

"There's a simple solution to this. I'm going to go find the little bastard and bring him in here to testify."

"It's not that simple. First of all, if you come at him with guns blazing, he'll get scared and run off. You know you frighten him. Also, he spends most of his time as a wolf, for God's sake. He's not going to know what to say or how to act. He doesn't even have any identification!"

Sighing, Jeremiah scrubbed a hand over his face, brushing across the two days' worth of beard growth. "Point," he conceded, "but I think you're underestimating the kid."

When Isla tossed him a look that said a whole lot of *yeah right*, he just chuckled. "Seriously. I mean, I guess he's no *vigile*, but our boy is a right powerful witch...er, wizard....hell, I don't know what it's called."

Isla waved a hand, indicating for him to continue. "Maybe he can cast some kind of spell to dispel suspicion or, shit, maybe he can conjure up a fake ID. We won't know until we find him and explain what's happening. Which is exactly what I am going to do."

"Point," she said, repeating his earlier thought. "You've got to handle him delicately, though. If you spook him, he'll run off and we won't see him for days."

Gathering her slender hand in his, he turned it over to press a kiss into her palm. "You can trust me. I'm going to fix this."

"I do."

Jeremiah rushed passed Chief Sinclair on his way out to go find Marduk. "Where are you going?" Chief asked.

Grabbing his jacket, he made sure the look he tossed Sinclair over his shoulder was murderous and brooked no arguments. "I'm going to find her alibi."

"You've got two hours before we lock her up for the night!" he snarled, clearly getting annoyed with Jere's forcefulness. "And no tricks, Rousseau."

Chapter Seventeen

Jeremiah drove his rented sedan down the coastal road at breakneck speed as he headed back to the cottage in Lochranza. He'd had the forethought to pick up some of his clothes for Marduk, as the wolf always poofed into his human form naked as a jaybird.

Grabbing a polo shirt and a pair of khakis, he bolted back out the door and headed south toward the turn-off for the mountain cabin. If Marduk was anywhere that he could be found, it would be there.

Pulling up to the cabin after negotiating the winding drive, Jeremiah noticed that all was quiet. There were no birds chirping, no squirrels rustling in the brush—and that was a sure sign that an apex predator had been spotted.

Turning in a slow circle to survey the tree line around the cabin, he suddenly found himself at a loss. How exactly did you call a wolf? Especially one that was a shapeshifter. Finally he settled on yelling Marduk's name at the top of his lungs. Hopefully even the beast would recognize its own name.

Hearing nothing still, Jeremiah tried calling out again. "Isla needs you!" he shouted. "Flea-bitten mongrel that you are," he added under his breath. Just when he was about to go inside and rack his brain to figure out where to look next, he heard a rustling in the brush behind him, causing him to freeze with his hand on the doorknob.

Looking over his shoulder, he caught sight of the great grey beast in the shadows at the edge of the forest, and he slowly turned his body around to face it. Still unsure of how much humanity Marduk retained while he was in wolf form, Jere was careful not to make any sudden movements.

The two of them shared a silent, tense moment as they stared at one another. After seconds that seemed like hours, the wolf sat back on his haunches, lowered his head, and waited. Jeremiah had the absurd notion that the two of them had reached a tentative understanding.

Wordlessly, he turned to disappear into the house, leaving the door standing open at his back. He was fishing around for a beer in the fridge when he heard the soft click of the door closing behind him. Jeremiah nearly dropped the bottle when he turned around to find a very human and very naked Marduk standing by the door.

"Oh, for the love—I'm never gonna get used to that."

Marduk looked down at himself, raised his ice blue eyes back to Jeremiah, and shrugged his shoulders. Muttering to himself, Jere tossed the throw from the couch at Marduk, hoping he would have the sense enough to cover up. "Wait here, I've got clothes for you in the car."

As Marduk dressed, Jeremiah quickly explained Isla's situation to him. "It doesn't matter to them that she would never do anything to hurt another person. All that matters is she can't verify where she was during the time frame, and they aren't going to let her go unless she can."

Lifting his chin, Marduk looked at Jeremiah, his artic glare seeming to glow. "Then we shall go down there and take her out ourselves."

Jere shook his head. "That's not the way things work in our world. We can't just go blow a hole in the police station and politely escort her out. She'll just be in more trouble. You are going to have to go down there with me and tell them she was with you."

"Then let us go." Nodding decisively, the younger man headed for the door. Jeremiah halted him with a firm hand on his shoulder.

"This is very dangerous. We need to be prepared. How long can you maintain your human form?"

"Your guess is as good as mine. I've never tested the limits. It will all depend on how much magic I use, and how much energy is drained doing so."

"Okay," Jeremiah said, drawing out the last syllable. "We'll just have to be quick then. And pray you don't poof back into a wolf while we're surrounded by armed policemen."

Jere rolled his eyes when Marduk merely shrugged again. Clearly the boy didn't understand the gravity of the situation. "Do you have any identification? They'll ask for it when we go in."

Marduk's eyes widened, he gave an offended sniff and scowled at Jeremiah. "Of course. I am *feradux*. Not some two-bit magician," he said, as if that should mean everything to Jere. Gingerly unbuttoning the cuff of his shirt, Marduk rolled up his right sleeve to reveal his forearm.

Before there had only been smooth, olive colored, bare skin over lean muscle—Jeremiah knew this because the boy was always parading around stripped to his birthday suit. Now the skin began to shimmer and, slowly, a design appeared starting from his wrist and coiling around to his elbow.

The markings were a series of slashes and coils, wrapping around strange symbols that were runic in nature, but Jeremiah could not identify their origin. There were words lining the underside of the forearm that he did recognize.

Quo vadis quae ego vadam – the simple translation being "wherever she goes, I shall go." As Jeremiah met Marduk's cool, calm gaze, he knew then that this young man would do as much as he could to keep Isla safe. This, at least, they had in common. When Jere extended his own right hand, Marduk nodded and shook it firmly. They were going to go get their girl.

"While that is spectacular artwork, that's not the type of identification I was talking about." He took out his Louisiana driver license and showed it to Marduk. "You need something that says who you are, otherwise your statement won't be worth the price of the paper it's written on."

"It won't be a problem. They will know who I am."

"Marduk, that's not the way—"

Holding up a hand to cut off the conversation, Marduk turned to open the door of the cabin and looked over his shoulder at Jere. "Trust me."

Taking a couple of deep breaths, Jeremiah thought it over. What choice did they have really, but to trust in Marduk's ability to sell his story to the cops? After the brief pause, he nodded sharply, grabbed the keys from the counter, and followed Marduk out the door.

Jeremiah entered the police station first, with Marduk at his heels. Once inside, the two men stood broad shoulder to broad shoulder and eyed the officers who had looked up from their paperwork. The policemen seemed instantly on alert, Jeremiah realized. One of the AFO's—or Authorised Firearms Officers—even went so far as to let his fingertips rest on the grip of his police issue.

Then again, the two of them probably made a pretty menacing picture. Both over six foot tall and well-muscled—Jeremiah with his brick-house build and Marduk full of hard planes and lean muscle—and both looking mad enough to spit nails. Jere couldn't blame the officers for being wary.

The majority of policemen in the UK did not often carry firearms, except under special circumstances, tending to sway toward extendable ASP batons. But Jeremiah supposed strange deaths and disappearances all over the island qualified as special circumstances, and the Strathclyde Police Force had called in the AFO's and armed up.

"We need to see Sinclair. Now." Jeremiah demanded it of them in a tone that dared anyone to question him. They were quickly shown into the Chief Constable's office, with its burgundy walls and huge cherry wood desk. When they were seated in the two chairs facing the desk, the officer who had brought them backed out of the room without a word.

It was then that Jeremiah realized that Marduk was projecting waves some sort of alpha male witch back-the-fuck-off-me vibe, so strong that it raised goose bumps on his arms. So that was part of the reason the officers were so intimidated. What other tricks did the boy have up his proverbial sleeves?

Finally Chief Sinclair entered the room and skirted the chairs to reach his desk, giving the two men a wide berth. "What've ye got for me, Rousseau?" he asked, his wary eyes flicking to Marduk and then back.

"This is Isla's friend, Marduk..." At a loss, Jere cut a side glance at the young man next to him.

"Custos," he said, emphasizing his already heavily accented speech. "Marduk Custos. I am visiting from my home in Rome."

"He is the one that was with Isla during the time that you have *accused* her of taking part in these disappearances," Jeremiah interjected with narrowed eyes and a voice dripping with menace.

Clearing his throat uncomfortably, Sinclair addressed Marduk. "That true?"

Those arctic eyes glinted like diamonds and appeared just as hard as Marduk studied the older man. "Yes, it is. I met Isla at her house around four o'clock on Thursday and stayed the night. And again on Friday, we were together at her house until she left to go visit Dr. Rousseau, where I'm told she spent the remainder of her time until she came here," Marduk finished, tossing a glance to his side at Jeremiah.

The other man nodded almost imperceptibly. Chief Sinclair pushed a yellow legal pad and pen toward Marduk across the massive desk. "I'm goin' to need you to make an official statement. If you please, write down what you just told me."

As Marduk scratched pen over paper to create his surprisingly elegant handwriting, Jere regarded the man in front of him. Sinclair looked weary, the wrinkles that had always been etched in his face seemed deeper than ever before.

When Marduk passed the written statement back to Sinclair, the chief extended his hand. After shaking first Marduk's hand and then Jeremiah's, Sinclair stood and bid the other men to rise as well.

"I just need to make a copy of your driver's license and get your contact information, and you boys can be on your way."

As Marduk peered into Sinclair's eyes, Jeremiah began to feel a crackling tension in the air. The atmosphere of the room became so thick that he could barely draw in enough oxygen to breathe.

Jere wondered why everyone else in the building didn't come rushing into the room to figure out what the source of the feeling was, but no one did. Maybe he had some weird sensor that went off when people around him were using magic, set off by his close proximity with Isla.

Continuing to stare, increasing the ever-present tension that seemed to be holding Sinclair transfixed to the spot where he stood, Marduk spoke in a low voice. "That won't be necessary, will it, Constable?"

Sinclair slowly turned his head from side to side, eyes wide, and answered as if he were hypnotized. "N-No...not necessary at all."

"Good," Marduk said crisply, fiddling with his cuff. "Now go and get Isla so that Dr. Rousseau and I can be on our way."

Just as quickly as it started, the spell was broken as Sinclair hustled out of the room, calling for an officer to fetch Isla for them. Jeremiah followed Marduk out of the office behind the chief, and he had to place supporting hands on the kid's shoulders when Marduk swayed on his feet a bit.

He could only imagine the amount of energy it took to maintain the kind of power that could, however briefly, control minds. The young man was much more powerful than he ever realized. It made Jeremiah worry about how much longer Marduk could hold his human form.

Deciding he didn't want to find out, he ushered Marduk out of the office and into the main room where Isla waited with a uniformed officer. Sinclair was nowhere in sight. Not wanting to push their luck, Jere grabbed her hand with one of his and placed his other on Marduk's shoulder, guiding them both out.

When they were safely piled in Jeremiah's rental and on the road back to the cabin, they breathed a collective sigh of relief. Jere heard the rear car seat creaking, and the faint sound of joints cracking from behind him. A glance in the rearview mirror told him that Marduk had lost the battle with his glamour and was now curled up in an exhausted bundle of wolf.

"Not a moment too soon," Jere mumbled, and punched the gas as the car ascended up the mountain.

ॐ

Jeremiah cast a worried glance at the woman beside him in the passenger seat of his car. She was looking tired and pale after her ordeal. Reaching out with his left hand, he brushed a caress down her ebony curls.

"How are you holding up?" he asked, rather lamely.

She gave him a weak smile, but the muscle that clenched in her jaw spoke volumes about how angry she still was over being accused. "I'm all right," she replied, sighing. "I just really need to relax and spend some time with the few people who actually care about me."

As she covered his hand with hers and leaned into his touch, her dimples flashed when she finally gave him a genuine smile.

"I thought you might say something like that...so I asked a few folks to the cabin tonight to have dinner. Consider it your release party," he said, giving her a lopsided grin.

She returned his smile, grabbing his free hand and kissed it. Jere stared at her mouth briefly before having to turn his attention back to the road.

When they arrived back at the cabin, they climbed out of the car and Isla opened the back door for Marduk, who bolted into the woods. She figured that was probably for the best, since she was hearing the sounds of cars approaching, gravel crunching under the tires.

Forgetting the wolf, Isla smiled and waved at Callum and Jack who climbed out of their ragtop jeep. Needing to be among friends and touched that Jeremiah had sensed that, Isla teared up a bit as she hugged her boys.

Callum squeezed her tightly and rubbed a reassuring hand on her back. "There now, me love. Don't cry."

Sniffling bravely, Isla turned to hug Jack as well. "How did the search go?" she asked, feeling a shadow pass across her face before she steeled herself.

Jack gave an angry jerk of his head. "Not a damn thing turned up. It's like those people just disappeared into thin air." He narrowed his eyes with the look that passed between her and Jeremiah. "You think this was the work of those demons, don't you?"

"Unfortunately, yes," Isla answered. "All of the other disappearances and deaths this summer seem to have been. We've got no reason to assume otherwise."

"It's probably a ploy, trying to draw us out and separate us. They want to get Isla alone so they can take her. Damned if I'm going to let that happen," Jeremiah said.

"Makes it doubly stupid that they don't have our best tracker on the island out there looking for those people. Not only would you be able to pick up their trail, but you'd possibly be able to save them once we found 'em," Jack said with an apologetic look at Isla.

Isla clenched her fists and shook her head. "Those people shouldn't have to suffer because of the stupidity of the local police. I say we launch our own search tomorrow at first light. It's Sunday and the season is ending, so we're clear of tours for the day. I was going to use the day for housekeeping at the office, but I think the Expeditions crew should form our own search party."

"We could get in a whole heap of trouble for that, Isla," Callum said, "interfering with police business and all that."

"It won't matter to anyone *what* we did if we find them. Plus, that terrain out there," she said with a broad gesture at the forest, "is our *office*. It's where we work. No one knows it better than us, and if we don't want to be seen, we won't be."

Jeremiah looked from Isla to the two other men and nodded. "I'm in. Y'all just need to prep me on what we're going to be dealing with, trying to go stealth," he said with a grin.

Jack and Callum shared a look between them, obviously communicating without words in the way of longtime lovers. "We're in too," Jack said. "We'll talk the others into it when they get there. But we have to agree that there'll be no hard feelings if someone doesn't want to risk it, aye?"

Isla nodded this time and leaned into Jeremiah when he placed a comforting arm around her shoulders. She was feeling much steadier now that some of the control was back in their hands. Smiling, she waved at the newcomers driving up to them.

Amy and Brynna climbed out of the Expeditions van as Kieran pulled up behind them and unfolded his coltish legs from his compact. Kieran received handshakes from each of the men, and then flushed to the tips of his ears when he received a hug from Isla. The girls doled out hugs across the board, and Jeremiah yelped when Amy reached around to squeeze his bum, sending Isla into a fit of giggles.

Jeremiah slid closer to Isla and stepped a little behind her, causing everyone to laugh. Kieran hauled a large cooler out of the back of the van and dropped it proudly at their feet. "We brought steaks and beer!" He jumped when Jeremiah clapped him on the back and shouted, "My kinda man!"

Isla stepped back to watch them all tromp into the house, laughing and joking with each other—the younger ones leaving the two older men to drag in the cooler—and it caused her heart to swell with pride. *There they are,* she thought. *My family.* She had gone so long without a family that she hadn't realized that they had created one of their own, here on their little island.

A cold breeze wafted in through the trees from the west, ruffling her hair as it swirled around her, causing her to shiver. Fall was coming. Samhain. This will all be over soon, one way or another, and Isla was going to make damn sure that her family made it through, even if she didn't.

Feeling a tingling sensation at the scruff of his neck, Jeremiah turned back to face Isla from where he stood on the porch. He was struck by the look of her. Her mane of ebony curls swirled around her, and her eyes sparked with hellfire that lit a jade glow in their depths.

He took her in from her tense, muscular body, to her chin lifted defiantly toward the trees. She was a lioness, guarding her pride. And he had one fleeting thought before he turned to join the others inside. *There she is.*

Jeremiah, Jack, and Callum spent the next half hour contemplating the steaks on the grill, as men often do. When he managed to extricate himself from the steak summit, Jere came back inside to find Isla. In the living room, Kieran and Amy were learning an Irish card game from Brynna that he was ninety-eight percent sure was completely made up.

Jeremiah found her in the kitchen, smiling to herself as she chopped vegetables for the salad dish. "Should I be jealous of those carrots?" he growled in her ear, and she jumped and shivered.

"No," she said, turning and allowing him to cage her against the counter. "I was just thinking about how I've been alone most of my life, and now all of a sudden," she made a sweeping gesture toward the living room, "here you all are. That makes me smile."

"Good," Jere said, kissing the tip of her nose. "You deserve to be happy for a change." Callum and Jack reentered the house, both carrying plates piled with steaks, and joined Jere and Isla in the kitchen to help finish prepping for dinner. Jeremiah was absently washing the cooking utensils while staring pensively out the kitchen window.

He jolted when a big hand clamped down on his shoulder and squeezed. "Something's on your mind," Jack said in a low voice in Jere's ear. It was more of a statement than a question. Jeremiah gave him a short nod, tossing a wary glance over to where Isla and Callum were rummaging through the fridge for condiments.

Jeremiah motioned for Jack to join him on the front porch, under the pretense of cleaning the grill. "What's up?" the older man asked.

"I've been thinking..."

Jack let out a snort. "That's your first mistake!"

"Yeah, yeah. Look, the last two searches we've gone on have gotten pretty risky. And not just in a dangerous terrain, *Man Vs. Wild* kind of way. In a demon possession, murder/suicide kind of way. I just feel that it wouldn't be right to ask these people" — he gestured toward the house — "to risk life, limb, and sanity without knowing fully what they're up against. You know?"

Jack nodded slowly, scrubbing a hand across his two-day-old growth of stubble. "I see your point. Their normal defenses for protecting themselves may not work against the threat they'll actually be facing."

"I believe that we need to tell them as much, or as little, about all of this as they need to know to protect themselves. I just don't know how Isla is going to feel about it."

Jere turned worried hazel eyes to Jack's face. "I love her, you know."

"I know."

"I'm gonna do everything I can to keep anything, especially me, from hurting her. But you've known her longer than I have. How's she going to handle this?"

"Looks like we're about to find out, mate," Jack said in a low voice as Isla and Callum came out on the porch. Both of them were smiling and chuckling as they came through the door.

"Oi, what's takin' so long out here?"

Focusing a shrewd gaze on Jeremiah, Isla's face fell when she saw his expression. "What is it? What's happened?" she asked nervously.

Leaning back against the railing, Jere ran agitated hands through his hair, causing it to stick up at odd angles.

"Nothing new has happened. Jack and I were just talking about this search we're planning. I still agree that we should do it, but we were wondering if it's really fair to drag the others into this without giving them some sort of idea of the...dangers they'll be facing."

He watched as the emotions flickered across her expressive face. Her eyes widened with shock, and he saw her stubborn jaw clench in defensive anger, and underneath it all was stone cold fear. But the wheels were turning, so he pressed his point.

"If we're searching for these missing folks, we can't keep an eye on Kieran and the girls every second. While they may be outdoor experts, they have no idea how to defend themselves against demons!"

Finally, he saw reluctant acceptance in her strong features, followed by a fierce determination. She straightened her shoulders and pierced him with a smoldering gaze. "You're absolutely right. I promised myself that I would make sure no one else got hurt because of me. They need to know what we're dealing with."

Enfolding her into his strong arms, Jeremiah rested his chin on the top of her head. "I know this won't be easy for you, but the three of us are behind you. Those kids in there love you, and I know they'll find a way to deal."

Callum rubbed her back briefly before returning inside to set the table. Jack gave her arm a reassuring pat. "Let's just have a nice dinner, forget about everything for a little while. Then we'll deal with the hard stuff, yeah?"

Isla nodded and allowed Jere to lead her back into the cozy cabin.

The spread was laid out on the thick cedar dining room table, and the seven of them sat down to tuck into it. They talked about their respective days at work, the impending end to the travel season—they even had a heated debate about who was going to take it all in the Women's World Cup.

Any mention of Isla's recent incarceration and the missing people was strictly avoided. Isla, Jeremiah, Callum, and Jack had been able to relax and enjoy the food and companionship shared with their friends. But as dinner was winding down, the tension crept back into the room and back into their bodies as they anticipated the discussion they had to have.

While Jeremiah and Isla cleared the table and did the dishes, Callum and Jack discreetly ushered the others into the living room under the guise of planning the search. They kept an eye on their friends from the kitchen as Callum spread out terrain maps on the large coffee table. The five of them had begun arguing about the best starting point and the spots they needed to cover by the time Isla joined them.

Jeremiah brought in a round of ice-cold beer for everyone, then lowered his big body to the rug, sat cross-legged and leaned over the coffee table to study the maps.

"I think we need to concentrate on the area of the King's Caves," Amy said. "What better place to hide, or hide someone, than a cave system?"

"I agree with Amy—" Kieran started. Brynna cut him off with a snort. "Yeah, you would!" It had been glaringly obvious to everyone but Amy that Kieran had been nursing a huge crush on her since the day he started at Expeditions.

Two red spots appeared over Kieran's sharp cheekbones and he kept his eyes on his hands, but he shook his head vehemently. "I'm serious. We definitely need to search the caves. There are so many crevices and dark corners that people could hide in. My vote is to follow the bluffs from Blackwaterfoot to the caves, and if we find nothing, we head back over Machrie Moor."

Interested now, Brynna tapped her chin with a hot pink fingernail, a color that clashed strongly with her fiery red curls. "The bluffs would be a good path to take if we don't want to be seen. We'd be above the beach but below the trail, and all of the brush and boulders will make for good cover."

Kieran straightened his shoulders a bit, happy that the women were agreeing with him for a change.

Jeremiah looked up and smiled at Isla as she walked round him to sit at his left side, his arm automatically drawing her closer to his side. Giving him a weak smile, she looked down at her hands as she flipped her grandmother's coin through her fingers. Jere could feel her body trembling lightly, and he wished like hell he could protect her from whatever her friends' reactions might be.

Ever the observant one, Brynna narrowed her eyes at her friend and frowned. "What's wrong, Isla? You look like you're about to jump out of your skin."

Taking a deep, steadying breath, Isla leaned into Jeremiah for strength and made eye contact with first Brynna, then Amy and Kieran. "There are some things that you all need to know about what you may be up against going on this search. Once you hear it, if any of you aren't comfortable being involved, there will be no hard feelings."

"Boss, we already went through this," Brynna spoke up. "We understand the risks and we're with you." The others nodded.

"I really appreciate that, I do. But you don't *know* all of the risks. You need to hear me out before you make that decision. This requires me to reveal some very personal information about myself that I am not entirely comfortable with—and you may not be either."

"Whatever it is, we'll deal," Amy said with her typical straightforwardness.

Isla shook her head. "You may not be able to deal, but I want to be clear that whatever your reactions are, I understand. Some of you may not even believe me," she stated, worrying her bottom lip with her teeth and looking back and forth between the three of them.

Kieran snorted and raked a hand through his shoulder-length, black hair. "Clearly it can't be too unbelievable, because it looks as though Cal, Jack, and Jeremiah already know, and they're still here. Don't keep us in suspense any longer! Spill."

Taking a death grip on Jeremiah's hand, Isla began her story in a shaking voice. As much as she wanted to rush through it, to get it all out and then wait for the inevitable backdraft to consume her, she didn't. She took strength from Jeremiah's strong presence and started from the beginning.

She told them of the night her mother attempted to take her life and of the strange brand that appeared on her skin. With Jeremiah's help, she explained his profession and what led him there to the island and how he tracked down Mhairi.

She gave them the rundown of all of the things they had learned from Mhairi about Alastore and his *auchrim*, and the many ways he has and will try to attack them. Brought up last and emphasized was the fact that they believed the demons had the ability to possess people or take over their minds.

"The threat from Alastore is very real," Isla finished, looking at each of them in turn. "That is the reason I felt the need to tell you all of this. I can teach you how to defend yourselves against him, mind and body, but you have to truly understand. This is happening."

Brynna and Kieran, who had been leaning forward during the story, sank back into the cushions of the overstuffed couch, while Amy remained motionless. The three friends looked back and forth among one another, temporarily stunned into silence.

Amy's lips twitched and Brynna's eyes twinkled when she looked over at Kieran. In a moment, the three of them dissolved into a fit of laughter. Isla blinked, her mouth hanging open in disbelief as she watched her friends laugh so hard that tears rolled down their cheeks.

"Jaysus Bosslady, you bloody well had us all goin' for a minute there," Brynna said, clutching her ribs.

Amy hooted and slapped Kieran on the knee. "I really think Ki was buying it the whole time!"

Gulping in a deep breath, Isla tried to tamp down her temper that rose viciously to the surface. Bad things tended to happen when she lost it. A squeeze to her hand let her know that Jeremiah was worried about her reaction as well.

She waited, expressionless, until the cackling and ribbing had died down. When her young employees realized that the others in the room were not joining in with the joke, three pairs of eyes snapped to Isla's face, all with matching frowns.

"Boss?" Brynna asked cautiously. It seemed as though seeing was believing, so Isla decided reluctantly that she would have to demonstrate. She looked to Jeremiah, silently asking for his support, and he nodded in return.

Isla closed her eyes and focused her energy in the way Marduk had taught her. It had become easy with practice, almost an immediate reaction to having the thought. Suddenly, all of the lights and electronic devices in the house shut off, plunging the group into darkness and silence.

"What the f—" Kieran's exclamation drifted off as everything turned back on. The three of them looked around warily, and Brynna rose up on her knees on the couch to look out the window. "Is there a storm coming? Or did you forget to pay the power bill?" she asked with a weak laugh.

Scrubbing both hands over her face, Isla shook her head sadly. Evidently, it was going to take much more to convince them. Reaching toward the coffee table, Isla held out her hand, and Amy's beer slid across the table to slap into her palm.

Hearing a chorus of shocked gasps, she thought she must be getting through to them. She quirked an eyebrow at the three kids who were now staring at her like she was the newest freak show attraction. "Need to see more?"

There was a brief moment of silence until Brynna and Amy began talking excitedly all at once.

"Can you read my mind?"

"Do you use spells or do you just think things and they happen?"

"Can you see the future? Can you start fires?"

Isla held up a hand for silence, and the questions trailed off. She quirked a half smile at them. "That's more like it. I'll answer all of your questions, but one at a time, okay?"

When they both nodded, Isla began answering. "I can't read minds. At least I haven't been able to so far, and that's just fine with me. Most of what I do comes from harnessing and focusing energy to manipulate the environment. I think there are some things that require spells, but I'm still new at this, so everything that I've learned seems to come from within."

"I can't see the future," she said, looking pointedly at Amy, who simply shrugged. "I seem to be able to manipulate natural elements—earth, air, fire, water, and of course energy, or atmosphere. So I'm sure I can start fires, but I stay away from anything destructive. People think the worst of me already, I don't need to give them any more ammunition."

Isla began to notice that Kieran had been extremely quiet since the *demonstration* and when she looked over at him, he was white as a sheet. His green eyes were wide and shadowed, and he was breathing rapidly like he was halfway to hyperventilating.

"Kieran, you okay brother?" Jere asked, causing all eyes to turn to the young man.

"I...uh...I...," he stammered his nonresponse, and Atticus chose that moment to vault into Kieran's lap causing him to jump. "Mother *fucker*!"

That earned him a hiss as the cat was dumped unceremoniously on the floor. Pinching the bridge of her nose, Isla glared at the cat. "Get lost Atty. Go find Smit and occupy yourselves elsewhere." There was a silent communication between them as the cat glared back at her before sniffing and bounding off into the bedroom.

That, apparently, was the last straw for Kieran. He leapt off the couch, muttering to himself, "She talks to fucking cats...and they understand her." The muttering tapered off into incoherent stuttering as Kieran hugged himself and paced back and forth, as if he was unsure of the easiest, and safest, way to get away from her.

Sighing, Isla stood up and reached for him. "Kieran—"

"No...," he said. "No! Don't touch me!" Isla shrank back as if she had been struck and swallowed a sob.

"I—I'm sorry," Kieran started, a tremor in his voice. "I just...I can't do this." He turned, grabbed his jacket and keys, and bolted out the door like his ass was on fire.

When Isla made to follow him, Jeremiah caught her hand and pulled her back. "Let him go," he said gently. "He needs some time to process. He'll be back, or he won't. It has to be his decision. Right now, there's six of us still here. Enough for a good search party. So we need to table this for now and get started with the briefing, yeah?"

Forcing back the tears that threatened to fall, Isla visibly steeled herself and nodded. "Cal, Jack, you were part of the police search. Why don't you start us off by telling us what you know."

When they had all settled back around the coffee table, Callum spread out a stack of pictures. "Swiped these off an officer," he said with a mischievous grin. "They had plenty, they'll never miss 'em."

Passing the pictures around, he began to list the particulars about each missing person. "Isla, you'd be familiar with this first one," he said, tapping a picture of a woman, probably in her mid-forties with shoulder-length, brown hair and warm amber eyes. "Claire Corrie, age forty-two. She's single and lives alone, but she has a brother and sister-in-law who live on the island as well. They got worried and called the police when she didn't show up for dinner on Thursday. No last known location."

Pausing briefly to have a sip of his beer, he picked up another picture of two young men who were smiling with their arms thrown around each other. "Freddie Miles and Asher Davis, tourists from San Francisco, age thirty-two and twenty-seven respectively. Word is they were on a honeymoon of sorts after a commitment ceremony last month."

Jack chimed in, filling in the details. "Asher and Freddie were last seen in the tearoom at Kildonan Inn, where they've been staying on the island.

Callum passed around the last picture for the group to look at. An elderly couple smiled out at them. "Douglas and Margaret Bànach, ages sixty-eight and sixty-three. Born and raised on the island, last seen at Thursday tea at the senior center. Unlike the first three people to go missing this summer, there are no reports of any of these new victims setting out to hike or camp. It's like they just disappeared."

"So, basically," Isla began, "we have nothing to go on. No idea where they started and definitely no idea where they've ended up?"

"That's about the whole of it, aye," Jack said grimly.

Amy leaned forward and pulled a hand-drawn map of the island toward her. "These gateways...do you know where they are?"

Isla shrugged one delicate shoulder. "No way to know for sure. The only time I've ever been sure I was near one, I was led to it in a dream."

"You saw it in your dream?" Brynna asked.

"No, I was dreaming I was searching for a missing child. I sleepwalked to a set of standing stones I've never seen before or since. I think that was Alastore's plan. To use a dream to lure me to the gateway where he could pull me in. He can't physically force anyone to do something. He has to use energy to control someone's mind, to make them do it on their own. Or at least, that's what we think. There's no tellin' what he'll be able to do when he gains more power."

"Damn," Amy said, and everyone nodded their agreement. "Isla, if we were to come upon a *locus* during a search, do you think that you would know?"

"I can't be sure," Isla said, chewing her lip, "but I think so. The one I ended up at that night was giving off a low-level energy buzz, kind of like walking past an electrical plant. I could feel it prickle my skin, and I felt a strong pressure in my head."

"Wicked."

Rolling her eyes at Amy, Isla turned her attention back to the maps. "I agree with what Kieran said. We can park at Shiskine golf course in Blackwaterfoot and set off on the walking path along the beach, below the bluffs. That way it will seem like we're just friends going on walkabout, instead of a rogue search party."

Pausing to listen to the chorus of agreements, she continued. "Once we reach the bluffs, we'll climb to the game trail halfway up the hill, right at the base of the bluffs. It's a rough path and it will be difficult terrain, but we'll have lots of cover until we get to the caves."

They talked and planned into the evening, and Isla spent a couple of hours working with Jack, Callum, Amy, and Brynna to teach them defenses against Alastore and his minions. She talked them through clearing their minds and putting up mental barriers to avoid possession.

"These are last resort techniques, of course. Our number one goal will be avoidance. Barring that, I will be the first line of defense. You'll only need to do these things if he gets to you."

Taking a deep breath, Amy rose gracefully to her feet and reached out a hand to haul Brynna up off the couch. "First light isn't too far off, so we'd better get home. We'll stop by the office to get some supplies and a set of two-ways."

Saying their goodbyes, the girls departed, leaving the four of them alone again. Isla sighed and flopped down on the couch, snuggling into Jeremiah's warmth when he settled beside her. He smelled of soap and rain, and the familiarity tugged at her heart.

"I really hope we find them," she said softly to no one in particular. A cold chill had settled in the room, causing her to shiver.

Jeremiah rubbed his hands over her arms, and then stood. "The weather's really cooled off lately. I'm going to build a fire." Choosing the fireplace over the cast-iron stove, Jere knelt by the pile of firewood on the hearth. Methodically, he began stacking the logs in a pattern on the rack inside the stone fireplace.

"Cal, can you run outside and get me some kindling?" Jere asked the older man.

"Sure thing, mate," Cal said, as he bounded out the door while Jack excused himself to the washroom. When they were alone, Isla slid to the end of the couch to drape her body over the armrest.

"You know, we never did tell them about—"

"I wonder where—," they spoke at the same time, both cut off by a scream from outside.

"*Bloody hell!*" Callum screeched. "Isla, grab the shotgun! There's a fucking wolf outside!" Cal's boots thudded on the ground outside as he ran for the porch.

"—Fuck."

"—Marduk."

Callum bounded through the front door and he slammed it behind him, locking it and pressing his back up against it, as if that alone could keep the beast out. Jack returned to the room to see his lover up against the door, panting, white as a ghost. He crossed the floor in three long strides and gathered Callum into his embrace. "What's wrong, love?"

Catching his breath, Callum buried his face in the crook of Jack's neck. "There's a wolf outside, Jack. Isla, I'm sorry I didn't believe you that time when you told me you saw one."

Rising to join the two men, Isla rubbed a hand over Cal's back. "Don't worry, Cal. It won't hurt us. I think you better sit down because I have another tall tale to tell you."

∞∞

After a dreamless sleep, curled into the warmth of Jeremiah's body, Isla awoke when it was still dark out. Shaking Jere lightly to wake him, they hurriedly dressed and migrated to the kitchen to get coffee and a light breakfast out before their fellow searchers arrived.

Hearing tires crunching on gravel, Isla pulled the curtains back from the kitchen window to see the Expeditions' van lumbering up the drive once more. "Ready or not, here they come," she said, putting the coffee pot and an assortment of fruits and local cheeses on the table.

The door swung open to reveal Callum and Jack, dressed alike in black t-shirts and camouflage cargos. Isla grinned at the sight of the two burly men, in matching clothes, all kitted out like they were going into a war zone.

Her mirth died when she had the fleeting thought that they probably were. The two men looked anything but funny when you took in the twin machetes and hunting knives that were strapped to their utility belts.

As the two men stepped further inside, they were followed by Amy and Brynna, dressed head to toe in black, hair slicked back into pony tails, and carrying similar weapons. Isla gasped when she saw a sheepish looking Kieran step across the threshold, trailing behind the girls.

Not hesitating, she walked over to him and enveloped him in a tight hug. With one last squeeze she pulled away, looking up at him with questioning jade eyes. "What are you doing here?"

The young man fidgeted and studied his fingernails for a moment while he gathered his thoughts. "I'm sorry I freaked on you last night. It was just a lot to take in all at once, you know."

Isla nodded sympathetically. "I do know. It happened the same way for me. I had no idea about any of this, and then the revelations started piling up all at once. If it weren't for Jeremiah, I would probably have gone insane."

"I grew up here, so I know all the stories about witches, pookahs, banshees, 'n such, but you know how my mother is. I was trained not to believe in those things, that it was sacrilege."

Kieran's parents were deeply religious, and he came from a very strict upbringing. Isla could imagine that it would be very hard for the young man to break through their preconceived notions to believe in something that couldn't be explained away by religion.

When he turned eighteen, Kieran had moved out and come to work at Expeditions. His parents had considered his leaving *abandoning* his family, and they had cut ties with him. Now barely twenty, the boy had no family that would speak to him, but he was happier than he had ever been, surrounded by his friends.

"I know you, Isla, and I care about you. You're more than just a boss to us, you're our friend...so I don't care if you are a witch or a purple polka-dotted dragon. I'm still going to stand by you, as you've done with me."

This time Isla did have to brush away a tear, as she quickly embraced Kieran again. "Thank you. That means more to me than you can know." Pulling herself together, she returned to Jeremiah and looked around at their small search party.

"Right then, let's go over our plan one more time while we eat, then get geared up and be off, yeah?"

They gathered around the small kitchen table and tucked into the light breakfast fare. Jeremiah cleared a spot to lay out their map of Arran. On top of that, he placed a wafer-thin piece of velum that had another map printed on it. This map was also of the island, but it was crudely hand drawn and had places named on it that some of them had never even heard of.

"I went to the booksellers when I first got to the island, and I found a little, self-published travel book that is nearly ninety years old. It's full of island legend and lore, but also has some great insight into the terrain and routes that may not be so well known on the modern island. It had this great map in it as well, with all of the old names for the towns, and it focuses more on landmarks and walking routes than towns and roads.

His excitement reminded Isla of a child on Christmas morning, and it made her smile. "It's a great find. We should take it with us, in a dry bag."

Nodding, Jeremiah shifted the maps so they were side by side and pointed to the same spot on both of them. "We'll drive to Blackwaterfoot and park at the Shiskine golf course, here, hopefully looking inconspicuous. Taking the walking trail to the beach from there, once we make it to the beach, we'll climb the hill to the game path at the base of the cliffs."

Isla took up where he left off. "We need to try and stay off of the main walks, so we'll stay on the game path as long as it's passable. Skirting around the Drumadoon promontory, we'll ascend to the King's Caves."

Turning to Jeremiah, Isla smiled. "You'd probably be interested to know that it is said that King Robert the Bruce took refuge in the King's Caves after killing John Comyn," she said, laughing when Jere's face lit up with interest.

"We need to stay together until we get to the caves, as the terrain will be very dangerous. Once we search the caves, we'll head back east over the moors toward Machrie. We may decide to split up at that point, with at least one group making it back to Shiskine—the safe way—to pick up the van. Agreed?"

There was a chorus of "Aye's" and "Yes's" in response to her question, so she continued. "Each one of us needs to pack light but smart. We need enough food to last the day and night, in case we can't make it back until morning."

Amy reached into her pack and started unloading the seven radios she had taken off the dock at Expeditions. "Channel five. Got to try and stay off the police channels." She passed out extra battery packs for the two-ways as well, just in case.

They filled their packs with food items with high-caloric content, to give them energy in case any of them got stranded. Kieran was given a bowie knife from Jack since he hadn't any weapons of his own.

They packed fire starter kits, an extra set of clothes for each of them, and their maps in dry bags. Each searcher had a canteen and a flashlight strapped to their utility belts as well.

Jeremiah barked out a laugh when Jack pulled some camouflage paint out of his bag.

"We're going full commando, huh?"

Jack nodded and laughed. "Silly, I know, but I figured it might help since we're trying not to be seen."

Jere flashed his wolfy grin and reached for the paint. "Why not? Every little bit helps." Each of them smeared lines of the black and green paint on their face, hoping it would help them blend into the brush on the game trail, as that would be their only cover provided by nature.

Jeremiah pushed his chair away from the table and stood, making brief eye contact with Isla, Jack, and Callum. "I'll go get Marduk," he said, knowing that he would have to provide the boy with clothing. They had let the wolf spend the night in the spare room of the cabin, knowing that it wouldn't do to have him show up on the doorstep stark naked.

The four of them had decided not to tell the others about Marduk's true nature, but his power would provide extra protection against the *auchrim*, so they couldn't afford to leave him behind.

Brynna gave Isla a puzzled look as Jeremiah left the room. "Who's Marduk?"

Isla's gaze shifted to the right before looking across to Brynna, causing the other woman to narrow her eyes in suspicion. "He's a friend of mine who's visiting. He'll be coming along with us, since he is as good a tracker as I am."

Six pairs of eyes turned toward the living room as Jeremiah returned with the tall, dark young man. Marduk was dressed in black cargo pants and a green t-shirt, and he was allowing his intricate tattooing to be shown. He stared back at the group with ice-blue eyes as they were introduced to him.

As Marduk had come into the room, Isla witnessed the shock of the others as the impact of Marduk's ambient power smacked into them, causing them to shift in their seats. It occurred to her too late that Marduk may not be aware of his effect on people, and he may not know how or have any desire to dampen it.

"Marduk, this is Kieran Donovan, Amy Williams and Brynna Murphy. You met Callum and Jack last night." Marduk nodded to the two men he had already met and shook hands with each of the newcomers.

When his palm touched Brynna's, she gripped it tight and looked up at him sharply. Addressing Isla without taking her eyes off of him, she spoke. "So he's like you, then?"

Momentarily shocked at the declaration, Isla sputtered as she choked on her coffee. "How did you know?"

Brynna shrugged a delicate shoulder and fingered her coffee cup. "He just has the same sort of"—she waved her hands in the air, seeming to search for the right words—"energy signature as you do. I never really noticed it until I felt it from someone else. Also, his tattoos seem to be of a similar style as your *signa*," she said matter-of-factly.

Impressed with the girl's powers of observation, Isla had the thought that Brynna may be a very valuable asset to the search as well. They waited while Marduk loaded his pack and painted his face like the others.

Jeremiah carried extra food for the young man so Marduk could fit a couple of extra sets of clothes in his pack, in case the need arose for him to shift, hopefully well out of the viewing range of the others.

Deciding they were finally ready, the group trooped out the door—first the younger searchers, then Callum and Jack. Isla moved to follow when she suddenly found herself pushed up against the wall behind the door, her mouth captured in a searing kiss.

Wanting to put all of his emotions that he couldn't find words for as they set forth to risk their own lives, Jeremiah gave no quarter. He plundered her mouth with a sensual dance of nipping teeth and sweeping tongue.

Nudging a knee between her legs to further trap her, he sunk his hands deep into her ebony curls, canting her head back to deepen the angle of the kiss. When he finally tore himself away with a strangled groan, they stood there staring at each other, gasping for breath. As he took in her flushed cheeks and her plump lips bruised from his kiss, he knew she was the most exquisite creature he would ever come across

Jeremiah nearly went weak in the knees when she gave him a brilliant smile and flashed those dimples that he wanted to kiss, along with every other inch of her. She strode over to him, swaying her hips in a cocky little swagger, and patted him on the back. Hard. "Atta boy," she said. "Time to get going."

With a wink and a smile, she sashayed out the door. Jeremiah blinked dumbly for a moment, trying to get a hold of his raging libido so he could concentrate on the task at hand. But he couldn't help but admire the view as he locked up and followed behind her. God, she was spectacular.

PART III

TERMINUS

Chapter Eighteen

The sun had only begun to rise as the van pulled into the public parking lot at the Shiskine Golf Club in Blackwaterfoot, and a heavy blanket of mist still clung to the ground, obscuring their surroundings.

Isla stepped out into the crisp air, scanning the beach and cliffs for any early hikers. The chilly, overcast morning worked in their favor, as each of them was wearing some sort of hooded jacket or sweatshirt to hide their painted faces, camouflage clothing, and weapons. It was hard to look inconspicuous when one was kitted out like a frontline soldier.

Gathering their packs and supplies, they piled out of the van and under cover of fog, they started down a wide dirt road that ran parallel to a misty, pebbled beach that was hugged by the grey Kilbrannan Sound.

This was the part of the route that provided the least cover and, even with the fog, they could easily attract attention. Spreading out, they walked two by two, keeping a distance of twenty feet or so, hoping they would look like couples or friends out for an early morning stroll.

Isla led the way beside Jeremiah, and he immediately pulled her close against his side. Selling the bit, she told herself with a grin. Looking behind them, Isla noted that they were followed by Amy and Marduk. The *feradux* trained sharp eyes straight ahead, but she knew he was scanning his periphery for any signs of trouble.

Brynna and Kieran were next, chatting and chuckling to themselves, arms slung around each other. The two had taken to each other almost immediately after Kieran had started working for Expeditions. They were as close as a brother and sister, and teased each other like them too.

Walking side by side behind them were Callum and Jack. Unlike the others, they didn't talk or touch. They just walked at a leisurely pace, shoulder to shoulder, close enough so that their arms or fingers were always brushing.

Eventually, they veered off the dirt road, onto a path that skirted the golf course, and it took them down a subtle incline toward the beach. They came to a halt where the trail dead ended into a barbed-wire fence.

After a cursory look around, they saw that there was no gate nearby. With gloves to protect his hands, Jack grasped two of the wires between the barbs and pulled them wide apart. The rest of the group stooped to climb through the space one by one.

Isla halted the group while Callum took Jack's place holding the wire, allowing him to slip through. From there they cut through a misty field that continued the slope down to the beach. The small group gathered on the shore at the base of the large hill that loomed over them, stretching to the foot of the cliffs.

On the shore they were totally out in the open, but it was too early for most day hikers, and they still had the morning fog on their side. Isla took a moment to survey their route and make a plan. The cliffs and hill lined a mile or so of the coastline, and the hill itself would prove a difficult climb. Covered with rhododendron, fern, thistle and other thick foliage, the hill was also home to hundreds of boulders and flat rocks that were nestled into its face. She knew it would be a difficult ascent, even for the Expeditions crew.

The rocky outcrops tapered off about halfway up and gave way to much denser thickets at the bottom of the cliffs. Though she couldn't see it, she knew that the area at the top where the brush was thickest was where the game trail would be.

From there the cliffs rose out of the mist, lumbering giants, great columns of feldspar and sandstone, neatly formed by the erosion of the coast, standing close to one hundred feet high. If someone were to stand at the top of the cliffs, they would be well over two hundred feet above where sea met shore.

"We need to go up single file," Isla began. "While I have every confidence in all of your climbing abilities, I want our most experienced climbers in the front and back of the group. And as much as I hate to play it safe myself," she said with a self-deprecating smile, "we need to protect our main defenses against the threat, which are Marduk and me."

The others nodded gravely, so she continued. "Cal will go first, clearing the way for Jeremiah and then myself. Amy, Marduk, and Brynna will be next, in that order. Marduk has the least experience among us with this terrain, so I want him in the middle," she said with an apologetic look to the young man, who simply shrugged and winked.

"Behind Brynna will be Kieran, and Jack will bring up the rear," she finished. "Everyone good with that?" After they all had agreed, Callum took over the briefing to prepare the group for the ascent, explaining the techniques for the benefit of Jeremiah and Marduk.

"Right then, we'll be doing what we call 'rock-scrambling' to get up this hill," Callum said. "This type of ascent walks a fine line between being a very treacherous hike and a very easy rock climb. We'll be free climbing, as climbing gear won't help us much here."

"Rock scrambling is like rock climbing, except you don't see any extreme verticals and your only equipment is your bare hands. Jeremiah, you'll remember some of this from your first search. We'll need to find hand and footholds that we can use to lever ourselves up, to where we can climb to the next plateau."

"You each need to look out for the person in front of you and in back of you when you can," Isla added. "Give each other room to move, but don't get too far apart."

Callum dug his fingers into the soft, dry sand on the shore, coating his hands, and encouraged the others to do the same. "This will help your grip. Not as effective as chalk, but it'll do. Ready?"

Cal took one more look at each of the faces behind him and waited as they nodded. While most in the group were experienced beyond their years in all things outdoors, Isla still felt responsible for all of them as the unofficial leader of the search, but she trusted Callum implicitly to take point on the climb.

Isla wasn't worried about Jeremiah, not really, as he could hold his own on a climb. She knew without a doubt that she'd give her own life to keep him safe.

Smiling a little, she looked at their little wildcat, Amy. It would take a tank to bring that one down. She was a bonnie lass, that was for sure, but she was also as hearty as they came.

Kieran was the least experienced of the Expeditions crew, and that was enough to cause Isla to worry a bit about the young man's safety. But Kieran had learned a lot in the two years he'd worked with them and what he lacked in longevity, he made up for with enthusiasm.

Brynna was nearly as tiny as Isla, but her small frame was packed with steely muscles and an iron will. If she had her way, she'd beat all of them to the top.

Her eyes softened as they fell on Jack—a man who'd been like a surrogate father to her in the past ten years. He was built like a brick shithouse and could stand up to more than all of them. That didn't succeed in stopping the hard knot of worry that formed in her gut when she thought of him possibly getting hurt.

Marduk was the wildcard. She knew Callum still wasn't clear on exactly *what* he was, and he certainly had no idea of the young witch's climbing abilities. She saw Callum give Marduk a skeptical look before looking away with a shake of his head.

Isla had witnessed the look and smirked at Callum's back. She was sure he had no idea how much dexterity, athleticism, and preternatural strength one gained from being part wolf. She knew that Marduk was probably safer than all of them.

The group set off at a quick pace, but since there was no trail up the hill, the going was tough. They picked their way through the brambles and stinging nettles, thankful for the thick BDU pants they wore and the long-sleeved outerwear they had used to conceal themselves earlier.

As the brush grew too thick to push through, Callum drew his machete and began to cut a narrow path for the hikers. They always wanted to leave the natural environment as intact as possible, so they were still squeezed and scraped on all sides by branches and thorns.

Brynna eyed the dark stranger in front of her warily. He was certainly well made, with a long sinewy body, darkly tanned skin...and those eyes. If they had met under different circumstances, she may have even acted on her natural attraction to him. But she didn't trust him. She knew he was a magick user like Isla, but there was something definitely different about him—which led her to believe that they'd not been given the whole story about the mysterious young man.

Power emanated from him in waves, and she felt it like little firecrackers bursting across her skin. Her own body longed to respond to it, despite her misgivings about the man himself. She kept a tight grip on her instinctive nature, willing herself to keep away from him while his power drew her like a magnet. And the tattoos? Those were a concern. If they meant what she thought they did, then she knew more about him than she wanted to.

While Isla was very brave for revealing her true nature to keep her friends safe, Brynna had her own secrets to protect. Ones that she wasn't willing to share for any reason.

Brynna had just begun to breathe hard when Callum slowed his pace. They'd arrived at the first cluster of boulders, and he was waiting for the others to catch up. "This is where it gets dicey, mates," he said, gesturing at a grouping of rocks that looked much, much larger than they had from the shore.

"Best thing will be to try and stick to the grooves in between the rocks wherever possible. There will be more handholds and better leverage. Go slow and choose your path carefully. Right, off we go!"

After dusting his hands with some more dirt from the ground, Callum began the climb up the rift between the two boulders. Brynna did the same and once again fell in behind Marduk. There were a few flat rocks along the way for the climbers to take a rest and wait on one another.

Callum, Isla, Jeremiah, and Amy had all made it to a large one and were waiting on the others to regroup. Brynna was watching Marduk climb, and she had to admit to herself a grudging respect for the man. He moved like Spiderman, easily finding the best spots to place his hands and feet.

Marduk had almost caught up with the others. He was clinging to the edge of the flat stone by one hand, while his feet were wedged in crevices in the rock below. Muscles rippled under golden skin as he leaned back to turn his face to the sky and sniff the wind.

Brynna's mouth went dry at the sight, and she wondered how the man wasn't even breaking a sweat—

Her thoughts were cut off abruptly as the piece of rock she had braced her weight-bearing foot on dislodged and plummeted down toward the beach. Brynna felt herself slide as she grappled unsuccessfully for something solid to grab onto. Bracing for the fall, she had the fleeting thought that she should probably curl up, protect her head and neck, when suddenly a strong hand shot out and latched onto her wrist.

Instinctively, she grabbed on with her other hand for a better grip. Crisp, artic eyes cut through her panic, and an alien thought pushed its way into her mind. *Relax your body. Got you.* Brynna blinked and stared, temporarily stunned into immobility. And that was apparently all Marduk needed.

Before Brynna could even form a cry for help, she was swung up and over Marduk's head to skid onto the flat rock, where the other searchers were there to catch her. After she was safely on steady ground, Marduk effortlessly vaulted up to join them and assisted Kieran and Jack up onto the ledge.

Sitting with Isla's arms around her on the large slab of granite, Brynna trembled and panted. She was experiencing the typical system meltdown after the adrenaline rush of a dangerous situation.

Marduk knelt in front of her and slowly extended his hand toward her, silently asking permission to touch. When he heard nothing but chattering teeth, he slid his hand into her warm auburn hair and grasped the back of her neck.

Peace. The thought fluttered around inside her head while an incredible calming warmth radiated out from his hand, stilling her shivers and calming her body. She wanted to protest at the invasion, but it felt so amazingly...peaceful that she couldn't bring herself to do it.

When he finally pulled away, her body mourned the loss, but her mind was at ease. "Thanks," she said sheepishly, "for saving me. And, you know...the other thing."

"My pleasure," came the softly accented reply, as he raised her hand to his lips for a light kiss. Amy snorted indelicately behind them and Callum cleared his throat.

"We should get movin'," he said. "I want to be past these godforsaken rocks quick as we can, yeah?"

Isla rubbed Brynna's back reassuringly while sneaking worried glances at the young woman. "Maybe we should go back. At least some of us..."

"No!" Brynna said, sharply, hopping gracefully to her feet. "I'm fine, no harm done. Besides, after what Gandalf over there did to me, I feel better than ever." She gave Callum and Isla a defiant look that just dared them to argue.

"Off we go, then," Callum said, and began cutting his way through the brush beyond the group of boulders. The others fell into their order, following his path. When Marduk walked past Brynna to take his place in the line, she tensed when he leaned close to her ear.

"'It is in Men that we must place our hope,'" he said and grinned. She would have laughed at his *Lord of the Rings* quote, glad that he hadn't taken her dig personally, if her knees hadn't gone all rubbery from witnessing the wicked smile. Was he flirting with her?

Silently admonishing herself for being distracted *again* by the charming boy, she resisted the urge to smile back. Steeling her expression and giving him a scowl, she waved her hand to signal that he should keep moving. "Let's go, there's work t'be done."

The group had to cross one more cluster of boulders before reaching the game trail, which they did, thankfully, without further incident. Finally the eight of them stood on the narrow ridge at the foot of the cliffs, surrounded by thick brush that towered above their heads, completely obscuring them from onlookers. Branches and thorns snatched at their clothing and hair as they made their way quickly along the game path.

Jeremiah turned back to look at Isla. "Feel anything?" She closed her eyes, he assumed to open up her energy receptors, as she'd taken to calling them, to see if she picked up on anything out of the ordinary. "Not a thing. At this point, I'm not sure if that's good or bad."

They had hiked just over a mile on the game trail when Callum stopped so abruptly, Jeremiah grasped the other man's shoulder to keep from slamming into him from behind. In front of Callum, the terrain plunged down into a deep valley between the hill that they were on and the smaller, rolling hills below.

"Looks like we've run out o' road, mates."

Peering over Callum's shoulder, Jeremiah raised a silent prayer to whoever was listening that they all made it through this in one piece. This descent would be treacherous.

"Safest way to do this will be to use gravity to your advantage. Slide or crab-walk your way down. Don't try to walk completely upright or you *will* fall. Got it?"

When they all agreed, Callum sat down on his backside and began to edge toward the drop off. "Alright girls and boys, hang on to your nut sacs. Here goes nothin'!"

After Callum disappeared from view, Jeremiah pulled Isla to him for a quick, hard kiss, before he slid over the edge after him. One by one, the searchers began the descent. Some slid on their feet, leaning back with a hand braced on the packed dirt to steady them. Others abandoned appearances, and coasted down on their asses.

Cal, Jere, Isla, Amy, and Marduk all made it safely to the flat ground at the bottom of the valley. Brynna skidded down the last few yards and hopped up beside them, dusting herself off. "What a rush!" she exclaimed happily.

Her excitement died as a scream bubbled up in her throat. They watched in horror as Kieran's foot hit a large rock about halfway down, flipping his body forcefully until he was sliding down the hill on his back, head first.

Jeremiah saw Jack reach for the boy and miss, barely catching himself before he went tumbling down as well.

"Shit!" Jeremiah shouted, and lunged toward the foot of the hill. Kieran was sliding wildly and beginning to get bounced around between the trees that lined the small trail, a bit like a pinball. Jeremiah ran as far up onto the path as his momentum would carry him, which was farther than he'd have thought, and anchored himself with a small tree.

As Kieran rolled past, Jere snaked out an arm and caught the boy around his middle. He knew that Kieran impacting him at the speed he was going would probably break his arm, so instead of trying to stop the motion, Jere let go his hold. Wrapping his body around the boy and holding on tight to shield Kieran from further injury, he allowed their combined body weight to straighten out their trajectory.

When they hit the bottom, Jere turned so that he would take the impact, and then rolled several times before coming to a stop. Both men lay completely still.

His eyes were squeezed shut against the pain exploding in his skull, but he heard Isla's strangled scream. She knelt beside Jeremiah and began running her hands over his body to search for injuries, while the others closed ranks and looked on with worry.

With a pained groan, Jeremiah released Kieran and rolled over onto his back with one arm thrown over his eyes. "Ow," he said in a gravelly voice, surprising a burst of hysterical laughter out of Isla.

"No kidding," she answered, and he tried not to wince as she continued to check him over. He was completely covered in dirt, most of his exposed skin was covered in scratches and quickly forming bruises, and he had a gash on his temple. But he was awake and breathing.

"What hurts? Can you tell if anything's broken?"

"I'll be fine," he said, taking several deep breaths before sitting up. He looked over to where Jack was leaning over Kieran and talking softly. "How's the kid?"

"A little banged up, but he'll live. Looks like you took the brunt of it," Jack answered. "If you hadn't done that, we might have lost him."

Oh, so carefully, Jeremiah got to his feet with the help of Callum and Isla. He shifted his weight, testing to see if anything was going to buckle, and he was proud of himself for only staggering a little. Jere looked down at his shaky but surprisingly sturdy legs. "Ain't gonna be pretty in the morning, but they'll do."

Callum let out a shaky breath and laughed. Before Jere had a chance to speak again, Isla's hand shot around his neck and she pulled his head down to seal her mouth over his in a ferocious kiss.

Her entire body trembled in his arms as she slid her hands up under his shirts to hold on tight. Jeremiah allowed himself to sink into the kiss, reveling in simply being alive and here with her.

He launched his own attack of nips and licks, until she let him in. Groaning, he wrapped his arms around her and pulled her against him tightly. When a chorus of whistles and catcalls reminded them that they weren't alone, they broke apart reluctantly, though Jeremiah kept her closely tucked against his side.

Kieran walked over them to stand in front of Jeremiah. He wore a sheepish grin on his dusty face, but his eyes betrayed the abject terror of the situation he had just escaped. "Sure I would've broken me neck if it hadn'a been for you, mate," he said, his accent obviously thicker from the adrenaline.

Kieran reached out a hand to shake Jeremiah's, and squeaked when the big man pulled him into a tight hug. "Don't scare me like that again, hear?" When he felt the boy nod, Jere released him.

Jeremiah searched Kieran's eyes as he spoke softly to the young man. "You good to go?"

"Yes, sir," he said, eyes fierce and determined.

Jeremiah nodded. "Alright then. Let's go."

Isla's hand on his arm halted his departure. "You two may need medical attention. I think we should turn back —"

"Like hell," Jere said, turning on his heel and walking off.

Chapter Nineteen

Isla sighed, staring at Jeremiah's retreating back. *Cursed manly pride*, she thought. She started after him, only to have Marduk block her path. His eyes were eerie, opened wide as if he were looking through her instead of at her.

"We have to keep going. Something is happening at the caves. Feel it." It was an order, not a question. Isla closed her eyes and expanded her energy receptors, and she felt it. A sizzle in the air, a crackling static that could only be caused by big power. Her hairs stood on end and the back of her neck tingled.

"Yeah, I feel it," she said, and watched as he cleared himself from his trance-like state. She motioned for him to join her with the others. "Okay, we'll go on. Brynna, Jeremiah, Kieran—I am trusting you to tell us if you need to stop for any reason."

Still a couple of miles from the caves, the group pressed on. They traveled a walking trail that had been worn into the rolling hills along the shore, and again they were sheltered by the bracken. As they were no longer climbing, they broke ranks and clustered together. Jack and Callum took the lead, while the younger searchers followed them. Isla, Jeremiah, and Marduk hung back to talk strategy for fighting Alastore.

"I don't know what we're going to find," Isla whispered, not wanting to alarm the others. "I can sense the presence of extremely powerful magick, but I have no idea who's in those caves." She flicked her eyes to Marduk, and he shook his head.

"I can't tell either. I should be able to sense the different beings, but it's like something is...scrambling the signal."

Jeremiah was ever the practical scientist. "Why don't we come up with the most likely circumstances and figure out how we'll handle them. Then when we get there, we'll improvise.

"Alastore has appeared to you a couple of times, but only in dreams or as an astral projection, am I right?" Marduk asked.

"Yes."

"I don't think he'll come at you himself at first. What's the point of being an evil entity if you don't use your minions?" he said with a half-smile.

"Hardy har har," Jere said. "Get to the point."

"Most likely he will funnel all his energy into his *auchrim*, so that they can materialize. They may try to fight you physically, or through magick, but they will most certainly try and get into your head to control you."

"Do you think the cave is a gateway?"

"There's no way to tell. Isla may be able to sense it if we get close, since she is connected to Alastore. But obviously that theory hasn't been tested."

"If the *auchrim* are in corporeal form, can we kill them?" Jeremiah asked.

"Sadly, no. Although you can cause them a great deal of pain," he said with a wicked smile. "Anything you do that would normally cause death—beheading, a break to the neck, stab to the heart...you get the idea—will send them back to the *locus*. So it gets rid of the immediate threat."

"So what if Alastore does decide to come at us?" Isla asked. Alastore hated her, so she felt sure that the demon wouldn't miss an opportunity for a personal appearance.

"Only you will be able to stand against him. If anyone else tries, he will use them against you. You can't let that happen."

"What about you?"

Marduk shook his head sadly. "I can fight *auchrim* until kingdom come, but my powers will be ineffective against the *Lochrim*, I'm afraid. When it comes to Alastore, I can't help you. I can only help you help yourself."

"Gee thanks, Yoda," Jeremiah interjected.

"'Much to learn, you still have,'" he said with a grin.

Isla rolled her eyes and kept walking. For being an ancient mystical creature, the kid sure was a walking movie encyclopedia. "So if we do find any of the missing persons, we need to get them clear of the *auchrim* as quickly as possible, so they don't get caught in the crossfire—so to speak."

"We must be careful though," Marduk answered, "because they can make you see things that aren't there, and make things that are there invisible to you. Trust nothing, question everything, because things will most definitely *not* be as they seem."

Each lost in their own thoughts and worries, they traveled along the walking trail until they saw the cliffs begin to taper off into smoother, rounder sandstone structures that curved toward a point of shore that stuck out into the sea.

The rocky outcrops in this area were as smooth as marble from constant crashing of the sea. Near where rock met shore, Isla could barely make out the yawning mouth of the first cave in the cave system.

Callum stopped just ahead and turned back toward the group. "Oi, up ahead is the Drumadoon promontory. Beyond that westernmost point will be the King's Cove, but the three caves are right there at the tip of the promontory. We'll be able to see all of them when we get closer. Final destination, kids!"

As they approached the point of the cove, the other caves came into view. The holes created in the sandstone by the mouths of the caves looked eerily like the face of a human skull. The trail ascended up a small hill that led to a grassy knoll, flanked on the east by the caves and on the west by jutting stones.

The first cave they came to was small and shallow, so much so that it couldn't even fit all of them in at once. Quickly realizing that nothing could possibly hide in a space that size, Isla urged them to keep going.

As the others shuffled out of the opening, Jeremiah was distracted by the ancient paintings and carvings on the walls of the cave. Running his hands along the walls, fingers dipping into the ruts made by carving tools, Jere felt as though he could almost feel the spirits of those who had come before them.

This is a place of great power. Jeremiah blinked, confused. Where the hell had that thought come from? Shaking his head as if he could clear it, he walked out to join the others. He still couldn't shake the prickling sensation that something had been in there with them.

As they approached the second and third caves, Jeremiah realized that these were actually two openings to one enormous cavern. The shape of it sort of reminded him of half of a doughnut. Filled with the same sea smoothed stones that populated the shore, the floor of the cave sloped up slightly while the ceiling tapered down to meet it.

There were even more archaic carvings, as well as interesting geological structures like stalactites and stalagmites, and a strange mineral calcification that turned certain parts of the cave walls a deep, blood red. It was certainly creepy, but fascinating.

Callum dropped his pack and turned in a slow circle. "This is as good a place as any to stop for a quick rest and some food, yeah?"

"Sounds like a good idea to me." He eased himself down to a flat stone, wincing as his bruised body protested, and Isla sat down beside him. She opened her pack to pull out their food supply. The rest of the searchers followed suit.

They had packed small sandwiches bought from a tearoom in town, along with fruit and some energy bars. After eating, Jeremiah lowered himself to the cave floor and stretched out his legs, closing his eyes.

He sighed contentedly when he felt Isla's fingers begin to comb through his hair. Climbing accidents, shapeshifters, and crazy homicidal demons be damned. He was alive, and he had his woman working her magic on him. Life was pretty damn near perfect.

That was the last thought he had before the earth began to shake. The whole cave began to rumble and quiver, causing the stones on the ground to bounce around like jumping beans. Cursing a blue streak when dust and pebbles began to rain down on them, Jeremiah leapt to his feet and tugged Isla up to meet him.

"Get a lot of earthquakes in Scotland?" Jere asked, only half kidding.

Isla shook her head and cast a wary look at the ceiling of the cave. "Uh, no. Not many, and definitely not like this."

"Must be a freak quake," Callum said, not sounding convinced. "Maybe there's an undiscovered fault line or something.

"Yeah, I'm sure it's something like — "

Isla hadn't even finished her sentence when the cave began to shake more violently, and a feral, unholy growl rose up from the bowels of the earth.

"Aaaaaand time to go, folks," Jeremiah said, hustling Isla toward the mouth of the cave. The others were right behind them as stalactites began crashing down on all sides.

Just when he'd thought they were home free, as soon as he crossed the threshold of the cave, he slammed into an invisible wall. The impact propelled him back so forcefully that Jack had to catch him.

Well didn't that just rattle his brainbox!

"The fuck?" Jeremiah shouted once Jack had set him back on his feet. He reached out to touch the empty space at the opening and his hand contacted the invisible barrier, as solid as if it were a concrete wall.

"We're trapped."

The growling rose again to a near deafening pitch, while the walls around them shook violently. Amy screamed as a stalactite crashed down from the cave ceiling to land inches from her foot. "What do we do?!"

Isla looked around the cave desperately, trying to think of a way to get them out of this situation. They were trapped in a cave that was coming down around their ears. *Think, damn it, think!* She couldn't help but feel responsible for the others, since she was the one Alastore was after.

Seeing the column of rock that separated the two openings of the cave, she noticed that it curved up and out into a low overhang that was fairly smooth. That was their only hope for protection from falling rock.

Grabbing Jeremiah's hand, she pulled him to the small alcove. "Come on guys, get under here," she shouted above the hideous growl. When they were all huddled together, sheltered from the debris, Isla racked her brain to find a way to get them out.

"What kind of magick is this?" she asked Marduk.

"I am guessing some kind of containment spell. He would lose too much energy from literally trying to form and hold it. He wouldn't be able to maintain it long enough."

"Are you sure it's Alastore?"

Marduk nodded, his ice-cold eyes sharp and deadly. "I already tried to counteract the spell. Couldn't budge it, which means only you can."

"I don't know how," she said while the sharp edges of panic dug into her stomach.

"Yes you do. You just have to say the words, and just let go of your power. It will do the work."

"What are the words?" she whispered.

She gasped as thoughts that were not her own insinuated themselves in her mind. "*Quid contineat oportet solvi. Sic fiat semper. What was once contained must now be set free. So mote it be.*"

Gathering her resolve, Isla drew strength from Jeremiah's hand grasping hers tightly, grounding her. She took in a deep breath, was preparing to gather her power, when something snapped inside her head. It was like a switch had been flipped, a door had been opened, and hundreds of anguished cries flooded her ears.

Screaming, crying, pleading...all rocketing around inside her mind. All the souls of all the people trapped inside Alastore's *locus*, begging to be freed. To be ended. It was too much. Too much pain, too much noise. Isla sank to her knees with a moan as a searing pain flashed through her skull.

Grabbing her head in her hands, she doubled over — in such a position that she almost looked like she was praying — and she screamed. And screamed. She screamed until she no longer had a voice, and still they came, her mouth gaping open to form the silent syllables.

Jeremiah knelt in front of her, placing his hands over hers and pulling them away from her head. "Isla, look at me," he said with a calmness she couldn't fathom in that moment.

When she finally opened her eyes to look at him, his face swam in her sight. Her eyes burned and her vision was hazed in red. Jeremiah cupped her face in his hands and tipped it so he could look in her in the eyes. "What's happening? What do you feel?"

"I can't...the people...screaming. So many...people," she stuttered, nearly incoherent.

Not sure what people she meant, Jere took a chance anyway. "The missing people?"

"Them...and so many...more," she said, breaking off with a strangled moan. When her eyes started to flutter closed, he shook her gently.

"I know it hurts, baby, but if you want to help those people, you've got to push through."

"I can't!" she wailed.

"Isla!" he said, punctuating it with another light shake. "Don't let him win. Don't let that evil win. You need to get mad about it. Use your anger. Fight!"

As she listened to Jeremiah's calm but firm voice, Isla began to take back the control of her mind. She had heard the voices, acknowledged them, and promised to help. But Jere was right. She couldn't help if she was down for the count, and she'd be damned if she was going to break her promise to those people. Putting up her mental barriers to allow herself to focus, she breathed through the pain.

Squeezing her eyes shut tightly, she shouted the words to the far recesses of the cave, so loud that it rose over the sound of the growling.

"*Quid contineat oportet solvi. Sic fiat semper!*"

And then she pulled the pin. Pulling energy from stores within her that even she didn't know were there, she allowed it to swirl and build in her chest until it exploded out of her.

A ripple of energy brushed past them and through them, as the mouths of the cave burst with a supernatural light, followed by a deafening boom. Isla felt herself being swept into strong arms and carried out while the shields were down.

Collapsing in the grass circle about ten yards away from the cave, Jeremiah held on tight to Isla as the others ran full blast to drop down beside them.

As they lay on the cool, lush grass, panting and gasping to catch their breath, it seemed as though all eight of them were now covered in dirt, bruises and cuts. But they were all alive.

Jeremiah looked down at her and she smiled at him with something akin to...elation.

Reaching up a delicate, but work-roughened hand to stroke his cheek, she batted her eyelashes dramatically and placed the back of her other hand across her forehead. "My hero," she said, in full swoon.

Jeremiah snorted and grinned. "Yeah, yeah. Get off me, woman!"

With one last pat to his cheek, Isla hopped up and dusted herself off. Reaching out, she helped pull Jeremiah up. Gathering all of her friends together, she looked at each of their faces in turn. "Those people are out there, somewhere. I had them in my head, begging for help. I'm going on. This is a little more than you signed up for, so if anyone wants to turn back, now's the time. Any takers?"

Seven pairs of eyes met hers in hard stares. And, yeah, they weren't going anywhere. Isla turned to look at the rock formations behind her. Beyond the sharp outgrowth of sandstone, around the corner of the promontory, was the third and largest cave.

Isla knew deep down to her core that they would find something there. What...was anyone's guess.

හ)(ශ

The King's Cave had a wide, domed mouth covered by an ornate iron gate. It was said that the intention of the gate was to protect the cave paintings and carvings from damage, but it was never locked.

The iron hinges squealed as Callum swung the gate wide enough for them to pass through. Isla and Jeremiah entered the enormous cave behind him. Though not too large in area, the main cavern expanded upwards with high, vaulted ceilings.

At the back of the cavern, Isla noticed that there were several narrow tunnels. God only knew where those led, or if they were even passable.

Cautiously, the eight of them stepped into the middle of the cave. Eerily quiet and dark, the cave had a very sinister atmosphere. The daylight from outside the mouth contrasted sharply with the stale darkness in the interior, leaving Isla struggling to adjust her eyes.

There was nothing but silence. Darkness. Stagnant air and water. But no missing islanders and, clearly, no demons either.

"Damn it!" Amy's quiet whisper voiced their collective thoughts. "I was sure we would find *some* kind of clue in here."

"I was too," Isla answered, frowning. "Still am, actually." She couldn't explain the feeling she had. Her skin crawled and her stomach jumped with uneasiness. Studying the recesses of the cave, Isla turned in a circle until her gaze rested on the far left tunnel.

She stared for so long, completely and utterly still, that the others began to fidget and clear their throats. She knew Jeremiah stood by, waiting patiently. She'd drawn a bead on something and was trying to work it out in her head.

Brynna shifted on her feet nervously. "Maybe we should —"

"Shh!" Isla hissed, holding up a hand. And then she heard it. A muffled voice, a sound somewhere between a moan and a sob, coming from the tunnel. Isla rushed forward, ready to leap to the rescue, when a hand on her arm stopped her.

Turning, she gave Jeremiah a questioning look. "Wait. Think," he whispered. "It could be a trap. You need to go in there expecting the worst."

At Isla's nod, he released her but followed close behind, ducking his head to clear the low sandstone ceiling. The tunnel was wide enough for two people to fit side by side but soon began narrowing.

After a few feet, it curved sharply to the left. Not one to make the same mistake twice, Isla peered round the bend to check out what was beyond. It was a dead end, but it wasn't empty. She gasped when she saw a body curled up on the cold ground.

Grabbing Jeremiah's hand, she pulled him up close behind her. "There's someone there," she whispered.

Slowly, they made their way around the corner and approached the figure cautiously. Hearing their arrival, the figure raised its head, face curtained by muddy brown hair. Wide, unfocused amber eyes stared up at them with blatant terror.

Isla looked at Jeremiah out of the corner of her eye and he nodded almost imperceptibly. Claire Corrie. They'd found her.

Not wanting to frighten the woman, Isla inched forward with Jeremiah close behind her. "Claire? Is that you? We've been looking for you."

Claire cringed away when Isla reached out to touch her shoulder. "P-Please...," she said through chattering teeth, "please go. They'll be back any minute!" Her voice rose in panic as she spoke.

"Claire, it's okay. We're here for you. The search party."

"No. No, no, no!" Claire screamed, covering her ears and rocking. "You can't help me! You have to go!" The woman let out an agonized wail and then opened her eyes. They had gone from amber to completely clear with shadows swirling in them.

Before they had time to process that new development, Claire seemed to be grabbed by invisible hands, yanked back through the stone wall. Isla stood there, momentarily stunned, staring at the empty tunnel.

Isla pinched the bridge of her nose to keep from screaming. "You've *got* to be kidding me. Astral projection?"

"Has to be. I don't think it would be physically possible otherwise. But it was a damn good one," he answered, frowning. "They must have siphoned a good supply of energy off of their new captures."

"They're not here, are they?"

"Doesn't seem that way."

Suddenly, Isla felt a tremor in the atmosphere. It wasn't like the earth shaking quakes from the second cave. It was as if the air had a pulse, and it was beating steadily, harshly, like the rotor blades on a helicopter.

She grabbed Jeremiah's arm at the same time that he spoke the words she was thinking. "It's a trap!"

The two of them took off down the tunnel, back the way they came, skidding to a halt when they reached the main cabin. The rest of the searchers stood shoulder to shoulder with their backs to them.

Standing between the group and the mouth of the cave was a throng of pale skinned, raven- haired figures. A fine mist swirled around the macabre gathering, further obscuring the searchers' escape route.

"It's a whole hive of the things," Jeremiah whispered. The *auchrim* merely stared at them, unmoving. Through the enveloping mist, they were strangely androgynous. Multiple copies of the original, a perfect simulacra of Alastore.

The creatures parted, making way for a lone figure to step forward. Well, if it wasn't the original himself.

Alastore was dressed impeccably in steel gray trousers and a black dress shirt. His black hair was swept away from his face and slicked back. He looked every bit the gentleman, from the sharp, patrician features, all the way to the tips of his black Gucci loafers.

He was the proverbial wolf in sheep's clothing.

Squeezing between Callum and Amy, Isla moved to stand in front of her friends. Jeremiah and Marduk flanked her on either side, bracing for the worst.

While the three of them knew exactly what they were dealing with, the rest of the searchers had been left in the dark. Callum's gruff voice echoed in the cavern.

"Just who in the *hell* is this joker?"

Fiddling with his diamond cufflink, Alastore raised an eyebrow and his lips quirked in a half-smile. Rich, disembodied laughter bounced around the recesses of the cave.

"*Legio nomen mihi est, quia multi sumus,*" came the quiet answer.

"What? What did he say?"

Jere cleared his throat and flicked a nervous glance behind him at Callum. "He said 'My name is Legion, for we are many.'"

"Demon that quotes the Bible. Cute," Amy said.

Alastore glided closer to where Isla stood, causing Jeremiah to surge forward. He was stayed by a calm hand on his arm.

"It was generous of you, witch, to bring us all of these extra souls. I can assure you, they will be put to good use." The demon smiled his gruesome, serrated smile, and actually winked at her. *Winked.* This time Jeremiah was the one who had to restrain her from going for his throat.

After a brief moment of stillness, Alastore executed a crisp about-face and walked back to his minions who, again, made way for him. Just as he passed the front ranks, he paused and turned his head toward the *auchrim* closest to him.

His voice was as gentle as it was deadly when he spoke. "Take them."

None of them had a moment more to think as the *auchrim* swarmed them, surrounding them on all sides. The cave was filled with a cacophony of hisses and screeches, and the eight of them were sucked into a cloud of scratching, biting, and clawing monsters.

Isla could hear Jeremiah shouting to them over the din. "We've got to separate. Divide and conquer!"

An auchrim immediately attacked her, but she spun around and caught him in the back with her knife. There was a bright flash of blue fire as the creature's body exploded into vapor. Isla immediately searched for Jeremiah and found him facing off with another one. Ducking under the arm of the screaming beast as it swung for him, he ran through it with his machete.

Caught off guard by the disappearing demon, Jeremiah left his back unguarded. Isla watched in horror as an *auchrim* grabbed him from behind, wrapping a bony hand around his throat, and dug its fingernails into the sensitive skin over his jugular.

Having just dispatched another demon with her machete, Isla spun on her heel when she heard Jeremiah yell. The sound was quickly cut off by the creature that was squeezing his neck.

She didn't think. She just reacted instinctively to protect her mate. Stretching out her arms, she summoned all the extra energy she could find and shot a fireball out of her hands. She prayed the two bodies locked in combat didn't turn as the flames hurtled toward the *auchrim's* back.

As the demon combusted, Jeremiah staggered forward, coughing and gasping for air. "Son of a —" He was cut off as another *auchrim* lunged at him, and he quickly raised his machete and relieved the thing of its head.

All around them, demons burst into flames, but it seemed like they just kept coming. Ants from an ant hill, bees from a hive. Wild laughter bubbled up inside Isla as she heard Freddie Mercury's voice in her head.

She stabbed another demon in the heart with her blade, watched as flames engulfed it, and it was vaporized.

Another one bites the dust.

She yelled at Kieran to duck, and she tossed a fireball at the *auchrim* who had been stalking him.

And another one gone.

Striking another demon with a mean roundhouse kick, flooring him, Isla pounced on the creature. It screeched as she placed a hand over its face, summoned her power, and blasted it home.

And another one gone.

During a brief reprieve, Isla searched the cave for the others. Brynna and Kieran were fighting back to back, as were Callum and Jack. Amy flipped a rather large demon over her shoulder. When it landed flat on its back, she pressed her booted foot into its windpipe.

The creature screamed and thrashed, swiping at Amy's leg with its claws. Calmly, coldly, she sliced the *auchrim's* throat with her machete and smiled as it dusted.

Another one bites the dust.

Isla backed up until she found herself pressed against Jeremiah's back. When he tried to speak to her, he had to shout over the sounds of battle. "They just keep coming. I think we might be in trouble here."

Nodding, Isla glanced worriedly around them. "Agreed."

Finally her gaze rested on Marduk, and what she saw astonished her. It appeared as though he was dusting demons with a mere thought. The sight gave her a little spark of hope, and an idea.

Nudging Jeremiah with her elbow, Isla made eye contact with him over her shoulder. "I have a plan. I have to get to Marduk. Cover me?"

At his nod, she started slashing her way through the fray, dispatching demons left and right while Jeremiah defended her back. When they finally reached Marduk on the other side of the cave, Isla pulled him aside while Jeremiah guarded them.

"That hands-free thing you've got going on? Can you teach me that?"

"Well, of course, but now's not exactly the time," Marduk answered.

Isla rolled her eyes and shook him softly. "Now is the only time we've got. What if we join our energies? Maybe we can end this."

Marduk tapped his chin as if he were pondering this, while Jeremiah slashed another *auchrim* that had advanced on them. "Uh, guys, if you've got a last-minute Hail Mary play, now's the time!"

Nodding, Marduk grabbed both of Isla's hands with his, forming a circle. "It's worth a try. Isla, I need you to close your eyes and concentrate on expanding your energy to fill the cave. To pull off something this big, we'll need to use a spell."

The words were disembodied—his lips never moved as he spoke them.

"*Per gyrum terrae, aerem, ignem et aquam, Domina magna virtus tua implico nobis minatur exitium.*"

He raised his eyes to Isla's face, silently willing her to repeat the spell. Together they chanted, hands clasped tight, until Isla could feel the power bubbling up from the deepest recesses of her soul, like a hot spring in a frozen tundra.

The pressure was so great inside her head and her heart that she thought she would explode from it. It was almost painful. Just when she thought she couldn't possibly take it anymore, that she would surely be burned to ash by the enormity of the energy, something inside her snapped.

A wave throbbed through the atmosphere, radiating out from their circled bodies. It was so powerful that it felt like a seismic ripple. All around them, demons began to burst apart, one after another, shattering like glass in an explosion. The others instinctively ducked as if they would be hit by shrapnel. When the air finally cleared of dust and debris, Isla sagged into Jeremiah, and he tucked her against his side. She noticed that he'd had to slip his other arm around Marduk's shoulders to keep him from collapsing as well.

When the two of them had recovered enough to stand on their own, Isla smiled up at Jeremiah. "It worked! We did it."

Grinning, Jeremiah bent his head to kiss her sweetly on the lips. "Yeah you did."

Their reverie was cut off by the sound of Amy's shrill scream. The three of them whipped around, searching the dark cave with their eyes to determine the source of her distress.

One *auchrim* had survived. Its corporeal form was that of a young male, dressed in jeans and a t-shirt. Isla gasped as she realized that the thing had a death grip on Kieran's face. The boy's head lolled limply as the creature's claws dug into his flesh. His eyes were glassy and unfocused, fixed on the creature's face.

"Kieran!" Jeremiah shouted, trying to get his attention as the *auchrim* leaned in closer and bared its teeth.

"Shit. *Shit!*" Isla hissed. When Jeremiah sent her a questioning look, she explained herself. "Kieran left early last night. We didn't know he was coming today, so he never learned how to defend himself."

Cursing under her breath, Isla turned back to the scene, and watched as a single tear rolled down Kieran's cheek. "What should we do?" she asked, at a loss as to how to help her friend without causing the demon to attack. A muscle ticked in Jeremiah's jaw as he turned steely eyes to her. "Distract him."

Without waiting for an answer, Jeremiah backed up slowly to fade into the darkness that swallowed the edges of the cave.

Swallowing down her worry for Jeremiah, Isla cautiously inched closer to where the *auchrim* held Kieran captive. Holding out her hands, palms up, in a gesture of submission, she began speaking softly to Kieran.

"Ki, just listen to me. Clear your mind, then imagine yourself in the place where you feel safest." She wasn't sure if Kieran could hear her, but the demon's attention was focused on her instead of Jeremiah, so she hoped that would prove to be the diversion he needed.

"Fight him, Ki. Don't let him take you." When she tried to step closer, the *auchrim* hissed and gripped Kieran tighter. Freezing, Isla looked around frantically for something — anything — to use to help free her friend.

Suddenly, the creature was jerked back hard, stunned into dropping Kieran and thrown bodily against the cave wall. As it tried to stand, Jeremiah pushed it up against the cold stone and closed his hands around its throat.

He would have rung the life out of the demon, Isla was sure he'd intended to, if she hadn't come up behind him and placed a hand on his tense shoulder. "Just finish it," she said, her voice thick with exhaustion.

Removing one hand, Jeremiah unsheathed his bowie knife and drove the point home.

Callum and Jack propped Kieran up between them as the group exited the cave and Isla followed, eager to be well away from an obvious hotspot of *auchrim* activity. Wanting to put some distance between themselves and the traumatic episode in the cave, the eight of them made their way down to the rocky shore.

Isla took comfort in the circle of Jeremiah's arms as she looked out across the cool, grey sea. Further down the beach was a cluster of cairns—stone altars erected by travelers as memorials and landmarks. Somehow it calmed her to know that others had come and gone along the same path they'd traveled, and survived.

Sighing, she pulled away from Jere and faced the rest of their small band of searchers. "Callum, Jack, take Kieran home. He needs to recover. Girls, you go with them. Jeremiah, Marduk, and I will go on toward Machrie and see if we can make it across to the Clauchland Hills before dark."

Callum began to protest, but Isla held up a hand to silence him. "I won't risk any of your lives any longer. But if I don't keep going, all that we've been through today will have been for nothing. Please."

"All right lass, we'll go on. You don't radio in by nightfall? We come get you. Understand?" Callum said.

Smiling, Isla kissed him on the cheek. "Got it, boss. Take the trail up to the top of the bluffs. It will be an easier trip for Kieran."

Nodding, Callum took up his position under one of Kieran's arms with Jack opposite him. Kieran gave a weak smile, and they set off for home.

And then there were three.

ℰ⟩⟨ℛ

Strange that their battle seemed to have waged on for hours, but when they emerged from the caves, it was only mid-morning. Once free of the caves, Isla, Jeremiah, and Marduk took the walking trail that led to the top of the cliffs in a gentle sloping incline. Grateful for the brief respite to their grueling journey, Jeremiah wrapped an arm around Isla's shoulders and smiled down at her.

"Those were some pretty amazing pyrotechnics y'all pulled off back there."

Marduk feigned shining a medal on his chest. "No big. All in a day's work in my world."

His lighthearted jibe surprised an indelicate snort out of Isla. Jeremiah chuckled and shook his head. "Seriously though, are y'all going to be okay to continue?"

He was happy that Isla appeared to give his question at least a little thought before she answered. "You know, I really feel fine now. It's like getting up and moving helped restore the lost energy.

Jeremiah pondered that as they made their way through the fields of low, mossy grass and grazing sheep.

Around noon, after making good time traipsing over the moorland, they came upon the Machrie standing stones. Tall and majestic, the ancient sandstone monoliths stood silently guarding the old, ruined farm buildings beyond.

Isla stepped into the circle, turning slowly and raising her face to the sky. "I don't feel anything bad here. This is a place of peace," she said softly, then blinking as if she had surprised herself.

Satisfied that the stones were not guarding a *locus* ready to rain demons down on them, they stopped for a brief rest and some food. A breeze blew in, swirling around the three of them, bringing with it the cool October air. Marduk looked over at Isla and she shivered at the look in those pale eyes.

"Samhain draws near," he said.

Nodding, Isla cuddled closer against Jeremiah's side, breathing deeply of his woodsy, masculine scent. "What do you think Alastore will do now?"

Marduk shrugged. "There is no way to know. He may lay low, gather all of his strength for the battle on Samhain..."

"Or he could come at us with all guns blazing, hoping to weaken us enough for him to win easily," Jeremiah supplied. Standing, he dusted himself off and began repacking his rucksack. "We'd better get going if we want to make it to the hills by nightfall."

"Are you picking up any signs of the missing people?" Marduk questioned Isla.

Isla shook her head as she slung her pack over her shoulder. "Not a thing. Not even a latent track. I just figured we'd head toward the old fort at Dun Fionn, as it's rumored to be a hotbed of paranormal activity on the island."

"We need to go then, we'll lose the light fast." Jeremiah looked over his shoulder at Marduk. "Why don't you go furry for a little while and do a little recon up ahead. Double back and warn us if you see anything out of the ordinary."

The young man sent Jeremiah a grateful smile that told him he'd been having trouble holding the wolf back. While Marduk poofed into the shape of his silvery wolf, Isla and Jeremiah trudged onward.

By midafternoon, they had reached the Clauchland Hills forest. Isla led the way on the forest walk that ascended to the summit of Dun Fionn from the dirt footpath they had been traveling on—an intermediate hike, much welcome after the strain they had endured that morning. As they entered the canopy, she noticed how much darker their surroundings were with the trees blocking the sun.

Isla and Jeremiah reached the summit just as the sun was beginning to sink below the trees. The curtain of forest parted to reveal a large stone cairn that marked the ruins of the old fort. They, along with several man-sized boulders, were nestled in a carpet of cool grass.

Unable to resist, Jeremiah kicked off his shoes and sighed as his toes sank into the lush green. From the old fort, he could see the waves crashing against the rocks down below in Brodick Bay.

To his left, Goat Fell, the sleeping giant, loomed a great shadow in the failing light. Closing his eyes, he breathed deep of the fresh mountain air mixed with sea spray that was so unique to the island itself.

He smiled as Isla's arms, delicate yet impossibly strong, wound around his waist, and she rested her chin against his shoulder.

"This is one of my favorite spots," she said reverently. "Whenever I feel alone or lost, I come up here to be with the mountains and the sea. It just puts things in perspective. You feel it too."

He nodded, turned, and pulled her into the circle of his arms. He tilted her face up to his and placed a kiss on those full lips. Briefly, his fingers sank deep into her ebony curls, and he deepened the kiss, unable to prevent his body's reaction to her.

Sighing, he pulled away, trying to remind himself of why they were there. "Getting anything?"

"Not a whisper. I'm beginning to imagine Alastore laughing as he watches us through some sort of crystal ball as we trudge along on our merry wild goose chase."

"Maybe. But what else can we do but sit on our hands until Samhain?"

She didn't have a good answer for him. It galled her that she didn't have any answers at all. And, as the sun finally cast her last shadow in the fort, she realized that they were out of time for the night.

"There's a small clearing under the canopy, just beyond that last boulder. That will be a good place to make camp."

The clearing was indeed small, providing them with just enough room to pitch their hike tent and build a small campfire.

Jeremiah was wary of camping out in the open with all of the dangers that were waiting for them, but the soft rustling of wildlife and the soft bubbling of a nearby burn put him more at ease.

The activity, or lack thereof, of the woodland animals would be their early warning system.

Isla pulled out some dehydrated vegetables and black beans from her backpacking kit to cook over the fire. They had plenty of energy bars and snacks, but nothing lifted the spirits like a hot meal, so he quickly set about building the fire.

After they'd pitched the tent and laid out the bed rolls, Jeremiah tried to raise Callum on the radio as promised.

"Callum? Callum? Come back."

Static.

He repeated the call and breathed a sigh of relief as the radio sputtered to life.

"Oi, Jeremiah! Come back!"

"Yeah, Callum. We're bedded down for the night on Dun Fionn, just inside the woods from the old fort. Over."

"Find anything, mate?"

"Not a thing. Seems like we've hit a dead end. We'll head home at first light and regroup. We should make it in to Expeditions by midmorning. Over."

"Sounds good. We don't hear from you by then, we'll send the cavalry."

"'Night. Over and out."

Clicking off the radio to save battery, Jeremiah joined Isla by the fire ring. She shivered lightly in the evening chill, so he pulled out the trail blanket to cover them. She sighed and leaned in.

"What do we do now? I thought for sure that locating the missing people would give us some clues as to how to beat Alastore. Samhain is close, but what the hell do we do when it gets here?"

Jeremiah shook his head and pressed a kiss to the top of her head. "Not sure, babe. This is new territory for me too. When we get back, I'll contact my friend Drew to see if he's gotten any more done on the translations. And I think we should try and see Mhairi again."

"I guess we should. If anyone knows how to stop Alastore, it would be her. I have to wonder why she won't just tell us. Don't you?"

"Maybe she doesn't know. Not specifically. But she may know something that could lead us to the answer. She's already given us a big part of it — *the blood is the key*."

After they finished their hiker's feast, they climbed into the tent and almost immediately fell asleep. The events of the day had taken their toll, and the two of them were engulfed with exhaustion.

Jeremiah was pulled halfway out of his bone-deep fatigue by the feeling of warm lips pressed against the pulse point in his neck. He moaned sleepily and lifted his chin to give better access. He shuddered when teeth nipped along his jugular.

The last thing he felt before sleep claimed him again was a hand sliding down his abdomen.

When Jeremiah awoke hours later, he was disoriented and alone. Shaking his head to clear his mind of the exhaustion and latent lust from his fervent dreams, he squinted to look around the tent. His gut twisted in panic as he imagined what could have happened to Isla. Had she been taken in her sleep again? She could be anywhere.

Taking a breath to calm himself, Jere emerged from the tent to look around. It was almost pitch dark, the only light coming from the dying fire and the bit of moonlight that broke through the forest canopy.

"*Isla!*" he hissed, not wanting to lose the element of surprise if something had gotten to her. Shivering in the cold of full night in Scotland's October, Jere tugged a wool sweater over his head and shoved his feet into his hiking boots.

Grabbing his hunting knife, he set off on the most obvious path, down to the river. Following the sound of the gently babbling brook, he trod soundlessly on the soft brush of the forest.

"*Isla,*" he whispered, straining his ears for any sound that would give him a clue. Hearing nothing but silence at first, he was just about to move on, when it came.

Faint and otherworldly, the tinkling sound of light splashing floated on the air. Cautiously, he approached an opening in the trees that he knew would lead down to the burn. Stopping short, he was taken aback by what he saw.

There in the clearing was a small pool, caused by the buildup of rock and sediment in the low-flowing river. Isla was submerged up to her chest, the water licking just over her full breasts, and she leaned back on her elbows against the bank.

Seeing Jeremiah, she smiled, causing her dimples to wink out at him. Despite his confusion, seeing that sent a shot of pure lust straight to his groin.

"Come in," she beckoned with no less power than a siren's song. "It feels lovely."

"Uh, Isla," he started, swallowing against the tremor of desire in his voice. "It's October. In Scotland. Don't think skinny-dipping is the best thing to be doing right now."

Her laugh rang out like a bell on a clear day, sending little shivers over his skin. He wondered if she was in her right mind, but other parts of him were really close to not caring.

Her laughter died as her gaze dropped to his lips. Wetting her own lips, her eyes traveled a scorching path down his body. "I think this is exactly what we should be doing," she murmured.

Aw, fuck it all, he thought as his brain short circuited. If he was going to freeze to death, what a way to go it would be. Anxious to join her, hypothermia or not, he stripped off his sweater and shirt. He had peeled his jeans halfway off, when he realized he hadn't taken off his boots.

Isla giggled as he stumbled in his haste to get them off. When he was finally, blessedly, naked, he summoned all of his mental fortitude to step into what he could only imagine would be ice-cold, murky water, and hoped he wouldn't squeal like a girl.

It was a shock to his system when the water he stepped into was the temperature of a hot-tub, and instead of the black, peat-infused, muddy color it should have been, he saw that the pool was as clear as bathwater, softly reflecting the moonlight.

Wading in until the water lapped at his hipbones, Jeremiah stopped to stare at her. She was a dazzling water nymph, her lush and curvy body belying the strength that rippled beneath it.

She stood and he was mesmerized by her luminescent skin as the water rolled down in glistening rivulets. He swallowed. Hard.

Isla bit her lip as she studied him until he began to fidget under her scrutiny.

Confusion clouded his strong brow as his unfocused eyes finally zeroed in on her face. "What the hell? How is this warm? I've never heard of any hot springs on Arran."

Again, the tinkling laughter sent shivers down his spine. "There aren't any," she said with a mischievous smile. "What's the point of being a witch if you can't make a little magic every now and then."

Lowering herself back onto her elbows on the mossy bank, Isla took a moment to enjoy the look of him. His shaggy, brown hair was wet at the tips from the gathering steam, and the heat in his hazel stare was enough to make her belly coil with need.

His impossibly wide shoulders and chest tapered down to rock-hard abs, which were now quivering as he breathed fast and shallow. Isla's own breathing grew shallow as her eyes followed the stark line of his oblique muscles into the deep V that disappeared into the water.

His worried gaze raked over her as if searching for invisible injuries. "Doesn't it sap your energy to keep it hot?"

"Surprisingly, no," she said, examining her fingertips coyly. "I feel great, actually. Energized. I think it may be because water is one of the elements and I can tap into its life force."

In that instant, his gaze became sharp, a slow, wolfish smile curling his lips. "So you're telling me that you and me are alone in a hot tub?"

Chewing on a fingernail, Isla nodded, suddenly feeling a bit like a jackrabbit caught in the crosshairs.

Just when she thought he would pounce, he surprised her by doing the opposite. Stretching his arms above his head, he fell back into the water until he was completely submerged. He stayed under for a ridiculously long amount of time, and the picture he made when he rose back out of the dark water made her mouth run dry.

Rippling muscles in his torso stood out in stark relief from the kiss of the dim moonlight as the water sluiced down his smooth skin. His longish hair was darkened from the damp and slicked back away from his angular face. The moon enhanced the shadows around his eyes and the hollows of his cheekbones, giving his face an almost predatory appearance.

He looked dangerous—and positively sinful. Gone was the goofy, easy-going scientist who lit up like a Christmas Tree at any prospect of learning something new. In his place was a dark, volatile, and unbearably sexy stranger.

Surprisingly, she loved both sides of him, but she was glad that this one had decided to come out and play. Slowly he waded his way over to her—how he could make it seem like a swagger in waist-deep water, she had no idea.

There was no doubt in her mind that tonight, their lovemaking would not be slow and tender, but as wild and fierce as their surroundings.

In a flash, he was on her, strong arms trapping her against the bank of the pool. Tilting her head back to look up at him, she nibbled on her plump bottom lip. He traced the path of her teeth with the pad of his thumb, and then tilted her chin up to claim her mouth in a bruising kiss.

Isla's heartbeat went into overdrive, and it was so loud in her head it was a wonder he didn't hear it too. He drew back a hair's breadth, still so close that his breath mingled with hers.

"Open for me," he commanded in a gravelly voice that turned her knees to water. There was really no other choice than to readily comply.

Her head swam as he deepened the kiss, stroking her with his tongue as if trying to taste every inch of her. And she was right there with him, teasing, nibbling, biting at his lower lip. She had learned that it was just that right amount of aggression mixed with her sweetness that lit his fire.

Unwilling to release her mouth, he growled his approval when she wrapped her legs around his waist. Her heart leapt in anticipation as he used his body to push her until her back was flush with the soft sloping bank. She couldn't help but rock against him as he sucked up a mark on her collarbone.

She could feel him fighting for control—he'd want to go slow for her, give her the adoration she deserved—but the raw wildness of their surroundings had her more feral side straining to be let loose. She tilted her head up to scrape teeth along his jugular.

From the way his hips bucked sharply, she knew she'd found a sensitive spot. His satisfied grin turned into a groan as she rocked against him again, enveloping him in warm, moist heat. As his hands roamed her body, his muscles bulged and his body practically vibrated from the strain of holding back.

"Isla...," he said, breaking off with a hiss as she reached down to take him in her hand. His body tense, he dropped his forehead to hers. "I — I can't..."

Understanding, her mouth curved in a wicked smile as she tilted her head up to brush her lips over his ear. "Then don't," she whispered, biting down on his lobe.

A strangled sound came from somewhere deep in his chest, and the wire snapped. He seized the hand that was taunting him, captured both of her wrists in one hand and pinned them above her head, and entered her in one hard surge.

Isla gasped and arched her back at the exquisite invasion, her heart thumping in her ears. She could see the pulse at his throat fluttering wildly, and it gave her a sweet sense of satisfaction to affect him that way and knowing he was right there with her.

She watched him through heavy lids as he gripped her hips tightly and surged into her. Muscles rippled, the chords of his neck strained, bulging veins stood out starkly under his golden skin. He was magnificent. He was relentless.

Those were her last coherent thoughts as he hit a spot that caused her eyes to roll back in her head and her mind to go blank. She could already feel her orgasm building, a warm coil low in her belly.

They had survived the unthinkable, a fate worse than death. In the wilds of the forest, surrounded by the warmth of her magic, she was tempted to give herself over to the sensation. But she wasn't ready — she needed more of him.

She wrenched her wrists out of his grip, causing him to lose his balance and fall forward, chest to chest and hip to hip with her. He merely growled deep in his throat, buried his hands in her curls, and thrust deep.

The new angle provided such an exquisite friction that she felt herself fly apart. Her release crashed over her until she gasped and clawed at him. He rode her through it, grazing teeth along her neck, causing her to shiver through the aftershocks.

Soon his breathing became laborious and he lost his rhythm. Reaching around, she dug her nails into his firm rear in encouragement, which seemed to send him over the edge. He sank into her once more before he was finally swamped in his own release.

He called out her name in a voice edged with sandpaper and bit down delectably hard on the fleshy part of her shoulder, sending her over another crest. They lay there, wrapped up in each other, hearts pounding and breaths coming in gasps, for what seemed like an eternity.

When he finally caught his breath and came back down to earth, Jeremiah raised his head limply to look down at her. With her wild curls drying around a face that glistened with a fine sheen of perspiration, he thought she looked like an angel. She was practically glowing.

He rose up on his elbows and regarded her more closely. She *was* glowing. Her skin had a goldish tint to it and, when he looked behind him, he saw that the pond was lit from underneath with some ethereal golden glow. Might have freaked out a normal person, but he had been dealing with the paranormal most of his life and, well, he was sleeping with a witch. Turning back around, he gave her a lopsided grin. "So…was it good for you?"

"You dork!" she said, but she laughed and splashed him. He swept her up in his arms and dunked them both. When they rose, Jeremiah sighed contentedly as Isla wound her arms around him. He kissed the top of her head.

"We should get some sleep."

"Mmm…sleep," she said, yawning.

He led her out of the pool and into the biting chill of the night air. Quickly drying them both off with his t-shirt, Jeremiah hastily pulled on his sweater and jeans while Isla did the same. Hand in hand, they sprinted back to the campsite.

When they reached the small clearing, Isla dove inside the tent and into her bedroll. Jeremiah spent a few moments outside banking the fire so that it would burn through the remaining hours of the night, and then joined Isla in the tent.

Completely exhausted, both from their earlier ordeal and their lovemaking, they fell asleep quickly, huddled together for warmth. Neither of them knew what the next day would bring, but for tonight—for the next few hours—they were safe in each other's arms.

Chapter Twenty

When Jeremiah and Isla returned from Dun Fionn the next day, they met the others at Expeditions before the first tour of the day. They wanted to regroup and go over what information they had — which they all agreed was absolutely goose-egg.

As the two returned to the lobby, hand in hand, Isla smiled at Kieran who was already back on his post at the front desk. "Hey Ki, why don't you tag along on Amy's hike today? I'm too beat to go out, and I would really like two guides on each tour until things settle down."

She saw the subtle blush that covered his cheekbones, and she knew it had a lot to do with his little crush on Amy, but she meant what she said. While the threat was upon them, she didn't want her guides out alone.

Kieran flashed her a brilliant smile and took off for the equipment room, tossing a look over his shoulder. "Thanks, boss! Radio if you need me!"

Shaking her head, Isla settled into the swivel chair behind the counter and waggled her eyebrows at Jeremiah.

"He's just excited to spend the next three hours staring at Amy's arse."

"Can you blame a kid?" Jere said with a snort. Isla rolled her eyes and turned her attention to the day's schedule.

"We've quite the busy schedule. What are you going to do with yourself today, Dr. Rousseau," she said, treating him to a dimpled grin.

"Need to get up with Drew and see if he's made any headway on those translations. Then I thought I'd go to the library in Brodick and do some research."

"And check your email. And Facebook."

"Yeah, so? I'm a social butterfly," he said with a wink. Leaning across the counter, he captured her lips in a tender kiss. It was an extreme contrast to the aggression of last night, but it was no less powerful.

"Pick you up here around four?"

Isla licked her lips and nodded. Jeremiah's eyes latched on to the movement, causing him to have to remove his ball cap and clutch it in front of his crotch to avoid embarrassment. He backed away slowly, without taking his eyes off her seductive expression.

The spell was broken when he backed into a lamp beside the front door, and Isla erupted into a fit of giggles. He was still smiling as he closed the door behind him and stepped out into the morning sun.

It was a bright, beautiful day, but he was learning from the locals that the grey clouds obscuring the summit of Goat Fell would mean a storm later on. Pulling his iPhone out of his back pocket, Jere checked for a return call or email from Drew. Nothing.

"Damn, brother, where are you?" he said out loud. It wasn't like Drew to go off the grid for so long, and Jeremiah had an uneasy feeling about it. With all of the strange things going on around him, he wasn't cool with his best friend disappearing on top of it.

Not normally one to bother his friend at work, he broke down and dialed Drew's office at Tulane.

A tinny, nasal voice sounded on the other end of the line. "Tulane University, Anthropology Department."

"Hello, this is Dr. Jeremiah Rousseau. I'm trying to reach Dr. Deveraux. Can you put me through to him?"

"I'm sorry, sir, Dr. Deveraux is traveling on University business for the next two weeks. Would you like to leave him a voice mail?"

"No ma'am, I've already left him one on his mobile. Is there any way you can tell me where to reach him? It's important."

"No, sir, I'm not allowed to give out that information. Is there anything else I can do for you?"

Biting back the urge to snap at the bored receptionist, Jere took a calming breath. "No, ma'am. Thank you."

Ending the call with a frustrated tap on the screen, he shoved a hand through his shaggy hair. "Damn it, Drew! Where the hell are you? We're running out of time. We're fixin' to have a demonpocalypse on our hands here."

Jeremiah couldn't help the uneasy feeling that washed over him as he had the thought that something was terribly off. Realizing that pitching a fit to his phone wasn't going to get him anywhere, Jere climbed into his rental and headed for the library.

Having just waved off the last tour for the day, an afternoon kayak trip led by Callum and Jack, Isla settled in to work on the accounting. Sitting at the old roll-top desk in the corner behind the front counter, she was deeply engrossed in paperwork when she heard the bells on the front door jingle.

Glancing up from her work, she cautiously eyed the stranger who stepped inside. Big. That was her first impression. The man was so tall and broad shouldered that his large frame filled the door frame and almost completely blocked out the light from outside, causing his features to be shadowed.

A fission of fear passed through, causing her to palm the hunting knife she kept in the desk drawer. Not moving a muscle, she narrowed her eyes at the shadow of the man's face. When he stepped into the light, her posture relaxed slightly.

His eyes were the color of a clear blue sky, and most importantly, they weren't swirling with shadows. He had spiky blond hair, carefully arranged to look effortless, and he had what she could only describe as classic all-American good looks.

Yes, definitely American, she thought as he gave her a toothy smile. She'd put money on that. He was dressed impeccably in steel grey slacks and a deep purple dress shirt with just a tiny bit of sheen to it. She was sure that he was kitted out in designer brands from his necktie to his polished black loafers.

As he approached her, she noticed he moved with a fluid grace and commanding confidence that spoke of old money. Someone used to getting his way.

"Canna 'elp ye, sir?" she asked, laying the brogue on thick. When confronted with strangers, she'd often play the part of the naïve, little island girl until she had a chance to assess them.

"Yes, ma'am, I hope you can," he answered, his manners and his lopsided grin strangely reminding her of Jeremiah. American, nailed it. She raised a delicate eyebrow and waited for the handsome stranger to continue.

Shifting to pull something out of his pocket, he presented her with an outdated flip phone. Unable to completely stifle the chuckle at the polished young man's antiquated piece of hardware, she unsuccessfully covered it with a cough.

Shrugging sheepishly, he grinned at her. "Yeah, I know. I'm kind of holding out for the iPhone 5."

"So what can I do for ye?" Isla prompted.

"Um, well, I think my battery has finally bit it. Do you know if there is an electronics store somewhere on the island? I'm only here for one night to visit a friend of mine, and right now I've no way to get a hold of him."

He spoke in a very careful and cultured way, making Isla think he must be well-educated, practiced in public speaking. There was a hint of something else in his refined accent that she couldn't quite place. French? No, that wasn't it, but something similar.

Giving up, she focused on his question. "No, mate, I'm sorry. Y'won't find anythin' like that on the island. Best take the ferry to Glasgow."

Leaning on the counter, the man frowned slightly and then sighed. "Thanks anyway. Since I won't be spending time looking for a cell phone battery, can I sign up for one of your tours. I might as well do a little sightseeing while I'm here."

Isla didn't buy for a second that the expensive-looking stranger had come here looking to go on a hike, or to ask her about cell phones, for that matter. But, as she didn't yet feel threatened, she played along, hoping he would eventually get to the point.

"Out of luck again, I'm afraid. I just sent out our last tour for the day. I can book you something for tomorrow if you'd like." If he noticed her slipping back into her regular accent, he didn't comment.

Blondie shook his head and smiled. "I'll be leaving early in the morning. Next time. I won't take up any more of your time. I appreciate the help, miss...?"

"Isla," she said, reaching out her hand for him to shake. "And you are?"

"You can call me Andrew."

"Nice to meet you, Andrew." Her brows disappeared under her thick bangs as he gallantly kissed her hand.

"*Non, Cher*, the pleasure is all mine." Okay, French it is, she thought. When he bowed over her hand like a country gentleman, she dissolved into laughter.

This was the scene Jeremiah was treated to when he quietly entered the lobby. Jerking her hand away, Isla gasped when she saw the murderous look Jere aimed at the stranger. Unsure of what to do, her eyes flickered back to Andrew.

Her eyes widened as Jeremiah advanced on Andrew. "Hey!" he shouted at the man's back. "You better keep your filthy coon-ass paws off my girl, hear?"

Andrew whirled around to face the other man, eyes angry and expression hard. "Listen here, *coullion*, I don't know who ya think ya talkin' to, but I ain't seen no ring on her fingah."

Whoa, where the hell had that come from, Isla thought. Gone was the cultured socialite and out came a manner of speech that was similar to Jeremiah's, but with the faint French behind it. Gasping, she gripped the hunting knife as she saw the man charge Jeremiah.

The men came together with a thud, and Jeremiah immediately had Andrew in a headlock. "Gonna teach you some manners, boy!"

"*Je vas te passe une callotte!*" Andrew shouted between gags.

"Like to see y'try," Jere answered, squeezing harder.

Isla rounded the counter and bore down on them, hunting knife at the ready. "Alright, break it up! Not in my house! Jeremiah, let him go." She faced a wheezing Andrew as Jere released him. "I think you need to leave now."

Her jade eyes threw sparks, and her chest heaved from the adrenaline from what she thought was a genuine fight about to happen. Her face changed to one of surprise, and then confusion when both men busted out laughing, clutching each other as they doubled over.

Sighing, Isla slapped the knife down on the counter and pinched the bridge of her nose. Andrew gave Jeremiah a leering smile. "That your girl?"

"Hell, yes!"

"Amazing," Andrew mumbled under his breath, making Jeremiah grin smugly.

Pushing between them, Isla glared at Andrew and then turned her fierceness on Jeremiah. "Excuse me, but what the hell is going on?"

Pulling her against him, he gave her a quick kiss and nipped her lower lip. "Sorry, baby. We're just kiddin' around. I'd like you to meet Dr. Andrew Deveraux, a colleague of mine. We've also been friends since grade school. Drew's the one I told you about, the one who's helpin' me with the translations on that book from Latium."

Understanding dawned, and she turned the full power of her dimpled smile on Drew. "You could have just said so!"

Smiling back at her, Drew punched Jeremiah in the shoulder. "You're a lucky man, brother. A lucky man."

Nodding, he wrapped his arms tighter around Isla. "What the hell are you doing here? I've been tryin' to get a hold of you for a week!"

"Long story, truly," he said. "If there's anywhere to get a decent cup of coffee around here, we could sit down and talk about it."

"Sounds good. You can follow us to the tearoom in Whiting Bay."

Drew cut his eyes skeptically at the back of Isla's head, raising his brows questioningly.

Jeremiah nodded. "I want Isla to be in on this too. She's somewhat of a local expert on the folklore around here, and she's been helping me research."

It was the truth, in a roundabout way, and Isla was grateful that he hadn't shared her secret. She knew Jeremiah would trust Drew with his life, but she wasn't ready to trust him with hers.

At the tearoom, they found a table in a back corner, out of the main path of most of the customers. After ordering three coffees, Jeremiah leaned forward expectantly. "So, first things first. What are you doing on Arran, and where the hell have you been?"

Drew paused while the harried waitress set down their coffees, along with a carafe of milk and an assortment of sugars.

"I'm taking a sabbatical this semester. Been traveling around doing visiting lectures. The cell phone's been on its last legs for a few days now, and I think it's finally dead." He spun the boxy-looking flip phone on the table.

Jeremiah snickered, holding his mug in front of his mouth to hide his smile. "He's holding out for the iPhone 5," Isla supplied with a grin.

"I'm lecturing at Edinburgh on Wednesday, so I thought I'd drop in on you since I've been out of touch."

Breathing an audible sigh of relief, Jeremiah relaxed a bit. "With all of the crazy things that have been going on lately, I was worried something had happened to you."

Drew gave him a questioning look but didn't press the issue. "Well there was one thing..."

"What?" Jeremiah asked, suddenly alarmed.

"Just before I left New Orleans for my lecture at UC Berkeley, my apartment was broken into."

"*Fuck!*" Jere hissed. "The book?"

"Relax, it's fine. I keep it in my safe, just in case. I think that may have been what she was after though."

"She?"

Drew nodded. "Yeah, I caught her in the act. One of my lectures got canceled at the last minute, so I came back home. There was no sign of a break in or anything—I didn't even know she was there until I made it into the study and I saw her trying to crack the safe.

She was dressed head to toe in black, straight out of *Mission Impossible*. Tiny, dark-haired, had a mean right hook."

"What made you think she was after the book?" Isla asked.

"Well, she didn't touch anything else. I combed the place after she left and not a thing was out of place. She just messed with the safe...the book was the only thing in there."

"Wait, after she left? Didn't you have her arrested?"

Drew gave Jeremiah a sheepish smile and absently fingered his jaw. "Told you she had a mean right hook. When I found her in there, I grabbed her, and she spun around and cold-cocked me. Didn't knock me out, but it rung my bell but good. Stunned me long enough for her to escape out to the terrace."

"Dude, you live on the sixth floor!"

Drew shrugged his big shoulders. "Can't explain it. When I cleared my head enough to walk straight, she was gone."

Jeremiah let out a low whistle. "You always did have a knack for gettin' tangled up with man-eaters."

With the comment, Drew choked on his coffee. "Ain't that the truth? There was one more strange thing about her, though."

Isla leaned forward and Jeremiah raised his eyebrows in question. "The symbol, on the cover of the book? She had a tattoo similar to it, right here." He tapped his index finger on his collar bone.

Wincing, Isla did her best to try and hide her reaction to that little tidbit. Unfortunately, just like Jere was a keen observer, so was Drew. He narrowed his eyes at her.

"So what have you gotten out of the translations?" Jeremiah asked eagerly. Drew opened his mouth to answer, but Isla held up a hand to stop him.

She glanced warily at an older couple at another table within earshot. "Maybe we should discuss this back at the cabin."

Nodding, Jeremiah pulled out enough cash for the check and a tip, and the three of them headed back to *Taigh na Beinne*.

₭Å

Once they were settled back at the cabin, Isla passed beers around. By the time he had a cold beer in his hand, Jeremiah was practically jumping out of his skin to find out about the translations.

"Alright, spill it," he growled.

Drew chuckled at his friend and sipped his beer slowly, winking at Isla. "I'm afraid there isn't a whole lot I can tell you. I've been over the scans you sent me hundreds of times, and most of it is written in a form of Old Latin that is virtually unrecognizable. Your only hope is to dig up someone who is an expert on this particular subculture."

"Damn it," Jeremiah whispered. "I was hoping we would get some answers."

"What is it you're trying to find the answers to?" Drew asked quietly, seeming to wait for Jeremiah to meet his eyes.

Jeremiah glanced where Isla stood with a wary gaze fixed on Drew. She rubbed her arms as if she was chilled. It was clear that she didn't trust the newcomer enough yet to tell him her secret. Sighing, Jeremiah scrubbed a hand over his face.

"There have been strange things happening on the island since I've been here. Abductions, what I believe to be possessions, to name a couple. I have reason to believe that these events may be connected to the *auchrim*. Paranormal activity is always strongest around Samhain when, supposedly, the veil between the two worlds is thinned. As we're getting close to Hallowmas, if anything is going to jump out at us, I want to know how to stop it. Is there anything in the texts about killing the *Lochrim* and closing the gateway?"

Drew regarded Jere with a steady gaze for several seconds before shaking his head. "There is nothing in the translatable part of the text that mentions killing the *Lochrim*. It vaguely alludes to cutting off its energy source to trap it, but it doesn't say how that's accomplished. I do believe, however, if one does manage to kill the *Lochrim*, that will close the *locus* for good."

Nodding, Jeremiah sat back against the couch cushions. Mhairi had said as much—nobody knows how or if the *Lochrim* can be killed. "So what *did* you learn?"

"A nice collection of random facts. The book spoke a lot about the power of the *Bruixi* witches, and where it comes from."

Isla sank down to the couch beside Jeremiah. "What did it say?"

"That their powers are primarily elemental. Not only does it exist inside them, but they can draw from the four elements of life to harness and expand their own power."

"Earth, Air, Fire and Water," Isla said quietly.

Drew eyed her speculatively but gave her an encouraging smile. "Exactly. While they are trained in spell casting among their cultural subset, it's usually only used in special circumstances."

Always the storyteller, Drew paused for dramatic effect. "More importantly, the book said that the *Vigilati* have—and I'm paraphrasing this part after drawing my own conclusion—have a predisposition, or possibly even a genetic marker that allows them to manipulate a single element more so than the others. And more so than a normal *Bruixi* witch."

Isla glanced at Jeremiah, eyebrows raised. "Interesting. I hadn't come across that in my...research."

Drew steamrolled on with his story, the fire of discovery lighting his eyes. "Also, the largest chunk of translatable text I came across doesn't deal with the *Vigilati* at all. It deals with another race within the *Bruixi* culture—it refers to them almost like a separate species—called the *Feradux*. Sound familiar?"

Jeremiah grunted and his eyes automatically went to the door, expecting Marduk to pop up at the mention of his kind, sort of like Beetlejuice. Satisfied that he wasn't going to see a naked wolf-boy walk through the door, he looked back at Drew. "We've heard of them, but there doesn't seem to be much known about them in general. What does the book say?"

"They are revered, and often feared, among the *Bruixi* society as being the most powerful beings, even more so than the *Vigilati*. Although they haven't the special powers needed to fight the *Lochrim*. The *Feradux* are bred and raised as protectors of the *Vigilati*, but when one of them misuses his power to hurt another, he becomes enslaved to a v*igile*. While the two still share a symbiotic relationship, the *Feradux* no longer has the choice to live on his own and meet his own needs. Their fates are intertwined—if his *vigile* dies, he will too."

"So is the *feradux* indentured to the *vigile* for life?" Isla asked, fiddling with a curl that fell over her shoulder.

"Not necessarily. In order to be released from service, the *feradux* must make a blood sacrifice for his charge. If he survives it, he's free."

"Interesting," Jeremiah said, scratching his chin. "So the shapeshifting is unrelated to the *feradux-vigile* bond."

Drew pegged him with a sharp glance. "Shapeshifting?" he asked, looking back and forth between the two. "There wasn't any mention of that in the book."

"Uh, well, it's something that has come up in our other research," Jere covered.

Sighing, Drew stacked up the copies of his translations that he had brought with him and handed them to Jeremiah.

"Look, I know there's something you're not telling me, and that's okay. I just want you to know that you can trust me, so if you need any help with anything, all you have to do is call."

When Jere raised an eyebrow at the last comment, Drew grinned. "Promise I'll get a new phone as soon as I get to Glasgow. I'll be in Scotland for the next three weeks, so I'm around if you need me."

"Thanks, brother," Jeremiah said, "'preciate ya." Standing up, Drew gave Jeremiah a one-armed hug and kissed Isla on the cheek.

"Gotta be up before dawn tomorrow to keep on schedule, so I need to get back to Brodick and try and find somewhere to stay."

"Don't be silly," Isla said, "you'll stay here, of course."

"Now, I couldn't impose on two young lovers," he said with a grin. "I think I passed a boarding house on the way in."

"Idiot. Boarding house?" Jeremiah tossed a set of keys to Drew, who caught them neatly, a reflex that went back to his college baseball days. "I'm staying here with Isla tonight, but you can stay in the cottage I'm renting."

"Alright, thanks. That'd be great!"

Scribbling down the address and rough directions on a piece of paper, Jeremiah handed it to his friend. "Just leave the key under the mat."

Drew picked up his briefcase and headed to the door, turning to wave at them one more time. "Remember, if you need me..." When Jere nodded, he turned to leave. "'Til next time, *mes chers amis*. Take care!"

Breathing an audible sigh of relief, Isla sank down onto the couch. "That was close. We need to be more careful."

"Yes, we do. For the record, I trust Drew with my life. The only thing he would do is help. He's come along on my investigations before."

"I believe you. I'm still just getting used to even my friends knowing my secret. Hell, I'm still getting used to knowing it myself."

Sitting down beside her, Jeremiah urged her to lay down with her head pillowed in his lap. "Of course you are. That's why I covered with Drew. It's not my secret to share. I just wanted you to know that he meant what he said. He'll be there if we need him."

Nodding, she smiled up at him. "What does *mes chers amis* mean?"

"It means *my dear friends*. It's just one of those things we say back home."

The phrase reminded him of being back in New Orleans, and he had to fight off a brief wave of homesickness.

"How come Drew uses so much French in conversation and you don't?"

Jeremiah laughed and shrugged. "There are certain areas that you'll hear more of the 'Franglish' than others. Drew lived down the bayou from New Orleans, in a much more rural area. My family used to live there too, until my dad died. After that, Mama needed to move into town to find a job."

He smiled when she rubbed his knee. "Also, Drew's grandmother is from France, and he is very close with her. The French, and the accent really, only come out when he lets his guard down or when he gets riled."

"I noticed that." She was silent for a moment, lost in thought. Jeremiah jumped when she suddenly socked him in the arm.

"Ow! What was that for?"

"For making me believe that you two were actually going to fight!"

He just gave her his big, wolfy grin and leaned in for a mind-melting kiss. When they finally broke apart, Isla curled into him and sighed.

It was nice to have another night of feeling warm and safe, he thought as they both drifted off to sleep.

⁊⁊Ⓒ⁊

It was full dark when Isla awoke to light scratching at the front door and a soft whine. Gently detangling herself from Jeremiah, she managed to rise without waking him. She knew that whine, so she opened the door for Marduk.

Slapping a hand over her mouth to stifle her laughter, she observed the proud wolf standing on the porch, soaked to the skin from the driving rain outside. Ice-blue eyes glared at her, which only made her shake harder with silent laughter.

She placed a finger to her lips as she stepped back to make room for him to enter. "Jeremiah's sleeping," she whispered. "Stay here, I'll grab a towel."

Still unsure of how much he understood when he was in wolf form, she regarded him silently. The animal dipped his head slightly in acknowledgement, so Isla went to the linen closet to pull out a towel.

Rubbing the silver fur until it stood on end, she made Marduk look more poodle than wolf. Standing, the wolf cast off any remaining water with a deep, full-body shake. Yawning, Isla returned to the couch and lay back down with Jeremiah, who curled into her without waking.

She knew they should go to the bedroom, but she was so tired and the living room was warm and comfortable. Marduk spun three times before curling up in front of the fire.

Isla smiled as she drifted off again, thinking that they made an odd little family, but that was exactly what they were.

An inhuman screech pierced the quiet night. Jeremiah and Isla bolted upright from their position on the couch. Marduk flashed into his human form and headed back to the bedroom to grab a pair of Jere's sweats.

Jeremiah grabbed the shotgun from the coat closet and loaded some shells while Isla peered out the window. He heard Marduk return to the room, and at the same time Isla gasped and wrenched the door open to run outside.

"*Fuck!*" Jeremiah shouldered the shotgun and took off after her with Marduk right on his heels.

Isla had stopped at the edge of the porch and stood, frozen, staring out into the rainy darkness. Beyond her, Jeremiah could see the silhouette of a man. His face was in shadow, but from the luminescent eyes swirling with shadows, he knew it was Alastore.

When the man stepped forward into the dim light cast through the open door of the house, it became clear that he had a victim. Mhairi Mackay stood in front of the demon, and he had a strong arm locked around her neck.

Jeremiah surged forward, determined to protect Isla's only remaining family, but Marduk stopped him with a hand on his shoulder. With a silent shake of his head, Marduk encouraged Jeremiah to think first and act with care.

Trust nothing, question everything, because things will most definitely not be as they seem. Marduk's earlier words came back to him, and Jeremiah gave the man a quick nod to let him know he understood.

Isla lifted a foot to step down off the porch. "Think, Isla. Breathe. That's not really Mhairi. She's at Sacred Hearts, guarded by doctors and nurses that didn't even want to let *us* in at first, remember?" he said in a low tone.

He saw a shudder rack her slender body but, much to his relief, she stayed put. Three pairs of eyes fixed on the pale, glowing arm that had the projection of Mhairi in a headlock.

Alastore threw his head back and cackled, before pinning each of them with a hard glare. "You think you can defeat me? I will lead you to your graves like lambs to the slaughter." His voice was demonic, and they could hear the echo of pure evil behind it. It sounded like a dozen demons living inside one body, speaking in unison.

Without warning, he wrapped his free hand around Mhairi's head and twisted in opposite directions. They heard a gruesome snap before the image of Mhairi crumpled to the ground.

A strangled cry ripped from Isla's throat as the three of them bounded off the porch. They ground to a halt as Alastore threw his hands up toward the sky, and the pelting raindrops burst into incandescent flames.

The pellets of flame singed their skin, forcing them back to the shelter of the porch. Isla wailed as the spectre of Mhairi seemed to dissolve under the onslaught of fire and rain combined. Alastore's head swiveled back to face them, his eyes gleaming with madness and hatred, pierced through to Isla's soul.

"The little witch thinks she can defeat me! I, who can make the sky rain fire?" He took a step forward and Isla stood her ground. He glared at her with his mouth turned up in a gruesome sneer. "I will *burn* your *life*!" he spat at her.

"You'll watch everything you care for turn to *ash* if you fight me!" He turned his cutting glare to the two men standing shoulder to shoulder on her right and absently gestured toward them. "These will die. *Everyone* will die."

Facing Isla again, he gave her a sickeningly sweet smile. "And you, my dear…You will watch things fall apart. And then, you shall be mine." She shuddered when he licked his lips and leered at her.

Isla would never be able to explain what came over her in that moment. As she focused on the images the demon pushed into her head—the pain and suffering, the dead and dying—it was the thought of Alastore turning his wrath upon Jeremiah that sparked the bone-deep anger inside her.

Storming off the porch into the maelstrom of fire and rain, she felt the breeze on the nape of her neck, when Jeremiah reached for her and missed. Storming toward Alastore, she stopped a few feet in front of him.

The balls of fire raining from the sky seemed to roll off an invisible shield around her and fury radiated from her body. "The hell I will!" she growled at him, gathering her energy low in her chest, preparing for a strike.

Marduk's deceptively calm whisper drifted over to Jeremiah. "He's goading her for a reason. Pushing her buttons. He may be trying to funnel her energy into himself, leaving her vulnerable for him to take her. Alastore does nothing without reason. Stop her."

Jeremiah palmed the shotgun and whispered back to Marduk. "If I shoot him, it's not going to stop him, right?" He waited for the other man to nod before continuing. "But it'll hurt."

Giving him a devious grin, Marduk nodded again. "It sure will. When he's in corporeal form, he'll feel the same pain a human would, he just won't die. It will send him back to the *locus* to recharge."

"Good enough for me." Jeremiah pumped the forestock of the shotgun, drawing Alastore's attention. The demon snarled at him but didn't seem overly worried. That didn't bode well.

Bracing the buttstock of the twelve gauge on his shoulder, he took aim and pulled the trigger. Nothing happened. Cursing, he expelled the dead round and pumped again. Trigger pull, nothing.

Howling with laughter, Alastore returned his attention to the 110 pounds of livid woman that stood in front of him. He cocked his head, like an animal hearing a strange sound. "So pretty, and yet so easy," he began, "*just like your mother.*"

"Dammit," Jeremiah hissed as he saw flames spike out from Isla's fingertips. She was playing right into Alastore's hands, but she just couldn't see it. Shoving the shotgun into Marduk's hands, he turned toward the house.

"I think he's somehow jamming the gun. Maybe if I find something with no mechanics, he won't be able to stop it."

"Hurry."

Well, duh. Jeremiah bounded into the house and began tearing through cupboards and rifling through drawers. He thought about grabbing a knife, but he didn't think any of them should get that close to the demon.

Inspiration struck when he found an unopened bottle of vodka, dusty and forgotten in a cabinet. Grabbing a kitchen rag, he ripped it in half. Emptying a third of the bottle down the sink, he stuffed the rag down into the neck, making sure that it was in far enough to soak up the alcohol.

He snagged a lighter from a drawer and rushed back outside. "Get her out of the way," he ordered Marduk as he passed, not even stopping to make sure the other man heard him. He didn't need to stop, because Marduk ran to catch up with him as he was lighting the rag on fire.

Marduk grasped Isla by the shoulders and yanked her back into his arms as Jeremiah tossed the burning bottle at Alastore's feet.

The projectile immediately exploded, engulfing the demon in a huge wall of fire. The surge of heat was so intense, Jeremiah backed up several steps. He stood, watching as the skin melted off of Alastore's corporeal form to reveal a blackened skeleton.

An inhuman screech rent the air as Alastore pointed a bony finger at them. "You're mine," he croaked as what was left of him dissolved into ash and flame.

"Yeah, yeah, and our little dog, too. Got it," Jere grumbled.

"Hey!" Marduk's indignant tone said he didn't appreciate the dog reference, but Jeremiah didn't much care. Pulling Isla away from wolf-boy, he enveloped her in a tight hug. Resting his chin on the top of her head, he allowed the shudders he had been suppressing to roll over his body. Giving her one last squeeze, he set her away from him and brushed past her, stalking into the house, slamming the door behind him.

When Isla eased her way in through the front door and into the open living area, she saw him standing in front of the fire. He faced away from her with one elbow propped on the mantle. The tension in his body was evident, from his tight shoulders, to his clenched fist, to the way he shoved the fingers of his other hand through his hair.

Standing behind him, she called to him softly, "Jeremiah."

He rounded on her, eyes snapping and body shaking with fury. He started to speak, then clenched a fist over his mouth to stop himself. Taking what appeared to be a few calming breaths, he dropped his hand. "What the hell were you *thinking*?"

She'd expected him to shout at her. That she would have been prepared for. It was the startling calmness of his voice in contrast with the anger in his posture that caused her stomach to drop. "I'm sorry, I..."

He held up a hand to silence her. "You'll let me finish." It wasn't a request. When she nodded, he began to pace fitfully. "After all the work we have done to dig up information on the *bruixi* and the *lochrim*, all of the friends who have risked themselves to help us, how could you risk throwing it all away like that?"

Still she waited, knowing he had to say his piece before he could get past it. "If we're all going to survive this, you have to be more careful. *Think*. Alastore pushes your buttons, tries to make you angry. What do you do? Give him what he wants!"

Whirling around again, his hair stood up in all directions and her heart melted just a little, despite his anger. "Unbelievable..." Letting him rant for a while, Isla waited and took it all in. She knew the anger was driven by fear, and the fear was driven by love.

Eventually the words ran out and the silence from her drew his gaze to her face. She looked up at him and couldn't help but smile.

"I'm sorry," she said, placing a tentative hand on his forearm. "When he threatened all of you...when he threatened *you*, I just lost it." She was embarrassed when her lower lip trembled, but she pressed on, needing him to understand.

"I know that doesn't make it right, for me to be so careless, but that's what happened. I've never known what it's like to have a real family. I've had to do for myself since I was a child." Cursing, she brushed a tear off her cheek.

"Then you came along and showed me. In just a few short months, you have become my home. It doesn't matter if I'm on my island, in the city, or in the States, as long as it's with you. You and Furball out there, and the folks at Expeditions *are* my family, and when faced with the prospect of losing that, I saw red."

Jeremiah pulled her into his arms and kissed her, long and slow. "I get it, I really do. But I'm just a foot soldier in this war, honey. You're the warrior — the only one who can end this. I'm not important."

Pulling him down to her, she kissed him fiercely, invading him with her very essence. Trusting him to hold her up, she wrapped her legs round his waist and held on tight. He shivered as she whispered in his ear. "I'm only a warrior with you holding me up. Do you understand me?" she said fiercely.

"You are just as important as me. If you don't survive this, I won't either. You want to be a soldier in this battle? Then live. Because if anything happens to you, I won't survive that."

He looked as if he might protest, but she bit his earlobe to shut him up. The time for words had ended.

Carrying her to the bedroom, he laid her down gently and began to reverently peel off her clothing. Quickly stripping himself, he slid into bed beside her. The storm had subsided, and soft moonlight filtered in through the window.

Crawling up her body, he covered her. The muscles in his arms rippled as he held himself up to keep from giving her all of his weight. A sudden intensity filled her, and she cupped his face in her hand. "Jeremiah," she said quietly, "I really need you to understand something. It worries me that you don't think you are an important part of this...situation that we're in."

He ducked his head, putting his face in shadow. "Look at me." She waited until his gaze rested on her face again, brimming with love and strength. "You are the *most* important, because without you giving me strength, this would break me."

"No, it wouldn't. You're stronger than you think you are, Isla."

"Maybe so," she answered, tugging on his arm and placing his hand over her heart. "But having you with me, in here, makes me unstoppable." She grinned at him. "I love my island, I love my job, but you are my home. Wherever you go, that's where I'll be. That is...if that's what you want."

He was silent for so long that she began to think he wouldn't answer and her smile faltered slightly. Finally, he leaned in and brushed his lips over hers.

Tilting his head, he deepened the kiss. When he lifted his head, his eyes were bright and his face was determined. "Darlin', if you think I'm letting you get away, you ain't got your head on straight."

And, oh, how she loved the way his accent got so thick when he was turned on. It gave her delightful little shivers all over.

"Seriously, love. In case I haven't said it well enough or often enough, I love you. You're it for me and we're in this thing together, for sure."

Rolling them to their sides, facing one another, he hitched her leg up over his hip. They both gasped as he slid into her in one smooth motion. They made love slow and gentle, the cool light of the moon glinting off their skin.

When Isla finally crested the wave of her release, Jeremiah was right there with her, pouring his whole self into her. Finally rolling apart, Isla curled into his side and closed her eyes. Everything would be fine, she thought.

Chapter Twenty-One

Jeremiah woke up to the incessant croaking of a bullfrog next to his ear. What...what? "What the – ?" he groused, his voice gritty from sleep.

Isla groaned and put a pillow over her face. "Oh dear God, make it stop!"

"What the hell is it?"

"It's your phone, genius. It's Andrew. He changed your ringtone to the frogs while he was fiddling with it," she mumbled and tossed a pillow at him. "Just answer it already."

Clicking the phone onto speaker, Jere glared at the goofy picture Drew had taken of himself to pop up when he called. "What?"

"Aw, now that's no way to talk to your best good friend. Where y'at, Cap?"

"Drew, what the hell time is it? Where are you?"

"Just settling in at my hotel in Edinburgh, thought I'd see if you had any questions about the rest of the translations," he answered, studiously ignoring the first question. "You?"

"We're in bed, you ass! It was a long night."

"Oh, I see. You're all bent outta shape because I interrupted you with your new little piece—"

"Mornin', Dr. Deveraux."

"I'm just pickin' atcha, *cher*. When are you gonna leave that *coullion* and run away with me?"

"Did you have a point?" Jeremiah growled at his friend.

"Sure did. The University set me up with a penthouse suite at the Balmoral. I was wondering if y'all would like to come up north and keep me company for a day or two. We could discuss the translations."

Jeremiah didn't get the feeling his friend had any new information. More than likely, he was just bored. "Don't think we're at a point where we can leave, but we'll think about it and get back to you."

"Sounds good, brother. Take care."

"Yeah, you too."

Sighing, Jeremiah rolled over and buried his face in the crook of Isla's neck, while she gently rubbed his back. Eventually they were able to drift back to sleep.

Another rude awakening came when Isla's phone began to vibrate...against Jeremiah's head. "You have *got* to be kidding me." He took the phone and padded out of the room, thinking that at least one of them should get some sleep.

"Hello?" he answered when he reached the living room.

"Ah...Yes. I was looking for Isla MacAllen. To whom am I speaking?"

"This is Dr. Jeremiah Rousseau." He clenched his jaw hard to try and keep the irritation out of his voice. Rubbing at a sore spot on his shoulder blade, he waited for the speaker to continue.

"Oh, Dr. Rousseau, good. This is Dr. MacLaren from Sacred Hearts. I was calling to talk to Isla about Mrs. Mackay. I'm afraid I have bad news."

Isla felt the mattress dip as Jeremiah sat down beside her. She didn't move, hoping he would give up and go away. After only four hours of sleep, was it too much for a girl to ask to sleep in?

A gentle shake to her shoulder caused her to grumble and peek up at him through her curls. "Darlin', you have a phone call." His tone caused a spark of worry in her, but she brushed it off, thinking he must just be tired.

Moaning a little, she stretched and yawned. "Tell them I'll call them back."

"No, Isla." He waited until she looked up at him again. The look in his eyes caused her heart to plummet. "You need to take this, baby."

Pulse drumming, she accepted the phone from him. "Hello, this is Isla."

"Isla, Dr. MacLaren here. I am afraid I have some bad news about your grandmother."

She listened numbly to the doctor for several minutes.. Finally she ended the call and stared down at the phone in her hands as if she was surprised to find it there.

"She's gone." Her voice was quiet. Brittle.

Sliding over beside her, Jeremiah gently took the phone from her and pulled her to him. "What happened?"

"Not sure, exactly. He used a lot of medical lingo, but the gist of it seemed to be that she died of natural causes. It happened in her sleep, around three a.m. He said she wouldn't have been in any pain."

For a moment, he looked as if he wanted to say something, but shook his head and smiled weakly. "I'm sure he's right."

"What were you thinking? You have to be honest with me, Jeremiah. I'm not going to break."

"Three a.m. The witching hour. I just wonder what time it was when Alastore made his *grande entrée*."

"I looked at the clock when I first woke up. It was two forty a.m. Which would have put the time he 'killed' the astral projection of Mhairi..."

"At around 3 a.m. Damn."

"His hands are all over this," she said. "I don't know how, and I don't know why, but he did this. We have to stop him before he hurts anyone else."

When neither of them were able to go back to sleep, they showered and dressed. As Jeremiah emerged from the bathroom, Isla pulled him into a tight hug, needing to feel his strength surrounding her. Her hands snaked up his back to rub in gentle circles, but he hissed and pulled away when her hand brushed his left shoulder blade.

"What's wrong? Are you hurt?"

He shook his head and gave her a pained smile. "It's nothing. I think I must have gotten burned by some of the fire-rain from last night." And just how ridiculous was that statement, she thought.

Isla decided that they should head into Expeditions for the morning. Having lost her only real family member, Isla felt a pressing need to be surrounded by her little makeshift family.

The lobby was bustling when they arrived. The morning tours were just going out, and Callum and Jack were returning with a group from an overnight camping trip.

Isla smiled as Amy led a group of young kayakers through the lobby with Kieran trailing behind. Just before he went out the door, Kieran turned. "Hey Isla? Almost forgot. Some fancy lookin' bloke came in looking for you. I told him you weren't in yet, but he wanted to wait. He's in the lounge."

Exchanging a worried glance with Jeremiah, she waived the young man off. "Thanks, Kieran, have a good trip and be safe."

"Will do!"

The lounge was created as a place where customers and employees could relax and enjoy the scenery. It had high, vaulted ceilings with exposed rafters, and picture windows along two walls. The view was one of the best the island had to offer. The floor-to-ceiling stone fireplace topped off the rustic coziness of the room.

When she came in, Isla saw the man standing in front of the western window with his back to her. Hearing them enter, he turned around and gave her a sad smile.

"Miss MacAllen?" His voice was smooth, cultured, with a hint of Slavic...maybe Russian. When she nodded, he stepped forward. "I am Alexei Vasiliev. I'm afraid I have some sensitive information to discuss with you." He cast a wary glance at Jeremiah.

"Mr. Vasiliev, this is Dr. Jeremiah Rousseau. Anything you have to discuss can be said in front of him."

Vasiliev appeared disconcerted at first but eventually shrugged and gestured toward one of the plush leather couches. "As you wish. Shall we sit?"

Isla sat at one end of the couch, across from Vasiliev, while Jeremiah sat on the coffee table, seeming to invade the newcomer's personal space with his presence. She had to bite her lip to keep from laughing at his obvious alpha posturing.

"Why are you here, Mr. Vasiliev?" She saw no need in skirting the issue.

"I have come to speak with you about your family's estate."

Confusion marred her brow as Isla tried to process the information. "I don't understand. There isn't any estate. I don't have a family."

"Perhaps you should start at the beginning," growled Jeremiah.

"Yes, of course. I am one of the solicitors on retainer to represent the interests of the patients at the Benton Heights Asylum in Edinburgh."

The name dropped like a stone in the quiet room, and Isla felt the dread welling in her to the tip of her toes. "What would you want with me?" she asked in a small voice.

"You are the daughter of Mrs. Eileen MacAllen, yes?"

"She birthed me, if that's what you're asking," she said coldly.

Obviously uncomfortable, Vasiliev cleared his throat. "I'm afraid Mrs. MacAllen is not well. She has requested that I draw up a will for her, and she is naming you as her beneficiary."

He paused for dramatic effect, as if he were expecting some sort of jubilation. When silence reigned in the room and all he got was a dead stare from Isla, he pressed on. "Of course, you would have to come to Edinburgh to sign all of the official documents, but she plans to leave everything to you when she passes. She has also requested to meet with you before the papers are signed.

Vasiliev jumped when Jeremiah cursed. Isla squeezed his knee, letting him know that she was okay. "Why now?"

"Pardon?"

"Why. Now? Are you aware of what happened between my mother and I, Mr. Vasiliev?"

"Alexei, please. I only know what little Mrs. MacAllen has told me...that because she was an alcoholic, you were taken from her at a young age and put in an orphanage."

She laughed, but the sound was hollow and humorless. "I haven't seen my mother in twenty years, *Alexei*. Not since she slit my throat when I was eight."

The dark-haired man's chocolate-colored eyes widened, and Isla lifted her chin back so that the scar was visible. "She had told me that my grandmother, who would have been my only other living relative, was dead, when in reality Eileen had kicked her out and told her never to come back. After my mother tried to kill me, I was put in an orphanage and I never heard from her again. I assumed that she must have died in prison or in whatever cage they put her in. No offense."

Vasiliev shrugged weakly, clearly shaken and off-kilter. "None taken, of course. I apologize for bothering you and bringing up these obviously painful memories. However, if you'll allow it, I do have a piece of advice."

When she gestured for him to continue, he nodded his thanks. "Whatever happened between you and your mother, she isn't going to be with us much longer. So if you need any kind of closure—if you have anything you've always wanted to ask or say to her—then I would encourage you to do so. I know it's none of my business, but for what it's worth, I am no stranger to unfinished business."

A shadow crossed his face in the space of a second, before he rose and shook hands with both of them. He handed Isla a business card with an apologetic smile. "Should you decide to visit, just give me a call and I'll set it up for you. Just think about it."

"Thank you for coming all of this way, Mr. Vasiliev. I'll show you out."

He raised a hand to stop her. "No need. I'll find my way." And then he was gone. Isla sank back down on the couch and stared at the card in her hand.

Jeremiah sat next to her and turned to face her. "You don't have to do anything, you know. You can just throw it away."

She shook her head. "Yes, I do. Vasiliev was right. If I don't go, I'll always regret not confronting her. And besides, the most important thing right now is learning how to defeat Alastore. She may have information that can help us."

Squaring her shoulders, Isla raised her eyes to Jeremiah's face.

"I'll call Drew and see if his offer to take one of the rooms in his suite is still open. We can drive up today and spend a few days in the city while Vasiliev sets up the visit."

Silently, he pulled her into his arms and kissed her deeply, and Isla knew he was trying to give her all the strength he had.

ॐ

As they stood in front of the Benton Heights Asylum, Isla felt a cold fist of dread surround her heart. The five-story stone building was an imposing figure, silhouetted against the early evening sky.

It resembled a medieval keep, complete with battlements and turrets. She wondered if it had been built to look that way or if the building had been converted. Iron bars on the upper level windows reminded her of what exactly the facility was meant to house. Dangerous criminals who were deemed unable to stand trial due to lack of mental faculties.

They approached by the front walk that wound its way through what probably used to be elaborate gardens, left to grow wild from lack of care.

Pausing at the front steps, Isla glanced around at the dismal setting and then turned back to Jeremiah. "Don't let me forget who she is."

He nodded. She knew that Jere would understand her first instinct would be to feel sorry for someone who had to live in this environment, and she may need a reminder as to why her mother had earned her place at the forbidding institution.

They were greeted at the front door, not by a doctor or medical staff, but by Alexei Vasiliev, the solicitor. The man looked rather eerie himself, like he belonged in the freakish establishment with his pale skin, dark hair and eyes, and coal-grey suit.

"I am glad you decided to come, Miss MacAllen. I am a strong believer in the importance of closure." He shook hands first with Isla, and then with Jeremiah. When they stepped into the foyer, the only sound that could be heard was their feet tapping on the marble floors and the distant beeping of a heart monitor.

As they descended a long hallway, lit by flickering fluorescent bulbs, Isla eyed the crumbling ceiling and the walls where the paint was peeling away.

Isla had to bite the inside of her cheek to keep from saying something about the conditions. Despite her resolve, she lost the battle.

"Who takes care of the...upkeep of the facility?" she asked with what could only be described as a haughty sniff.

Vasiliev did have the good grace to look apologetic when he answered. "The asylum is running on a skeleton crew right now with just enough staff to care for the remaining residents."

"Remaining residents?"

The young man nodded while ushering them into the stairwell. "Yes. The current residents will be the last to live here. Benton Heights lost government funding and private donations have long since stopped coming. It was decided that the current residents would be allowed to stay until the time that they pass away, after which the facility will close for good."

"Why not just transport the residents to other institutions?" Jeremiah asked as they reached the third floor and exited the stairwell.

Alexei stopped in his tracks and turned slowly, pinning them with an intense stare. "Make no mistake, while this is not a prison, *all* of the patients here are extremely dangerous and are in various stages of mental decay. Please don't forget that."

He started down a narrow corridor and they followed him. "Benton Heights had neither the security nor the resources to transport the residents. And, frankly, no one would take them. Since most of them could not survive in a prison environment, due to severe psychoses, it was decided to let them continue on living here."

They stopped in front of a thick metal door with a small, square window inset in it. There was a cracked nameplate underneath the window that read *E. MacAllen*. Taking a deep breath, Isla looked over at Jeremiah, and he nodded. Yep, this was happening.

"Are you ready?" Alexei asked.

"As ready as I'll ever be to confront my would-be murderer," she mumbled. The solicitor knocked lightly on the door but didn't seem to expect an answer. Sticking a key in the lock, he shoved the heavy door open with a creak.

The three of them stepped into the dimly lit room, and then Alexei nodded to them. "I'll wait outside. Take all the time you need."

There were similarities with Mhairi's room at Sacred Hearts—sparsely furnished with a bed, table, and rocking chair, and a crucifix above the bed. However, Eileen's room was dusty and unkempt with water stains on the ceiling and cracked linoleum on the floor.

It was the wall beside the bed that immediately drew their attention. There were dozens of drawings taped to the walls. They looked like the scribbles of a child, but the subjects were eerie screaming figures and what appeared to be runic symbols. There were also incoherent writings carved and painted into the eggshell paint, some under the pictures and some over.

Eileen lay on the bed on her side, facing away from them. At least, Isla thought it was her. Her face wasn't visible from that position. She jumped at the sound of metal scratching across the linoleum as Jeremiah pulled up a chair for her.

Sorry, he mouthed. Slowly, she lowered herself onto the chair and wiped sweaty palms on her jeans. She cleared her throat once, then again. "Hello, Eileen. Mr. Vasiliev told us that you had asked to see me." Her voice was gravelly, and she couldn't catch her breath. She didn't sound like herself.

The frail body in the middle of the bed rose up and Eileen turned to face them. No matter how much mental preparation she had gone through to get ready for that moment, it still struck Isla like a punch to the gut.

Her face was gaunt, her body skeletal. Black hair was scraped away from her face into a severe bun, lips pinched from age and hard living. But her eyes were bright, sharp, and exactly how Isla remembered them. In-*fucking*-sane.

The unfocused eyes rolled toward her and zeroed in on her face. "Thought I'd killed you."

Isla felt Jeremiah tense from where he stood behind her, arms crossed like a bouncer, glaring at Eileen. The statement didn't faze her too much—she had expected hatred, so mild unpleasantness was tolerable.

"You certainly tried," Isla answered, careful to keep her tone bland. Eileen cleared her throat gruffly, as if her voice hadn't been used in years.

"No...I mean I thought you were dead. It wasn't until I had Alexei start researching my family tree to settle my estate that we realized you were still living. I'm surprised you kept my last name," Eileen finished coldly.

Isla pinned her with a jade green glare, refusing to be intimidated. "I kept my father's last name. Besides, I've nothing to hide." Eileen snorted, but didn't comment on who exactly her father *was*. Isla didn't want to show her hand too early.

"Mhairi was alive too, contrary to what you told me growing up."

"Was?"

"She passed away two days ago at her assisted living facility."

Eileen shrugged a bony shoulder, but her eyes were sharp. "Did you see her before she died?"

"Aye. Once."

While the older woman digested that, she focused her attention on Jeremiah. "Who's this?" Jeremiah remained still and silent, allowing Isla to direct the conversation. He continued to scowl at the woman.

"This is Dr. Rousseau. Jeremiah."

"A doctor? My dear, I've already been committed."

It was Jeremiah's turn to snort. "If I were in charge of your care, you'd be more than committed. I'm a doctor of parapsychology." He narrowed his eyes at her, gauging her reaction.

Raising an eyebrow at Jeremiah, Eileen sneered at her daughter. "He's your lover." It wasn't a question.

"My personal life isn't any of your business."

Ignoring Isla's comment, Eileen looked Jeremiah up and down. "He's handsome. The handsome ones are always dangerous."

Isla rolled her eyes and pinched the bridge of her nose. "Spare me the motherly advice. We're way past that. Why did you ask to see me?"

Shrugging again, Eileen stared at some point on the far wall. "Just to see if you'd come, I imagine. Why did you?"

There wasn't any reason to lie. "To get some closure, I guess. Maybe some questions answered. You going to try and kill me again?"

Eileen stared at her and grinned happily. It was eerie to face a woman who looked so much like her mirror image, staring back at her with madness clouding her eyes. "No need. Your days are numbered anyway. The demon will come to claim you soon," she said in a sing song voice.

Gritting her teeth, Isla took a calming breath to keep from strangling her mother. "Well, since you brought it up, what can you tell me about Daddy Dearest?"

Pursing her lips, Eileen glanced at the window and then turned back to Isla. "Charlie was—"

"We both know that I wasn't talking about Charlie. Tell me about Alastore." Eileen shrank back against the wall and hissed as if she'd been bitten. "Don't speak his name to me!"

Isla wasn't proud of the little tingling of satisfaction she got from rattling Eileen's calm exterior, but it was there nonetheless. She waited a beat until the woman's body relaxed.

"How did he come to you? I got the feeling it wasn't your intention to be unfaithful to your husband."

Eileen shook her head vehemently and tears gathered in her eyes. "No, never. I loved my Charlie. *He*," she spat the word, "began coming to me in dreams, taunting me with my darkest fears and most depraved desires. I would often wake up somewhere else in the house, or even outside, with no memory of how I got there."

Isla's eyes widened, and although a sharp intake of breath was the only sound she made, Eileen's fierce gaze zeroed in on her. "It's happened to you, too."

"Only once."

Laughing humorlessly, she continued. "How it starts. He finally came to me one night when Charlie was in the city on business. I always used to think that he approached me disguised as Charlie, but in retrospect, it was much more simple than that."

"How so?" Jeremiah asked, leaning forward in the chair he had pulled up for himself. Isla smiled to herself at his inquisitive nature.

"I think somehow he put the suggestion in my mind that I was really seeing Charlie. Occasionally, the truth would sink in, and their faces would become interchangeable. The demon was so handsome and compelling in his own right that I just turned a blind eye to what I knew inside. That this was not my husband."

The unexpected swell of sympathy that rose inside of Isla scared her just a little. "Why would he do that? Seek out an average human woman to seduce? What does he gain from tricking you into bed?"

"You." Jeremiah spoke up, and Isla was surprised to see Eileen nod at him, respect evident on her ravaged face.

"Exactly right," she said. "This 'average human woman', as you put it, would be the mother of the next generation of one of the most powerful witch bloodlines ever to exist."

Isla snorted, disbelief coloring her face. "That's not what you used to say. The old ways that Mhairi practiced were anything from pure nonsense to devil worship, according to you!"

Shaking her head sadly, Eileen lifted a shaking hand to pat at her hair. "I did say those things, yes. Part of it was denial—I didn't want to believe such things existed—and another part of it was pure selfishness. It was a part of my mother that I would never get to share...never get to understand. Adolescent frustration turns into hurt and anger...and so on and so forth."

Isla's eyes widened as it occurred to her that she had never once considered Eileen's perspective. What it would be like growing up with a mother who was a powerful *bruixi*, knowing that she would forever be ordinary. "I can see how that may have been hard," she capitulated.

"Let's get back to Alastore," Jeremiah said. "What do you think he sought to accomplish by setting out to create a *Lochrim-Bruixi* hybrid?"

Looking at him as she would a slow child, Eileen leaned forward to pat his hand. To his credit, he only recoiled slightly. "To create the ultimate weapon, dear. An offspring that he could nurture and train in his depraved ways, with the power to destroy the race."

"That's why you tried to kill me."

Eileen nodded, and it chilled Isla to see the utter lack of remorse in her face. "He would have taken you. Used you as a weapon to destroy us all. Whatever my feelings toward my mother, I am positive that the *vigilati* are the only barrier between our world and a hell like no one has ever known."

"Bullshit. Let's not pretend you didn't go bat-shit crazy and start believing that Isla was the devil's daughter. *And* let's recognize that Isla was a living, breathing reminder of your weak-willed infidelity, and rather than directing that anger toward yourself, where it belonged, you took it out on an eight-year-old child!"

Isla gasped, and Eileen screeched as she reared back her hand to slap him. He snagged her wrist before she could connect and squeezed just a little harder than was necessary. She clenched her teeth and glared at him.

"We can sit here like normal human beings and have a rational discussion about a mutual enemy, but what we aren't going to do is forget who and what *you* are."

Jeremiah gaped at the older woman when she dissolved into a fit of maniacal giggles. He dropped her wrist like she was a leper.

"Doesn't matter!" More cackling. "None of it matters. He's found you now and he will have you!" Hearing her mother parrot the words Alastore had said days before caused Isla's skin to crawl.

"He still visits me, you know. I know about all of his plans for you. Samhain approaches, dear."

Jeremiah slapped heavy hands onto his knees and stood up. "Yep, time to go. That's enough, Isla." Smiling sadly, she nodded to him and stood. "Goodbye, Eileen." They turned and headed for the door.

"You will be the downfall of your people, Isla. Remember that," she called happily. Isla froze, shoulders tensed, and slowly turned back around to face her mother.

"There's one thing that Alastore didn't figure into his perfect plan."

Eileen cocked her head like a curious puppy, so strangely childlike in manner that it seriously gave Isla the creeps. "And that is?"

"Free will." Turning on her heel, Isla stalked out of the room, leaving Jeremiah to catch up.

The drive back to their hotel in Edinburgh was quiet, the air thick with worry and unspoken thoughts. Jeremiah let it go for as long as he could, and then he broke the silence. Reaching out, he wound one of her silky smooth curls around his fingers.

"Proud of you," he said, giving her a lopsided grin.

She laughed and, as always, the husky sound sent lust racing through him like a shot of adrenaline. "What for?"

"Are you kidding? You held it together better than I did back there. I'm sorry I lost it, but she was trying to manipulate you. To make you forget."

"I know she was," she replied, and paused. "It's nice though, having someone want to fight for me. I've been on my own so long that I've gotten used to only relying on myself." Grabbing his hand, she pressed a kiss to his palm, causing him to shiver.

Forcing himself to concentrate on driving, he squeezed her hand and disentangled his own to place it back on the wheel. "What did you mean, free will?"

She was silent for a long while, before she took a deep breath. "What I meant was if Alastore's goal was to create a hybrid that he could train for his own purposes, what assurance did he have that the *Lochrim* side would win out? As easy as it would have been for him to turn me against the *bruixi*, it would have been just as easy for them to do the same against him. So it follows that as much damage as I could have done to my own people, I should be able to do to him and his. The fact that I grew up alone, away from any knowledge of both the *bruixi* and the *auchrim*, makes me the wildcard. Classic nature versus nurture."

Understanding dawning, Jeremiah's mind began to race. "So if he believed that you had the power to destroy the *vigilati*, it follows that you should have the power to destroy him too."

"Exactly." Her dimples winked as her smile beamed out at him. "It seems as though he may not have anticipated not being able to win me over. Or the fact that I would have a supernatural crime-fighting dream team backing me up. With you and Marduk helping me, I *will* find a way to destroy him."

As pride swelled in him at her bravery, fear for her clenched his gut. Four days until Samhain and whatever showdown fate had planned for them.

"Jeremiah." Her voice jolted him out of the web of his own thoughts.

"Hmm?"

"We should tell Drew what's going on." When he looked at her in surprise, she explained. "As much as we gained from the meeting with Eileen, we still don't know how to kill Alastore. Now, more than ever, we need to know what is in that book. I think he'll be able to help us more if he knows what we're looking for."

Jeremiah let out a breath he didn't know he'd been holding and smiled. "I think that's a good idea. And for what it's worth, you can trust him."

"I trust you."

"Besides, Eileen said something to me after you walked out that I need to run by Drew. Maybe he can help me figure out what she meant…"

Jerking up straighter in her seat, Isla turned to face him. "What did she say?"

As he'd turned to make his exit, Eileen's voice had stopped him once more. "Have you felt the laqueum *yet?" He froze, but didn't look back at her. "My daughter is not the only one whose time runs out on Samhain."*

"She asked me if I've felt the *laqueum* yet."

"What does that mean?"

"I'm not entirely sure. I have some ideas, but I want to pick Drew's brain about them. Hopefully something was mentioned in the text that might bring me some clues. I'll give him a call and ask him to meet us at the hotel."

Chapter Twenty-Two

Drew sat facing them with a stunned look of disbelief on his face. Mouth hanging open, he looked back and forth between Jeremiah and Isla as if he expected one of them to say "syke!" and take it all back.

Having just given Drew the cliffnotes version of *bruixi* lore and a quick rundown of recent events on the island, the two of them shared a worried look, hoping they had made the right decision.

"You're telling me that she's a witch," Drew tipped his head toward Isla, "and the two of you are embroiled in some kind of armageddon battle between good and evil, the prize being the salvation or destruction of humanity. Do I have this about right?"

His voice was tinged with the slightest bit of hysteria and he laughed humorlessly.

"Drew, man, you've been in investigations with me before. You know that there are things in this world that defy explanation. Isla is one of those things."

"I'm not fond of parlor tricks, but I can prove it if you like," Isla said calmly. Drew looked uneasily at her, as if afraid she may actually be telling the truth.

"Go ahead, Isla. I think he needs to see it."

Stretching out her fingertips toward Drew's water glass on the other side of the coffee table they sat around, Isla used her energy to push and pull it to her. Waving a hand over the glass, the water congealed into an orb of liquid that floated out of the glass and hovered over her hand.

She held it out to Drew, who dipped his finger into it and drew it back to stare at his dripping wet skin. With a flick of Isla's wrist, the ball exploded into vapor, causing Drew to jump.

He scrubbed a hand over his face and leaned back in the plush chair he sat in. "Okay," he said finally.

"Okay? Okay what?" Jeremiah's voice was tense, until he felt Isla's calming hand on his knee.

"Okay, you're in love with a witch. I believe you, I just need a second." Standing up, Drew walked to the fridge and grabbed three beers.

"Why are you telling me this now?"

"It was my call," Isla spoke up. "Jeremiah wanted to fill you in when you visited Arran, but I was afraid. I've had people who merely *suspect* that I'm a witch turn on me. I'm somewhat of a pariah where I live, and I just didn't want to have to worry about another witch hunt—pun intended."

"I can understand that. It's hard to know who you can trust with your vulnerabilities," Drew conceded.

"But after visiting my estranged mother, we were left with more questions than answers about my lineage and the threat we're up against. We really need to get everything we can out of the book you're translating, and I thought you would have a better chance if you actually knew what you were looking for."

Laughing genuinely for the first time, Drew seemed to relax a little. "Well, I appreciate that, *cher*."

Sitting back and taking a swig of his beer, Jeremiah looked at Drew. "So, do you have any questions for us before we get to work?"

"Yeah, one. When I visited you, you mentioned shapeshifters—I don't buy for a second that this is something that just came up in your research. Are you ready to tell me about that now, too?" He raised an eyebrow, and Jeremiah knew without a doubt that his friend was issuing a challenge.

"Isla?" he questioned, not wanting to push her.

"Drew, you remember reading about the *feradux* in your research, right?" When he nodded, she continued. "Marduk is my *feradux*, and he spends most of his time as a wolf. The animal side serves as sort of a spirit guide for us, I think. He is here to protect me and help me however he can, but he cannot fight against Alastore."

"Where is he now?"

Isla shrugged a delicate shoulder. "Back on Arran, I suppose. He can only maintain his human form for so long, so I figured he wouldn't be able to make the trip—"

A brisk knock interrupted her. Drew frowned as he stood to answer the door. His penthouse suite was on a private floor, and any visitors had to have a key card to take the elevator all the way up.

He opened the door to reveal a tall, lanky stranger. A dark-haired young man with ice-blue eyes and a sardonic smile. Obviously stunned, Jeremiah watched Marduk as he walked through the door past a slack-jawed Drew and across the room, and lowered into a spot on the floor at Isla's feet.

"*Merde!*" Drew exclaimed, slamming the door and returning to his seat. Jeremiah fist-bumped the Marduk and Isla patted him on the shoulder.

"How did you know where to find us?" Isla asked, fondness evident in her tone. He shrugged a lean shoulder.

"You called and I came, *domina*. That is our way."

Taking pity on his friend, Jeremiah introduced their new visitor. "Drew, this is Marduk. Apparently he could make the trip after all. Marduk, my good friend, Dr. Andrew Deveraux. He is going to help us with our research so we can find a way to defeat Alastore."

Rising to grab a beer for Marduk, Jeremiah clapped Drew on the back. "Ready to get to work?"

Drew pulled out his laptop and set it on the coffee table. Jeremiah did the same, and Isla snuggled close to him to be able to see the screen. "So what are we looking for, specifically?" Drew asked.

"Any mention of the *Lochrim* in general and of Alastore in particular. That will give us a starting point for translations."

Looking back down at his screen, Drew nodded. "I wrote a program to help search through the texts. I can plug in a particular word and the algorithm searches the images of the pages. At least I hope it does. Haven't had time to test it yet."

"You're such a nerd, " Jeremiah teased, "but it benefits us, so I'll allow it. There is one other word we should search for—*laqueum*. Eileen mentioned that word to me before we left."

They researched in silence for about an hour—Drew pouring over the texts with his program and Jeremiah and Isla doing internet research and rough translations of excerpts from the text. Marduk stretched out on the floor and appeared to take a nap.

"Think I got something," Drew murmured, staring intently at the screen. "My program found several mentions of *laqueum* in this passage. It will take me a few minutes to translate it...if I'm able to at all."

Pursing his lips, Drew studied the writing and began to scribble furiously on a notepad he'd pulled out of his computer bag. His lips moved silently as he formed the words that he translated in his head.

Finally he put down the notebook and raked a hand through his spiky blonde hair, causing it to stand up in all directions. "Well, this is interesting."

Closing his laptop, Jeremiah sat forward. Isla shook Marduk who awoke with a light snore. They all watched Drew intently as he began to explain his findings.

"Up until now, we've been operating under the assumption that the *bruixi* genetics pass from maternal grandmother to granddaughter. It was implied that the father's DNA has no bearing on that outcome."

Isla looked warily at Jeremiah. "I never really thought about it. So much emphasis is put on the matriarchal lineage. For lack of a better term, I assumed the father was just a sperm donor."

"Exactly. But according to the book, *bruixi* mates are chosen by the gods. They are men who have latent power that has lain dormant all their lives, but those powers can be unlocked when they are united with their mate."

Jeremiah cleared his throat and clutched Isla's hand just a little too tight. "How do they know? How do they know they've found the right mate?"

"The text puts forth three ways to tell. One, the two of them will be drawn together by circumstance or unseen forces, even across great distances. Two, the male will have come in contact with a *bruixi* sometime in his early life. And three, once the couple declare their devotion to one another, a *signa* will appear on the male's body, matching that of the *bruixi*."

"Are you serious?" Isla exclaimed. "It really says that?"

"I am, indeed. It is called the *laqueum*. The word actually translates to *snare* in new Latin, but in context, I believe it is closer to *bonding*. Have any of these things happened to you, Jere?" Drew raised an eyebrow at his friend.

"Well, I did come in contact with someone who I know now was *bruixi*. And I traveled from Louisiana to Scotland to find Isla based on a few rumors of a witch on the island. But I don't have any mark on me."

Drew frowned, and Jeremiah caught Isla staring at him intently. "What, Isla?"

She clamped her lips tightly and shook her head, flicking a gaze toward Drew, and then turned wide eyes back for Jeremiah. It was obvious that she didn't want to speak in front of Drew.

Jeremiah ran a hand over his face and turned to his friend. "Give us a minute?"

"Of course," Drew said and nodded toward the bedroom. "Why don't you two go in there and talk while the kid and I keep reading?" Marduk snapped his teeth at Drew but said nothing.

Once they were alone, Isla lunged for Jeremiah, tugging at the hem of his shirt. "Take this off!"

Laughing, he grabbed her questing hands and glancing at the closed bedroom door. "Now's not the time, darlin'. We have company."

"Oh, swallow your ego for two seconds and take off the damn shirt!"

"Yes, ma'am," he said, grinning. He tugged the t-shirt over his head, muscles rippling under the tattoos encircling his arms, and he smirked at her. "Now what?"

She roamed her hands over his skin, up his arms and over his shoulders, and again he winced when she brushed over his left shoulder blade. Gently, she explored the area with light brushes of her fingertips.

There were raised lines underneath the skin and, like cat scratches, they were welting up and turning red. Tracing the circular pattern with her fingertips, she allowed a ghost of a smile to touch her lips.

"I thought so."

"What? What do you see?" Jeremiah turned his head, panicking as if a spider were on him, and struggled to see an area of his body that he obviously had no access to. She gestured toward the triple mirror in the massive bathroom, and he turned so that he could see the reflection of his own back. He could see the reddened and raised lines underneath the skin of his shoulder blade. It looked as if, indeed, a signa was forming under his skin.

"Holy shit," he breathed, turning to sit down on the bed before he fell down. He was startled when he suddenly had his arms full of warm, willing woman. Isla straddled him, grasped his face in her hands, and kissed him. He opened for her as her tongue caressed the inner recesses of his mouth. His eyes crossed as she sucked on his tongue and rocked against him.

Remembering they weren't alone, he reluctantly broke the kiss with a nip to her bottom lip. "What was that for?" he asked, panting hard.

"For being mine." She smiled brightly and kissed his nose. "It looks like you have my *signa*. It's still under the skin, but I have a feeling by Samhain, it will look just like mine."

He caressed Isla's cheek for a moment before rising, crossing his arms over his lap to hide the little *problem* she gave him.

They headed back out to the main suite and showed the others what they'd found. He looked at Drew, his brows knitted together. "So, what, does this mean I'm a witch too?"

"Not exactly. Right now, your powers are dormant, and they exist only to fuel Isla's energy to be able to use her power. In time, you may be able to learn how to do some tricks of your own."

The three of them laughed at that thought, but were startled by a flash of blue light and a burst of smoke. At Isla's feet was a silver wolf, who whined and laid his head on her foot.

Drew stood abruptly and backed away, knocking over his chair. "Oh my God —"

"Take it easy," Jeremiah said calmly. "You know the *feradux* are shifters."

Reaching down, Isla ruffled the fur behind Marduk's ears. "He must have drained his energy finding us. He can't hold his human form for long once he's depleted it. Marduk, why don't you go into the bedroom and rest?"

Nudging her leg with his cold nose, the wolf rose and slunk into one of the two bedrooms in the suite.

Taking a deep, shuddering breath, Drew righted his chair and sat back down. "Well, now I've seen everything."

Stretching out, Isla rested her legs across Jeremiah's lap, and they returned to their research. This time, they skimmed the scans that he had made from the ancient book. Silence reigned in the room for another hour or so.

Yawning, Isla leaned into Jeremiah and squinted at the screen. "What's that?" She pointed to scrawled handwriting in the margin of the page and seemed to struggle a bit with the pronunciation as she murmured the words.

"Vetera novis per loqui et respondere monent."

As soon as she read the words, Jeremiah knew it was a mistake. Isla looked down at her arms and scratched at them, as if bugs were burrowing underneath her skin. She looked over at him, her eyes wide with fear, and he felt helpless to stop what was happening.

Jeremiah watched in horror as Isla threw her head back with a loud gasp, as if she struggled to pull air into her lungs. Her body bowed against the back of the couch as she twitched and convulsed, the tendons and veins in her neck standing out in relief.

Fear lanced his heart as he grabbed her arms to try and still the violent shaking. "Isla! Answer me, sweetheart. Breathe!" Marduk bounded back into the room, oblivious to his nudity, and stood behind Jeremiah, staring nervously at his charge.

"What happened?" he demanded.

"She read some words in the book...I don't know if it was a spell, or what. Do something!"

Before he could respond, Isla finally drew a deep breath and her body fell still. When she stirred and sat up, she looked out at them with empty eyes.

Jeremiah ran his hands over her face. "Isla, honey. Talk to me. What happened?" He began to panic when she just sat there like a limp ragdoll. Her face began to flicker and change, like an old tube TV stuck between two stations. Slowly the static coalesced into a face that was etched in his memory.

She had stick straight ebony hair, dark skin, and milky opalescent eyes. The most recognizable feature, however, was the large *signa* that writhed and shivered on her left cheek.

Jeremiah was stunned, rooted to his spot like an oak tree. *Impossible!* The spectre that was once Isla swiveled its head around to stare at him through those hollow eyes. "Hello again, young one," she said in a gravelly voice.

"Wh—Who are you?" Jeremiah flicked a glance over to where Drew sat, transfixed, which assured him that his friend also had no idea what was going on.

"My name is Leora. I am the *Bruixi* goddess of fire."

Jeremiah continued to stare. "Of course you are," he grumbled. "Who else would you possibly be?"

The image of Leora frowned at his sarcasm. Well, that was just too damn bad. He'd had about all he could stand of the hocus pocus for the night. He frowned right back at her.

"If you're a goddess, then why were you telling fortunes in the *Vieux Carré* with all of the other gypsies?"

"To watch over you, my darling. Your survival was imperative. *Is*, rather. And, as you well know, I was right to be concerned."

"How did you get here?"

"The little one here must have stumbled upon a channeling spell. Her power is so great, she has but to speak the spell and it is cast. She need not put any effort behind it."

"Why am I so important?"

"Because you are to be the mate of the most powerful *vigile* ever in existence. You are to be the mate of the leader of the *Praedos*. Your fates are now inextricably entwined. She cannot survive without you, nor you without her. It will take both of you to win this war."

"If you know so much about all of this, surely you can tell us how to defeat Alastore."

Leora shook her head regretfully. "Unfortunately, I cannot, because it has never been done. The one thing I do know is that Isla is the only one who can do it. Her particular...lineage is perfectly suited for it, but only she can harness that power."

Rubbing his eyes wearily, Jeremiah sighed. "Can you at least tell us how we will find the *locus*?"

"The way will be lit by the Samhain moon," she said with a half-smile.

"Well, that's not cryptic at all," he muttered, and she laughed. "Thank you for watching over us. If you would, please release Isla so she can get some rest."

Inclining her head, Leora smiled at him. "If either of you should have need of me, you need but speak the spell, and I will come."

With a flash and a pop, Isla's face was restored and she slumped over into Jeremiah's waiting arms. As she stirred, she clutched her head and squeezed her eyes shut. "There has *got* to be a better way to have a conversation with an ancient *bruixi* goddess," she said weakly.

Laughing uneasily, Jeremiah tugged her close to reassure himself that she was unharmed. "Do you remember anything that was said?"

He felt her nod against his chin. "I heard everything, clear as day. It was like I was there...only I wasn't."

Kissing the top of her head, Jeremiah looked at Drew and Marduk. "I think that's enough for tonight, boys. Let's all get some sleep. Marduk, you can bunk out here for the night."

As they split up to go to their respective beds, Jeremiah couldn't help but wonder what would become of all of them.

₭℞

It was the evening before Samhain when the small group gathered at *Taigh na Beinne*. Drew had come back to the island with them, refusing to take no for an answer. The four of them, clearly on edge, sat around the fire, bodies coiled with tension.

Sighing, Jeremiah surged to his feet and ran agitated fingers through his hair. "This is about ridiculous."

Isla knew exactly how he felt. She could do nothing but worry about the battle to come.

"Nothing is going to happen until after midnight anyway, so there's no sense in worrying about it right now." Tapping furiously on his phone, he dialed Callum and told him to round up the crew and head to the cabin.

In less than an hour, the cabin was alive with activity, filled to the brim with friends talking, laughing, drinking. Only Jeremiah, Isla, and Marduk chose not to imbibe, needing to keep clear heads for the battle ahead.

While Drew was being introduced to the Expeditions staff, Isla sat back and watched her friends, her heart swelling with pride and affection. This is family, she thought. As her eyes roamed over them, she saw Drew flirting shamelessly with Amy, with a disgruntled Kieran watching from off to the side.

Creeping over to him, she bumped his hip with her own and smiled. "Why don't you just tell her how you feel?" she asked, gesturing at Amy with her water bottle.

Kieran looked back at Amy talking with Drew. "Are you kidding? She's...and he's... She thinks of me like a little brother. She said that!"

Isla placed a hand over her heart in mock pain. "Ouch! Kieran, maybe it's never occurred to her to look at you that way because you keep your feelings to yourself. You won't ever know what she would think until you give her a chance."

The young man merely grunted and continued to glare at Drew. "Who would ever take me over him?"

Setting her water bottle down, Isla grabbed his hands and tugged him around to face her. "If you don't believe in yourself, then there's no point in expecting others to! You are handsome, smart, and resourceful, and anyone would be lucky to have you."

Grinning, Kieran bent down and kissed her cheek, his shock of black hair falling over his forehead to tickle her skin. "Thanks, Mom."

He winced when she punched him in the shoulder. "Go on, get over there!" As she turned around to search for Jeremiah, her gaze landed on Brynna in a corner, nervously eyeing Marduk. *Wonder what's gotten into the little Irish*, she thought, but decided not to worry about it. Her friends could take care of themselves and she needed to let them.

Isla sauntered over to where Jeremiah was chatting with Jack and molded herself to his side. The way his arm automatically went around her warmed her to the core. In her periphery, she saw Amy excuse herself from Drew and go outside for some air. She smiled to herself when she saw Kieran follow shortly after.

Amy stepped out onto the porch and breathed deep of the crisp night air. She shoved her hands into the pockets of her hoodie to fight the biting cold. She enjoyed spending time with her friends, but she had to get some air and escape the slick *Doctor* Deveraux.

The man was perfectly nice and incredibly gorgeous, but something about his cocky smile and perfectly pressed clothes reeked of old money. That man had most likely wanted for nothing in his life, and because of Amy's own hard experiences, his attentions annoyed rather than intrigued her. She had no doubt that he expected her to trip over herself at the opportunity to fall into bed with him, and she didn't plan to give him the satisfaction of being right.

She yelped when someone crashed through the door behind her. Afraid Deveraux hadn't taken the hint, she turned, but smiled when she realized it was only Kieran. Breathing a sigh of relief, she started toward him only to draw up short when she saw the look in his eyes. It was dark and intense, almost...hungry.

Her sweet, loyal Kieran was nowhere to be found. That was the last thought that passed through her before he shorted out her brain.

He had followed her with the intention of merely talking to her, possibly taking Isla's advice to tell her how he felt. Best-laid plans went to dust when she turned around, deep blue eyes wide with surprise, hand at her throat. Her cheeks were flushed pink from the cold wind whipping over her skin—her plump lips were open slightly on an inhale. The sight of her shot through him like a punch to the gut, and all of his carefully thought out words flew out of his head.

Burying long, slender fingers into her thick blond hair, Kieran held her still as he captured her mouth in a searing kiss. It was as intense as it was unexpected. She tensed at first. He felt her ball up her fist against his chest as if she wanted to push him away. But just when he thought she would, her body relaxed against him and she opened for him.

Keeping one hand threaded deep in her hair, he let the other one glide up and down her back. Silently cheering when he felt her start to kiss him back, he cupped her jaw to tilt her head and deepen the kiss.

She pushed away from him suddenly, eyes wild and chest heaving, as if she had just remembered where they were...and *who* they were. He'd known there would be some resistance, given her previous opinion of him, so he didn't allow himself to get discouraged. He simply waited patiently, much like one would wait out an unruly child's temper tantrum.

"You can't—we can't...," she sputtered. "Kieran, you know I love you, but babe, I've got five years on you...," she began rambling about all of the reasons why this was not a good idea, eyeing him warily when he smiled. "We're friends, and relationships, hooking up—whatever this is—ruin friend—"

Her rant was cut off when he pressed a finger to her lips. "Shut up." She gasped as he swooped in for another assault, but this time she matched him in intensity. Carding her fingers through his midnight-black hair, she gave as good as she got, nipping at his lips and stroking his mouth with her tongue.

Amy let out a little whimper as Kieran's hands slid down to her ass and jerked her against him, bringing her in full contact with his arousal. She tugged on his hair to bring them even closer, her head spinning.

This was an unexpected development. He could feel her hesitation, and he knew it was because she'd always looked at him as a friend—a younger friend who needed protecting. But he most definitely was *not* a child, and he could take care of himself.

He felt the moment when she gave in. Hooking a leg around his hip, she plastered herself against him, and he shuddered at the feel of her. His hand was just starting to wriggle between their bodies, when they heard the doorknob turn and jumped apart guiltily.

They waved dumbly at Brynna, who ran out to her car to get something. Amy started for the door then stopped to look over her shoulder at Kieran. "Let's go tell Isla we're leaving. Take me home?" He gave her a dazed nod and followed her inside.

Isla smiled to herself as she watched Kieran ushering Amy out her front door like his pants were on fire. She was happy for the two of them.

"You're looking pretty pleased with yourself. What's up?" Jeremiah asked. Isla shrugged and grinned at him.

"Not a thing. Just happy to be here with you, and all our friends." Not buying it for a second, Jere just shrugged and squeezed her tighter, turning his attention back to their friends.

Chapter Twenty-Three

As evening fell and the full moon rose, the house began to clear. Brynna left shortly after Kieran and Amy had, with Callum and Jack following an hour later. Jeremiah looked around at who was left—their motley crew of demon hunters.

Drew was passed out on the couch in front of the fire, and Marduk was yawning in the recliner, no doubt exhausted from trying to keep from going furry all night. Clearing his throat quietly to get their attention without waking Drew, Jeremiah gestured back toward the bedrooms.

"We should all get some sleep, because who the hell knows what we're going to be facing, come the witching hour. Marduk, go on into the guest room. No one will bother you." The young man nodded, stretched, poofed, and trotted off toward the back of the house.

Practically vibrating with nervous energy, Isla paced around the kitchen. "How can I possibly sleep? Too much to think about...it's like Christmas eve, only Santa is an evil, soul-stealing demon."

"Well, that's not creepy at all," he said, chuckling. Moving into the path of her pacing, he grasped her hands and kissed the protest from her lips. "Just go take a long, hot bath and relax a bit. It'll help you get to sleep later. I'll clean up out here and be in to tuck you in when you're done."

She snorted at his cocky wink but followed his advice, heading back to the master bath. She tossed a saucy look over her shoulder at him, causing the grin to disappear and his eyes to fill with sensual promise.

After cleaning up the mess from the impromptu gathering, Jeremiah headed back to their bedroom. That thought caused him to stop in his tracks. When had he started thinking of it as their bedroom? When had he started to think of *Taigh na Beinne* as home?

Shrugging, he decided that he liked the idea. Pausing in front of the door, he had an idea that caused him to retrace his steps to the guest room. Knocking softly, he entered, knowing he would receive no verbal acknowledgement from the wolf. He laughed when he saw the grey lump of fur in the middle of the king-sized sleigh bed. Whoever said canines prefer sleeping on the floor never met Marduk.

Jeremiah plopped down on the mattress with a bounce, earning a low growl from the sleepy beast. "Hey Fleabag," he said, as he nudged the warm mass. "Sorry, I need you to humanize again for just a minute. We gotta talk."

Marduk snarled, but then Jeremiah heard the telltale pop and flash of the shift. "What?" came the disgruntled response.

Rubbing tired eyes, he tossed Marduk a blanket. "First, cover up. I've been doing a lot of thinking about what's going down tonight." He paused and Marduk just stared, waiting for him to finish and not volunteering anything.

"I'm not sure if Isla is ready for this. Her powers are too new. And I don't know that I would survive losing her."

"There really isn't any choice in the matter. This is happening. The Samhain moon has risen, and when it is at its pinnacle, Alastore *will* come for her."

"Yeah, about that. I kind of have a plan...and I need your help." Jere had the grace to look sheepish as Marduk eyed him warily.

"I'm listening."

"I want to look for Alastore myself."

Marduk blinked, gaping at him, and then laughed. "You? What do you have to fight him with, your bare hands? You can't possibly hope to defeat him on your own, a mere human!"

He said *human* the way Jere's people would say *swamp sludge*. Like it was the most repugnant thing he could think of.

"Nothing. I have nothing but my bare hands and my intellect. But I have to try. Her life is worth much more than mine! If something happens to her tonight, I would never forgive myself for not having tried."

Marduk inclined his head, conceding the point. "I think it's a suicide mission, but I get why you want to do it. What do you need me for?"

Staring guiltily at his hands, Jeremiah took a deep breath. Then he pierced Marduk through the heart with anguished hazel eyes. "Keep her here."

"*I beg your pardon?*"

Wincing at the incredulity in Marduk's voice, Jere pressed on. "I just need you to buy me a couple of hours. I figure, in that amount of time, I will have figured out one way or another how this is going to go."

"Let's pretend for one moment that I would actually do this thing that you ask. How would you propose I do it? As you well know, she is quite powerful."

"I don't know. Isn't there some sort of *feradux* spell that can seal a room? You're the magician here, brother."

"I suppose I could come up with something like that. The problem is that confining her walks the very fine line between protecting and helping her and hurting her. If I go against her, it will have terrible consequences for us all."

"Isn't there a way around it? After all, if I pull this off, then it *will* be helping her."

"Point. I could put a caging spell on the bedroom that would prevent her from leaving and from using her powers to free herself—"

"Great. Do that."

"*However*, if she realizes that I am doing it...if she calls me by name and asks me to release her, there is nothing, and I mean *not a thing* that can prevent me from doing so. Understood?"

Jeremiah nodded gravely. "I'll leave after I'm sure she's sleeping deeply enough not to hear me get up. I'll tap on the door when I pass by and that will be the signal to cast the spell."

As Jeremiah hopped off the bed, Marduk grabbed his arm. He raised an eyebrow in a silent question.

"You realize she may not forgive you for this."

Jere stared down at his hands before answering. "I know. But that's a chance I have to take. If it saves her life, it will be worth that and more."

The wolf-boy looked at him and shook his head. "May not even be an issue, since you'll probably end up dead anyway," he said, his smile taking the sting out of the words.

"Gee thanks, mongrel. Just be ready."

Just after 2 a.m., Jeremiah silently slid out of bed. He looked back at Isla, who was sleeping on her stomach, the covers tugged down to reveal her bare back. Her skin was flushed rosy from the warmth of sleep and their earlier lovemaking.

He wanted nothing more than to curl up beside her and shut his eyes to the world. But he didn't have that luxury. He had to protect her. His love. His life.

Dressing painstakingly slowly to keep from making noise, he crept out of the bedroom and down the hall, softly tapping on Marduk's door to give the signal. He gathered a rucksack with a few choice weapons, a flashlight, and his Saint Lauren medal. The Patron Saint of survivors had been with him in times of struggle ever since Katrina, and he was counting on her now.

Without a word or a sound, treading carefully so he didn't wake Drew, he left the house and plunged into the night.

Marduk placed a hand on the door to Isla's bedroom and pushed his power down his arm and through his fingertips. He envisioned it as a light that enveloped the entire room that enclosed his *domina*.

This was to protect her. This was what he was born to do, he thought as he began reciting the spell.

> "*Spiritum sanctum in captionem hujus regni.*
> *Luna non splendebit in lumine est.*
> *Sed invocato nomine feradux ponet eam liberi.*"

He repeated it over and over, allowing its power and meaning to trap his *domina* in a gilded cage.

"Hold the spirit in this hallowed realm. Let not the light of the moon shine on it. Only invoking the name of the feradux shall set her free."

ഇ�രു

Trudging through the shadowy forest, Jeremiah was unsure if he was going the right way. The full harvest moon cast a ghostly glow that filtered through the thick canopy of trees.

Stepping into a clearing of sorts, he noticed that the ground spread out before him had an...aura. A blood-red haze rose from it, and it reflected the eerie light of the moon.

The Samhain moon will light the way. It looked as though Leora had been right. Sucking in a breath, he cautiously followed the trail through the woods, keeping his eyes peeled for anything unusual. Relatively, of course.

Soon the terrain began to look unfamiliar, which was odd since he had explored nearly every square foot of that island with Isla, especially the areas around the cabin. Eventually the dense wooded area thinned and gave way to a wide-open field. One that Jeremiah was sure he'd never seen before.

Crouching down in the tall grass on the outskirts of the field, he surveyed his surroundings. The flat tract of land was bathed in the same wine-colored glow as the trail had been. The Blood Moon taunted him, as if it announced the presence of the malevolence Jeremiah could feel swirling around the open landscape.

In the center of the field was an enormous stone circle that looked to be close to two hundred feet in diameter. Jeremiah thought to himself that it was nearly as large as Stonehenge and looked to be made of similar Sarsen stone.

There was no way he and Isla would have missed this. The *locus* must only be visible during Samhain, and most likely Beltane as well.

Keeping low, he approached the structure carefully. He circled around it, taking in the lay of the land, familiarizing himself with the battlefield. He noticed that one of the stones had some strange runic glyphs carved in it, the symbols pricking at something in his memory that he couldn't quite place.

Leaning in to see better, Jere ran his fingers over the depressions in the stone. Pulling out his iPhone, he snapped a couple of pictures for later, hoping Drew could help him translate the symbols.

He was so engrossed in studying the ancient markings that he never saw the attack coming until it was too late. Each arm was grabbed by a pasty-skinned, shadowy-eyed *auchrim*, and they held him in place with an unnatural strength.

Alastore materialized in front of him, impeccably dressed as always. But this time his eyes were red-rimmed and the eye glyph etched in his forehead vibrated with a bizarre red glow, almost matching that of the Blood Moon.

This time there was no pretense. Jeremiah could clearly see that Alastore was done trying to appear human. His mouth gaped open, serrated teeth dripped saliva.

Jere's eyes widened as the demon gripped the sides of his skull, black-tinged nails digging into the skin. For the second time in his life, he found himself staring into a pair of dead, opalescent eyes with shadows dancing inside them.

He felt the familiar tug at his consciousness, as the edges of his vision began to dim. He felt a wrenching sensation deep within the core of him, as if his soul was literally being ripped out of him.

Head spinning, his knees weakened, and all he wanted was to let go and allow himself the sweet oblivion of sleep.

No! Something screamed at him to fight. He had to push back. He had to end this for Isla's sake. Summoning all of his will and what was left of his ravaged strength, he concentrated on the energy that coiled inside of him. He had no idea what he was doing, but he had to try something.

He imagined his energy to be a lit fuse that would burn and build until it eventually exploded. Alastore and his two minions were thrown back and landed hard about twenty feet away from them.

Taking only a moment to puzzle out what happened, Jeremiah looked down and checked himself over. Everything was intact and he hadn't, in fact, exploded. Something, though, had to have sent the nasties flying. And boy did they look pissed.

Striding toward him aggressively, Alastore thrust out his hands and a wall of fire erupted between them, causing Jeremiah to have to leap backwards to avoid getting burned. He was well aware that while it may be conjured by magick, the demon fire could burn like any other.

Alastore kept blasting at him with those bursts of unholy fire as he approached, the flames nipping at Jere and singeing his clothes. One final thrust of those flames caused Jeremiah to trip in an effort to avoid it, and he tumbled back inside the perimeter of the stone circle. Inside the locus.

Well, shit, he thought. This was bad. Jeremiah's heart lurched as he realized he had failed. God help them all.

Wake up...

Isla groaned in her sleep and tugged a pillow down over her head to shut out the whispered voice. She needed just a little more sleep. Just a little more before she could face the battle for the fate of all humankind.

As the warm blanket of sleep began to slowly cover her again, the voice returned, sharp and insistent for all its whispering.

Wake up...Isla, you have to. Wake. Up.

The single voice became many, hissing in her ears and through her head. They were accompanied by a dull tugging sensation on what she could only describe as her brain stem.

Disgruntled and unwilling to move, she snaked an arm out to Jeremiah's side of the bed, hoping to rouse him to take care of whatever *problem* had arisen now. Her hand reached nothing but cold, empty sheets.

Instantly awake, Isla sat bolt upright in bed, trembling with a feeling of dread that she couldn't explain.

With dilated eyes, she searched the recesses of the inky darkness, already knowing she wouldn't find Jeremiah, but she had to look. "Jeremiah?" she said in a small voice. "This isn't funny. Are you here?"

She paused only for a moment, not really expecting a response. Somehow sensing that this was the beginning of their battle, she took the time to dress, silently and in the dark. Packing a few essentials into a backpack, she shouldered it and started for the door.

She turned the handle and...nothing. The door wouldn't budge. "What in the bloody hell?" Trying it again, this time putting some muscle behind it, she cursed when she got the same result. Not even a quiver from the two inch thick panel of cedar.

The edges of panic gripped her as she darted for the north facing picture window on the adjacent wall. Pulling aside the thick drapes, she paused for a moment to stare up at the moon. It was enormous and shone bright the color of a finely-aged Chambord liqueur.

One didn't have to be a witch to take that as a bad omen. Frantic now, she unlocked the window and tugged at the lip. Again, nothing. Not even a shiver of the glass or a creak of the wood.

"'The game is afoot,'" she murmured. Realizing that this was clearly some plot related to the battle with Alastore, she thought the Shakespearian quote seemed rather fitting.

Going back to the door, she placed both hands on it and surged her power into it. She was met with such resistance that the energy surged back up her arms and into her body with a rather painful shock.

"What magick is this?" she said, repeating her earlier words from the caves.

Rubbing her arms, she stepped back, utterly confused. She didn't believe that Alastore had the power to come into her home and manipulate her surroundings. She didn't really know how she knew that, only she figured if he had been able to, he would have done so by now.

So who else would have a power that rivaled her own and would wish to use it to keep her confined? A feeling of complete betrayal ripped through her as the answer formed in her mind. "*No!*" she hissed, but she knew it to be true.

Summoning all of her physical strength, she pounded on the door with both fists, while pushing out her power to rattle the whole house. "Let me out!" she screamed, punctuating each word with a bang on the wood. "You can't keep me in here! I will eventually find a way around this spell, but we don't have that kind of time! Marduk!"

She gasped when the door instantly sprang open, freeing her. Of course. He wouldn't disobey a direct order. It would be interesting to hear his justification for this one, but there was no time now.

Bounding down the hall, she skidded to a stop when she found Marduk in the living room, on his knees with his head bent, while Drew still slept soundly on the couch. "Forgive me, *domina*," he said softly, and raised his artic eyes to her face. She saw great sadness in them, but no remorse. *Forgive me*, he'd said. Not *I'm sorry*.

It was obvious to her that he had done this in some misguided attempt to protect her. It was clear that, while it saddened him to have gone against her, he had thought he was doing the right thing. She placed a hand over her heart as an inconceivable thought occurred to her.

"Oh my God. He put you up to this." It was a statement, not a question, as she could guess what had happened. Her love would do anything for her not to risk her life to fight Alastore. But what he hadn't taken into account was the *laqueum*. If he died, most likely she would follow, either instantly or shortly thereafter.

Isla dropped to her knees in front of Marduk, gripping his face in her hands. "Marduk, where is he?"

His eyes reflected his anguish as he drank in the sight of her, as if it could be the last time he would ever see her. "He went to the *locus*. I don't know where it is, but if Leora is to be believed, the way should be clear to the two of you."

Leaping to her feet, she dashed to the door and out into the night, trusting that Marduk would be behind her.

When Isla arrived at the moonlit field, she gasped at the sight of the stone circle. Somehow this had been completely masked from her the entire ten years she'd lived on the island. Seeing the danger in merely striding up to the structure and expecting to find Alastore simply waiting for her, she chose to skirt the field and travel around to the western point of it with the jagged edges of the forest to conceal her from view.

Approaching from the west, there was no choice but to travel out in the open. She saw the moonlight reflecting off an object on the ground, some thirty feet away from the perimeter of the circle.

As she came nearer, she realized with a start that it was Jeremiah's rucksack. Her heart pounded wildly as she searched the field for any signs of life. It comforted her a bit to hear the rustling of the brush as the wolf snaked his way through the trees, doing some reconnaissance of his own.

Isla knew, without a shadow of a doubt, that Alastore was using Jeremiah as bait to lure her into the *locus*, where she would be at her most vulnerable. She knew just as surely that she was powerless to do anything but walk into the trap.

Cautiously, she advanced on the stone circle, traveling east. When she approached the perimeter of the circle, she stuck close to one of the ancient monoliths and peered into the circle from behind it.

The circle was lit on the inside by a ring of flames that burned from an unseen source, one in each of the spaces between the stones. The flickering fires caused moving shadows to dance in the ghostly pit.

Isla could tell by the constant internal feedback, and the feeling of pins and needles running rampant under her skin, that this was indeed the portal to the realm of the *Lochrim*. Clapping a hand over her mouth to stifle a cry of distress, she spotted Jeremiah off to the side, near the northeast point.

He was lying on his side with his back to her, so very still, and she noticed a trail of blood that had trickled out of his ear. Not a good sign. She couldn't tell from that distance if he were merely unconscious...or worse.

Knowing it was wrong, but not being able to stop herself, she ran to him, breaching the wall of the locus and feeling it like little stab wounds all over her body. She had nearly reached him when Alastore appeared in front of her, without the usual flurry of explosions and puffs of smoke.

Having to stop in her tracks to avoid crashing into him, Isla glared at him.

"Hello, daughter," he crooned, causing her skin to crawl. "Come to join me?"

With her ebony curls whipping in the wind, Isla threw her head back and laughed mirthlessly. "Not a chance, you soul-stealing bastard!"

Alastore's eyes flashed but he didn't rise to her baiting. "You are the illegitimate daughter of a human peasant and the *King* of the *auchrim*. Who's the bastard?"

"I know exactly who I am and where I came from. And I was born to destroy you." Launching a surprise offensive, she sent a spiraling ball of flame shooting toward his chest. He screeched as it singed him, but it didn't seem to do much damage.

He flew at her with superhuman speed, bursting apart into mist just before passing completely through her. She couldn't help but breathe in the mist as it wafted over her, and she felt him inside her, choking the life out of her.

She fell to her knees, clawing at her throat in a desperate attempt to breathe. Sending a concentrated energy wave through her own body, she burned up the particles of the mist that were strangling her life force.

Not missing a beat, she leapt up and spun to face him as he rematerialized. She raised her hands to the sky, murmuring a spell that she heard whispering in the back of her mind, in a voice that sounded suspiciously like Mhairi's.

Clouds gathered instantly and thunder shook the ancient stones. Alastore barely had time to look up before lightning struck him, hard and fast, knocking him to the ground. After her storm dissipated, Isla saw him crumpled in a heap on the ground.

Not wasting any time, she rushed to Jeremiah and rolled him over on his back. Putting her head to his chest, she could hear his heart beating weakly and his breath rattling in his chest. She cupped his face with her hand, and his image blurred as tears filled her eyes. "Jeremiah? *A ghràidh*, please answer me." There was no response.

Temporarily blinded by grief, she had made a grave error in turning her back to her enemy. Alastore surged up behind her and pushed a blast of dark energy towards her that sent her flying.

Her back crashed against one of the giant stones, stopping her flight and causing her to drop to the ground, striking her forehead on a rock. Stars burst behind her eyes as she landed and then reeled in a sickening lurch.

She didn't entirely lose consciousness, but she was stunned into momentary paralysis. She could only watch as Alastore stalked her, charging his power until it radiated from him in a fearsome aura of blue flame.

Stretching out a hand toward her, he prepared for the kill shot. Just when she thought he would have lashed out at her, a streak of grey shot out of the surrounding darkness and collided with Alastore.

Marduk dug his sharp fangs into the demon's arm, causing him to shriek in pain. Isla knew it also channeled the offending energy into his own body, so that Alastore could not use it to strike at her.

With a sharp yelp, the wolf's body dropped like a stone, crumpling to the ground at the demon's feet. Alastore gave it a kick, causing it to roll over next to Jeremiah's lifeless form.

Isla let out a keening wail as she saw the two most important people in her life lying on the ground at the feet of her enemy, casualties of war. She struggled to her feet as twenty years' worth of anger and resentment bubbled to the surface.

Hands curled into claws, she lunged at the source of all her pain. Alastore's eyes widened in surprise — she was sure he never expected a physical attack from a magickal being, but she was also a strong, fit, feisty human woman willing to use all of the weapons in her arsenal.

She raked her fingernails down his cheeks, carving deep furrows in the skin and causing blood to flow like a river. When she pulled her hands back, she stared at them, covered in the blood of evil...the blood of her father.

The moment distracted her enough for Alastore to launch his own physical attack. Reaching for her belt, he snagged her twelve-inch hunting knife from its sheath and reared back to stab her.

He was gunning to pierce her heart, she knew, but as he plunged the knife home, she turned slightly and threw out her arms defensively. So instead of the fatal blow he'd intended, the knife was buried to the hilt in her left shoulder.

Instantly, she took an internal inventory and knew that, though the knife had missed hitting any major organs or vessels, it was buried so close to the shoulder joint that her left arm was rendered immobile. She wouldn't die from the stab unless she bled to death, but having a broken wing certainly lowered her odds of defeating the demon.

Too much of her energy was being diverted to the wound to summon any great power to fight Alastore with, but she blasted him with a fireball hoping to slow him down to give her time to think.

She grasped the hilt of the knife and gritted her teeth as she slowly pulled it out of her. Pain exploded in her shoulder and her vision dimmed. Once again she had to struggle to stay conscious.

Looking down at the weapon that was soaked in her own blood, she watched the rivulets of her life force trickle down to mingle with her father's blood on her hands.

The blood is the key.

Out of nowhere, she remembered Mhairi's words and an idea occurred to her. What if Mhairi hadn't meant that the figurative *blood* that she shared with her father was the key to his destruction. What if she meant, literally, the actual blood.

Giving herself no time to question her plan—there really was none because this was a last resort—she pretended to double over in pain, sinking to her knees. The demon wouldn't be able to resist kicking her when she was down.

He stalked her. His predatory smile was as gruesome as it was foolhardy. He stood in front of her where she knelt, head down with her bangs obstructing his view of her eyes. That was the one thing that could give away her intentions.

Evil incarnate, Alastore fisted a hand in her hair and jerked her head back to force her to look at him. Before he had a chance to see her eyes, she reached up and plunged the knife deep into his heart—the knife covered in her own blood.

Releasing her, he stepped back and stared at the knife protruding from his chest. He gave a weak laugh, because normally if his corporeal form was injured or killed, it wouldn't affect him.

But his face began to show panic as his veins began to stand out black, in contrast to his pale, thin skin. Gasping for breath, he staggered backwards, gripping his throat. Suddenly his entire body was engulfed in his signature blue flames, and he began to burn.

Oh, how he burned. Skin and muscle peeled away and turned to ash, revealing a bloody skeleton underneath. Screaming like a siren, Alastore's corporeal body began to disintegrate before Isla. It seemed as though her blood inside him had locked his essence to his body, so that if the body was destroyed, so he shall be.

Finally, with a burst of sulphur and smoke, he exploded into a cloud of dust that floated away in the October breeze. Not sparing a moment to revel in her triumph, Isla returned to her *càirdean tuislichte*. Her fallen friends.

Chapter Twenty-Four

Isla sat on the cold ground inside the stone circle that no longer vibrated with vortexical energy. She was between the bodies of her greatest love and her loyal protector, both barely clinging to life.

She was still unsure what Alastore had done to Jeremiah but knew that it had to have been severe to hurt such a strong and vibrant force of a man. Sitting with a hand on each of them, she channeled all of her remaining energy into them, aiding their hearts to beat and their lungs to breathe.

Using her power, she searched through them, looking for any damage and repairing what she could. She stopped briefly to call Drew, knowing that if they didn't get help, they would all die out there.

She made the call and a sleepy Drew answered. "Yeah?"

"Drew, I need you to come get us."

Drew came instantly awake and alert. "Where are you? Are y'all okay?"

"Listen carefully. You need to take my pickup truck because we're all injured and, as of now, only one of us is conscious. Marduk will need to go straight to Jack, and Jeremiah and I need a doctor."

"Got it," he answered calmly, though she heard the worry in his voice.

Isla dug the handheld GPS unit out of her pocket that she had brought as an afterthought, and read off the coordinates to him.

"Plug that into the GPS in the truck and it will lead you to us. Hurry."

"Hold on, I'll be there soon!"

Dropping the phone, Isla returned to focusing her powers to heal Jeremiah and Marduk. She'd never tried this before and had no idea if it would work at all, but she to do something.

Suddenly, the ground started to rumble and Isla looked above her to see hundreds of ghostly figures rising up from the circle and floating off into the sky.

"All of the souls Alastore trapped," she murmured. "They're free now." Startled by a sound behind her, Isla turned to see several people walking around the stones, looking confused and disoriented.

They were dirty and their clothes were torn, but they looked unharmed. They seemed to be unaware of her presence, too confused by their surroundings to notice, so she left them alone. Those must have been the people Alastore hadn't gotten to yet, and among them were the missing from the island. They were freed as well.

Hearing a groaning noise, she turned back to Jeremiah and was met with cloudy hazel eyes. They were unfocused but open. He gave her a weak smile, showing one wolfish canine. "Hey there beautiful," his gruff voice cracked, but it was music to her ears.

She flung herself on him and sobbed, finally let go of all of the worry and fear she had been consumed with since she'd found him gone. "Don't you ever scare me like that again," she scolded.

Jeremiah gingerly sat up, rubbing at his temple. Feasting his eyes on his brave warrioress, covered in blood and dirt, hair knotted and clouded around her head, he'd never seen a more beautiful sight.

He leaned forward to capture her lips in a searing kiss and allowed his hands to roam over her skin—something she never thought she'd get to feel again. When his hand brushed over her shoulder, she winced and pulled back.

"Easy there, tiger. I have a few battle wounds." He inspected the stab wound in her shoulder and frowned at her. "Isla, this is really deep. We need to get you to a hospital!"

She shrugged her good shoulder, and told herself it could have been much, much worse. "I'm fine, love. You need to get checked out too because you were unconscious for a long time. And Marduk needs to get to Jack. He'll never be able to take human form to go to the hospital, so he needs a vet."

Both of their heads turned when they heard an engine roaring and saw headlights cut through the dark night. Jeremiah gave her a questioning look.

"I called Drew. We needed a ride," she said. As the truck neared the circle, Isla realized that they were all safe, for the moment anyway. The overwhelming relief mingled with an adrenaline crash, combined with blood loss, caused her to see spots in her vision. Just as Drew parked the truck and rounded the hood to come help them, her world went black.

It was a chilly November day on the Isle of Arran. The wind was high and the sky was cloudy. Isla sat on top of a huge boulder that jutted out of the sea. There was a group of them that formed a line from the shore, like giant stepping stones.

Jeremiah pulled her closer and wrapped his coat around her, and she leaned back against his chest, and they watched the waves violently crashing against the rock. Jere knew this was one of her favorite places.

Resting his chin on the top of her head, he took a deep breath. "So what happens now?"

"What do you mean?" she asked, turning her head.

"Well, I'm kind of wide open. My family is in New Orleans, and I'd love for you to meet them someday, but I can live and work anywhere. I don't care if I'm on this island, in the States, or on a boat in the middle of the ocean, as long as I'm with you. Where's home to you?"

"You are," she said, tilting her head up to kiss his chin. "You are."

"You have your house here and your business. Maybe we should just stay here."

"Callum can run Expeditions. I'm more of a silent partner, really. I just enjoy working. Gives me something to do."

"Okay...so you want to travel? See the world?"

"You really want me to meet your family?" she asked shyly.

"Of course, Isla. They'll love you. And Mama 'n them would kill me if I didn't let them meet the woman I'm going to marry." He became suddenly unsure of himself. "You're going to marry me, right?"

She laughed, and the tinkling sound was one that he would never get tired of. "That was a hell of a proposal, but yes, I'm going to marry you."

She fell silent and Jeremiah could practically hear the wheels turning. "What are you thinking about?"

"You know how, when you met me, I had no idea what I was, or what I could do?"

"Yeah..."

"What would have happened to me if you had never come? If I had never learned about my powers?"

"But I did come. Where are you going with this?"

"What if there are other people out there like I was, with no idea what they are or what threats they are facing? How many *embulibruixi* are out there? I feel like I need to help them. If any good is to come of what happened here, I need to track down others like me...especially other *Praedos*. We've got to teach the *bruixi* to defend themselves."

"So you want to travel around the world, searching for witches and teaching them how to use their powers? Just the two of us?"

"Three." Two heads swiveled around as Marduk leapt up on the rock behind them, looking as fit and hearty as ever after his ordeal. "I would go with you, *domina*, if you'll have me."

"But, Marduk, you're free. You made your sacrifice. I'm not your *domina* anymore. You can maintain whatever form you like. You can go where you want and make a life for yourself."

"You may not be my *domina* anymore, but you are my family. You and Jeremiah are all I've got. Plus, you could use my expertise."

Isla looked at Jeremiah and he shrugged. Turning back to Marduk, he slapped the young man on the back. "Welcome aboard, dog-breath," he said, ducking as Marduk swung at him playfully.

"That's wolf-breath to you, buddy! So where shall we go first?"

"Believe it or not, I think we need to go to New Orleans. Not just to see my family and plan a wedding, but to do some research. The *bruixi* book was nearly stolen from Drew in New Orleans, which means there is someone out there that knows something. That seems to be as good a starting point as any. How 'bout it?"

Isla nodded, smiling. "I think that's a great idea." They stared at each other for long moments until Marduk cleared his throat. "I'm going to meet up with Drew to make travel plans. Don't be long, you two."

The two of them stood there on a rock in the middle of the sea, the wind whipping through their hair and the waves crashing around them. Isla couldn't think of anywhere she would rather be, than with the man who had saved her life and her heart.

Looking into his warm, hopeful eyes, she didn't need the power of clairvoyance to see her future. It was laid out before her, and all she had to do was hang on tight.

www.ingramcontent.com/pod-product-compliance
Lightning Source LLC
Chambersburg PA
CBHW070758180626
46818CB00001B/8